# FORTUNE'S SON

## THE TASMANIAN TALES 1

### JENNIFER SCOULLAR

PILYARA PRESS

Fortune's Son
Version 1.0
ISBN: 978-0-6483089-0-4

# ALSO BY JENNIFER SCOULLAR

*To Peter Bishop, Varuna's foundation creative director and this book's original champion*

# CHAPTER 1

F unny, but on the day it happened Luke had never felt so cocky. As he set off in the cart that grey afternoon through Hobart's wintry streets, he felt like he owned them. Felt like a king. Youth will do that to you.

Storm clouds piled high in the leaden sky as he drew rein in the lane behind Abbott House. The imposing double-storey home, with its fashionable Battery Point address, was a far cry from Luke's humble cottage in working-class Wapping. Yet he wouldn't have swapped them. For all its grandeur, there was something cold, even sinister about the home's forbidding stone façade.

The force of the gathering gale caused the old pony to whinny and shy like a colt. Luke glanced up at Mt Wellington, its peak shrouded in cloud. Better hurry, the rain would hit soon. He knocked at the kitchen door, cap in hand, head bowed to the bitter southern blast. After a long wait, the housekeeper answered his knock. He was a favourite of hers, and knew it. A handsome lad with even features and bold, brown eyes, women already found his larrikin style and quick wit appealing. But instead of allowing him into the kitchen and out of the weather, perhaps even offering him a treat of freshly baked bread, she seemed oddly flustered and tried to close the door in his face. Luke jammed his boot inside to block it.

'I've come for my sister, Mrs Dunsley. Where is she?'

The housekeeper avoided Luke's eye and tried again to force the door shut. With a shove he entered the cosy kitchen, which smelled comfortingly of cinnamon scones and roast beef. Generally he'd find Becky there, chopping vegetables or polishing the silver tableware required for the evening meal when Sir Henry Abbott was in town. This time she was nowhere to be seen.

'Your sister will be here directly,' said Mrs Dunsley. 'She'll be taking the master his tea, is all. How about a nice piece of corn bread and jam? Or would you rather some cold lamb and chutney? I think I can find a glass of warm buttermilk to go with that.'

Bread and buttermilk? Why wasn't she cuffing him round the ears for his cheek? And since when was it the job of a lowly kitchen maid to take the master his tea?

Ignoring her protests, he pushed past into the hall. Faint sobs came from the parlour to his left. Bursting through the door he found Rebecca on the floor – blouse undone, skirts pushed up around her waist, lip split and bleeding. On top of her lay a trouser-less Henry Abbott, so intent on his pleasure that for a few seconds he failed to notice Luke enter the room.

He was only fourteen years old, but Luke could more than hold his own in a street fight. Working at his uncle's blacksmith shop had given him powerful arms and a strong, straight back. Even so, he may well have been no match for the much older and heavier Sir Henry if it had not been for the power of his outrage. And the sight of his sister's rumpled clothes, skinny legs, and bloody, tear-drenched face caused any respect he might have had for his superiors to vanish.

Luke dragged the surprised man off Rebecca by the collar of his fine starched linen shirt, choking him in the process. Then hurled him half-naked and headfirst against the wall. Henry Abbott tried to stand, revealing a broken nose and two chipped front teeth. Dimly, Luke was aware he should stop, but he didn't. He drove his fist hard into Abbott's temple, rendering the master of the house unconscious.

'Luke, you shouldn't have . . .'

Turning his attention to Becky, he gently helped her to her feet, murmuring words of comfort, adjusting the crying girl's clothes. Then, cradled like a child in arms, he carried his sister past the astonished Mrs Dunsley out to the cart, gee'd up the impatient pony and drove home before the storm struck.

His mother, Alice, was in the kitchen when Luke guided Becky through the front door, down the hall and into her little bedroom. 'Is that you, Luke?'

'Don't tell Mama,' whispered Becky. 'I'll die if you tell Mama.'

Her sobs were loud enough to summon Alice from the kitchen. 'Whatever's wrong?' she asked. 'Luke? Becky?'

Luke took his mother's hand. 'No . . .' said Becky, but Luke was already leading Alice from the room, shutting the door behind him.

As Luke recounted the events of that awful afternoon, all colour drained from his mother's face. 'You have to get away, this very minute,' she said, her voice low and urgent. 'Pack a change of clothes while I get some food. Hurry.'

'Go?' said Luke. 'Why should I go? I'm going to make Abbott pay.'

'It'll be you who'll pay, my darling,' said Alice. 'Who knows what they'll charge you with.'

'Let them put me in the witness box.' Luke crossed his arms over his chest. 'I can't wait to tell the world what sort of scum Abbott is.'

'I'll pack your bag myself then.' Alice turned on her heel, running down the hall towards the lean-to on the back porch where Luke slept.

She tossed a few things in his canvas pack with shaking hands. Becky appeared in the doorway, her face pale, and swollen around the jaw and temple. She'd have a black eye by morning. Alice turned and hugged her daughter fiercely enough that it hurt them both. She had to pull herself together. She mustn't let fears for Luke overshadow what had happened to their sweet Rebecca. Alice touched the girl's face with infinite tenderness, and choked back a sob. Where would

Becky end up now? At the jam factory or flour mill? Work for girls in those places was like slow murder. And what if she fell pregnant?

'Luke will be all right, won't he?' said Becky. 'Papa will know what to do.'

'Yes, yes . . . shush now,' Alice said soothingly, but she knew better. Thomas couldn't fix this. Luke had to leave, and leave now. It was his only hope. The coppers wouldn't be far off and there'd be no fair trial of the kind Luke imagined. Even if Rebecca could face the shame of testifying, the word of a servant girl was of dubious value against the statement of a wealthy and important man like Henry Abbott.

Alice's mind worked furiously as she grabbed boiled potatoes and cheese from the kitchen. The only person alive who might help them was Daniel Campbell. He'd gone out of his way to aid their family before. Giving Thomas work. Taking Luke into his school. A kind man. A respected man, with standing in society. But he was somewhere up country, many days' ride distant. Thomas must go for him anyway.

Thomas. She drew a long, shuddering sigh. Any minute her husband would burst in the door with that cheerful smile, declaring his family was worth ten of other men's. How would she tell him?

Alice dashed back to Luke, thrust the pack into his hands, and pulled him down the hall towards the back door. 'Go bush, up the mountain, to that little camp of yours. They'll never find you there.'

'I won't run, Mama. It's not me that's done wrong.'

He'd grown so tall, her son, and he stood there, an immoveable object.

They looked at each other, eye to eye, as the pounding at the front door began.

'Please, Luke,' Alice said.

But then the door flew open and two constables trooped in.

'Luke Tyler,' said the biggest man in a rough voice. 'I'm arresting you for the grievous assault of Sir Henry Abbott.'

Becky appeared at the doorway, shivering and hollow-eyed. The look on her face said it all. She shook her head as if doubting the truth of what was happening.

Luke stood his ground, confident that justice would prevail. Even when they shoved him against the wall. Even when they seized his arms. Only when they chained his hands behind his back did Luke react. He exploded with impotent rage, roaring like an animal. The chains held tight. What could he do?

'No.' Alice grabbed hold of Luke. 'You can't take him. You can't take my son. He was protecting his sister, that's all.' She tried to prise the constables' fingers from his arm and was slapped away.

'Don't cry, Mama,' Luke called as they dragged him out. 'I'll be back soon, I promise.'

Alice ran into the street after them, into the rain and gloom. Icy fingers gripped her heart so tightly it could barely beat. A fog wrapped around her mind, stealing her senses, making her stumble. She fell on the slippery road, landing hard in the mud. When she looked up, Luke was already gone.

# CHAPTER 2

L uke took a bite of bread, then hurled it to the putrid floor. 'Call this breakfast? It tastes of nothing but weevils and mould.'

His frail, bearded cellmate pounced on the prize and wolfed it down in between hacking coughs. Luke was both sickened and overcome with pity. 'Here, greybeard.' He handed over a morsel of hard cheese. 'Have this too.' The sick old man needed it more than he did. After three days in this stinking, freezing cesspit, Luke was to go before the judge that day and tell his story. With any luck he'd be home by sundown.

Morning crawled by. Bars at the high window cast striped shadows on the wall, his only way of marking time. The iron shackles bit into his skin, and minutes felt like hours. He filled the space by imagining how his parents were feeling. His mother? Sick with worry. His father? Wild and angry. Trying to find a lawyer. How much would that cost?

He listened all the while for the sound of footsteps in the hall outside. At last came a voice and the clang of keys in the lock. A guard opened the gloomy gaol cell, roughly cuffed Luke's hands, and led him blinking into the wan winter sunshine.

Just a short walk. Part of the old chapel on site had been

converted to a courthouse. Luke put on a brave front, but averted his eyes from the high iron gate to the right. The execution yard and gallows lay beyond. Passing them stole his courage. In the shadow of the gate, Luke felt like the frightened child he was, frantic for his family.

The guard took him to a back entrance of the courthouse, and down a hall with cells either side. They stopped outside an imposing carved door. 'Wait here.' The guard idly chewed tobacco, as Luke shifted nervously from foot to foot, wishing his clothes weren't so filthy and his feet weren't so cold. He rubbed his frozen hands to regain some feeling.

A loud knock sounded from the other side. 'In you go, son.'

He found himself in a crowded, oak-lined courtroom. Grand and civilised. It reminded him of Mr Campbell's library. Luke took to the dock, feeling more hopeful.

'Luke . . . Luke!' His mother's voice. He tried to find her in the sea of faces in the public gallery. There, at the side, and Becky too, waving. He waved back. Where was his father? Where was his lawyer?

A fat, red-faced clerk swore Luke in and read out charges of aggravated assault and attempted robbery. Robbery? Where had that come from?

'How do you plead?'

'Not guilty.' Luke's voice sounded faint and faraway in his ears.

The proceedings were a confusing blur. The bewigged judge looked half-dead, his sunken face marred with acne scars, and great grainy circles under hollow eyes. Luke found himself shivering, unable to stop. The prosecutor, with the voice of a sergeant major and a handlebar moustache, boomed out the case against Luke. It bore scant resemblance to the truth.

'This young felon forced his way into Abbott House with a scarf tied over his face, knocking the elderly housekeeper to the floor. He then helped himself to the family silverware. When Mrs Dunsley attempted to rise, the defendant made to strike her again. It was only the timely intervention of Sir Henry Abbott that saved her from further injury.'

The judge frowned. A cry of protest rose from the gallery. 'You're a lying piece of crap!'

Luke's heart leaped with hope. His father? He eagerly searched for him. No, not his father, but big Uncle Hiram at the back, with his fist in the air and standing head and shoulders above the rest. As Luke watched, two constables bundled him out. Luke's throat tightened as the prosecutor continued without mention of Abbott's assault on his sister.

'The defendant dropped the silver, struck Sir Henry in the mouth and fled like the coward he is.'

A murmur ran through the crowd as Henry Abbott emerged from a door at the side of the courtroom. Luke's teeth ground together, and his body stiffened. Abbott walked right by, and shot him a brief contemptuous look before taking the stand.

How Luke hated him. The way he walked, and the sound of his voice and his cruel face. He hated his cold blue eyes. He even hated the smell of him.

Abbott spoke clearly, calmly, his evidence a pack of lies incriminating Luke and casting himself in the role of a hero. On being dismissed he left the courtroom without a backward glance.

Next, a nervous Mrs Dunsley testified. No wonder she couldn't meet his eye. She confirmed Abbott's cock-and-bull story in every detail.

'No further witnesses,' said the prosecutor. 'As open and shut a case as I've seen, your honour.'

The judge nodded sagely and peered at Luke over horn-rimmed glasses. 'Have you anything to say in your defence?'

Luke's mouth was so dry it was hard to speak. He licked his lips, but no spit would come. 'They're lying, sir,' he managed. 'I didn't steal anything.'

'That's for me to decide. Did you strike Sir Henry Abbott and Mrs Ida Dunsley?'

'Not Mrs Dunsley.'

'And what about Sir Henry?'

'I was protecting my sister, Rebecca. She'll tell you.'

'Do you call her as a witness?'

Becky and his mother had pushed their way to the front of the crowd. Luke went to speak, then stopped, open-mouthed. He studied his sister with a growing sense of horror. Her arms were clutched around herself, shoulders curled forward and chest caved in. She rocked softly back and forth, eyes downcast. Confusion washed over him. He hadn't thought this through.

His mother gently pushed Becky forward. She raised her head, revealing a face drained of colour and eyes like a wounded fawn before the hounds.

'Well?' asked the judge.

'No,' said Luke, finding his voice. 'I do not call my sister as a witness.'

His mother clamped her hand to her mouth, eyes wide. Becky began to cry.

'Then you will speak in your own defence?'

Luke's heart was racing. Telling the truth would humiliate his sister in front of all these people. And for what purpose? He had no hope of being believed now. A silence fell on the crowded courtroom and the answer came to him. He swallowed hard, searching for courage. 'I've changed my mind.'

'Luke, no!' came his mother's cry. She fell to her knees. Instinctively he reached his cuffed hands for her, but a guard shoved him back.

'I plead guilty to all the charges.'

The judge's bloodless lips creased into a thin smile. 'A wise move, for I don't suffer liars well in my court. Are you sorry for your crimes, boy?'

'I am sorry, your honour.' The words stuck in his throat. 'And I beg God's forgiveness.'

The judge picked up his pen and started to write. For an agonising few minutes, all Luke could hear was the scratching nib.

At last the judge looked up. 'Luke Tyler, you have pleaded guilty to the charges laid against you: namely that you did on the fifteenth day of July, in the year of our Lord 1882, callously and with malice aforethought commit an aggravated assault on Sir Henry Abbott and Mrs Ida Dunsley. Furthermore, in the course of the assault, you did attempt to steal a quantity of valuable silver tableware.' He shuffled his papers. A baby's thin wailing sounded from somewhere. 'These are very serious crimes, however, I am a merciful man, and will take into account your youth and contrition.'

The judge struck his gavel three times. 'Luke Tyler, it is therefore ordered and adjudged by this court that you be sentenced to fifteen years hard labour.'

The gavel came down one last time to seal his fate.

# CHAPTER 3

Would it never stop raining? Luke bent his head to the blast and trudged into camp with the other prisoners at the end of another ten hour work day. He sucked the smooth stone in his mouth, a trick supposed to keep hunger at bay, but it wasn't working. His belly clenched in pain and all he could think about was dinner. He could already taste it, see himself sopping up the possum stew with a hunk of bread. His mouth watered as a sodden guard slammed the timber gates behind them.

Mr Collins, the new superintendent, watched them from the porch of his hut. He was portly, with a florid face and bushy beard. Luke stared enviously at the column of smoke rising from his chimney. At his warm coat and dry clothes. The shivering men shuffled into a rough line and waited. Once Luke stopped moving, the cold sank deep into his marrow. The wind redoubled its fury, piercing through his thin clothes with icy needles.

Collins stumbled and swore as he stepped off the porch. 'Line up, you ragtag bunch of bastards.'

Luke groaned to hear him slur his words. He'd been drinking, which meant he'd been gambling, which meant he'd been losing. Which meant the men would almost certainly go hungry tonight.

'We're missing a man,' said Collins. A web of red lines flared up his cheeks.

The guard stepped forward. 'I've checked 'em twice, sir. They're all there.'

'Are you saying I can't count?' Collins' eyes bulged from their fleshy pouches. 'I'll have you flogged.' He took a swig from a flask he found in his pocket.

The prisoners shuffled about in the rain, rubbing their hands together and stamping feet, as the guard counted them for the third time. When he turned around again, Collins had already vanished, retreated to the warmth of his hut. 'Get off with you,' said the guard, and made a dash for his quarters. The tired prisoners did the same.

The prison farm stood a mile from the small gold-mining town of Hills End, nestled in the foothills of rugged ranges. More than five hundred convicts had once lived there, in huts they built themselves from bush timber. Guards told stories about the heyday of British transportation, when thousands toiled in such camps as little more than slaves, building roads, drains and bridges. They were log-cutters and quarry men, even used as beasts of burden to pull carts full of timber and stone. But the convict ships came no more and the work camps and their inmates had been largely forgotten. As these lost men served out their sentences or absconded into the bush, the prison population had declined to less than fifty.

Luke pushed in the door of his leaky hut. The rain had turned the dirt floor to smelly mud, and it seemed almost as wet inside as out. He climbed onto his bunk and sank back on the straw – cold, wet and hungry. Pulling the filthy blanket around him, he slammed his fist into the wall.

'Steady, lad, you'll have the roof in,' came Bob's voice from the bunk below. 'Come here and I'll lend you a dry shirt.'

Old Bob Nelson was the most senior inmate, and seemed to lead a charmed life. He pilfered shirts from the laundry, food from the kitchen, tobacco from the guards, and never got caught. He was also the unofficial leader of and spokesperson for the prisoners.

Luke stripped off his wet clothes and hung them over the end of his bunk. He pulled on the dry shirt Bob offered him, wrapped himself back up in the blanket, and tried to stop his teeth from chattering. 'I swear, Bob, we'll starve before spring gets here.'

All the recent talk in camp was of what to do about Mr Collins. He wasn't an excessively harsh man and, being bone-lazy, did not push the men beyond endurance as some had in the past. But he did possess one major flaw – he was an inveterate gambler and never missed an opportunity to try his luck. The problem lay in the fact he was both stupid and illiterate. Unable to read, write, or accurately perform even the simplest calculations, Collins invariably found himself on the losing page of the bookmaker's ledger. At such times he would down great quantities of rum and swap his mild disposition for one of vile ill-temper -dishing out random beatings and refusing to feed the men.

'I've got an idea.' Bob produced a biscuit from nowhere and handed it to Luke. 'Get your pants on.'


Bob knocked on the half-open door of Collins' hut. Luke could see the superintendent slumped on a chair by the fire, muttering curses and swigging from a nearly empty bottle of rum.

Bob stepped into the crude doorway, looking as respectful as possible. To Luke's surprise, Collins beckoned them in. He was in the maudlin stage of drunkenness. Rage would come later.

'What is it?' asked Collins, staring into space.

'If you please, sir,' said Bob. 'The men and meself feel uncommonly grieved by your rotten luck, and we think we can help turn it around.'

'Nothing can lift this curse that's upon me.'

'Here's me idea. Luke's your man. Real quick at calculations is young Luke. Why, he's beat the best of us at cards ten times over. Why don't you take him along next time and no bastard'll swindle you. He's sharp as a tack, is Luke.'

Collins looked up. Luke was well-known around camp as a card sharp, with an uncanny ability to remember cards played. For a time the superintendent seemed lost in thought. 'Think I'd trust one of you thieving scoundrels?' he said at last. 'Get out, and you'll see no dinner tonight.'

'Great plan,' said Luke, as they returned to the hut.

Bob winked and gave him another biscuit. 'Give it time, lad. Give it time.'


The stars were out by the time Luke climbed into the bunk and closed his eyes. He flinched as Henry Abbott's face swam into view. The man who'd violated his sister and unjustly condemned him. One day he'd settle the score.

Luke groaned and scratched at the bedbugs. Who was he kidding? The truth was, he was a coward. There'd been chances to escape, and each time he'd lost his nerve. Early on in his sentence, a boy made a bold but poorly planned bid for freedom. He almost starved in the bush before being recaptured, flogged and sentenced to a timber-gang - a punishment usually reserved for the roughest men. He returned a year later, barely recognisable, with failing health and a broken spirit. The memory was never very far away. So Luke always convinced himself to wait until he was a little older, or wiser, or healthier, or warmer, or closer to Hobart before trying. Yet as prisoner numbers dwindled, rumours grew that the camp might close down altogether. A return to the more secure Hobart Gaol would make escape almost impossible.

Luke's empty stomach growled like an angry animal. He rocked back and forth in an effort to keep warm, and received a thump and shout from below. Arrgh! Time to go to his happy place. He'd long ago learned to tune out the present, leaving his mind free to roam in the painless past. It was the only thing that had kept him sane over the last four years. Recalling memories of home and family. Memories of school and his teacher, Daniel Campbell. For Luke was well educated at a time when most boys of his station had no formal teaching at all.

Hobart's government schools were bleak, unpopular places. Alternative schools sprang up, run by emancipists and charitable benefactors. Campbell College was such a school. Lessons were first held in an old wool store adjacent to Coomalong, Mr Campbell's Hobart home at Sandy Point. Luke's father was one of the tradesmen engaged to remodel the building into classrooms. A former convict, he'd always resented his lack of formal education. When Mr Campbell offered Luke a place in his new school, Papa jumped at the opportunity. Luke had loved Campbell College, its spacious grounds and native gardens such a contrast to the smell and squalor of Wapping. By simply imagining the rutted roadway that led there, overarched with blue gums, all things became tolerable.

He found a memory. A day-long ramble with his teacher up Mount Wellington. The cool, timbered slopes as familiar to Luke as his own street. There, among the wattles and sassafras, among the chorus of currawongs and the buzz of bees, Luke's thirst for knowledge grew.

'What's this?' he'd say, over and over, on finding a bird's nest or a lizard or any manner of thing. He dropped a brilliant beetle with vermilion bands into Daniel's hand.

'Ah, a *Buprestidae*, and a very pretty one at that. Some are metallic green, others azure blue and gold. I imagine you found this on a tea-tree blossom?'

'Do you know all about beetles?' asked Luke.

'I've collected more than six hundred species in Tasmania alone, but gave up with many still to go.'

'Why?'

'Somehow, I no longer wished to kill them. I still look for beetles, as before. When I find an old friend I admire him awhile, then let him trundle away in peace.'

With extravagant care Luke replaced the beetle on the tea-tree.

He learned to recognise each bird call. He noticed everything from tiny ants to a camouflaged eagle's eyrie in the soaring canopy of a mountain ash.

'The she-eagle's mate was shot long ago,' whispered Daniel. 'It took her years to find another. When lightning struck her nest, she rebuilt it in the splinters of the thunderbolt.'

Luke clambered through the bauera bushes to the other side of the tree, craning his neck to examine the eyrie from every angle. The fluffy white head of an eaglet poked over the broad, tangled mass of leaves and branches.

Daniel cautioned him to silence and pointed skywards. A vast, moving shadow glided above them – the crooked-beaked she-eagle with a rabbit gripped tight in her talons. Luke had seen eagles before: bedraggled corpses strung along fences by farmers or huddled captive in cages. But this graceful, beautiful bird – he could no more imagine taking her life than he could his own.

'My dad says they eat lambs,' said Luke. 'He says they should be shot.'

'They eat rabbits and cats and carrion. Our foolish farmers don't know what a friend they have.'

With Daniel by his side, Luke learned that wild Tasmania was far from the harsh and forbidding land that townsfolk portrayed it to be. To those who loved and understood her, the island was Eden itself: boasting abundant game, reliable rainfall and a temperate climate very much like England. Daniel taught Luke about bush food – fern roots, native plums, kangaroo apples and giant land crabs that grew more than a foot long and weighed ten pounds. Where to seek shelter in a mountain storm. How to light a fire, track game, find fresh water.

One day the pair sat on a mossy log overlooking a little spring. A wayward swamphen chick wandered further and further away from its parents, darting for a hovering damsel fly that always remained out of reach. As they watched, a snowy goshawk plummeted to earth, seconds later clutching the lifeless baby bird in its grasp.

'See, Luke? Unwary youngsters make easy targets for hungry hawks.'

'It doesn't seem fair,' said Luke. 'To die for such a small mistake.'

'Perhaps, but the harsh consequences of mistakes are common and, I might add, they're not confined to careless baby birds'.

One day Daniel took Luke to a new part of the mountain. Here blackened soil and smouldering piles of branches extended into the distance. No bird sang. Red mud seeped like blood from the wounded earth, oozing downhill in jagged channels that cut the naked ground. A lone wallaby hopped forlornly across the vast, empty slope.

'Why?' Luke's voice cracked with emotion. 'This land's too steep to farm.'

'The brewery,' said Daniel. 'The Government granted them a large slice of this mountain. They burn even the biggest logs in their furnace. The same thing happens all over the island, and all over the world.'

'Where will the eagles live?' Luke's misery turned to anger. 'When I grow up I'll protect the eagles. I'll protect the forests.'

Daniel smiled. 'Perhaps you will, my boy. Perhaps you will.'


Luke had a more powerful secret weapon than memories of his home, family and school – one that worked even in his darkest hours. When floggings or hunger or solitary confinement threatened to drive him mad, he'd think of Bluebell, his tomboy princess.

He'd given Belle that nickname because she loved blue flax lilies and often wore them in her hair or behind her ears. A girl utterly unaffected by the hardships that ruled the lives of common people. A sweet, shining creature from another world. At fourteen, he'd made up his mind that one day he'd marry her. And, although he'd never told Belle of his plan, he'd sensed they had an understanding.

They'd first met when he was ten and she was eight. At first Belle had been jealous of her father's new protégé. Luke won her over with a three-legged quoll. He rescued the half-grown native cat from a steel-jaw trap and arrived with it one morning at Coomalong, the Campbells' gracious home adjoining the school. Luke pulled it from the burlap sack, half-dead from blood loss and shock, its mangled foreleg hanging from a sinew.

'What have we here?' asked Daniel as Belle stroked the velvet softness of its spotted fur. 'That leg must go,' he said after a quick examination.

Belle made a small, strangled sound, then ran to the house in tears.

Luke assisted his teacher to remove the leg, then cleaned and bandaged the little stump.

Belle named the quoll Pallas, and became her devoted nursemaid. Pallas recovered, sleeping in Belle's dressing-table drawers by day, and making herself useful catching mice in the kitchen at night. She even learned to ambush rabbits in the garden, substituting speed with cunning, stealing into low branches and launching herself upon her prey from a height, like an owl.

Pallas was the first of many waifs and strays that Luke brought to Belle: possums, magpies, bandicoots, cockatoos and a little wombat that dug a hole under the house and ate the garden. Groundsmen no longer mowed the sweeping lawns, now kept in good trim by an assortment of kangaroos and wallabies. Belle's mother, Elizabeth, made some half-hearted attempts to curb Luke's penchant for collecting wildlife, but in this she received no support from her husband. He thrived in the midst of this growing menagerie, using the animals in class discussions, following them round with a notebook and making endless sketches.

One of Daniel's preferred pastimes was to sit in the garden while Luke and Belle copied John Gould's magnificent full-colour plates and he read aloud from the text. He often held forth on his pet subject – the destruction of the island's native species and the need for national parks.

'Quolls, like our sweet little Pallas, relentlessly trapped for their pelt. Devils labelled vermin. Then there's the thylacine.' He turned to an illustration of two native tigers and read the caption. '*Thylacinus Cynocephalus, the pouched dog with a wolf's head*. Of course it's neither wolf nor tiger. It's the world's largest marsupial carnivore. You can't imagine what an important animal it is to the zoologist.'

Luke looked up from his sketching. 'Then you'd outlaw the trapping of tigers?'

'Certainly. Otherwise they will be lost to us forever.'

Belle became obsessed, drawing nothing but native tigers, bringing the animals to life with a few simple pen-strokes. She was quite the artist.

'I wish I had a tiger cub for a pet. Can you find me one, Luke?'

He'd tried hard to fulfil her request, but it seemed there were no tigers to be had. Even then, Tasmania's unique thylacines were rare as diamonds.

Luke rolled over in bed and smiled, picturing Belle's bright, expectant face, wishing he'd been able to make her wish come true. Thumps and yells sounded from out in the night. Collins would have a sore head tomorrow, and the whole camp could sleep in. Luke yawned. His body found a more comfortable position, and his mind found another memory.

# CHAPTER 4

B ob's suggestion must have stayed with the superintendent. Come next Saturday race day, Luke joined Collins on an outing to Hills End. He was first subjected to a string of the most dire and bloodcurdling threats imaginable should he try to escape. He had to wear tattered prison clothing, stamped with broad arrows, branding him a criminal for all to see. Yet no threats or humiliation could detract from his excitement. Being out in the real world for the first time in four years was a dream come true. Trotting down the same roads he'd slaved for years to build. Trotting into town, past shops and dogs and pretty young girls in ribboned hats. He could almost imagine being free again.

With Luke's capable assistance, Collins not only avoided falling victim to unscrupulous bookmakers, but also came away with a tidy profit. That night the prisoners enjoyed a golden syrup and damper supper, requested by Luke and agreed to by a for once happily inebriated Mr. Collins.

On the first few occasions Collins watched Luke like a hawk, bringing along Curly, the gang foreman, and two guards for added security. Curly proved more trouble than he was worth, somehow managing to down such a large quantity of liquor that Luke and a guard were twice required to carry his supine body back to the cart for the journey home. The gambling trips continued without Curly and, eventually, even without the guards.

In camp, Bob and Luke were regarded as heroes, and the nightmare of Collins' drunken furies became a thing of the past.

Luke often contemplated running, on these trips to town, but each time fear triumphed. He had no clue as to what to do or where to go. There were rumours of successful escapes, of some men making it to Hobart, but nobody knew for sure. However everybody knew what happened to the rest; they perished in the bush or were recaptured with ten years added to their sentence. In any case, going home would put his family at risk. Harbouring an escaped convict was worth a decade in prison. So instead he meekly returned to camp with Mr Collins, always swearing to himself that at the very next opportunity he'd give his foolish captor the slip.

Saturday afternoon, the last day of winter. The prisoners were weeding a vegetable plot under the close supervision of Bob, a successful market gardener in a previous incarnation.

Dick Collins called Luke over. 'We've hit the jackpot, son,' he said. 'There's a dog fight in town. Nothing better than a good dog fight. Harness Blossom and keep your wits about you. You're in for a real treat.'

The day had been cold and raining, but the clouds parted as they began their drive. Luke enjoyed the sunshine on his back and the smell of warm, damp earth. All around he saw signs of returning spring. Welcome swallows gathered mud for their nests from puddles along the rutted track. Pairs of black-faced cuckoo-shrikes (known as summer birds because their annual arrival heralded the end of winter) flitted in the branches of the same blue gums they nested in last year. Luke doffed his cap to them. Brave birds. Each year they dared the dangerous flight over Bass Strait from mainland Australia to raise their broods in Tasmania. He could use some of their courage. Imagined making that journey in reverse, flying to the mainland where no one would know him.

Flowers budded on leatherwood and waratah. Tiny, golden pompoms of wattle blossom lent a sun-kissed appearance to the forest, even when high clouds strayed across the face of the sun. Beetles and butterflies, bees and moths emerged into their first and last spring.

The old bay mare plodded along the bumpy road, unmoved by Collins' cursing or the half-hearted bite of Luke's whip on her flanks. After half an hour they reached the outskirts of Hills End, a mining town nestled in the foothills of the ranges. Mr Collins directed Luke down a washed-away track flanking the township on its northern perimeter.

Soon they reached a large, ramshackle building, framed by rough bush timber and clad with six-foot strips of stringybark. The low ceiling consisted of the same material. A ragged stone chimney discharged a thin stream of smoke from the roof. Other men were also arriving: on horseback, in carts and on foot. A series of muffled barks and howls could be heard from the barn.

Luke climbed down from the cart, tied Blossom to a rail and followed Collins inside. He'd never been to a dog fight. It took some time for his eyes to adjust to the gloomy interior. The only light came from four poky, high-set windows, one on each wall. Smoke filled the air. A long trestle served as both a bar and a betting table. The place stank of blood and sweat.

At the centre of the room, two men stood in a shallow pit of filthy sawdust. Each held a dog. One looked like a dingo, with a mangy, yellow coat and half-starved frame. It cowered from its owner, lips drawn back in a snarl. The other was a young black kangaroo-dog, much larger than the dingo, straining excitedly against his chain.

A man at the bookie's end of the bar shouted for quiet, and the rabble crowded round the pit. Both men unleashed their dogs and stepped back. It was over before it began. Though taller and heavier than his opponent, the black dog was sorely disadvantaged by youth and inexperience. As he rushed in on his foe, the dingo delivered a savage bite with lightning speed. The young dog fell stricken to the floor with a gaping wound low on his flank. The dingo didn't press his attack, but shrank back to watch.

The wounded dog struggled to his feet and stood panting, dazed and bleeding. Stumbling forward a few paces, he lay down, head on paws, as shock set in. A wide, dark stain spread on the ground beneath him. He whimpered a little. A disgruntled punter dealt the mortally wounded animal a kick to the head. Twitching violently, the dog rolled onto his side, bared his teeth one last time and lay still. His owner unceremoniously dragged him away through the jeering crowd.

Luke felt a burning in his throat. Years of incarceration had accustomed him to human cruelty, but he'd lost nothing of the respect and love for animals that he'd known as a boy. If anything, his admiration for them had increased in inverse proportion to his growing contempt for humanity. He shut his eyes tight and cursed beneath his breath. Old memories would not help him now.

Collins, whisky in hand and already half-inebriated, motioned Luke to join him at the betting table. Luke assisted the overseer by outlining to him the odds available on upcoming fights and then placed his bets for him, ensuring he wasn't cheated in the process. Collins settled happily in for an afternoon of drinking and sport, insisting that Luke remain by his side.

The next bout proved equally sickening. Two experienced and well-matched dogs fought for ten minutes before one succumbed to pain, blood loss and exhaustion, allowing its opponent to seize a death grip on its throat. Even the winning animal, Luke saw, would likely die from its injuries. He couldn't stand it. Every part of him wanted to turn, to walk out the door and away from the smell and the smoke and the blood. To take his chances out in the wild. To not be part of this world.

The next fight was ready to begin. A man dragged a shaggy, black dog forward on a rusty chain – the biggest dog Luke had ever seen. He looked like a bear. If I'm ever lucky enough to own such a dog, he thought, that's what I'll call him – Bear. There was no snarling from the animal, no impatient bloodlust. He seemed instead confused and scared. When unleashed, he did not launch himself at the heavily built brindle mastiff he was pitted against. Instead, he launched himself at the crowd in a frantic effort to escape. It took a whiplash to his muzzle before he could be contained. Although obviously no fighter, his remarkable size engendered a flurry of bets.

When the mastiff charged, the bear dog seemed taken by surprise and suffered a bite to his shoulder. Luke felt rage rise within him as he watched the magnificent dog being forced to fight. Natural agility kept him safe for a few minutes; he turned and twisted to avoid the mastiff's tearing fangs. Luke could stand no more. His muscles tensed as he prepared to leap forward and try to stop the fight. A desperate howl of pain came from the ring. Luke stiffened, certain the black dog must be down. He peered around a fat man with a whip who'd moved in front of him. But as he caught a glimpse of the ring, and the hooting and hollering grew louder, he saw it was the brindle dog in trouble with the bear dog's teeth at his throat.

The mastiff lay still, and its owner stepped forward. Bear sprang to face him, and the crowd melted back. Seizing his chance, the dog leapt from the ring. None were game to block his path. He burst through the door and fled towards the trees with a mob of men at his heels. Luke was one of them, silently thanking the dog for giving him not just the opportunity but also the courage to run.

The rest of the rabble stopped at the tree line. Some useless calling, then the men drifted back to the shed. Some raised rifles, shooting after the fleeing dog, but he was out of range. Not so Luke. A bullet whizzed past him. The next winged his shoulder. He watched the bright blood stain his shirt as he ran, but nothing could stem his elation. Luke vanished into the gully, ignoring the pain of his wound, fleeing with as much energy and determination as the great dog. He needed to put a great deal of distance between himself and town before Collins missed him.

# CHAPTER 5

C oorinna followed the stream down the mountain, three half-grown cubs by her side. Upon first glance in the failing light, she might have been mistaken for a wolf. But Coorinna was a native tiger, the world's largest marsupial carnivore. Once upon a time, her kind had roamed without fear, from mountains to ocean in freedom and safety. But human settlement had long since driven them from the fertile open plains of their old hunting grounds. In the dense forest, prey was scarce and hard to catch. Her striped flanks were hollow from hunger, so tonight she risked hunting the lower pastures.

Coorinna stopped suddenly, forefoot raised. A dog lay in the ferny hollow ahead, blocking their path. She understood all too well the danger he posed. Her mate had been killed by shepherd dogs. Since then she'd raised her cubs alone, high on the range where man seldom ventured.

She waited a long time before leading her young in a wary arc around the sleeping dog and continuing on her way.

Bear opened his eyes. In the gloom, four shadows slipped wraith-like through the trees. He sniffed the air. Not people, not dogs; an unfamiliar scent. He licked his sore shoulder, and padded to the mossy stream for a drink, snapping in vain at a darting minnow. For weeks he'd had nothing but a few scraps of rancid offal, and his hunger raged. Bear whined, then wagged his tail, and followed the strange band of animals back down the mountain.

For more than an hour he trailed them. Timbered ridges gave way to patches of grassland. His nerve almost failed him when the tigers passed a disused shepherd's hut; men could be dangerous, he knew that now.

A full moon rose behind the hills, sharpening the shadows. The tigers stopped in a pandanus thicket on the rim of a grassy clearing. Bear crouched low. He smelled sheep. Moonlight showed them grazing with lambs in the open. One ewe with a newborn was foraging away from the flock, straying close to the waiting tigers. Bear did not regard the sheep as food and harboured no desire to kill them. In other circumstances he might have felt compelled to protect them. Instead he watched while Coorinna edged downwind, closer and closer to her target.

Abruptly Coorinna exploded from the scrub, and the ewe was down before she knew what hit her. The cubs went after the lamb. It ran for a few yards, then doubled back, vainly seeking its mother's protection. But she was already dead. Coorinna released her grip on the ewe's throat and lay down, breathing hard. The hunt had already exhausted her. She watched her cubs bound after the lamb. This would be their first kill.

The tigers settled down to feed. They'd not eaten for many nights. In Coorinna's emaciated state she wasn't fast enough to catch the swift mountain wallabies and she lacked the strength to kill kangaroos and wombats. Until now her cubs had been too young to be useful. The discovery of this lambing flock grazing unprotected was the answer to her prayers.

Bear licked his lips and crept forward, smelling warm meat. He was downwind, and so intent were the tigers on their meal that they didn't notice the dog until he was almost upon them. Coorinna whirled to face him with bared fangs, thrashing her powerful tail to-and-fro like an angry cat.

Bear kept coming, showing neither aggression nor hesitation. Coorinna backed off, stiff-legged. Bear fell on the ewe carcass, gorging himself, while the cubs fed on the lamb. Coorinna stood guard in front of them.

When Bear had eaten his fill, he walked to the edge of the clearing and lay down. Coorinna returned to feed at the sheep carcass, occasionally curling her lip and hissing at the watching dog. The sated cubs took to pouncing at each other, occasionally barrelling into Coorinna as she fed, earning sharp nips for their trouble. One started off in Bear's direction, but was warned back by its mother's threatening growl.

The bones were stripped bare when Coorinna led her cubs back up the mountain trail. With a wave of his tail, Bear rose and trotted after them. A chorus of shrieks and screams rose from the surrounding bush, and a dozen pairs of intense yellow eyes followed him. The devils had been there all along, hidden in the shadows, waiting for the tigers to abandon the kill. They descended on the carcasses, screeching and snarling in competition for prime spot. Bear broke into a run as the bloodcurdling cries grew louder. Compared to whatever lay behind him, the little tiger family seemed almost like familiar friends.

# CHAPTER 6

Luke trailed Bear ever higher into the mountains. Lessons in bushcraft came flooding back, lessons learned as a boy at Daniel's side.

'The earth is a manuscript rewritten each day,' his teacher had told him. 'As we go about our business, we leave a ripple that betrays our passing. Footprints are a part of this tell-tale ripple. Another is the warning cry of the currawong as we walk too close to his nest, the honeysuckle stem broken as we pass, the carelessly discarded core of our apple. Animals are no different. Tracking them is like reading. First we painstakingly learn the simplest letters. They join into words, combine into phrases and so we can read the book of the animal's life.'

Daniel always impressed upon Luke the sacred responsibility this information bore with it. 'Such skills unlock secrets. Treasure this knowledge and use it wisely. Disturbing wildlife can cause much harm, leading them to desert their young or abandon feeding grounds or flee into danger. Remember, you are a guest in their home and always show respect.'

Luke didn't find it difficult to follow Bear's frantic flight through the forest to freedom. Why he chose to follow the dog was not so clear, but it seemed as good a plan as any. His escape left him more conscious than ever of his own cowardice. He couldn't avoid it. A voice screamed in his head to return before it was too late, though logic told him it was already too late – the die already cast. His penalty would be severe, whether he surrendered now or was taken against his will. Only this thought prevented him from returning to camp, prevented him from throwing himself at the superintendent's mercy, from begging forgiveness and accepting whatever beating or punishment came his way.

It seemed to Luke that fear now entirely ruled him. How had he become so spineless? He thought back to his childhood in Hobart – so innocent and cocky then, full of brash charm, with an eye for the girls and never shy of a fight. His mother and sister, how they adored him, unable to refuse him anything once he trained his smiling brown eyes on them . . . Afternoons in his Uncle Hiram's blacksmith shop.

'He'll get on, that lad, there's no doubting it,' his father would announce to nobody in particular as Luke brought down hammer on anvil to fashion a red-hot piece of steel into a horseshoe or engaged a customer with a winning grin. His uncle agreed. Everyone agreed. How wrong they'd been.

The toe ripped off his boot on some rough ground. He kicked at the rocks again and again until his toes bled, filled with contempt for himself. Yet part of him acknowledged that he *had* finally escaped. For years he'd planned and plotted and schemed and dreamed of this, and doing it nourished a kernel of pride.

Luke ripped a strip from his shirt, tied his boot together as best he could, and forged on. Following the dog gave him a purpose, pointless as that purpose was. Focusing on tracking also distracted him from the seriousness of his predicament. How grateful he was for the bushcraft Daniel had taught him. It could spell the difference between life and death in the days ahead.

Hour after hour, Luke climbed into the rugged uplands. Some-times he glanced back, but saw no sign of pursuit. Open bush gave way to taller forests of eucalypt, southern myrtle and blackwood. Thick scrub and tangled logs slowed his progress, but also made it easier to track the big dog. His blundering through the undergrowth left an obvious trail.

At last Luke emerged from a timbered ridge onto an open button-grass plain, cradled between craggy cliffs. A shadow rippling along the ground, made him look up. Overhead soared two dark shapes, gliding in lazy, dignified circles across the vivid expanse of blue. He watched the eagles enviously, so far removed from the wretchedness of his own earth-bound existence.

The emerald carpet of cushion plants provided a delightful contrast from the grey-green forest, and soft, spongy comfort for Luke's aching feet. But now it proved much harder to follow Bear's tracks.

Luke recalled his teacher's words. 'The clues to the next track are in the present one.'

Although always kind, Daniel was an exacting taskmaster. When Luke found it difficult to age a trail, his teacher had taken him into Coomalong's garden and cleared a level patch of soil, removing twigs and pebbles and roughly smoothing it with the side of his hand. He used a stick to make five impressions in the soil, each roughly half an inch deep – a paw print.

'Memorise this mark. Also the prevailing wind, time of day, position of the sun.'

Six hours later, before Luke normally went home for the day, his teacher again summoned him into the garden to examine the print. Although it didn't look any different, Luke studied it carefully and wrote down the weather conditions.

Daniel gave him a satisfied smile. 'I've asked your father if you may stay with us at Coomalong this week. Would you like that? Good.'

The housekeeper showed him inside to a guest bedroom. There he discovered his own little trunk, lovingly packed by his mother, sitting in the middle of a soft featherbed.

Luke spent the evening wolfing down tender corned beef and cabbage dumplings, followed by mounds of pudding and clotted cream. After dinner Daniel challenged him and Belle to poker, a game they all took seriously in spite of playing for peanuts. When his wife complained about the children staying up late at such a questionable game, Daniel said he was teaching the mathematics of chance. Eventually Mrs Campbell wrested them away for a supper of warm milk and honey sandwiches. Luke went to his room, tired but happy, and sank into his soft bed.

Just as he was drifting off to sleep, his teacher roused him. Mr Campbell was carrying a notebook and oil lamp. 'Get dressed, my boy. Hurry up.'

Luke pulled on his trousers and jacket. In the excitement of being invited to stay, he'd forgotten to ask the reason for his visit. He was about to find out.

They trooped to the back garden. Light drizzle fell on the ground where the mock paw print lay. Daniel lowered the lamp so Luke could see. It looked a little different now: shallower, less distinct. He examined it for a while, making sketches, taking notes.

'Good, good,' said Daniel. 'I'll see you again at four o'clock this morning. You'll repeat the process every six hours for the next week, observing how the track deteriorates with time. That is how you learn to age a trail.'

He'd certainly learned from one of the best.


Luke scouted ahead and picked up Bear's tracks in a boggy patch beside a stream. He stopped to drink, cupping the clear, sweet water in his hands, gulping down long draughts.

Late afternoon melded into dusk. Shadows gathered, casting the jagged face of the range into stark relief. An icy wind chased after the departing sun, piercing Luke's ragged clothes. He shivered with weariness and cold, and the bullet wound to his shoulder throbbed painfully. Still, he was loath to abandon Bear's trail.

In the half-light he came to another creek. There, beneath a screen of pandanus leaves, he found a fern-frond bed trampled flat, still holding the impression of the sleeping dog. Luke curled up in the soft nest and slept.

· · ·

The tigers discovered Luke as they stole, soft-footed, back to the safety of the mountains. The playful cubs, with full stomachs and egos boosted by their first hunt, almost pounced on him as he slumbered. Coorinna called them away just in time. Bear, following a few minutes behind, showed more caution, giving the sleeping man a wide berth.

In the morning, Luke faintly recalled three inquisitive, twitching noses on little whiskery faces, bright eyes reflecting the moonlight. He thought it a dream. As he tried to rouse himself, the full extent of his predicament hit him. The bone-numbing chill of the Tasmanian highland night had seeped into his body as he slept, fingers of frost stealing his strength, enticing him to lie still just a little longer.

He tried to move, but his arms and legs were stiff and unyielding. At first he was pleased his shoulder didn't hurt, until he realised it was simply numb with cold. When circulation returned, it ached again with a vengeance. After several painful minutes of effort Luke coaxed his reluctant limbs to stretch. He clambered uncertainly to his feet, stumbled, and fell hard back to the ground, wondering where on earth his balance was. At last he managed to stand, hands still frozen, feet dead lumps of wood. Stamping toes and rubbing fingers, Luke lurched to the creek to drink. At first his hands didn't register the bite of icy water in his cupped palms, but soon enough his extremities felt like they belonged to him again.

As morning sunshine filtered through the gum trees and the pastel sky promised a warm spring day, Luke forgot his misery. An unfamiliar realisation hit him. He was free. Free to freeze, perhaps. Free to starve. Free to succumb to loneliness and madness, but free nonetheless. And he knew that he would not trade the sweetness of this freedom for a lice-ridden bunk, a meagre meal and the doubtful comfort of his cutthroat companions back at the work camp. With no better plan, Luke kept on after Bear.

For some reason the dog had changed direction. One set of prints had become four or even five. In miry ground below the creek he found the tracks of another large dog and what looked like puppy pug-marks. If Luke read the trail correctly, Bear was following a wild pack, his own tracks always overlapping the others.

It was with a great deal of apprehension that Luke descended the mountain, aware that by doing so he headed back towards town. His nerves played tricks on him. Once he was so sure he could hear men crashing through the bush, that he hid for an hour in a soggy, leech-infested depression behind a rock.

Eventually the forested slope opened onto a broad, grassy clearing. On its western edge was a ramshackle hut. Luke watched for a long time in the shelter of the trees, until curiosity overcame caution. He abandoned Bear's trail and hurried to the hut.

Nobody had lived there for a long time. Grass grew high all around. Sheets of bark lined the crude split-log walls, and wire loops tied the frame together. The weight of native honeysuckle had pulled the door askew, and part of the roof was caved in. Luke didn't mind. What a stroke of luck!

He pulled back the creeper and pushed through the rickety door. There was even a rough stone fireplace, mortared with crumbling clay. A rock lay at his feet. He picked it up and wedged it back into the tumble-down chimney. A smile spread over his face. He looked around. A crooked meat safe in one corner. Some dusty boards and a frayed hessian bag. In the bag he found a half-full gunpowder flask, two empty rum bottles and a rusty knife. In another corner lay a battered axe head, some wire, a broken broom and a cast-iron pot. Not much to most, but to Luke it felt like Christmas.

Dusting them off and trying to ignore his aching hunger, a million uses for each item sprang to mind. He forgot about Bear. He even forgot he was on the run. Luke swept the floor with the old broom. Tomorrow he'd cut a young tree to replace the split handle. He placed the boards on some stones along the wall to make a handy bench. He took the old pot and bottles down to a little creek that bubbled in a gully beside the hut. He washed them and filled them with water. On his way back he picked some early waratahs, his mother's favourite flowers. He used a bottle as a vase and stood the scarlet blooms on a level stone above the fireplace. It felt like home already.

Next to eat. Fashioning a rough snare from wire, he went back to the creek, where rabbit droppings pointed to a fresh warren. He dug a shallow hole, buried the loop at the base of a springy sapling, fashioned two notched pegs, and hammered them in on either side. Bending the sapling to the ground, he fixed the wire snare to its free end, carefully slotting the slender trunk into the notched peg. A trip-stick, laid across the path and wedged into the notches, completed the trap. Any rabbit knocking the stick would be ensnared and flung into the air.

Luke returned to the hut, and sat down to rest with his back against the wall. Fatigue and hunger were taking their toll. He glanced at the sun sailing high in the sky. Late afternoon at best, and rabbits wouldn't come out until dusk. His empty stomach couldn't wait that long. Time to go fishing.

He baited a bent wire hook with a wriggling worm, unravelled a thread from the hessian sack, and tied the line to a stick. Down to the creek he went and promptly caught a plump, spotted trout. Luke stopped to collect bracken root and warrigal greens on the way back to the hut. Now for a fire. Gathering kindling, leaves and dry grass, he poured a tiny portion of gunpowder from the flask onto the rudimentary stone grate. Using the axe head as a flint stone, Luke struck it again and again against the fireplace. Before long sparks flew, igniting the tiny pile of powder with a bright flash. Smoke wafted, followed by flame.

Luke whooped with delight. Before long, a fire crackled happily in the dusty hearth. Stripped fern root went into the fire to roast. Fish and greens went into the cast-iron pot, balanced on two large rocks either side of the grate. His first meal as a free man. The succulent fish melted off the bone. It was the most delicious meal he'd ever tasted.

The chill of approaching night nipped the air. Luke gathered bracken and fern fronds, piling them high against the wall away from the gap in the roof. He tested his new bed. Comfortable as the feather mattress at Coomalong.

As twilight fell, Luke checked his trap. A rabbit dangled in the wire snare. This was too good to be true. Luke hurried home to roast it on a stick. But with darkness came a growing sense of unease. Were they searching for him? Had a reward been posted for his capture? The lurking fear of discovery remained, yet nothing would make him abandon his refuge that night.

He finished the rabbit, washed his pot, refilled his bottle and snuggled down in his ferny bed. To distract himself from the nagging pain in his shoulder, Luke focused on the waratahs. Bold, fiery flowers – each scarlet torch a mass of individual blossoms. Daniel had told him that 'waratah' was a native word for 'beautiful'. Luke tried to remember the botanical name. That was it. *Telopea* from the Greek 'telepos', meaning 'seen from afar'. He gazed at the fire. An echo of the waratah was there in the flames. Red fingers leapt and danced, offering up shapes of animals and trees. The image of a dog glowed brightly and died. Luke's eyes grew heavy and he slept.

Hours later, the moon looked over the mountains to see the figure of a giant black dog standing like a statue in the clearing, staring at the hut. Raising his head, Bear sent a howl, long and mournful, into the empty expanse of sky. He took one last lingering look before melting into the shadows, leaving the moon to journey alone across the starry heavens.

# CHAPTER 7

Dawn drifted down through the hole in the roof. Luke opened his eyes. For a long time he lay, heavy-lidded and sleepy in his ferny bed, savouring the unfamiliar experience of waking in his own time, in his own place. With drowsy satisfaction he reviewed the previous day. He was finally free. Now all he had to do was figure out what came next. Perhaps he'd stay here for a while, let any search die down before moving on. One thought still nagged. He'd lost Bear. The big dog would be long gone.

Luke jumped up, shivering, and grabbed a stick to poke the fire. His shoulder hurt where the bullet had grazed him; a bullet meant for Bear. Thank God it had missed its mark. Hot coals hid under grey ashes, and with the help of a little kindling he coaxed a flame to life. Luke squatted by the fire for a few minutes, warming his hands, then picked up the cast-iron pot and pushed out the door. He should have saved some rabbit for breakfast.

Morning lay shrouded in a cloud that had crept, ghost-footed, down from the range overnight. Moisture dripped from each leaf and flower and twig. He prayed it would clear to a fine day. Rain, before he fixed the roof, would make life here very difficult indeed.

Luke stepped onto the grass to empty his bladder. What was that?

A movement at the northern end of the clearing stopped his breath. This was it; they'd come for him.

A mob of wallabies emerged from the mist. Luke exhaled, feeling a little foolish. The idea of wallaby stew took over from his fear, making his stomach clench and his mouth water. The animals cocked their heads, then bounded as one for the forest. Something had startled them. Bear? Luke edged round to where the mob had vanished in the trees. It was hard to get his bearings in the grey blanket of cloud.

His foot connected with something heavy. It rolled away a little. A useful rock for the chimney restoration project, perhaps? His hands found it on the foggy ground. It felt smooth and hard. Luke picked it up. Then, with a gasp, he dropped the object back to earth. A bleached white human skull bounced against his foot. Gaping eye sockets, staring up at him. Luke stepped back. All round, emerging from the mist, lay more scattered bones. A human femur bore tell-tale teeth marks of some wild animal. He gulped and picked up the skull again to examine it. Apart from a few missing front teeth it was intact. Was this the original owner of the hut?

Luke tried to convince himself it was good news. He had nothing to fear from a dead man. But a lingering sense of horror remained. His thoughts turned, despite himself, to dark scenarios. Foul play. Murder. Or did the man fall ill far from help? Did the devils, tigers and wild dogs come for him prematurely, feasting on his living flesh while screams echoed unheard off the granite tors?

Luke swore aloud. What use was he when his imagination regularly scared the wits out of him? He forced himself to collect the bones into a pile. At the very least they deserved a proper burial, and although he knew nothing of such things, he would do his best. Using the axe head and a stout branch he tried to dig a grave in the stony ground. Time and time again, tree roots and shale caused him to start over. He had to move further and further into the open, where the earth was more yielding and the ground clearer of roots. The task seemed to take forever and, all the while, the skull stared accusingly from atop its stack of bones.

He'd made good headway when, behind him, a dog barked – too

high-pitched for Bear. Luke froze. A man appeared from the forest, rifle raised. At his heels ran a cross-bred terrier, yapping furiously. Luke dropped his tools and raised his hands. Competing emotions ran riot through his brain: disappointment, despair, apprehension – even relief. Whatever happened next, death or capture, was out of his hands.

Minutes ticked by and the standoff continued. Finally the man lowered his gun. 'And who might you be, young fella?'

Surely this man knew he was an escapee? Ragged prison clothing, if nothing else, gave the game away. Perhaps he was playing some cruel game of cat-and-mouse by feigning ignorance?

'I asked your name,' said the stranger. 'Have you no tongue in your head?'

Why on earth didn't he just get on with it? Luke resolved to force his hand, reaching for the axe head lying on the ground. A bullet whizzed past his shoulder. It angered him, made him bold.

'You bloody well know who I am,' he said. 'So take me in if you can, or shoot me, but don't waste my time.'

The stranger laughed. 'A word of advice, son. Don't jump to conclusions. You go round announcing yourself a fugitive to the wrong folks . . . you're asking for trouble. Me? I take people wholly as I find them, and I ain't got nothing against you so far. So what say I lower me gun and you step away from that sorry-looking axe head and we have ourselves a friendly talk?' As a sign of good faith the stranger placed his rifle on the ground and stepped aside.

With nothing much to lose, Luke approached him with an outstretched hand. The stranger grinned and Luke took a good look at him – grey beard, untidy silver hair sticking out from under a broad-brimmed rabbit-skin hat, fifty or so. He wore a blue serge shirt and loose moleskin trousers held together with a leather belt. The garb of a trapper, or perhaps a prospector. Cautiously they shook hands.

'Angus. Angus McLeod. What say we retire to that hut? If there's any chance someone's gunning for you, lad, you'd best keep out of the open.'

They passed the pile of bones, topped by the watching skull. Angus doffed his hat and made the sign of the cross.

'Rest in peace, Clarry.'

'You knew him?'

'I did. A good bloke, was Clarry. Bit of a hermit. Built this place and lived up here the best part of forty years. Must've been seventy if he was a day, but still fit as a fiddle. I'd drop by twice a year, buy his skins, sell them in town. Never saw another soul, did Clarry. Abbott's foreman let the old man stay in return for watching the sheep sent up here for spring pasture. Clarry protected them from them native wolves. Vicious brutes. Kill thirty sheep a night, they do, just for sport. Follow a man for days through the bush just waiting for a chance to rip out his throat while he sleeps. They drink blood, y'know, like damned vampyres. Used to be plenty around here, but they're thin on the ground now. Old Clarry snared a fair few in his time – my word, he did.'

'How can you be sure that's Clarry?' asked Luke.

'Who else would it be, way out here? But there's a surer way of telling.' Angus lifted the skull, indicating the gap in the teeth of the upper jawbone. 'Clarry had his top front teeth knocked out in a bar fight. Never could say his *s*'s after that. Yep. This is Clarry all right, no mistake.'

'*Abbott's* foreman, you said? You don't mean Henry Abbott, do you?'

'One and the same. Holds every piece of good ground hereabouts. King of the wool kings and owner of the richest mining leases. King Midas, they call him.'

Luke's blood ran cold. Henry Abbott. The man who'd raped his sister, torn his childhood and family apart. Henry Abbott. Owner of this land. Owner even of the tumbledown shack that Luke wanted to call home.

In a daze, he followed Angus and his little terrier inside the hut and sat down on the plank of wood rigged up as a makeshift bench. The dog smiled and wagged his tail. Luke patted him. The dog climbed onto his knee. Angus, looking around, gave a long drawn-out whistle.

'Somebody's given this place a right going over. Stolen everything not nailed down. Likely done Old Clarry in as well. I know what they was looking for, lad, and I don't reckon they found it, neither. Clarry had a fortune hidden away somewhere. The tight-fisted old bastard made good money from trapping, and he hoarded every penny. Lived off the land, save for what provisions I brought him after selling his skins. Clarry didn't keep his loot here, though. Stashed in the bush, he told me. Guess nobody'll ever know now.'

The little shack took on a more sinister feel, as Luke tried to digest this new information. Its owner hadn't peacefully passed from old age. There was robbery at least and maybe killing as well. And all in the place where every blade of grass, every clod of earth, even the bleached murdered bones themselves belonged to the hated Henry Abbott.

A long silence ensued. 'Seems like I'm doing all the talking here, young fella.' Angus took off his hat. 'Your turn.'

Luke pushed the dog from his lap, stood up and moved over to the fireplace, shuffling from foot to foot. What to say? Angus would be able to tell a lot just by looking at him. He wore the sparse beard of youth and, even by bushmen standards, was filthy and bedraggled. Coarse government-issue prison clothes. Hands blistered and calloused. Hair oily and matted. Soles near worn out of his shoes.

'Son, you as much confessed to me you was running from the law,' said Angus. 'The look of you confirms it. What I want to know is how and why. Seems to me it might make for an entertaining yarn.'

When Luke started talking, he couldn't stop. He told Angus everything. From his happy childhood in Hobart to the nightmare of Rebecca's rape, from his unjust sentencing to his years of brutal incarceration, from his spur-of-the-moment escape to his discovery of the hut, and then his plan to give old Clarry a decent burial.

Angus gave a whistle, rose to his feet and stood for a long while, staring at the fire.

'That's some story. Abbott put you in this spot, you say. The same

Sir Henry Abbott that owns this town? That owns this here hut we both be standing in?' Angus whistled again. 'Blimey, so you're the fella that knocked his teeth out? Fair dinkum, son, there's a fair few folks round here'd give you a medal for that. Clarry used to have a good laugh about his own gap-tooth grin. *If it's good enough for his lordship, then its good enough for me.* They say Sir Henry's nose was never quite straight again, and that he always smiled with closed lips to hide the flash of gold caps in the front.' Angus fell into a fit of chuckles. 'I'll tell you something for nothing – Abbott doesn't have many friends around these parts.' He put on his hat. 'I suppose you could use a feed, son. Then maybe afterwards we can see about giving old Clarry that funeral, like you planned. Right kind of you, that was.'

A wave of relief swept over Luke, threatening to turn his legs to jelly. He sat back down.

'That's right, take a load off. See if you can't spark up that fire, and me and Scruffy here'll go and get the tucker.'

Luke gave Angus a long, grateful look.

'One more thing,' said Angus. 'What's your name?'

'Luke. Luke Tyler.'

Angus doffed his hat. 'Pleased to meet you, Luke.'

Feeling a little steadier on his feet, Luke stoked the fire. Soon a fine blaze crackled in the hearth. Angus returned with wallaby steaks, damper and a juicy apple each. It was an ample lunch and for the first time in a very long time, Luke ate his fill. After feeding Scruffy the scraps, Angus beckoned for Luke to follow him outside.

At the back of the hut stood tethered an enormous red-and-white bullock, bearing three large packs overflowing with skins and tools.

'Meet Toro. Stronger than any horse, half the cost and twice as amenable.'

Toro bellowed a welcome. Luke rubbed the friendly beast between his sweeping horns, while Angus unfastened a shovel and pick from the pack saddle. 'Let's give Clarry that decent burial you was talking about.'

With the help of the right tools, they were able to bury Clarry within the margin of the trees. 'No need to advertise,' said Angus. 'If folks in town don't know what's happened to Clarry, then we'd best try to keep it that way. Wouldn't do for the law to come poking about now, would it?'.

They gathered stones and built a rough cairn to mark the spot.

The winter sun was as high as it would rise, when Angus, with hat in hand, stood with Luke and Scruffy before the grave. Bowing his head, he haltingly recited a few words from the Bible.

*'Lord, you have been our dwelling place in all generations.*
*Before the mountains were brought forth,*
*Or ever you formed the earth and the world,*
*Even from everlasting to everlasting,*
*You are God.*
*Amen.'*

Luke gazed up at the snow-dusted peaks, which formed a dramatic backdrop to the sacred scene. He'd lost any faith he might have had, but a sense of wonder overcame him all the same. In that moment he saw something divine in the mountains presiding over his freedom and in the sheltering forest. Luke's eyes filled with tears and, for once, all fear left him.


Angus stayed for the rest of the afternoon. Fetching clothes from one of his packs, he threw them to Luke. 'Here. Do me a favour. Burn them lice-ridden rags you're wearing, along with that bracken bed you slept in last night. And while you're at it, go down to the creek and wash the bugs out of your hair. I'll not be lending clobber and blankets to any flea-infested convict.' Luke grinned and caught a bar of carbolic soap as it whizzed through the air at his head. 'And it's probably more than me life's worth letting you get your hands on this here cut-throat razor, but apart from helping to delouse you, a haircut and shave'll help disguise you. I'll wager even your own mother wouldn't recognise you then.'

Luke flinched at the suggestion. After all this time, his mother may well not recognise him. He headed down to the creek, carrying his new trousers. Stripping off, he stood naked in the icy water, washing months of grime from filthy skin. Lock by lock, he cut off his lousy, matted hair and watched the tufts sail downstream. He shaved his scalp and face with the blunt blade right down to skin, leaving red welts like a rookie shearer; then scrubbed his head with the harsh stinging soap till it burned.

Luke stepped from the cleansing stream onto a sunlit rock, feeling reborn. He'd endured the tormenting itch of lice for so long it had felt normal. Finally free from its crawling irritation, the contrast was startling. He raised his eyes to the mountains and was struck by a realisation. He'd endured fear for so long, it too had felt normal – intrinsic to his being. The presence of the quiet peaks gave him courage.

Luke put on his new trousers. Heading back up to the hut, naked to the waist, he met Angus coming down to replenish his waterskins.

'Christ,' said Angus. 'Someone's given you a flogging or two in your time.'

Luke shrugged. His back was covered in an old wickerwork of raised scars. His sore shoulder was red and inflamed.

Angus took a closer look. 'A bullet winged you then, did it, lad? That looks right nasty. Come back up to the hut and I'll bandage it. Clean it up with a little iodine as well.'

Luke shot Angus a grateful smile. The shoulder now ached constantly.

'I thought they'd banned floggings,' said Angus as he tended the wound.

'Not everybody's read the rule book. Solitary's worse. I once spent thirty days alone in a cell without windows. Sends you mad. Does something awful to your brain until you're sure you'd be better off dead. I'd rather a good whipping any day.'

Angus gently squeezed his arm. 'That's all behind you now, lad.'

He supervised the burning of Luke's clothing, then, leaving some provisions and a blanket, he said goodbye. 'You'd best be lying low for a few weeks. Not many people know about this hut, nor is it easy travelling between here and Hills End. You should be safe enough, though keep your wits about you.'

Luke buried his face in his hands, dreading the thought of being alone again.

'Don't you worry, son. I'll not let you down, nor give you up to the coppers neither. I'm off to Hills End now, but I'll be back when I reckon any hullabaloo's died down. Of course, that might take a might longer than usual, considering it was you what knocked his lordship's teeth out.' He chuckled and wiped his mouth with his sleeve. 'I'll guarantee there's a reward posted, and a big one too. But generally these things die down pretty quick. There's plenty of ne'er-do-wells in Hills End and the normal go is *no questions asked*. When things settle, I'll fetch you. Come gold panning with me, if you like.'

'I'd like that, sir,' said Luke, overwhelmed with gratitude. 'I'd like that a lot. How can I thank you?'

'By taking care, son, and keeping out of sight.' Angus doffed his battered hat. 'It's been a grand pleasure.'

With that, he untied his unusual packhorse, hoisted Scruffy onto Toro's broad back and set off down the mountain.

The trio wended their way from sight. Luke stowed away the contributions from Angus, and headed out to set his snare. Despite the bandage, his shoulder throbbed painfully, and despite the cooling day, he felt a little hot behind the eyes. He'd meant to go fishing, but weariness defeated him. Instead he collected fresh ferns and firewood for the night and returned to the hut. He made a billy of tea, ate a little salt-beef and damper. Then he lay down under the clean blanket and fell asleep.

Sometime in the early hours as his fire lay low, little more than pale embers, Luke woke to Bear's mournful howl. Resounding through the still night, it swelled in power until it caused the very hut to quiver. It echoed off the tors, rebounded in the gullies, filled the vast wilderness.

Luke thrilled and shivered at the sound. The great black dog, so instrumental in his flight to freedom, was calling to him. The cry became the howl of his own heart. Luke drifted off to sleep, certain of a bond that couldn't be denied.

# CHAPTER 8

O ver the coming days, Coorinna and the lost dog maintained their odd friendship. Often the lonely she-tiger cocked her head, ears straining to detect the call of her kind. Her sensitive nose tested the air over and over for the scent of another thylacine. She was ever disappointed.

All through the bush, life renewed itself. Spring was in full flux. Tender shoots of grass sprang fresh underfoot. Waratah and leather-wood flowers unfurled. Eager seedlings emerged from the warming earth, vying for the sun's strengthening kiss, and stands of native beech burst into bright leaf.

The quickening of sap in the forest was matched by the urgent desire of bush creatures to go forth and multiply. From the lowliest minnow to the lordly wedge-tailed eagle, all sought the comfort and satisfaction of a partner. The uplands throbbed with fertile vitality. Yet Coorinna remained unmated.

Her cubs, untroubled by their mother's restlessness, explored all their mountain home could offer. Each night there were new smells to investigate, new creatures to chase, fresh tarns to splash through with faithful Bear as escort. But their cautious mother was unwilling to travel too far. With unerring accuracy she always delivered the little pack safely back to their den by dawn.

Though unsuccessful in her efforts to find a mate, in other ways Coorinna's life was greatly improved. The active assistance of Bear and her growing cubs meant their hunting forays rarely failed. Coorinna grew strong. She no longer discouraged Bear. His unfailing good nature and the cubs' confidence in him allayed her fears.

The first few times Bear ventured inside the den he was swiftly repelled. But persistence pays and within days Coorinna's attacks lost their fury. Soon she accepted him deep within the comfortable lair, which she'd lined with ferns and moss. She even tended his injury, unable to resist cleaning Bear's festering shoulder with her neat, efficient tongue. The grateful dog lay very still, acknowledging her assistance with an occasional tail thump. Thanks to Coorinna's constant attention, the infection soon abated and Bear's wound healed.

Luke wasn't so fortunate. His injured shoulder continued to plague him, growing more and more painful each day. It was one thing to bid his fears goodbye in the cleansing creek with a new set of clothes and Angus's company. But it was quite another to maintain a positive outlook through the dreary days that followed. He didn't hunt or trap; he felt too ill. He called for Bear and left out damper, but the dog never came. More than Luke's shoulder ached now. His heart ached too – with despair and loneliness. A week passed. More.

His imagination filled the forest with strange, half-seen forms, and he stayed close to the hut. The sight of old Clarry's grave in the shadow of the trees never failed to disturb him. All too often now, he imagined his own to be the next set of bleached bones to be scattered carelessly over the grass. Luke spent his days watching for Angus to return. Though on guard against strangers, he saw no one. It was as if he'd dropped off the face of the earth.

He slept more and more, finding comfort in the dream world.

In sleep, Bear always came when called. With the big dog at his side, baying at a dream moon, Luke returned effortlessly to his family or travelled the world on wings of steel forged by his own hand. At other times, he sat in judgement upon a snivelling, pleading Henry Abbott, unceremoniously consigning him to the hangman's noose.

Luke became eager for sleep. He neglected his wound. And for some reason, he didn't feel hungry any more. The days melted into each other with seamless tedium.

One morning he didn't leave the hut at all. The hearth lay cold and Luke stayed in bed, mind muddled with fever. That night Bear's howl seemed to travel back with him from the dream world. Sometimes he heard a whimper when he thought he was awake.

Luke stumbled to his feet, pissed on the dead fire and collapsed back to bed, trembling and delirious. A bitter south wind had blown the door open and the hut was freezing. Yet Luke felt unbearably hot, and tore off his shirt. He could swear he saw Bear, but he didn't trust his senses. Thresholds of reality and imagination blurred as infection took serious hold.

For three days and nights Luke battled the fever: barely conscious, eyes closed, head aching, dreams no longer pleasurable. The creaking of the walls in the wind became the creaking of the old pony cart, carrying his trembling sister home from Henry Abbott's house. The moaning and wailing of storms through the forest became the cries of his mother as the constables dragged him away. His jaw clenched weakly, muscles quivering, twitching, exhausting his sick body even further.


Bear stood beside Luke's bed. Despite the company of his strange pack, he yearned for something more, something lost. He yearned for the companionship of man, to sleep before a fire, to feel the touch of a hand. To hear a loving voice.

As morning passed into afternoon, Bear maintained his vigil. There was comfort in proximity to the sleeping man. Bear licked

Luke's arm, where it sprawled across the floor. It was bathed in perspiration. He made a thorough job of it, cleaning every inch of bare skin. He pulled at the filthy shoulder bandage until it came away. He cleaned the oozing wound with his tongue. Then he lay down beside Luke, relishing the feel of the man's limp hand pressed against him. There he remained for many hours, until Luke's stirring broke the spell. Bear didn't go far: just down to the creek for a drink before settling contentedly on the sunny doorstep, where he snatched an hour or two of sleep. It was late afternoon before he returned to the tigers.

A cooperative strategy was developing within the pack. Bear took his cues from Coorinna and proved an apt student. With a functional family group of two adults and three half-grown cubs, Coorinna could use the time-honoured hunting practices learned from her mother. Stronger, and growing sleek of hide, she now targeted wallabies, her favourite food.

The two smaller cubs would show themselves to a group of wallabies foraging at the forest edge. With instinctive precision they chased their prey in the direction of Bear, Coorinna and the male cub who hid crouched some distance ahead. When the wallabies came bounding along, the waiting predators singled out the weakest animal and launched an attack.

The big dog learned quickly. Ten thousand years of domestication was hardly enough to extinguish two million years of evolution for such basic instincts as predatory aggression. Given the opportunity to track prey or pursue a moving target, the wolf in Bear made a sudden resurgence.

He became a formidable killer: finely tuned, controlled and intelligent – a worthy honorary thylacine. Even large kangaroos couldn't withstand the assault of two hundred pounds of muscle, teeth and bone. When his fangs found their throats, he braced his forefeet, hurled himself backwards like a spring released, and it was over.

This became Bear's routine – hunting with the pack by night and spending his days at the hut. The cubs were curious about where Bear disappeared to each day, but a stern glance from their mother discouraged their adventurous attempts to follow him.

Luke woke to the musical sound of magpies. His thirst burned, but the searing heat was gone from his brow. His body felt cool, almost cold. His head no longer throbbed and his shoulder barely pained him. He tried to move his legs, but they refused to obey him. Luke turned to see if his water-pot was within reach.

Bear was sitting by the door. For a while Luke imagined himself still asleep and fought against waking. The dog was even larger than he remembered: shinier, fatter, his huge frame blocking the doorway. Luke reached out and Bear flinched. Luke called, but his parched throat made no sound. He tried to stand. On the third attempt he succeeded.

Luke gulped down the few drops of water in the pot, soothing his swollen tongue. Now perhaps he could speak. He called to Bear. The dog shivered, as if afraid. Luke was afraid too – afraid that Bear would leave, that Bear would desert him.

Bear backed from the hut, out of sight. Luke stumbled to the door. Would the dog be gone? No, there he was – waiting, watching. Relief swept through Luke, threatening to drain the strength from his legs. Steadying himself, he picked up the pot. He tried to whistle but his lips were too dry. Instead he patted his thigh several times in what he hoped was an encouraging way, and cast a friendly, expectant glance at Bear. Then he moved off towards the creek.

To his delight the dog followed, maintaining a discreet distance. Luke reached the creek, gulping down great draughts of sweet water. Energy seeped into his dehydrated body. Bear watched while Luke sat on a rock, drenched his face and hands, and refilled the pot. He inspected his injured shoulder. The wound shone pink and clean. Luke grinned and started for the hut, this time managing a whistle. Bear responded with an uncertain wag of his tail and Luke whooped with delight.

Bear remained at the hut staying at arm's length, until the afternoon shadows grew long. Then, with a sharp bark of goodbye, he abruptly disappeared up the timbered slope. Luke cursed the mountain that stole the dog, calling uselessly into the bush until cold and exhaustion drove him inside to find a fitful, restless sleep.

# CHAPTER 9

Belle Campbell came downstairs from her bedroom. In riding trousers she could easily have been mistaken for a boy, if not for her mane of golden-chestnut hair. She followed the sound of raised voices through the house and into the library. Mama and Papa were arguing about her again.

'I simply must take Belle to Hobart,' said Elizabeth. 'Most girls of her age are preparing to enter society. Instead she's running wild as a tomboy out here in the wilderness.'

'There's no hurry,' said Daniel. 'She's only sixteen.'

Belle clamped a hand to her forehead and groaned. Why did her parents always talk about her like she wasn't there?

Daniel took a textbook on fungi down from the shelf. With a sigh, Elizabeth prised it out of his hands.

'Almost seventeen,' she said. 'And Belle needs time. Learning to behave like a lady might not come easily to our daughter.'

'I'm sure it won't.' He took the book back. 'She's bound to find the constraints of polite society as insufferable as you did, Lizzie.'

Belle stepped between them. 'Why don't you ask me what I want?'

Daniel beamed. 'A capital idea.' He opened the book and scanned the index. 'You decide, Belle.'

'I'll go if Grace goes, but only for a week. We have to be back for the birth of Star's foal.'

'I was thinking of a longer stay,' said Elizabeth. 'Plays, shopping, balls. We'll have lots of fun, but I'm afraid Grace can't come this time, darling.'

'Then I'm staying. Much as I love you, Mama, it's boring when it's just us.'

'You have your answer, Lizzie.'

Papa didn't look up from his book. That was bound to make her mother mad.

'We both know it's not so simple, Daniel. In this case you must choose for her, and you must choose Hobart.'

He closed the book. 'I will do no such thing. What would you have Belle do? Pay lip service to the modern notion of female independence that you yourself taught her, Lizzie, and then passively submit to her father's demand? You would think less of her for it.' He gave his wife, then daughter an affectionate kiss. 'In any case, I'd miss you both, and I can't go to Hobart. My work here is too important.'

Belle grinned. It was two against one. Her mother didn't stand a chance. 'What about the little school you've started, Mama? What will happen to the children if you leave?'

'You are my main concern,' said Elizabeth. 'Not other people's children.' She rested a hand on Belle's shoulder. 'You must spend less time rambling around the countryside by yourself, and more time with people your own age.'

'I can do that here,' said Belle. 'Binburra isn't the end of the earth. There's Grace, and the Longbottom girls and Edward Abbott. Edward asked us to a party just last week, but Papa said no.'

Daniel scowled. 'You know how I feel about Henry Abbott, Lizzie.'

'This isn't about you and your feelings, it's about our daughter. And Edward is not his father.' Elizabeth took Daniel's hands in hers. 'Shall we try a compromise? Belle and I will stay here, at least for now, if you will make an effort to be more social with our neighbours, including the Abbotts.'

'Please, Papa.' Belle gave him her most winning smile.

'If it's what you want,' he said at last in a gruff voice.

'It is. It's exactly what I want.' She threw her slim arms around him. 'Bye now.'

'Where are you going?' asked Elizabeth.

'For a ride up to the falls. I saw a platypus family there last week, and I promised Papa I'd find their burrow. I'm going to draw them. You should see the babies, Mama. They're so sweet.'

Belle slipped out the door before any more questions could be asked. She couldn't wait to saddle Whisky, her impatient palomino filly, and head up the waterfall track. She loved these mountains as much as her father did, but her mother was right about one thing. It would be good to see more of her friends, especially Edward. The compromise brokered between her parents would give her the best of both worlds.

Daniel returned to his books, angered by the prospect of rubbing shoulders with Henry Abbott, but pleased Belle would stay.

Three years ago the family had moved from Coomalong, their city home, to this country estate more than one hundred miles north-west of Hobart. Daniel had been watching the wholesale clearing of land for timber, mining and grazing in the area with increasing alarm, soon realising that the only way to preserve the forest, might be to own the forest. So he'd acquired this vast tract of land in the foothills of the highlands. By most standards, the property wasn't particularly valuable. It contained some cleared pasture, but the greater portion was virgin country, reaching high into the rocky uplands all the way to the cliffs of the central plateau.

Daniel created an independent board to oversee the running of Campbell College so he could spend most of the year in the country-side. He named the estate Binburra, a native word for beech tree. And, indeed, the more remote, mountainous parts boasted dense stands of Tasmanian beech, along with sassafras, southern myrtles, blackwood and leatherwood. Huon pine, a relic rainforest species prized for its astonishingly durable timber, grew along rivers and damp alluvial flats in the ranges.

Daniel loved Tasmania's trees, particularly its southern beech. One of a few truly deciduous Australian trees, it reminded Daniel of the true beeches of his native northern hemisphere, to which it was related. Like its northern cousin, it changed colour in autumn from modest green to rust-red, orange and brilliant gold. A miraculous contrast with its evergreen forest companions. Another favourite was the leatherwood, a lovely little tree that flourished in the highlands. It bore fragrant white flowers with exquisite red-tipped stamens, equal in beauty to any English rose.

The government didn't share his appreciation of Tasmania's wilderness. A Land Settlement Act allowed for easy selection of such land at a pound an acre, offering generous deferred payment plans. Thousands of acres were sold, the very object of the exercise being to encourage their clearing for agricultural use. All over the island, primeval forests were being logged, smashed, burnt, uprooted, fenced, ring-barked and poisoned into oblivion.

By protecting the forest, Daniel hoped also to protect the vulnerable tigers, devils and quolls. The chief reason he bought Binburra in the first place was because thylacines were reportedly snared there.

Daniel turned the page to an illustration of a strange little ostrich-like bird. He sighed. Tasmanians had already consigned their very own dwarf emu to the history books. Growing numbers of naturalists, scientists, and even some more enlightened members of the public believed thylacines would soon follow the emu into extinction.

But the unfortunate truth was that most colonials still remained fanatically loyal to their heritage, intent upon creating a little Britain at the opposite end of the world. Tasmania's bizarre marsupial carnivores did not fit with the pretty rose gardens and neat hedgerows that flourished as tributes to Mother England. The irony, not lost on Daniel, was that they paid homage to an idealised England few of these second- and third-generation colonists had ever seen.

Daniel was in for another disappointment. In the same year he purchased Binburra, prospectors found alluvial gold at Hills End, the nearest settlement. Worse, a substantial reef of gold was discovered right under the township itself. A train line was built. Daniel's dismay grew in tandem with the premier's delight.

The find received a beat-up in the Hobart Mercury and it wasn't long before the three illiterate prospectors who discovered the gold were swindled out of it. Hills End Resources was born, with Henry Abbott the managing director and majority shareholder. He already owned most of the prime timber and pastoral land in the district. Now he also owned the town, including a large estate eight miles west of Binburra on the other side of Murderer's Hill. Abbott named the property Canterbury Downs. The first thing he did was to clear and sell its ancient forests and replace them with pasture.

It got worse. Last year a group of conservative politicians and pastoralists had formed a society dedicated to the deliberate spread of introduced species throughout Tasmania. It boasted the governor as patron and the premier as president. Henry Abbott, a keen sporting shooter, was also a founding member, hopeful of importing all sorts of exotic game. Pests, more like it.

Daniel joined an opposing group, the Royal Society, the first scientific body in Australia dedicated to protecting native habitats and creating national parks. The society achieved some limited success, forming a few small reserves, but its proposed conservation reforms were regularly blocked in parliament by the powerful pastoral and mining lobbies.

Daniel wept for Hills End and became utterly consumed with his conservation efforts. An image of young Luke Tyler came to mind, as it so often did. How he'd love to have Luke by his side to help. He missed his intelligence, his enthusiasm, his compassion. What a waste. That was Abbott's fault too. Elizabeth didn't know what she asked. How on earth was he supposed to share a drink with Henry and pretend all was well?

# CHAPTER 10

Almost three weeks passed before Luke spotted Angus and his heavily laden bullock coming back up the mountain trail. So many futile hours watching and hoping meant he'd almost given up on them. His swag was already packed with his meagre belongings. Soon he and Angus would be gone from Abbott land, exploring far and wide, scouring the ranges for gold. What an adventure. He might just find his fortune.

Bear uttered a deep growl. Scruffy pricked his ears at the sound and, with impudent daring, ran on ahead, yapping wildly. Bear ignored the little terrier, but Angus was something else again. The dog had learned to trust Luke, but this trust did not extend to strangers. He pressed protectively against Luke's leg, hackles raised and a rumble rising in his throat.

Scruffy leapt into Luke's arms, squirming with delight. Angus halted Toro at a safe distance. 'What've you got there then, lad?'

Luke put down the wriggling terrier and spoke to Bear. He walked off, stiff-legged and lay down a few yards away. Luke told Angus about the dog's mysterious appearance at the hut.

'So, this is the hound that helped you escape, eh? A fugitive from the law too, I'll wager. There's talk in town of a rogue black dog

56

leading a pack of them native wolves. A devil dog, they're saying, as big as a lion and twice as vicious. Him and his wolves've been killing sheep a dozen at a time. There ain't likely to be two dogs of that size and description hereabouts. Nope. There's your killer, all right. One and the same.'

Luke looked at Bear with a sinking feeling. Could this be true? Bear *did* disappear every night without fail, announcing his departure with a single bark and trotting northwards into the forest, leaving Luke to spend the long hours of darkness alone. He returned each morning at first light.

Luke already knew the dog was hunting his own food. Caked blood on his ruff told the story, and he was never hungry for breakfast. But leading a pack of native tigers to attack sheep? It seemed preposterous. Then Luke remembered the odd pug marks he'd seen alongside Bear's paw prints on his second day of freedom. Daniel had taught him to recognise tiger tracks. What was the distinction between tiger and dog prints? Luke thought hard. In thylacine paws, two grooves ran across the pad. These lines were absent in a dog's print. He tried to visualise the tracks and saw furrows running from heel to toe. Tigers. Improbable as Angus's story sounded, Bear's nocturnal wanderings, combined with the sightings and tracks, seemed to confirm it.

'You can't take that dog with you when you go into town,' said Angus. 'He'll be recognised faster than you.'

'Why would I be going into town?'

'That's what I've come to tell you, you daft lad. There's jobs in town down the mine, just going begging. I've told the foreman me nephew needs work and he's happy enough to have you. We'll need to change your name, of course. Sir Henry's posted a fair bounty on your head, but I've done some quiet asking about and that work camp you was in ain't there no more. They moved those poor fellas back to Hobart not two weeks past, and the coppers have given up looking for you You'll have to leave the dog, though. What do you say?'

'No.'

'What sort of a damn fool answer is that? I go out of me way to save your sorry hide and find you honest work and you turn me down flat. What's the flaming matter with you?'

'Sorry Angus, I won't leave Bear.'

The dog jumped up and licked his face as if in thanks. On hind legs, Bear matched Luke's six-foot frame. Still weak from illness, he was knocked flat on his back. Angus reached for his rifle, watching Bear warily. Scruffy joined in the game, jumping on Luke's chest, making him howl with laughter.

Angus lowered his weapon. 'Well, I'll be damned!'

Still laughing, Luke pushed the animals aside, climbed to his feet and brushed dirt and leaves from his clothes. He hugged the dogs and half-heartedly reprimanded Bear, who continued to eye Angus in a hungry way.

The old man snorted and led Toro behind the hut, unloading some items from the bullock's pack and picketing him on a juicy patch of grass.

'Can you stay for dinner?' Luke asked.

'Aye, on condition that great mongrel of yours doesn't think I *am* dinner.'

Bear chose that moment to give his customary goodbye bark. Then he disappeared at speed into the forest. Scruffy chased after him for a while, but the little terrier's legs couldn't keep up.

Before long, wallaby steaks sizzled on the fire. Angus smoked his pipe and watched Luke stoke the flames. 'Your mind's made up then?' he said. 'You'll not come with me to town?'

'Not without Bear.'

'You're making a big mistake,' said Angus. 'Think about it. If you won't leave the dog, and the dog can't go to town, that leaves you well and truly stuck out here in no-man's-land.'

'It's not no-man's-land, though, is it?' said Luke, throwing a stick on the fire 'It belongs to that bastard Abbott. I should've killed him when I had the chance.'

A long silence followed, interrupted only by the hiss and spatter of fat in the pan.

'And stop calling Abbott, *Sir* Henry,' said Luke. 'He has no claim to the title.'

'Is that so?' said Angus. 'He sure acts lordly enough.' Another long silence. 'How's your shoulder?'

Luke told him of his bout of fever, and Angus checked the wound, pronouncing it healed.

'What did you do while you were away?' asked Luke.

'Sold my skins and some gold – for a good price too. I've rented a room from a widow in town. Damned fine woman is Molly Swift. I might take that job in the mine meself, seeing as you ain't interested. Settle down for a bit. I tell you what, these old bones sure do appreciate a soft bed. I might even consider marrying up with her, if she'll have me.'

'She'd have to be pretty hard up,' said Luke with a grin.

'Well, that's gratitude for you.' Angus snorted. 'I didn't traipse all the way up this goddamned mountain for me own pleasure. And all I get back is insults. So, if you're too clever to take me advice, tell me, what do you plan to do?'

'We could go fossicking. Bear could come with us.'

'I ain't going fossicking. I done told you that already. I'm fixing to court Widow Swift. Sorry, son. I know I said as we'd go prospecting up the mountain, but me plans've changed.' Angus took off his battered old hat and wrung it in his hands. 'Stop staring at me, will you? All hopeful like.'

Luke silently served up the steaks with boiled potatoes. Afterwards, as they sipped billy tea, Angus's expression brightened. 'Here's a thought. There's a fella that owns a run not far from here. I hear he's looking for an odd-job man. Fixing gates, a bit of fencing, cutting shingles. Do you reckon you could make a go of something like that?'

Luke nodded.

'His place ain't more than a few hour's walk due east of here. You could earn yourself some money without as much as showing your ugly mug in town. He might even let you bring your lousy dog, so long as it behaves itself. He's a funny sort of bloke. Hasn't got any stock, save a few cows and horses, so there's no fear of that mongrel of yours killing his sheep.'

'What's he do with his land?'

'He just keeps the place natural-like.' Angus frowned. 'Even puts trees back into perfectly good paddocks. Got more money than sense, I guess. Still, I've never heard a word spoken against him by any honest man. He runs some sort of school for poor kiddies in Hobart. Apparently you couldn't meet a nicer fella.'

Luke's fork hovered in mid-air. 'What's this bloke's name then?'

'Daniel Campbell.'

The news left Luke choking on a piece of potato. Angus eyed him curiously. 'I went to that school,' Luke managed at last. 'Daniel Campbell was my teacher.'

'Was he now? That's a stroke of luck. Did you two get on?'

'Yes, we got on.' Luke marvelled at the understatement. After his parents, Daniel had been the most profound influence of his life: mentor, counsellor, confidante. How often throughout his long incarceration had memories of his teacher kept him sane.

And Belle. Might he see Belle again? She'd be almost seventeen now. A wash of emotion left him trembling. He had Bear to thank for another miracle. If not for the dog, he might have gone to town with Angus, might have gone down the mine, risking life and limb, and for what? To line Abbott's pocket, that's what.

Angus peered at him. 'Taken a shine to the idea, have you, lad?'

Luke nodded, still a little tongue-tied.

'Righto, leave it to me. I'll swing it for you, nothing's surer. Happy to help.' Angus beamed. 'I'd appreciate it if Scruff and me could stay here tonight and have a bit more of a yarn. That's if you won't mind and Widow Swift won't miss me too much, of course.'

Luke snorted and Angus clouted him over the head with his hat.

Late into the night they chatted about their lives. Luke's childhood in Hobart, Daniel Campbell, Becky ... Angus had lost his wife and son to typhoid fever some years back. 'If me own boy had lived, he would've been close to your age.' The fire burned low before they turned in. With Angus snoring in a swag nearby, Luke was happier than he could remember. Scruffy snuggled contentedly beside him.

The night wore on. Luke lay awake, too excited to sleep, and marauding doubts began to steal his happiness. He wished Bear was beside him as well as the little terrier. Fears about Bear and the dangers he faced in the forest set in. Old worries about his family. How was Becky? How was his mother? His father. He missed him with a fierceness that four years hadn't managed to dull. Why wasn't his father in court on that last day? And what about the forthcoming reunion with Daniel? After all, Luke was one of his many students. Perhaps he'd overestimated his significance. Perhaps Daniel wouldn't even remember him?.

Luke went over and over the past, reliving memory after memory. Trying to put himself in his teacher's place, trying to judge how important their connection really was. It wasn't until Bear crept into the hut along with the faint light of piccaninny dawn that Luke fell into a blessed, dreamless sleep.

The sun sailed high above the peaks when Luke finally stirred. Angus handed him a plate piled high with fried damper and bacon. Luke hadn't eaten such a fine breakfast in years. With wagging tails, the dogs scrounged for the scraps Angus threw them. Bear didn't look like a bloodthirsty killer. He even tolerated Angus patting his head in return for a piece of rind.

After breakfast, Angus saddled Toro and packed his kit while Luke, took pot shots at trees with stones. He'd been counting on heading off with Angus. Now he faced being alone again.

'Cheer up, lad. I'll not be gone long, you'll see. A week or two at most. Time enough to pay me humble respects to Widow Swift, pay me rent and see your teacher for you. Be back for you before you know it.'

'Are you really going to take a job down the mine?' asked Luke.

'I don't know, lad. Honest labour it might be, but it's heavy and punishing work. Perilous too. They say you never can tell when them treacherous shafts will flood. No, I think that's work more fit for a man of your vintage. Perhaps I'll start up a store instead. Molly, Mrs Swift to you, says as how she'd like a store. Grand ideas she has, that one. Wants to sell everything from hams to hats and all manner of goods in between.' Angus chuckled to himself, fondness written large across his leathery features. Then he fetched two sacks from his pack and gestured for Luke to join him in the hut. 'Here's your supplies.'

He tipped a veritable treasure trove of goodies onto the floor: a round of cheese, flour, jam, salt, candles, rope, a small bag of sugar and potatoes, even some boiled lollies. Another parcel contained two new blue serge shirts, a hat and a used pair of leather boots. Luke could hardly believe his eyes.

'I can't thank you en—'

The two dogs chose this moment to tumble, mock-fighting, in through the door. Bear made for the cheese before Luke snatched it up. 'Leave off.' The big dog obediently lay in the corner, tail patting the floor, brown eyes beseeching Luke for forgiveness.

'He sure don't seem like no killer to me,' admitted Angus. 'But I'm afraid folks've already made up their minds. If he shows up in town they'll shoot him on sight. Remember that lad, won't you?'

Luke nodded, scrambling to save his lollies from Scruffy.

'Take care then, Luke . . . and one last thing.'

Angus pulled a long cloth-wrapped parcel from his pack saddle. Luke whistled through his teeth. A rifle.

'How can I ever—'

'Pay me back once you're on your feet.'

When Angus was out of sight, Luke set to work storing the provisions and washing breakfast dishes. How good it felt to be excited about the future again. He wasn't going to mope around this time, waiting for Angus to return. With a rifle he could go hunting. Perhaps a good feed of meat would keep Bear from wandering.


Luke and Bear spent the rest of the day exploring, following the creek upstream, where waratahs and leatherwoods bloomed in the gullies, and grass-tree spikes were bright with flowers. Spinebills and lori-keets foraged in yellow-gums, and the scented air droned with bees. A sparkling day. No wallabies though. Nothing larger than an echidna demolishing a bull-ant nest.

The steep slope levelled out to an open stringybark woodland. Bear stopped and sniffed the ground. Boot prints lay in the damp earth, a day or so old. Luke took cover and unslung his rifle, scanning the forest for movement. All was still – wait. What was that? Something dangled from a tree up ahead.

He crept forward to investigate. A dead possum, swung from a noose. There was another, and another. A lucrative trade existed in possum skins, and fur trappers made good livings. Possums tended to take the easiest route to the ground. Whoever set these snares had taken cruel advantage of this, leaning poles against trees, and setting looped wire snares halfway along their length. Unsuspecting possums clambered headfirst down the poles, straight into the noose. Luke took the possum down and secured it to his belt. It made more sense to steal this trapper's catch than to waste bullets of his own, and he never enjoyed killing.

He noticed the strangled devil as he cut down another possum: a squat, powerfully built animal with short legs, large jaws and a white blaze across its black rump and chest. It must have had the same idea as Luke, becoming trapped as it descended with its stolen possum meal.

Luke took a closer look and made an unexpected discovery – three shivering baby devils holding fast to their dead mother. Curious, Bear inspected the babies as Luke pried them loose. They wriggled wildly and Luke, reluctant to hold the tiny creatures too tightly, lost his grip. They fell as a tightly huddled mass, landing on the broad, warm back of the dog. Immediately they snuggled down into Bear's thick black fur and clung tight.

Luke grinned. 'Looks like you're Mother Bear now.'

He gathered half-a-dozen more possums and started for home. They took a convoluted course and Luke was careful to disguise his trail. It bothered him that a trapper was working so close to the shack.

It bothered him even more that Bear might run into this stranger one night. The dog followed carefully after Luke, mindful of his precious passengers, occasionally stopping to nose the babies. His tenderness was touching.

Back at the hut, Luke examined the little devils. They had fat tails, heads that seemed too large for their bodies, and sweet whiskery black faces with drowsy eyes. Two bore their mother's white blaze, but the smallest one was completely black. Bear lay down. The tired little devils snuggled into his coat and went to sleep.

Luke skinned the possums and pegged out the hides, planning to slow-cook any surplus meat on a smoky fire to preserve it. He fashioned a snug pouch from hessian, and filled it with dry grass to form a cosy nest. Then one by one he peeled the babies from Bear's back and placed them in their new home. 'There.' Luke stroked the dog's soft muzzle. 'At least if you disappear up the mountain tonight, you won't have passengers.'

Now what to feed them? He'd discovered to his cost that the little devils had sharp teeth. Perhaps they were old enough to wean. Luke painstakingly diced possum pieces into a fine mince. Bear gobbled up any bits of gristle or bone tossed his way, although he'd already eaten two skinned carcasses.

Luke grew more and more hopeful that Bear might stay. But just when it looked like the dog had settled for the night, he padded to the door and disappeared. Damn. These overnight adventures were far too dangerous.

Caring for the three little orphans soon took his mind off Bear. Luke made a thin slurry of possum mince and cold tea, practising funnelling it through a large hollow reed. With a bit of prodding, the concoction flowed without too much trouble. As the last rays of light fled the sky, Luke grew impatient for the babies to wake. He could use the company.

After dinner he lit one of his few candles. He swept the floor and made his makeshift bed, preparing for his visitors. And, as the sun dipped below the horizon and the bush retreated into gloom, the devils woke up. He prepared a pot of warm meat slurry and filled the thick reed, pinching the bottom to prevent leaks. Plucking a baby from the hessian pouch, he sat the shy little creature in the broad palm of his hand and manoeuvred the reed into its mouth.

To Luke's delight it sat up, clasped the reed with tiny hands and lapped up the mixture. The others followed suit. Afterwards, Luke washed their dirty faces and watched them wrestle and play. They were endlessly entertaining and Luke couldn't wait to show them to Daniel – and to Belle.

After native tigers, devils were Belle's favourite animals. Most people thought them stupid and vicious. Bush myths abounded. Lone drovers dreaded taking a fall from their horse with night coming on. They feared being devoured alive in the darkness. But Daniel, like Belle, thought them charming and worthy of protection. This was an unpopular view, and more than one parent had told his teacher so, accusing him of filling their child's head with nonsense. At one time even Luke had had his doubts.

But now he was proud of the little marsupial carnivores known nowhere else on earth. How Belle would love these orphan babies. The thought triggered a crushing wave of loneliness. Luke went to bed, listening to the little devils' yelps and snarls, and the sound of things being knocked over. Sleep was a long time coming.


When Luke woke in the morning, Bear was dozing before the fireplace, the little devils curled up asleep between his huge paws. Luke smiled. He was certainly collecting an odd lot of companions. His mouth watered as he thought about a breakfast of billy tea, damper and jam. How his luck had changed.

# CHAPTER 11

Angus breathed hard, trudging along the steep, tree-lined drive
to the Binburra homestead. The two-storeyed house nestled in
a semicircle of peppermint gums halfway up the hillside. The usual
sheds and stockyards stood to its left, but in other respects it was
quite different to other grand homes in the district. There were no
conifer-dotted lawns, no serpentine paths. Instead of the usual collection of roses and lavender, wild bush gardens of boronias and bottle-
brush spilled untidily into the paddocks. A fine-boned palomino filly
paced impatiently up and down the rails by an old shearing shed.
Dappled-grey coach horses and a few jersey cows grazed in a front
paddock, failing to make much of an impression on the lush grass.
Scattered gum and wattle tree saplings sprouted unchecked all
through the pasture. The forest seemed intent upon reclaiming the
land.

Angus reached the front gate and looked around, fearful the
station dogs might take a dislike to Scruffy. He heard no barking. All
was quiet. He opened the heavy timber gate and secured it behind
him. He tied Toro to a stout post, allowing him sufficient rope to pick
at the spring grass. Then he advanced to the front door, hat in hand
and Scruffy in tow. As he was about to knock, a tall, distinguished

man opened the door. Early forties, clean-shaven, greying hair and piercing blue eyes. The pair regarded each other for a few moments, taking measure. Angus was first to speak and came straight to the point.

'You be Mr Daniel Campbell, sir? Then I'd appreciate it if I could talk to you in confidence, on behalf of a young fella I know. A friend of both me and yourself, as he tells it. Luke Tyler.'

The man before him looked stunned. There was no doubt that he recognised the name.

'You know him, then?' said Angus. 'Young Luke?'

'Yes,' said Daniel. 'Yes, indeed. Why, it must be more than four years now since Luke was jailed. Spirited away so none could find him. Just a boy, and a more shameful travesty of justice I've not seen before or since. Tell me, man, have you news of him?'

'Yes, sir, I do. Angus McLeod and very pleased to meet you.'

Angus offered his hand, wondering if it was presumptuous, but Daniel grasped it warmly with both of his own, and urged Angus to continue his story.

Angus considered his words carefully, reluctant to compromise Luke's safety by giving away too much. However, he considered himself a reasonable judge of character and a gut feeling told him to trust this man.

'The truth is . . . Luke's done a runner. He's living rough in the hills not too far from here. A fine lad that deserves better than he got. Anyway, he won't come into town for work and he can't go on as he is . . .' Angus hesitated, wanting his request to come out just right. 'He speaks very highly of you, sir. I got to thinking that perhaps you might see fit to offer the lad a job, seeing as you're after a handyman?'

'Of course. Come inside while I fetch my wife. She'll be as thrilled as I am by this news.'

Angus declined Daniel's invitation and stayed respectfully out on the verandah. While he waited, Scruffy began to yap and growl. Turning to look down the drive, Angus saw a rider on a piebald mare approaching, with a packhorse following. A black kelpie dog trotted at their heels. Angus watched the newcomer dismount and hitch his horses to a rail. Scruffy ran to play with the kelpie.

From the looks of him, the stranger was a possum scalper, pack saddle piled high with skins. He introduced himself as Jim Patterson, and joined Angus on the verandah. The two men made small talk. Jim said he was on his way into Hills End to sell his hides. He'd decided to make the detour to Binburra after overhearing some interesting news at a musterer's camp a few nights back. All the talk there was of a pack of native tigers led by a huge wild dog. Their killing spree was causing carnage among the high country flocks. The story was drawing hunters from miles around as tigers were rare enough these days. In Jim's opinion the rogue pack might be holed up somewhere at Binburra, and he'd come for permission to trap there. Angus could just imagine what Daniel would think of that.

His ears pricked up when Jim complained of raided snares. 'Cut straight through they was, about six miles due west of here. When I catch the bastard he'll be sorry.'

Angus frowned. It was foolish of Luke to betray his presence like that. Why couldn't he just do his own hunting? Jim came across as a shrewd opportunist and it was good to know that Daniel was sure to send the man packing. He didn't fancy Luke's chances should Jim stumble across him.

Daniel returned and beckoned Angus inside, but stopped short when he saw the trapper. When Jim politely made his request, Daniel sent him away with angry gesture. 'There'll be no trapping or hunting here. Not now, not ever.'

Again Daniel beckoned Angus inside. Jim pressed his point, trying to explain about the sheep-killing tigers and his hunch that they were using Binburra as a base.

Daniel turned on him. 'Get the hell off my land! I don't care a jot about any damned sheep. Are you too stupid to realise it's wild dogs killing the stock? A pack of tigers led by a dog. It's ludicrous. Go peddle your ridiculous rumours elsewhere.'

The two men glared at each other. Then Jim tipped his hat, unhitched his horses, whistled his dog and rode off.

This time, Angus accepted Daniel's invitation to go inside. He followed his host to a small parlour left of the entrance hall. A beautiful woman stood by the window, stylish with a graceful presence, blonde hair worn up in a deft French twist. Although wearing a simple day dress, she still presented a picture of easy elegance. Daniel introduced his wife as Elizabeth. Angus was suddenly acutely conscious of his soiled, smelly clothes and dirty boots.

Elizabeth seemed to sense his discomfort. She smiled and shushed him when he tried to apologise. 'Now, now, sir. Think no more of it. Apparently we've important things to discuss. My husband tells me you bring good news to us of Luke?'

'Yes, ma'am.'

'Then this is cause for celebration. I'll ask our housekeeper, Mrs Scott, to bring us some tea and cake. Unless you'd prefer a drop of whisky?'

'Lizzie, tea and cake can wait. Do you recall talk a while ago of a prisoner escaped from the work camp? Well, according to Angus here, that was Luke. Apparently he's safe and hiding out in the hills just west of here. He needs our help, Lizzie. What do you say?'

Elizabeth's mouth turned down a little at the corners. Here was trouble. 'To aid him would put us at odds with the law, would it not?' she said. 'We must take account of that, Daniel, no matter how grave Luke's predicament. We have Belle to consider.'

'Pardon my speaking out of turn, ma'am,' said Angus. 'But it seems to me that you might give the lad a job under a false name. If he gets nicked, who's to say that you good folks knew who he was or that he was on the run?'

'Yes, of course,' said Daniel. 'We must help Luke, Lizzie. Our risk is slight at best. We'll invent a new name for the boy. Adam. Adam McLeod, your nephew, Angus. And you must bring him to us as soon as possible.' He pressed several pounds into Angus's palm. 'Take this for your trouble.' He turned to his wife. 'My dear?'

At last Elizabeth nodded her assent. 'Yes, Mr McLeod. We look forward to your return.'

As Angus turned to go, a pretty girl dressed rather like a boy came in, followed by Luke's rogue dog, right there in the parlour. Angus stood speechless and confused. His stare was mistaken for admiration.

'I see you're intrigued by Belle's dog,' said Daniel. 'Isn't she a beauty? Most people have never seen one quite like her before.'

Angus took a closer look and observed that the dog was slightly smaller than Bear and possessed of a finer head. But the overall appearance and expression was identical.

'What sort of dog is that?'

'Sasha is a Newfoundland,' said Belle.

'That's a fine animal, miss,' said Angus, trying to hide his surprise.

'Indeed she is,' agreed Daniel. 'Six specimens of the breed were imported this year from England, and we were fortunate to acquire this bitch for my daughter. She cost me an arm and a leg, but Belle's had her heart set on one since she was a child.'

'That reminds me, sir. I'd best let you know that Lu-- ah, that Adam's gone and found himself a dog for company. He and that mutt are nigh on inseparable.' Angus hesitated a moment. 'It's friendly enough, so I expect there won't be a problem with the little lady's dog. But Luke and him are a package deal.'

'Of course Adam may bring his dog. It will be company for Sasha.' At the mention of her name, Sasha looked up and wagged her tail. Daniel patted her fondly. Angus imagined their amazement when Luke showed up with Bear. 'When can we expect to see you both?'

'All going well we could be here by lunchtime tomorrow. Would that suit you, Mr Campbell?'

Daniel shook Angus's hand. 'Indeed it would.'

'And thank you again for all you've done, Mr McLeod,' added Elizabeth.

Angus saw Belle shoot her mother a curious look, as he followed Daniel onto the verandah, glad to be back outside. He untied Toro, whistled up Scruffy and, with a friendly wave, started down the drive, anxious to tell Luke the good news.

# CHAPTER 12

L uke and Bear lay on the grass outside the hut as the afternoon shadows lengthened. Angus had been gone for a week now. Surely he'd be back soon. What if Bear was on walkabout when he returned? Tonight he'd better tie the dog up.

Luke attached a stout rope to Bear's collar and fastened it to the doorpost. He laid his own blanket down and tempted Bear to settle there with a bribe of wallaby stew, but the dog was restless and wouldn't eat, unhappy with the new arrangement. Afternoon wore into evening. A breeze blew up, whistling down the chimney, as the first stars pricked through the roof of the night sky.

Bear could feel the tug of the darkening forest. When he rose to leave, Luke stroked and talked to him. He loved the smell of this man and the comforting sound of his voice, but as each hour passed his agitation grew. Ignoring a command to stay he padded to the door, only to be stopped short by the rope. He whined and lay down again, ears cocked towards the night.

It was then he heard the call – a series of sharp barks, not quite dog-like, coming from somewhere close to the hut. Bear was transformed. He fought against the rope like a wild thing, smashing the bench as he thrashed about, causing the frightened baby devils to dive for cover into Luke's empty boots.

For a time the rope held. Bear stopped his struggle for a moment, panting and trembling. Luke tried to soothe him, talking low and soft. The call came again. Bear sprang back like a thing possessed. The knot at his collar unravelled just as the weathered doorpost snapped. With one powerful bound Bear burst from the hut and vanished into the night.

If ever Luke had doubted Bear's association with the tigers, those doubts were gone. He hated them for the irresistible hold they had on his dog. He swore and kicked the splintered doorframe. Then a loud cooee sounded from nearby. Luke grabbed his rifle as Scruffy ran through the door.

The terrier caught the devils' scent and pounced on Luke's boots. Muffled squeals and snarls competed with his eager barking and Luke's frantic yells and curses. Angus pushed open the door just as Luke extracted a wriggling Scruffy from under the bench. He tied the terrier to the wall, well away from the devils who boldly emerged from cover to take a closer look at the yapping dog.

Angus eyed the babies dubiously. 'They're vermin. You do know that, don't you lad? Like overgrown rats, just more vicious. There's a bounty on their heads.'

'If a bounty makes them vermin, then I suppose I'm vermin too,' said Luke. 'And Bear as well. Out here I can't afford to be choosy and, anyway, they're good company.'

Angus grunted, unconvinced. He removed his hat and warmed his hands by the fire. Luke watched him, too scared to ask the question. A long moment passed. At last Angus turned around.

'The job's yours, Luke. We leave for Binburra in the morning.'

A broad grin split Luke's face. He quizzed Angus on every detail of his meeting with Daniel. Angus faithfully reported the day's events, patiently repeating parts when requested. He frowned as he told of

Jim Patterson's arrival. 'It wasn't smart to pinch that bloke's possums. He's on the lookout now.'

Luke was too excited to heed the criticism. 'Did you see a girl? Daniel has a daughter. Was she there?'

'Aye, the lass was there,' said Angus. 'A pretty little thing. On my oath, I swear she's got a dog the spitting image of yours. When I first seen it, I thought it *was* yours. A little smaller maybe, but not by much. Apparently hers come all the way from England. I forget what sort of dog they said it was. Where's your mongrel anyway? Gone walkabout?'

Angus noticed the rope tied to the broken doorframe. 'That's the right idea. Patterson vowed to kill that dog, and them wolves too. He's not the only trapper here about, neither. Next time, tie him up like you mean it.'

After dinner the two stayed up late into the night again, talking and chuckling at the devils' antics. How good it was to have a friend like Angus. Somebody to take his mind off tomorrow. Between his excitement over the coming reunion and worrying about Bear, Luke doubted that he'd ever sleep again.


Out in the shadowy forest, Bear wasted no thought on tomorrow. He was one animal with Luke and quite another one with Coorinna. Swiftly he overtook the tigers. The animals greeted each other and continued on the hunt, slipping wraith-like through the trees. The dog's senses sharpened when he travelled like this. Each indrawn breath painted a picture and his panting tongue tasted the breeze. The fresh passage of an old buck kangaroo, the alarmed flight of a low-roosting mopoke owl, the abandoned hole of a wombat and the nervous scuttle of a marsupial mouse in the leaf litter at his feet – such things he identified with the ease of the tigers. Sounds imperceptible to man rang loud and clear for Bear. The clicking of a beetle on a fern frond, the snap of a land crab's claw, the quiet, high whisper of a bat's soft wings, the breeze in the grass. He heard and saw and tasted and smelled and felt the night, tingling with vitality and the deep satisfaction of knowing his place in this world.

The baying of distant dogs caused Coorinna to hesitate, a snarl on her lips. But this wasn't the barking of tame dogs, to be sooled by a human master on the prey of his choice. It was the howling of the wild pack. They posed little danger to Coorinna and her cubs while there was an abundance of sheep. Nonetheless, she gave them a wide berth.

Life was becoming even more difficult in the forest. Farmers felled timber to open up pastures. Sheep carcasses laced with poison appeared along the retreating forest edge. Strong wires attached to cruel baited hooks hung from trees. Coorinna taught Bear to avoid these treacherous offerings. Thylacines were fastidious, intelligent predators who preferred to kill afresh each day. Devils, though, were natural scavengers, and scores died slow, painful deaths from feeding on contaminated corpses.

Coorinna alerted Bear to other hidden dangers. Several nights past they came across an unfortunate wild dog, caught by her front paw in a steel-jaw trap. The device was concealed along a bush trail, set to indiscriminately mutilate whatever came along. Bear and the tigers skirted the injured dog. She whimpered with pain and blood loss, every movement an agony. Bear whined in sympathy, but was quickly summoned away by an anxious Coorinna. From a faint scent at the scene the animals understood that this was the work of man.

The pack flushed a wallaby and gave chase: through gullies, across creeks, along ridges. As the tired wallaby hopped an arc around a rocky outcrop, Bear copied Coorinna's hunting technique, cutting across its path. Seizing his prey by the tail, he threw it to the ground and swiftly sank his teeth into its soft throat. The kill was over in seconds.

With full bellies and the night still young, the cubs wanted to visit the tarn in the next valley, one of thousands of little lakes gouged into the landscape by the force of long-vanished glaciers. Pouncing on roosting ducks and swans was their favourite game. But Coorinna led her disappointed young back to their lair, suspicious now even of their home forest.

The bored cubs roamed around, searching for bettongs or bandicoots to bother. Their irritable mother lay down, snarling at some imagined menace or else staring motionless into the night.

Bear stayed close by. To amuse the restless cubs, he bowled them over and over again with one huge paw. And while night turned into morning, they played together at the den's mouth. Dawn came, fading the moon, sending rosy streaks of light to colour the clouds of the eastern sky. The drowsy young tigers retired to sleep and Bear made his customary departure, to spend the day at the hut.

Luke had been waiting and watching for Bear since first light. He yelled with delight as Bear emerged from the trees and trotted to meet him. Dried blood stained his chest. Angus declined to mention it.

Luke took the dog down to the creek for a scrub. 'Please be on your best behaviour today.'

Bear responded by shaking himself, showering Luke in a rainbow of spray. Luke finished the job, washing himself as best he could and then putting on his most presentable clothes. With one final check of the hut, he closed the ill-fitting door and they headed off.

Their journey seemed to take forever. If they'd made a beeline across country it would have halved their travel time. But Angus wouldn't follow the direct route, demanding an easy and accessible path for Toro. The mountain slopes were full of beech trees, Angus said. Bushmen called them 'tanglefoot'. In places, their twisted, intertwined, ground-hugging branches formed impenetrable barriers to foot travel.

As it was, they compromised and followed the forest boundary south-east towards town for two hours, until it intersected with the road to Binburra.

To begin with, Bear seemed to enjoy himself, padding along at Luke's side, occasionally dashing after Scruffy to investigate a wombat hole or hollow log. But when they turned onto the Binburra track, he hesitated. Luke took a length of rope from his pocket and tied it to the dog's collar. It was clear from Bear's raised head and cautious movements that he was on high alert.

An hour later they were in sight of the homestead. Luke was quiet, meeting Angus's attempts at conversation with monosyllabic replies. And then he found himself running ahead, frustrated by Toro's plodding gait and impatient to come face-to-face with his past.

# CHAPTER 13

Daniel leaned on the verandah rail, lost in thought. Luke had been a boy of such potential, such promise. To be snatched away like that, unjustly imprisoned, denied any hope of a decent life . . . how devastatingly unfair life could be. Daniel had searched for Luke, but Henry had used his influence to spirit the boy away. It was like he'd dropped off the face of the earth.

And there was more to this tragedy. Daniel rubbed a hand across his heart. Thomas Tyler had fallen on their frenzied ride home to Hobart to help his son. He could picture it as if it happened yesterday – the wombat hole, the somersaulting horse. Thomas prone on the ground with his neck at an impossible angle.

Daniel traced a knot in the floorboards with his boot. The scene still haunted him. Did Luke even know of his father's death? If not, it would fall to Daniel to convey the terrible news. But not straightaway. Luke needed time to grow strong. Time to adjust to his new life, his new identity. Poor Luke. He deserved so much better.

It was Elizabeth who'd first noticed Luke's intelligence and zest for knowledge. The boy swiftly learned to read and write and do mathematics. But he didn't stop there. Luke devoured philosophical tomes, studied art, thrilled at the adventures of Greek and Roman mythology. Homer became a particular favourite. He explored the works of Dickens, Thackeray and George Borrow, and marvelled at the latest scientific theories.

Luke's chief passion, though, was the natural world. He'd spend hours reading Darwin, sketching animals, rescuing waifs and strays. There was never a smarter, more compassionate boy, and Daniel had taken particular pride and pleasure in his progress. He scanned the hill below the homestead, impatient for Luke to arrive. Wondering how much the brutality of prison life had changed him.

It was late morning before Daniel spotted two men and a red-and-white bullock coming up the track. He ran to meet them at the gate. At first he failed to place his former pupil in the figure of this broad-shouldered, tanned young stranger who watched him with penetrating brown eyes. But as Daniel searched Luke's face there was a shock of recognition. He could see the dearly loved boy in the man, at once familiar and strange.

For Luke there was no such prevarication. Here stood the rock of his childhood. Sometimes over the last few years he'd wondered if his life in Hobart was merely a dream, whether that first day of imprisonment marked his birth. But Daniel, in the flesh-and-blood, standing before him, confirmed the reality of Luke's past. This was the sweetest experience of his life. His troubled face relaxed into a smile.

'It's good to see you again, sir.' His voice was low and charged with emotion.

Daniel strode forward and wrapped him in a joyful embrace. 'Welcome, Luke.'

Bear bristled and growled, the snarl dying in the animal's throat only when Luke stroked his head, reassuring him with hands and voice.

'My goodness, Luke. Wherever did you find such a treasure?'

'Bear's a runaway pit dog, sir. We were both on our own out there so we sort of teamed up.'

'Pit dog, my foot! He's the finest example of the Newfoundland breed I've ever seen. You don't just find a dog like this out in the bush. It's not possible.'

'What breed did you say he is, sir?'

'A Newfoundland. Considered by many to be the noblest of all dogs. "One who possesses beauty without vanity, strength without insolence, courage without ferocity, and all the virtues of man without his vices." So said Lord Byron about his Newfoundland, Boatswain.'

Luke was intrigued. The words described Bear perfectly.

'You'll have to tell me all about him,' said Daniel, laying an affectionate hand on Luke's shoulder. 'But first I must hear all about you. Although that story is for my ears alone. Despite the injustice of it, the fact remains that you're a fugitive from the law. My daughter, Isabelle, won't be told who you are. Your appearance is different enough to maintain the pretence. We'll introduce you as Adam McLeod, Angus's nephew. The ploy protects you too. It removes the possibility of Belle inadvertently giving the game away.' Daniel inspected Luke's face. 'Can you keep up the charade, for all our sakes?'

Luke swallowed hard. It felt wrong, disloyal even, to forsake his name. And lying to Belle? That would be unbearable. But . . .'You have my word.'

Daniel shook his hand. 'Excellent. Now we must reacquaint you with my wife. To further the sham, please address us formally whenever Belle or others are about. In private you may call me Daniel.' Luke nodded. It would be unwise to slip between forms of address, but he was still deeply moved by the offer. 'Well, Luke, I mean Adam, let's get on with it.'


Belle galloped down the waterfall track. Her ride up the mountain had been wonderful. So many interesting things to see: nesting lorikeets, dancing egrets, hatching tadpoles. She was late home as usual. Hours late. She'd missed lunch again, and her mother would be cross. When would Mama stop treating her like a baby? She rode Whisky round to the stable, and spotted the bullock tethered below the house. It had been here before, only yesterday. She'd fed it some milk thistles. Why was it back?

As Belle passed the house she stopped dead, seeing double. How could it be? Her dog Sasha lay on the verandah, but also followed obediently at her horse's heels. Belle trotted closer. Bear stood and barked in loud alarm. Sasha surged on ahead and the two seemingly identical black dogs circled each other, stiff-legged. After a few moments they waved their graceful tails in unison, a gesture of acceptance and welcome.

Belle squealed with excitement, scarcely believing the evidence of her eyes. Somehow her father had procured a mate for Sasha. She jumped off Whisky and approached Bear slowly, sensitive to his body language, careful neither to startle nor threaten. Soon she sat between the two enormous dogs, gladly submitting to their great licks, while little Scruffy frolicked on and off her knee. Scrambling to her feet, she rushed inside to find her father. He and her mother were in the dining room, presiding over an extravagant afternoon tea. The only guests appeared to be Angus McLeod, whom she'd met the previous day, and a rough young man, his nephew.

'Belle.' Why did Mama seem so tense? 'This is Adam McLeod, our new station hand.'

Belle took in his wild look and filthy clothes. What was going on? Why on earth were these men being wined and dined like this? For once in her life Belle was speechless.

It didn't last long. She rushed over to her father, threw her arms around his neck and planted a long kiss on his cheek. 'Oh thank you, Papa. He's beautiful. Where did you get him? How on earth did you keep it a surprise? Does he have a name? Sasha already adores him.'

Daniel gently disengaged himself from his daughter. 'Whatever are you talking about, Belle?'

'Don't play games, Papa,' Belle scolded. 'You know exactly what I'm talking about. My new dog, of course.'

'He's not your dog, my darling,' said Daniel. 'He belongs to Adam here.'

Belle gave Adam a disbelieving glare.

'I'm afraid it's true, dear,' added her mother. 'But I do agree he's beautiful. How lovely that he and Sasha have made friends.'

Belle was too shocked for words. Again she looked over at Adam, only to find him openly gazing back – a brazen, full eye-contact stare. Such insolence. Belle left the room to hide her disappointment, teeming with unanswered questions. At the top of the list was how on earth a farmhand could afford to own an animal worth a hundred pounds or more.

Out on the verandah she took a second look at the new dog. He was nothing short of magnificent. But his coat was matted and tangled and full of burrs. If Adam couldn't care for him properly, then he didn't deserve to own him. Belle stroked his great head and fondled his ears. Such a perfect mate for Sasha. She would get her father to buy him. One way or another, this marvellous dog would be hers.

# CHAPTER 14

For Luke the next few weeks passed in a happy blur. Each morning, as soon as Bear arrived home at the hut, the pair headed off across country to Binburra. It involved bush-whacking through rugged terrain, but was a much shorter route than the Binburra track, taking little more than an hour. And with the help of a machete, each trip saw the trail grow broader and more accessible.

Although Luke's days were ostensibly spent doing odd jobs, in reality he spent most of his time assisting Daniel. Lewis, the station manager, soon gave up asking him to mend fences or re-roof the sheds.

'Not now, Lewis,' Daniel would say. 'Adam and I are busy.'

Lewis then looked to Davey, the stable boy. This did not go down well with Davey, who complained to Daniel. 'It's not fair, sir. Why should I have to do Adam's jobs as well as my own?'

'It can't be helped,' said Daniel. 'I need Adam with me.'

Luke learned how to catalogue new material in Binburra's extensive private library. The natural history section housed one of the finest collections in Tasmania. He tended the native seedlings being propagated in glasshouses, studying the names and growth requirements of hundreds of indigenous plant species. His favourite task was

assisting on day-long field trips, collecting seeds, cuttings and specimens. If only Belle would come along. It would be like the old days.

'Come with us today,' said Daniel one morning as Belle trotted
past on her palomino filly. 'We're inspecting the platypus burrows you
showed me. Bring your paints.'

Luke stopped stowing collecting jars in the pack. Would she
say yes?

'You'll love it,' said Daniel, 'and so will Sasha. It's been weeks since
you came with me up the mountain.'

Belle's lovely face creased in anger. 'That's because you no longer
ask me. You always ask Adam.'

'I'm asking you now,' said Daniel. 'And as for Adam, helping with
field trips is part of his job.'

'Well, you don't need me then, do you?' Belle rode off, spurring
Whisky into a gallop up the waterfall track.

'I believe she's jealous,' said Daniel. 'Remember your first days at
school?'

As if he could forget. They were burned into his memory.

'Belle was jealous of you then, at first. But she came round. Shame
we can't tell her who you really are.'

More than a shame. An agony. He tried not to look too often into
Belle's green eyes, for fear that she would finally recognise him. He
did not always succeed.

Daniel called Bear over and strapped a fully laden pack on his
back. The dog barely noticed the weight. He was a handy packhorse in
ridge country too steep and thickly timbered for riding.

'I've solved the mystery of where he came from,' said Daniel.
'When we imported Sasha from England, five other Newfoundlands
arrived with her. It seems your Bear was mistakenly left behind on the
wharf and stolen overnight. He's from champion stock, a valuable
animal. There's a handsome reward for his return.'

Luke put a protective hand on Bear's collar. 'He's mine now.'

'No argument there,' said Daniel. 'He'd have been well insured, and
anyone who'd forget about a magnificent dog like this doesn't deserve
him.'

Luke tried to imagine his dog roaming the tame English country-side he'd seen in pictures, and failed. Bear's home was these rugged highlands. He belonged to wild Tasmania now.

'Come on,' said Daniel. 'We've got work to do.'

These excursions transported Luke instantly back to childhood. At the end of the day, he almost expected to wave goodbye and go home to his parents and sister. 'I've written a letter to my family,' Luke told Daniel shortly after he arrived at Binburra. 'Saying that I'm here and I'm safe. Will you send it please?'

A shadow crossed Daniel's face. 'One letter, yes, but only to tell them you're well, not where you are. Remember you're a fugitive. Home is the first place the law will look. So much easier for your family if they genuinely know nothing of your whereabouts.'

Hard as it was to hear, this advice made sense. Protecting his loved ones meant everything. Still, one letter would be enough to lay their fears to rest. Enough to bring peace to a bereft mother. Enough to make a father glow with joy and pride. The thought sent a warm flush through him. Luke closed his eyes for a moment, imagining his father's face when Mama read him the letter. Each dear feature etched so clearly in his memory, it felt as if he could almost reach out and touch him.

'I'll keep writing letters, though,' he said, grinning. 'Even if I can't send them. Even if Papa can't read them.'

Daniel rubbed his forehead and then lowered his head. The silence hung heavy between them.

Luke's smile slowly died. 'What's wrong?'

'I should have told you . . .'

'Told me what?'

Why wouldn't Daniel meet his eye? A mounting fear snatched at Luke's heart. He'd never seen his teacher so grave.

'It's your father. I'm afraid . . .' Daniel looked up, his expression that of infinite warmth, infinite compassion. It was far more fright-ening than his bowed head had been. 'I'm afraid he's dead.'

'Dead?' It made no sense. Papa was still young, in the prime of life. A powerful bull of a man. Luke couldn't recall him ever being sick, not once. Men like that didn't die. 'When?'

'Some time ago.'

Luke struggled to understand. 'And you are certain of this, completely certain?'

Daniel pressed his lips together in a way that left no doubt.

'How?'

'A horse-riding accident.'

Luke heard himself gasp. That could do it. A fall could kill any man, even a man like his father. Tears flooded his eyes, leaked down his cheeks. Poor Mama. Poor Becky. Daniel seemed to be talking, but Luke couldn't hear through the rush of blood in his ears. Dreams of one day returning to his old life? They were just that – dreams.

Luke sank to the ground. A moment later Daniel joined him. They stayed like that for the longest time. Through his fog of grief Luke felt strong arms wrap around him.

'I cannot take your father's place, Luke, but know this. I care for you like a son. You have a family here . . . always.'

These precious words soothed like butter on a burn. His old life was gone. His father was gone, but, by some miracle, he still had his teacher. Binburra was more important now than ever – his sanctuary, the one place he belonged.

It was a wrench then, at the end of each day, to leave Binburra and make the arduous trek back to his lonely shack. Daniel often urged him to stay. 'Sleep in the shearers' quarters, or have a room in the house if you'd rather.'

Yet Luke never stayed. His excuse was having to feed the little devils, but he also wanted to conceal Bear's vanishing act at night. One afternoon, when he lingered later than usual chopping wood, the dog took off without him. Luke hurried home and spent a sleepless night wondering if Bear would find his way back to the hut. The dog showed up as usual the next morning, but not unscathed. A bullet had grazed his hip.

Luke shuddered as he washed and cleaned the wound. What would happen if one morning he wasn't there for Bear when he came home? Would the dog's wild nature claim him? Would he melt into the forest, throwing his lot in with the doomed tigers? With hunters swarming the hills, their death was just a matter of time.

Tying up the dog proved useless. Even when he fastened him securely, he couldn't stand Bear's distress and inevitably freed him. Luke was bound to the hut as surely as he'd once been bound by prison walls. It was maddening.

And then there was Belle. He'd been sure she'd recognise him. It hit him hard when that didn't happen, but the truth was that he barely recognised her either. They'd both changed so much. She'd grown from a skinny child into a stunning beauty, with flashing green eyes and the body of a woman. And no matter what he did or didn't do, said or didn't say, she remained implacably set against him.

His refusal to sell Bear hadn't helped. Daniel made offers, each more generous than the last, willing to part with a small fortune in order to please his daughter. But friends weren't for sale. Luke hoped that Belle wouldn't ask him for Bear herself. He would hate saying no to her. As time went on, he realised he needn't have worried. Belle barely acknowledged his existence. However, she did take every opportunity to hijack Bear, luring him with pats and treats and walks. The dog was a willing truant, enjoying being spoiled and playing with the increasingly coquettish Sasha.

Belle's animosity towards him cut deep. How could he get through to her without revealing who he was?

Late spring sunshine broke through the clouds. Luke was cutting fence rails, and Daniel was digging post-holes beside him. Unlike most gentlemen farmers, he enjoyed getting his hands dirty and often pitched in with the chores. They looked up as Elizabeth came down the path towards them carrying their lunch in a basket.

Daniel dropped his spade. 'What've we got today, Lizzie?'

Luke laid down tools and washed his hands in a tin drum of water, placed to catch drips from the shearing shed roof. Lately it seemed to do nothing but rain. How he longed to swap his long walks and leaky hut for a cosy little room at the homestead.

Daniel had finally convinced him to bring the baby devils to Binburra, so they were building them a secure enclosure. A hollow log filled with hay in the corner of the shed served as a snug den and the wire-netting run would allow them to safely explore outside.

Elizabeth admired their handiwork. 'Don't forget we're having dinner at the Mitchells' tonight. Hope the weather holds. We must leave by five. Remind Belle if you see her.'

Luke and Daniel sat down in the sun to eat, their backs against the warm tin shed. Luke looked about for Bear, thinking to share his sandwiches. The big dog was gone again. Probably off somewhere with Belle. He was getting jealous of that dog. If only he could remind Belle of their childhood friendship. It was a connection he craved.

'Another damned dinner party,' said Daniel. 'I suppose Belle must have her friends.'

Luke suddenly wished he could go to the party. Spend time with people his own age, have some fun. *You're a fool,* he told himself, and banished the impossible idea from his mind.


After lunch, as they put the finishing touches on the devil run, Belle arrived with the two Newfoundlands trotting ahead of her, tails waving. Bear's handsome coat was washed, combed and trimmed. Belle pointed to the new pen. 'What's this?'

Her father told her about the devils, and how she must help him keep meticulous records of their progress. The prospect of raising the little orphans captivated her, and she couldn't resist interrogating Luke. *Where did you get them? How old are they? Do they have names? What do they eat? Can you pat them?* He answered all her questions as accurately as he could, delighted she was talking to him. His voice was low and respectful, but he couldn't stop staring. How beautiful she was. Belle blushed and turned to hide it. Too late. It was the most charming thing he'd ever seen.

Daniel didn't seem to notice. 'Your mother asked me to remind you about dinner at Grace's tonight.'

'Will the Abbotts be there?' asked Belle.

Luke frowned and stalked away. How he hated Belle having anything to do with the Abbotts. His sister's bloody, tear-drenched face appeared before him. Daniel clearly didn't know about the rape or he'd never allow his daughter near the man. Should he tell him? Surely four years was long enough to keep Becky's secret?

# CHAPTER 15

'W hatever's wrong with Adam?' asked Belle, staring after him. 'He's a very strange person, Papa.'

'Leave the boy alone,' said Daniel. 'Perhaps he has a set against the Abbotts for some reason. Lord knows I do.'

Belle smarted at the rebuke, feeling the sharp sting of tears at her eyes. She retreated with Sasha to the upstairs verandah, her favourite thinking spot, with its stunning view of Binburra's ranges. She wished Papa would get along with the Abbotts. Henry's son, eighteen-year-old Edward, was Belle's firm friend. It was to him she turned when small-town life threatened to smother her. Edward always understood. Giving their chaperones the slip, they'd lie by the duck pond or hide in the conservatory, planning the exciting lives they'd lead.

'I'll join the Navy,' said Edward. 'Explore the coasts of Africa and India, maybe discover whole new countries.'

'I'll sail to Europe,' said Belle. 'Live in Paris, study at *la Sorbonne* . . . Graduate in botany and biology, earn the eternal admiration of my father . . . then marry a struggling zoologist of whom Mama thoroughly disapproves.'

'I'll become a zoologist then,' offered Edward.

'No. You must marry an exotic African princess, swathed in gold jewellery, with a diamond-encrusted bone through her nose.'

Belle loved their talks. She cared for Edward like a brother. It upset her that Papa had no time for him, and for no better reason than that he didn't like his father. Granted, Sir Henry was an arrogant man. Contemptuous of his wife. Hard on Edward, his youngest child and only son. Dismissive of his daughters, who'd been sent to England to find suitable matches and married off as soon as they were of age. He was unpleasant, but as far as Belle knew, Henry had done nothing to hurt their family. Why, then, did Papa despise him so? His hatred seemed almost personal.

Sasha pricked her ears and trotted to the railing. From their vantage point they could see Adam trudging out the gate with Bear at his side. Why didn't he bunk in the old shearers' quarters or the cart shed like their other farmhands? He must have some reason to make the long trek into town each night. A girl?

Adam and Bear had almost disappeared from sight when she saw them veer off the beaten track and turn west, straight into the forest. There was nothing in that direction, no settlement – no human habitation of any kind. How odd. She watched for a long time, but they didn't return to the road. Where were they going?

Her mother called from downstairs. 'Hurry and change please, Belle.'

Belle enjoyed social evenings, but she hated dressing for them. Millie, their housemaid, doubled as a lady's maid on such occasions, dutifully laying out her young mistress's clothes in the bedroom. Belle grimaced at the blue velvet dinner dress, with its wide bell-shaped sleeves and elaborately draped skirt. She absolutely refused to wear a corset, a decision her mother supported, although she still wore one herself. She said she liked her fashionable twenty-two-inch waist too much. But she had no wish to inflict this torture upon her daughter, pointing out that many modern doctors denounced the use of these undergarments.

The two halves of the corset were reinforced with whalebone, and hooked together in front and laced up at the back. Belle couldn't breathe in them, and hated that countless whales had died in the advancement of the ideal female figure. They made girls look ridiculous, with breasts pushed unnaturally forward to balance an equally exaggerated behind. Bustles, wool-stuffed pads or tiers of stiff frills were worn to further plump out the rump. Squashing all that flesh in was no easy task, hence the need for a lady's maid – someone to stand behind and strain the laces tight. Mama told horror stories of the damage they sometimes caused: fractured ribs, collapsed lungs and the displacement of livers and spleens.

'Don't complain so,' said Elizabeth, as Millie eased Belle into layers of petticoats, chemises and drawers. 'When I was a child, Grandmama insisted I wear crinolines. They were made out of starched linen and horsehair and were so rough and stiff that they rubbed my skin raw in places. They were better than the fashion that followed, though. Cage crinolines – they looked more like trellises for grapevines than articles of clothing. Honestly, Belle, I couldn't sit down or fit through doorways. When the wind caught underneath, I feared I might fly away. And when I walked, the thing bounced up and down like a monstrous, swinging birdcage, unless I took dainty, mincing steps like this.'

Elizabeth demonstrated the technique, accompanied by peals of laughter from Millie and Belle.

'I'd be grateful, if I were you, Miss Belle,' said Millie, as she sprinkled her mistress with lavender water. 'Dressing up in all this fine silk and velvet and lace. Your corsets are lovely too. I'd look right pretty in one, wouldn't I, ma'am?'

Elizabeth smiled and agreed. Belle went to the wardrobe and fished out several of the offending garments. 'Here, have them, if you like pain so much.'

She tossed them to the delighted Millie, who immediately held them up one by one against her body. Apparently she didn't see that cinching the tiny undergarments upon her full figure would be an impossible task.

Now Elizabeth joined in the laughter. 'Very well,' she sighed. 'You may have them, Millie. Perhaps you can alter them in some way.

Now, Belle, we must do something with your hair. Up, do you think?'

At precisely six o'clock, the coachman, Harrison, drew the dark-blue double-brougham to a halt in front of Binburra's homestead. The stylish pair of matched greys set off on the trip to the Mitchell estate at a spanking trot. Two elegant brass lamps, mounted either side of the cabin, cast swaying rays of light, their hazy radiance competing with the twilight. Moths and beetles drawn to the soft glow kept pace with the horses, zooming around in a fine display of aerial acrobatics.

Ancient trees loomed strange and mysterious in the gloom. Belle gazed out the window at the dark forest that had swallowed Adam, searching for some trace of his passage. She longed suddenly to shake off her frills and flounces and follow him into the wild mountains.

Elizabeth observed her daughter as she stared out the carriage window, lost in thought. Hard to believe this elegantly dressed young lady was the same girl who'd been swimming her horse in the creek a few hours earlier. Belle would not easily fit the mould society had ready for her. She was too strong-willed, too boldly intelligent. Elizabeth had been the same, struggling against the constraints imposed upon girls. How fortunate she'd been to find Daniel, a man who not only tolerated her independent spirit, but admired her for it. Belle was growing up. When she married, she'd need a husband with those same qualities.

Elizabeth very much approved of Belle's friendship with Edward Abbott and hoped one day it might lead to more. A love match was her dearest hope for Belle. By anyone's standards other than Daniel's, Lord Campbell's granddaughter paired with Sir Henry's son equalled a highly desirable union. Edward's mother, Jane Abbott, was also for the match. She and Elizabeth had talked of it privately. They felt sure that, considering the obvious affection between them, Belle and Edward's engagement was merely a matter of time.

The tired team trotted up the curved driveway of Clarendon Hall. It had started to rain. Grace and Edward waved to Belle from the broad bluestone verandah. Elizabeth eyed the young man approvingly. He cut a handsome figure. Tall with a sunny, open smile. Casually handsome in buff breeches and soft open-necked shirt. Sandy hair tousled by the breeze.

Edward ran to meet the carriage, with eyes only for Belle. He took her hand, helped her down. She wasn't very good at walking in those heeled kid-leather boots.

'Let's go see the new colt,' said Belle.

The three young friends headed down to the stables, laughing and talking.

Elizabeth smiled. Next thing, Belle would be kneeling in the straw to pat the foal, and smelling of manure instead of lavender. 'Take your coat. And try to look after that dress,' she called after them, then hurried inside to see if Ada Mitchell could use a hand.

These dinners were an ordeal for Ada. She strived so hard to achieve the comfort and enjoyment of her guests that she ruined her own. Elizabeth discovered Ada anxiously supervising last-minute meal preparations. Her capable staff took the opportunity of Elizabeth's arrival to usher the lady of the house respectfully from the kitchen, thus allowing them to get on with their work.


Daniel joined the men smoking on the verandah. Henry Abbott was talking business as usual, complaining loudly to his host about a new pumping unit that had broken down. Water was always a problem in the mines. Reefs of gold-bearing quartz lay within immensely hard rock. Five hundred million years ago, superheated water had flowed down fault lines and fissures in the earth's crust, dissolving gold from out of the surrounding stone. As the boiling streams cooled, they formed rich deposits that followed the course of these ancient flows. The danger of flooding inevitably accompanied any attempt to exploit such inaccessible veins of gold.

Mother Earth would not easily concede her riches, but Abbott planned to defy nature. He'd invested in four immense pumps, imported from Cornwall. They were the latest innovation and had cost a fortune. But for Henry, no price was too high if it meant the power of the underground rivers might be defeated.

The massive machines spewed eight million gallons from the mine every twenty-four hours, reaching depths of fifteen hundred feet. Enormous steam engines provided power. Each engine moved two pump rods down the shaft and each rod worked three pumps, swallowing vast amounts of water. The combined weight of rods and pumps exceeded a thousand tons.

Despite this impressive display of engineering, pumps and flows constantly battled each other. All too often the subterranean rivers won, cutting production and company profits. Incensed by these delays, Henry pressured his managers to extend the hours of the miners. Sometimes men laboured knee-deep in water or were sent down shafts subject to unexpected flooding. Even so, failed pumps inevitably left productive pits unmined for days and even weeks. James Mitchell was listening sympathetically to Henry's grievances.

Daniel poured himself a drink and stood close enough to eavesdrop. He quite enjoyed listening to Abbott's misfortunes. Soon the topic shifted to one far closer to his heart. Henry wanted a local levy on sheep. Funds would go to the newly-formed Hills End Tiger and Eagle Extermination Society, of which Henry was president. Stock protection associations, comprising wealthy members of the squattocracy, were becoming fashionable. Although purporting to speak on behalf of the entire farming community, Daniel noted their agenda invariably suited the wool kings best.

Abbott's levy was no exception. He proposed that farmers pay halfpenny per head if they owned under a thousand sheep. Those with over a thousand head paid a farthing, half the tariff of their smaller, poorer neighbours. On top of this obvious inequity, the funding flowed directly back into the hands of the very wealthy pastoralists who were behind the associations in the first place.

Daniel couldn't leave such nonsense unchallenged. Downing his whisky, he strode over to join the conversation.

'Don't be taken in by this garbage, James. Henry's running his own agenda. This levy amounts to compulsory subscription of every farmer hereabouts to his damned association. We all know its membership is falling. Little wonder, thanks to the rarity of tigers and eagles and the abundance of ways Henry invents to line his own pockets.'

James slapped his thigh and laughed. 'By George, he might be right, Henry. Parliament won't raise a levy based on the odd rogue tiger.'

'I'd hardly call it the odd rogue tiger,' said another man. 'I've eyewitness accounts from my musterers, all trustworthy men. They tell of a dozen or more bloodthirsty beasts, hunting in an organised pack, led by a colossal black dog standing as high as a horse. The demon dog, they call him. It's not unusual for them to leave twenty sheep, dead or dying, for the shepherds to find in the morning.'

'It's true,' offered another. 'I've lost fifty sheep these past two weeks. A few killed or maimed, the remainder entirely devoured.'

Daniel's laugh was filled with scorn. 'What? Thirty-eight sheep entirely devoured by tigers, bones and all? Utter rubbish! You'll find wild dogs and thieves more likely candidates.'

'I confess to taking Daniel's side in this.' James opened an edition of *The Mercury* and read aloud from a letter to the editor. *"'There are more enemies to sheep and lambs than tigers and eagles. Wild dogs for one. But I believe we have a greater evil to contend with . . . a greater pest, namely "the Duffer", who travels far and fast, and can't be snared or trapped. Tigers rarely kill more than one sheep a night. Whereas Mr Duffer removes sheep in fifties, aye, and in hundreds, and leaves neither skin, bone nor sign behind him."'*

James passed the newspaper around the group of farmers. Henry snorted in disgust, took a goose-liver appetiser and marched inside. As he went, he cast a look of pure malice at Daniel, who smiled and raised his glass. Beneath his breath Daniel muttered, 'Hope you choke on your pâté.'

# CHAPTER 16

L uke woke next morning at first light, having shivered through a cold and miserable night. He called to Bear. The big dog was an excellent warmer-upper, but he didn't come. His wallaby-skin rug lay empty by the hearth. Pulling on an extra coat, Luke went outside to brave the morning. To the north, mountain peaks lay shrouded in mist. To the south, pillows of cloud piled high upon each other, billowing to the roof of the sky. A silver rim outlined the thunderhead. A storm was on its way.

He stood for the longest time, scanning the gully's edge, expecting any moment to see Bear emerge from the trees. But the only movement came from the strengthening wind, roaring through the leaves and branches, whipping them into a frenzy. What to do? Had his fear turned to reality? Had the forest claimed Bear? Daniel was expecting him, but Luke would not leave till Bear came.

High aloft, a pair of wedge-tailed eagles wheeled across the leaden face of the sky, harnessing the turbulence of the coming storm. Flight feathers in their upswept wingtips opened wide, tempering the force of the gale that battered the mountain.

They surveyed the earth with eyes that could see rabbits half a mile away. To the east, high on the crest of the range, the she-eagle spotted movement. Reading the wind, she altered the angle of her wings and veered into a new flight path. Her mate followed close behind her, attracted by the same desperate scene.

Three half-grown tiger cubs sat together on a stony ridge. They presented an easy target, making no effort to seek cover. Instead they remained dangerously exposed, peering over the edge of the track. In the shadow of rocks beside the trail, Coorinna's body hung from a wire snare drawn tight around her throat.

Jim Patterson had finally outsmarted his quarry. A growing obsession with the demon dog had caused him to venture high into the uplands, where he'd chanced upon a narrow mountain track. It showed signs of recent use, not in itself unusual. What caught Jim's trained eye was a tuft of thick, black fur snagged on a wattle branch, fur unlike anything he'd ever seen. Soft and wavy, nothing like the coarse black hair of devils. The stony ground made tracking difficult, but he persevered, following the trail uphill. In a patch of soft earth where a spring bubbled from the hillside, he found what he wanted. The footprints of a dog and a tiger. He paused to get his bearings and hurried back to camp.

Gathering bundles of bracken, he placed the fronds in a can of water along with ten wire snares, and set it on the fire. Boiling snares with ferns removed the scent of man and metal. After ten minutes he fished out the wire loops. Using a piece of clean hessian like a rough mitten, he carefully wrapped the snares in fresh gumleaves, ensuring his skin didn't touch the wire. Next he stood by the fire, allowing smoke to billow over his body and the snares, permeating his clothes from top to bottom. Chaining his kelpie to a tree, Jim began the long climb back up the mountain.

He positioned the trap right where the precarious path down the mountain narrowed to the width of just a few feet. On one side rose a sheer rock face – the other fell away to steep, ferny cliffs. No room for his victim to sidestep the danger. Rubbing his hands in dirt to further disguise his scent, Jim carefully set the snare. Anchoring its free end to a stump, he rested the loop between two bauera bushes flanking the trail. To hold the noose open, he used painstakingly collected filaments of spider web, wound with delicate care at intervals along the wire and attached to leaves and twigs. After he'd completed his work, invisible gossamer threads held the noose in the path of any large animal using the trail. Clever Coorinna's luck had finally run out.

With wings folded against her body, the she-eagle dived. The cubs cowered in fear of the shadow as she screamed earthwards. And a furious snarl rose in Bear's throat. He sprang from his vigil by Coorinna's body. In a measured leap he flung himself into the air, his snapping jaws almost snatching the eagle from the sky. She banked and somersaulted, letting the wind restore her to the sky.

Bear crouched over Coorinna's frightened cubs. Now a new sound startled him; something was coming. Jim Patterson rounded a bend in the track. Ever so slowly he raised the rifle to his shoulder. Bear recognised the action, familiar with the bright flash and deafening noise that inevitably followed. Once before, the pain of seared flesh had accompanied that same noise, that same threatening gesture. Before Jim could properly take aim, Bear hurled himself back up the path and around the corner, driving the cubs before him.

Jim swore out loud and lowered the rifle as the animals vanished into the forest. He slid down the shaly slope to examine Coorinna's body. He scoured the ground up and down the trail for evidence of other tigers. Apart from the spoor of the half-grown cubs, nothing more was to be found, aside from Coorinna's own tracks. The scoffing words of a local landowner came back to him.

'There's no pack of tigers around here. The odd one maybe, is all. Feral dog packs? Now that's a different story. But not tigers. You'd make more money selling a live tiger to a zoo than trapping one for its scalp.'

Taking cutters from his belt, Jim snipped the wire noose and shouldered the strangled tiger up the bank and onto the path. Perhaps the farmer was right. On an impulse Jim decided to track the tiger cubs to their lair, wherever that was, and take them alive. That was where the big money was. And as for that monstrous brute of a dog, his scalp also carried a generous bounty.

Jim glanced at the threatening sky. Black clouds boiled in from the west. The weather was closing in, but the prospect of capturing the animals was too sweet to resist. Ignoring the elements, Jim hauled Coorinna's corpse into a tree and started off after Bear and the cubs.

Tracking them was simple. It wasn't possible for large animals to move through such thick forest without leaving an obvious trail. Trees sheltered him from the worst of the storm as it gathered strength and fury over the range. Only when forced to cross rocky, open ground did the driving rain almost knock him off his feet. Hour after hour, he pursued his quarry, battling the cold and growing exhaustion.

Jim finally lost their tracks when he came to a creek at the edge of a clearing. He stopped to catch his breath. A hut loomed out of the rain. Wait, he knew this place. Years ago Clarry had disputed Jim's right to trap here, and he'd agreed to move on. Since then the two men had remained civil, if not friendly, to each other.

Jim abandoned the trail. If old Clarry could put him up for a bit, he'd continue his chase in the morning when the weather cleared. He ran across the clearing to the hut, shook off the worst of the rain, and pushed inside. A broad-shouldered figure, back turned, stood before a fire. Too tall for Clarry. Jim raised his rifle and trained it on the stranger, grateful the noise of the storm had allowed him to enter unheard. 'Turn around slowly.'

The figure swung to face him. A young man, his firearm safely out of reach.

'Who are you?' asked Jim. 'Where's Clarry?'

No answer. Perhaps there was advantage in this. A bounty was on offer for an escaped prisoner. Henry Abbott himself had posted a fifty-pound reward. If this was the bloke, the tigers could wait.

'Hands up, son.'

Desperately Luke lunged for his rifle. Jim kicked it away, firing a warning shot into the roof of the hut. Luke lost balance, his head smashing against the stone chimney.

In that instant, Jim was thrown to the ground from behind. With a terrifying snarl Bear went for his throat. The trapper screamed as the dog seized him by the scruff of the neck, shaking him as a terrier shakes a rat. Bear threw Jim on his back, and stood over him, mad with rage and fear. Luke lay as if dead on the floor. First Coorinna, now Luke. And both were somehow connected to this man who lay whimpering before him.

If Jim had stayed quiet, offered no threat, he might have escaped. Instead, he reached for his rifle.

Bear struck. Jim folded his arms over his face and throat, trying to shield himself from the dog's slashing fangs. First his oilskin coat-sleeves were torn to shreds, followed by his flannel shirt. Soon his arms were ripped and bleeding. He was weakening. His hands fell to the floor. Bear struck again. Seizing the man's unguarded throat, he hurled himself backwards, tearing the carotid artery. Blood spurted in time with the beat of Jim's heart. Soon he lay, glassy-eyed, on the muddied, gore-drenched floor.

Bear went to investigate Luke's still form. His master still lived. Bear lay down beside him and barked to summon the cubs. If the young tigers heeded his call, well and good. If not, they must fend for themselves. Bear would not leave Luke's side tonight.

# CHAPTER 17

When Luke came round, Bear's warm, comforting body lay pressed against him. The dog licked his face, rousing him, bringing memories of the armed intruder rushing back. His head ached and felt heavy as lead. Perhaps he'd been shot? Slowly he sat up and looked around the hut.

What he saw astonished him. The stranger lay dead in the middle of the floor, an ugly, gaping wound at his throat. Bear pushed his head against Luke's hand. Caked blood matted his coat. Luke looked from the dead man, to Bear, then back to the dead man, struggling for another explanation, but there was none. Absurdly, he wondered what Belle would think of Bear now – all her careful grooming ruined.

The dreadful reality was sinking in. Bear had killed a man, living up to his reputation as a demon dog. Yet without his intervention, Luke would be on his way back to prison – or dead. He knew, given the choice, he'd take death over captivity.

Luke couldn't stop staring at the dog, stunned by what he'd done. Bear smiled back, wagged his tail a little and then curled up on Luke's ferny bed. This was a first. Luke called to him and patted the dog's own mat, indicating where he should lie, but Bear remained on the bed. Luke went over and took him by the collar. Still he refused to move.

A rustling beneath the bracken caught Luke's eye. Had the young devils found themselves a new daytime den? But a quick check of their improvised pouch confirmed all three babies sound asleep within.

Bear nuzzled the bed. What was that? A tawny, whiskered face with bright eyes peered up from among the fronds. Luke gently parted the bracken. How on earth? Three young tigers cowered between Bear's body and the wall. It made no sense. Luke closed the door to stop the animals escaping into the forest. For once Bear showed no sign of restlessness despite the late afternoon hour. He lay contentedly beside the cubs.

The bloodied corpse in the centre of the room demanded Luke's attention. Its dead eyes seemed to follow Luke about the room, as if pleading for help that could never come. He threw a blanket over the body to avoid seeing the stranger's face. Then he drank some rum, feeling it burn his throat and warm his freezing body. Sitting down on the bench, he tried to process what had happened, marvelling at Bear's split-second timing and the savagery of his attack.

What now? Luke didn't fancy the grim task of burying a man barely cold, but bury him he must. The truth could only be concealed if the stranger's body vanished. At least this time Luke had the proper tools for the job. He struggled to drag the body to the door, pausing for a moment to tie Bear up and place the devils' pouch in the old meat safe, which doubled as a cage. The hut now housed quite a menagerie.

Luke chose a soft patch of ground near Clarry's grave and proceeded to dig. Wet earth gave way easily, and before long the trench was deep enough to receive a body. He paused to retrieve a few rounds of ammunition from the man's belt. Then, with a shove of his foot, the body slid and fell, landing face-up. Urgently Luke shovelled dirt into the grave. Earth rained down on the stranger, but no matter how quickly Luke shovelled, he couldn't bury the image of the man's dead eyes and the gash in his throat.

There. The job was done. Luke wanted to say a few holy words, as Angus had done for Clarry, but he had no right. This man's death felt like his fault. So he received no sacrament, however humble.

In the hut, Luke shovelled the blood-soaked dirt from the floor into a burlap sack. Then he lugged it down to the creek. Dark, sticky earth stained the stream a muddy red. Luke repeated this process again and again, obliterating all evidence of Bear's crime, then fetched fresh river sand and ferns for the floor.

Was his imagination playing tricks or did the sour stench of death lie just as heavily in the air as before? Luke levelled the ground as best he could and lit a fire. The twilight sky was streaked with rosy clouds, indicating that the storm had passed. Luke's spirits lifted enough for him to light a fire and cook a rabbit for dinner. He cut another into pieces for the devils. They were awake now, and growling hungrily from the confines of their makeshift cage.

Luke fed them and allowed the babies a run around the hut. The devils began digging where the man had died. Had they smelt his blood? Revolted, Luke locked them away again.

The tigers lay quiet, hiding as best they could behind Bear. Luke chopped up his last rabbit and tried tempting them with pieces of meat. Bear gulped down the offerings, but the cubs shrank from Luke. So he retreated to the opposite side of the hut and sat down on the bench, quietly observing. Bear's lack of fear appeared to give the biggest cub confidence. It poked its head up and sniffed the air. He threw it a lamb shank that he'd turfed from the meat safe, to make room for the devils. These days Abbott's sheep had him to fear as well as wild dogs.

Since Bear and the cubs had appropriated his bed, Luke resigned himself to sleeping on the floor. He made himself as comfortable as possible by the fire with the help of the wallaby skin rug and blanket. Lying head in hands, he watched the flames, while the day ran over and over in his mind.

So many questions filled his throbbing head. Who was the dead stranger? Why did he come? Did he stumble across the hut or had he come on purpose? Would there be others? Luke got up to check his rifle, but his eyes fell first on the stranger's firearm, which lay discarded in the corner. He took it back over to the fire.

The biggest, boldest cub stopped gnawing on the lamb shank and hissed at him. What the tigers were doing in his hut was one more puzzle.

Luke opened the breech and checked it was loaded. He couldn't help being pleased to have acquired such a serviceable firearm, whatever the means. Well-maintained and far more modern than his own imprecise weapon.

He lay down and the questions began again. What time was it? What would Daniel be thinking? And Belle? She'd been expecting him to arrive bright and early at Binburra with a bag of baby devils. A knot formed in his belly. He'd let her down. She'd spent hours turning his humble enclosure into a devils' paradise. She'd even picked out names for them after quizzing Luke in meticulous detail about their personalities.

Belle. In spite of her privileged upbringing, she had plenty of compassion and a truly independent spirit. In a world where girls were given little choice other than to conform, Belle defied convention.

And who'd have thought that the serious girl he knew as a child would have grown into such a beauty? Luke stopped himself right there. Belle didn't even know who he was. He was yearning for something that couldn't be.

It took Luke a long while to fall asleep, one hand on his new rifle and one eye on the door. The devils growled and wrestled. The tigers wriggled in the bracken. Occasionally one cub explored a little, before hissing and bolting back to Bear. The big dog slept on, snoring softly. Despite his unease, the presence of the animals was a welcome contrast to the standard loneliness of his nights. When sweet sleep finally claimed him, he dreamed he was home with his family.

· · ·

Several miles to the east, Belle too found sleep didn't come easily. All day, the tension in the household had risen in a steady, inexorable way. And all because of Adam.

He hadn't arrived for work, even though she'd waited for him and the little devils all morning. He'd probably made them up and didn't wish to be caught out in such a stupid lie. This wasn't the first time a farmhand had proved unreliable – far from it. Why were her parents so upset? She kept finding them huddled together, speculating in whispered tones over Adam's whereabouts. When Belle interrupted, she was ushered away. Her parents were withholding something from her, that was plain. Adam had been treated more like some long-lost son than hired help ever since he'd arrived. She was sick of being shut out. What was so special about him? Belle burned with curiosity.

A knock came at the door. 'Still awake, Miss Belle?'

It seemed Millie couldn't sleep either. The girls were more friends than maid and mistress, and often talked at night. It was how Belle learned all the local chatter: who was sweet on who, who wasn't talking to their mother, who had tickets on herself. This time however, the gossip was a bit too close to home.

'So Adam's gone and done a runner.' Millie sat down at the dressing table. 'Wouldn't surprise me if the silver's gone with him. He's a dark horse, that one.'

'He is a bit of a mystery,' said Belle. 'But he never struck me as dishonest.'

Millie sprayed a little Eau De Cologne behind her ear. 'Well, I wouldn't trust him. Adam swans in here, keeps to himself, barely talks to the rest of us, and before you know he's the master's favourite. That's put a few noses out of joint, especially Davey's.'

*And yours too, Millie?* Belle wanted to ask, but was too kind. It was common knowledge that Millie held a particular grudge against Adam. On arrival he'd apparently dismissed her flirtatious advances, and since then she never missed an opportunity to stir up feeling against him.

Millie took two boiled lollies from the silver bonbon dish beside the mirror and popped them in the pocket of her night-gown. 'You do know what they're saying, Miss Belle?'

Belle flopped down on the bed. 'No. Tell me.'

'They're saying ...' Millie dropped her voice. 'That Adam is the master's bastard son.'

Belle let the words sink in, too shocked at first to speak. Her face slowly dissolved into a mask of anger. 'How dare you say that, to me of all people.'

'Sorry, Miss. I'm just telling you what they're saying.'

Belle leaped up and poked Millie hard in the chest. 'If I hear one whisper of you spreading such vile rumours again, I'll have you dismissed.'

Millie backed out the door, muttering apologies.

Belle turned the ridiculous proposition over in her mind. Could Adam be her brother? It would explain Papa's obvious affection for him, but not why her mother, too, held him in such high esteem. No, her father wasn't a philanderer. This was malicious mischief, nothing more. Yet, there was something special about Adam. Where did the truth lie?

Belle went to the window, and looked over the paddocks to the forest beyond. The sky, clear after the storm, sparkled with starry radiance. A fat full moon sailed low over the mountains and rested on a peak, too lazy to climb higher. Sasha padded over to stand side by side with her mistress. Together they stared into the mysterious night. And a plan formed in Belle's mind. Tomorrow she would find Adam and learn his secret.

# CHAPTER 18

In the morning Belle dressed as if she meant to go riding. Elizabeth packed her a picnic lunch, seeming glad to get her out of the way. The rain-washed sky shone pale-blue and free of clouds. Belle waved goodbye to her mother and trotted up the waterfall track, her dog at her heels. When she reached the top paddock, which was used to spell the carriage horses, she dismounted, unsaddled Whisky and turned her loose. The filly kicked up her heels and cantered off to join the herd.

Belle doubled back with Sasha at heel. Keeping to the perimeter of trees, she found the place where Adam had left the track two nights ago, marked by broken ferns. Filled with nervous anticipation she entered the forest.

Tangles of moss-encrusted logs blocked her way. Crowns of mountain ash, myrtle and blackwood formed a high canopy, blotting out the sky. The scrubby understorey of dogwood, laurel and bauera would have proved impenetrable in the steep gullies if not for a rough machete-hewn trail. It would be easier than she'd imagined to track Adam down.

Green starbursts of ancient richea plants, some as tall as a man, struggled towards the dim sky. It was eerily quiet. No bird sang. No animal moved. No grass grew in this damp gloom, which seemed empty of life, except for huge leeches. Belle stopped with a grimace to remove one from her arm.

Dozens of little creeks intersected the mountainside, though none large enough to block her way. After mountain storms, these gentle streams turned into swift-flowing torrents, powerful enough to sweep a man away. Alarming evidence of yesterday's flash flood lay all around. Debris trapped high in branches, a lifeless young wombat smashed against a rocky bank.

At each crossing, Belle half-feared she'd find Adam's drowned form as well. But Sasha forged on ahead, drawn by a familiar scent.

'Luke would not leave without telling us,' said Elizabeth. 'He's far too fond of Belle, for one thing. Someone must have turned him in.'

Daniel scowled and slapped at a fly. 'I should go into town, ask around.'

'Take Lewis to help you. Find Angus McLeod. He knows where Luke's shack is, and can be trusted.'

Daniel got ready while Old Bill, who was in charge of the horses, saddled Solomon. Elizabeth sat on the verandah, stomach churning What if Luke had been arrested? What if Daniel was implicated and charged with harbouring an escaped prisoner? Elizabeth watched Daniel and Lewis canter out of the gate, and recede from view. Still she sat, gazing across the forested valley, marking the sun's measured climb above the hills.

Time slipped by. Morning had crept nearly to noon when Elizabeth saw a group of mounted men approach at a gallop. She stood up, her heart thudding. Stiff with apprehension, she recognised Allan Grant, who worked for the Mitchells. With a sinking feeling she also recognised Tom Howard, Abbott's station manager: a small weasel-faced man with a vicious reputation. He was flanked by a dozen local farmers.

The riders thundered through the gate right up to the verandah steps.

A man she didn't recognise dismounted, as was customary, and removed his hat. 'May we speak to your husband, ma'am?'

Elizabeth eyed the rifle hanging from his saddle. She stood as tall as she could and with an assurance that belied her fear. 'Mr Campbell is away on business.'

The man shifted from one foot to the other, as if unsure how to proceed. 'We'll come back later,' he said at last. 'This doesn't concern you, ma'am.'

The others nodded in agreement, all except Tom Howard, who pushed forward to the front of the mob, waving down the protests of those around him

Elizabeth glanced at the house. Millie and Mrs Scott were peering through the front parlour window, while Bill hobbled towards her as fast as his arthritic knees would allow.

Remaining mounted, Howard demanded to speak to Daniel.

Elizabeth breathed deeply and steadied herself. 'I told you, sir. My husband is not home. What *is* this about?'

Several of the men wheeled their horses around as if to leave, but not Howard.

'We've come for your dog, ma'am. We mean to shoot it.'

'Whatever do you mean?' asked Elizabeth, amazed as much by the insolence as the threat.

Howard thrust out his chin. 'We've eye witnesses among us that can prove your dog's been leading that pack of killer wolves. You'd best turn the animal over to us now.'

'That's absurd,' she said. 'Our Sasha spends each night sleeping beside my daughter's bed. Why, that dog won't even harm a baby rabbit if she stumbles across one in the garden. You're mistaken, sir. Go hunt your rogue dog elsewhere.'

'Could we at least see the dog, ma'am?' asked another man.

'You may not. My daughter and her pet are not here.' Elizabeth did not falter as Howard snorted. 'Sirs, I assure you, you're quite wrong. Our dog is no killer. If you wish to take this ridiculous matter further you must speak to my husband when he returns. Good day to you all.'

Old Bill reached the verandah steps and gestured angrily for the men to leave. 'Don't come bothering the mistress again with your nonsense. Should be ashamed of yourselves, harassing a woman when her husband's not about.'

Howard shot him a poisonous look. Then he wheeled his horse around, and the men clattered from the yard.

Elizabeth watched them ride away. 'How strange.'

Bill frowned and removed his hat. 'With respect, ma'am, if the truth be known, I've been half-expecting this. Word around town is that killer dog's the spitting image of our Sasha.'

'How could any other dog be mistaken for . . . ?' The blood drained from Elizabeth's face. 'Send Davey to find my daughter and fetch her home.'

A few miles to the west, Belle and Sasha were making good progress. They emerged blinking from the deep forest shade into an open, grassy meadow. On the far side of the clearing stood a tiny ramshackle dwelling with a smoking chimney. Sasha headed straight for it, tail waving. Why on earth would Adam choose to live in this remote place?

Belle glanced up at the dramatic backdrop of mountain peaks, trying to orientate herself. From the angle of the ranges she guessed the hut lay on Abbott land.

'Adam,' she called, approaching the shack. 'Adam, are you there?'

Inside the hut Luke dropped his billy in surprise. He swore as scalding water splashed his arm. Grabbing his rifle, he turned to see Sasha nose her way through the door.

'Adam?' came the call again. Before he had time to think, Belle poked her head around the door. 'There you are.' She entered without an invitation. 'This place smells.'

Holding her nose, Belle looked around the filthy interior, now crowded with two oversized dogs. Her gaze lingered on a bunch of scarlet waratahs gracing the crude fireplace – beauty in contrast to squalor – then settled on Luke.

What must he look like? Bedraggled clothes, caked in mud. Gaunt face and wild eyes. Hands still clutching the rifle. Belle began to back away.

Luke sprang forward, grabbed her by the arm and pulled her inside. He stood, his back to the door, blocking her exit. It hurt to see the fear on her face. 'I'm sorry.'

'Sorry? Why exactly are you sorry? For disappointing my father or for manhandling me like a common brute?'

'For both.'

'If you're truly sorry, then you'll lay down your rifle. It frightens me.'

After a long hesitation, Luke placed the rifle at his feet, but remained standing in the doorway. What on earth was Belle doing there? She'd been told he lived in town. How would he explain about the hut? Belle stood, head high and bright eyes blazing, demanding just such an explanation. His mind ran through an assortment of implausible stories, hating the thought of lying to her.

There was another option. He could throw himself on the mercy of his childhood friend. In spite of the promise to Daniel; in spite of the fact that she now seemed to despise him. It suddenly felt so right he could barely breathe.

Belle tried to push past him. Luke took her by the shoulders and sat her firmly down on the plank bench. She watched him warily. 'What are you doing here?' she asked. 'What hold do you have on my parents? And why can't I leave?'

Luke sat down on the floor, his back against the door, his eyes fixed on hers. Belle blushed, but this time she didn't turn away. 'I'm going to tell you a true story,' he said. 'You can go when I'm finished, but not before. Do you understand me, Belle?'

His bold words stunned her into silence. She managed a nod.

Luke concentrated on letting down his defences, on being as unguarded and stripped bare as he could be. 'Don't you remember me?'

A puzzled look swept over Belle's face. Her green eyes were dark and searching, searching his face.

'Think harder, Bluebell.'

Her puzzlement turned slowly to wonder. 'Luke ...' His name was barely a whisper on her lips.

He poured out his story, leaving nothing out, not even Becky's rape. Even Daniel didn't know about that.

'Henry Abbott?' she said. 'Oh no. . .'

Belle asked an occasional question here and there, but mainly she just listened. When he'd finished she went to sit beside him with shame in her eyes. 'I should have known you.'

Luke shrugged. 'I barely know myself.'

She hugged his broad shoulders, kissed his face and then laid her head against his arm. The tenderness of her response was so unexpected, so precious, that for a long time he dared not move. He touched the fragrant softness of her hair, and she stirred. Again she kissed him, this time on the lips. Drawing her to him, he returned the kiss. The sweetness of her. The feel of her in his arms ... Then he was reeling from the impropriety of his behaviour.

Shaken, he stood up, turned his back on Belle, and refilled the billy.

'Would you like some tea?'

Belle looked around the filthy, scantily provisioned shack and laughed. 'Yes, please. With sugar and lemon and a little iced cake.'

Luke made a face at her. The male cub chose this moment to poke his head out of the bracken and growl.

Belle gave a small scream, and he dived for cover. 'That wasn't a devil, was it?'

'No,' said Luke. 'That's a tiger. You're sitting on the devils.'

Belle jumped up and peered beneath the bench. The black fur of the little creatures was just visible in the straw of the rusty meat safe.

'Devils *and* tigers?'

Luke launched into a new explanation.

'You mean Bear is that demon dog, the one with the bounty on his head?' Belle shook her head in astonishment.

'That's right. And I'm that desperate escaped criminal with an even bigger bounty on mine.'

'You're *no* criminal, Luke. Don't you dare call yourself that. It's Henry Abbott who belongs in prison.'

How good it felt to hear Belle say those words, to hear her so completely on his side. Like a dream.

'And of course Papa knows who you are. Mama too?'

Luke handed Belle a mug of tea.

'So, for all this time they've deceived me.'

'Your parents wished only to protect you. You mustn't blame them.'

By her expression, she was going to blame them anyway. Luke sipped his tea, feeling light as air, free of so many heavy secrets. But he spared her the story of Bear's deadly attack on the stranger. No one must ever know about that, not even Belle.

Bear pricked his ears towards the door and growled. In a flash, Luke had the rifle cocked and ready. Motioning Belle to silence, he pushed open the door enough to gain a view across the clearing. Two riders were approaching at speed. Luke recognised the lead horse: Daniel's rangy black stallion. Angus followed close behind on a bay thoroughbred. Luke lowered his rifle as Daniel reached him. It took Angus some time to wrestle his headstrong mare to a halt.

'Damn this cantankerous animal. Give me Toro any day.'

'We didn't have all week,' said Daniel.

With a grin, Luke took the reins of the fractious mare. Angus clumsily dismounted, then led the horses off to be tethered. 'I'm going to get water,' he called over his shoulder. 'Give you a chance to talk.'

'What happened to you yesterday?' said Daniel. 'We've all been worried sick.'

As Luke was thinking how to answer that, the freshly dug grave of the stranger in eyesight, Belle poked her head out of the door. 'Papa?'

'Belle?'

'I had no idea she was coming, sir,' said Luke, wetting his lips. 'Honestly. She just showed up.'

Belle emerged from the hut, hands on hips, and a defiant tilt to her chin. 'I know everything, Papa. Luke told me, just as you should have done. No, Papa, leave him alone. I'm no child to be sheltered from the truth. Luke has answered my questions honestly, which is more than I can say for you and Mama.'

'I want to talk to Luke alone,' said Daniel, turning to him, taller in his anger.

'You won't believe it, Papa. Luke's captured three tiger cubs, healthy and unharmed. I've named the biggest one King, and the other two Mindi and Bindi. They're in the hut.'

'Tigers? Is this true?' In his excitement, Daniel's mood swiftly changed. 'That's marvellous. However did you do it?'

Luke shrugged. It sounded too ridiculous to say the cubs walked in of their own accord. He told Bear to go inside and lie down, hoping the dog's calm presence would reassure them. Then he showed the rare youngsters to Daniel, gently parting the bracken to reveal each one in turn. Despite some hissing, the tigers didn't seem too concerned.

Next, Daniel inspected the meat safe containing the sleepy devils. 'Remarkable! Tell me everything.'

Luke could offer a reasonable amount of information about the little devils, but of the tiger cubs he was largely ignorant. He didn't know why they'd come, why they'd so inexplicably attached themselves to Bear or where their mother was. It had only been twenty-four hours since their arrival and they'd spent most of that time hiding.

'Have they eaten?' asked Daniel.

'The largest cub has,' said Luke. 'Not sure about the others. But I do know they seem much happier when Bear's with them.'

'Odd animal associations can form when a species is thrown off balance,' Daniel said.

'I've heard accounts from Rhodesia of lone lionesses adopting antelope fawns after their pride was killed by hunters, caring for them as they would their own young. Cheetahs adopting orphaned jackal puppies. Polar bears protecting wolf cubs. In times of need, in search of comfort, differences don't matter. We could all learn lessons of tolerance and compassion from these creatures.'

Luke listened, fascinated. There was no need for secrets now. He told them his theory about Bear hunting with the tigers.

'Entirely possible, my dear boy. Although I admit that at first I discounted such stories as nonsense.' Daniel beamed at Bear, who graciously raised his head and wagged his tail. 'So here we have the demon dog, eh? Who single-handedly has cast such fear into the ignorant?' Bear walked over for a pat. 'This splendid creature, alone in the wilderness, chose unusual companions – as, I might add, did you, my boy.'

Daniel shot Luke a glance of such open admiration that Luke fairly burst with happiness. The world had changed utterly in the space of an hour.

'We have these apparently orphaned thylacines, bonded to Bear as surely as to their true parent,' said Daniel. 'This is a natural history experiment too good to waste. I implore you, Luke, for the safety of Bear and these magnificent cubs, let's bring them to Binburra without delay.'

'Of course.'

'Wait here and I'll bring a cart to collect you. Ah, here's Angus now.' Daniel clasped Luke's hand. 'Goodbye. I'll be back before dark.'

'What about me?' asked Belle.

'I can't have an extra rider slowing down my horse. Since it's improper for you to remain here with Luke unchaperoned, you must go home whichever way you came.'

*Unchaperoned.* Luke felt Belle's lips again on his, and a confusing jumble of feelings swept through him. Desire, which he tried and failed to suppress. Shame. Rightness.

'I walked for hours through the forest,' Belle said. 'Surely, Papa, I can wait here for the cart?'

Belle looked so beautiful. Luke longed to have her all to himself again. What would Daniel say?

'Oh, very well then.' Daniel's mind seemed already to be on something else. He mounted his impatient stallion and set off at a gallop, while Angus was only half in the saddle. Angus lost his stirrups, hanging on precariously as his fleet mare raced after Daniel's horse.

Luke stood next to Belle, laughing.

'I'm starving,' said Belle, as the riders faded from sight. 'I don't suppose there's anything to eat?'

Now they were alone, Luke was suddenly shy. 'I'll cook you something.'

Yes, that was it. He'd prepare a proper feast, a last supper of sorts, celebrating his final afternoon here and the things for which he was grateful. Not only protecting the cubs but finding them a powerful ally. Pleasing Daniel in the process. Being able to leave the hut. And Belle. Belle standing before him in her muddy trousers, her fingers tracing the blooms of the waratahs.

No longer burdened by so many secrets, the tension in his body was slipping away. He could feel it in his shoulders, his jaw, in the skin of his face. But still he was holding onto something. Deep inside lay the knowledge of Bear's fatal attack on the stranger. Luke did not want to bring it to the surface. But it lay in the pit of his stomach, a kernel of anxiety that never entirely left him.


Belle watched Luke place a leg of lamb and some potatoes into a cast-iron pot. She'd never seen a man do even simple cooking before. How very impressive. She was even more impressed when Luke removed his shirt to cut firewood. Strong, sure strokes, expertly executed by muscled arms. A flush of warmth washed through her. It seemed incomprehensible that he was the same person she'd all but despised a few short hours ago.

The sun also showed off its strength, scattering the clouds and lighting up the bush. Belle caught sight of Luke's scarred back and gasped. The sound of axe on wood drowned out the small sound. Belle held her tongue. There'd be time for questions later.

She followed Luke inside, where he mixed flour, salt and water into soft dough, kneaded a flat loaf and slid it into coals at the edge of the hearth. Soon they were feasting on fresh damper spread with golden syrup while waiting for their dinner to cook. When the lamb was ready, he served her a plate with potatoes and warrigal greens. The meat melted off the bone. Belle had never shared a more scrumptious meal, although she politely refused the cooked land crab still in its shell.

Afterwards they finished with tea and the end of the tinned sweets. Belle manoeuvred close to Luke, hoping to rekindle the giddy intimacy of that kiss – her first kiss - but he kept well clear. It didn't matter. Just being alone with Luke like this was enough.

They whiled away the rest of the afternoon talking and packing up Luke's few possessions. 'Wouldn't it be wonderful if we could just stay here like this forever?' said Belle, oblivious now to the mud and the smell. The little shack felt like a palace.

The barking dogs announced visitors. Luke's sudden fierceness as he snatched up his rifle unnerved her. A dray drawn by a dignified clydesdale mare trundled towards the hut, a beaming Angus at the reins. The cart carried a sturdy crate piled high with hay, usually used for transporting poddy calves or lambs.

'Now this is more like it,' Angus declared as he drew the rig to a halt. 'One more ride on that crazy mare is more than my life's worth.'

Her father brought up the rear on Solomon. 'Hurry,' he called. 'Only three hours, maybe less, before dark.'

With the help of some blankets, they caught the tigers and transferred them, growling and hissing, to their crate. Luke unceremoniously shoved Bear in as well. Then he wedged his meagre bundle and the meat safe containing the little devils, at the rear of the driver's seat.

Luke took Belle's hand and helped her onto the dray. She squeezed in beside him, thrilled at the feel of his hard body pressed against her.

'There's no more room,' she told Sasha. 'You'll have to walk.'

Taking the strain, the patient clydesdale and its unlikely entourage began the bumpy journey back to Binburra.

# CHAPTER 19

Christmas had come and gone, and the full heat of summer scorched the range. A frowning Elizabeth watched Belle and Luke canter their horses down the hill towards the house. Lately, whenever she searched for her daughter, she could be found by Luke's side. Elizabeth considered herself modern enough, but she knew it was courting trouble to allow the pair to spend so much time alone together. When Belle visited Edward at his estate she was always properly chaperoned. It was true the pair often slipped off by themselves, but at least there was the semblance of propriety. It annoyed Elizabeth that Luke and Belle behaved as if they were still children, taking off whenever they pleased.

Her own mother had always enforced strict rules of conduct for girls. 'An unmarried woman under thirty should never be alone in the company of a man. If a suitable companion cannot be arranged then she should remain in the home or, at the very least, confine herself to the garden.'

How outraged Mother would have been by the behaviour of her unconventional granddaughter. More outraged with Elizabeth, perhaps, for allowing the situation to arise in the first place. For the first time she wondered if her mother's way was right. She ran her hand across her eyes and moved from the window to the next one. The truth was that neither she nor Daniel had much control of their headstrong child. And the situation was growing worse, keeping Elizabeth awake at night. She wished things could go back to the way they were before Luke arrived.

The horses drew up at the gate. Luke sprang from his saddle, took a firm, familiar grip on Belle's waist, and lifted the laughing girl to the ground. Elizabeth decided there and then to take her daughter to Hobart for the rest of summer.

A group of unfamiliar riders came into view, heading for the homestead. She hurried to the verandah and called out a warning, but Luke had already spotted the horses and made himself scarce. Elizabeth ran inside to alert her husband. She found him reading in the library.

'Riders, Daniel. Are the dogs away?'

Daniel closed his book. 'I'll check.'

Recently, Bear and Sasha had been restricted either to the house (much to their housekeeper's dismay) or to the tigers' pen. Although there'd been no more visits from angry farmers, it was clear the dogs would be shot if they roamed. The nearby hills were crawling with hunters keen to claim the demon dog bounty.

Elizabeth had hoped the attacks on sheep would stop now that Bear and the cubs no longer hunted at night, but the killings continued unabated. This didn't surprise Daniel, who'd maintained all along that feral dogs and duffers were mainly to blame.

The riders drew to a halt at the front of the house and Elizabeth went to greet them. Allan Grant, the Mitchells' foreman, dismounted and politely removed his hat. Strung across his saddle lay the body of a large black dog. For a moment her heart forgot to beat.

'We've come to apologise, ma'am,' began Grant. Daniel emerged from the side of the house and shot his wife a reassuring look. 'Mr Campbell, sir, as I was just explaining to your lady wife, we're here to apologise. I shot this brute earlier today along with two others. It's not your dog, is it, sir?'

'Indeed, no.'

'That's what I thought,' said Grant. 'This here's our culprit.' He gestured to the dog's corpse. 'I caught him pulling down a ewe, bold as brass. A ragged bunch of a dozen or more got away. Quite a few streaky brindle dogs among them. It got me thinking that folk's imaginations have been playing tricks on them and that you, sir, were right all along. This big black bastard here's been leading a motley pack of striped mongrels, not wolves. Apparently he's a rogue fighting dog that gave his owner the slip a few months back, and I'll collect a fine bounty for him. So it seems we owe you an apology, sir, on two counts. First for accusing your animal. And second, for not taking you serious when you said wild dogs was to blame.'

The other riders muttered their assent as Grant mounted his horse. 'You must think us a mob of bloody fools to believe something as daft as dogs and wolves teaming up. Especially since you say there ain't no wolves left in these parts anyways.'

There was silence, apart from the jangling bits of the restless horses. The apology had left Daniel speechless.

'Why, thank you, Mr Grant,' said Elizabeth. 'Your apology is accepted. My husband and I are grateful that you've resolved this unfortunate business'

'Of course,' said Daniel, taking her cue. 'Good day to you.'

With a nod the riders departed.

Elizabeth and Daniel stared at each other, astonished. For once a misunderstanding was working in their favour. Mrs Scott came to tell them lunch was ready, and Elizabeth went to find Belle. The shooting of this other dog simplified things. With the bounty claimed and Bear and Sasha safe at Binburra it seemed a perfect time to raise the idea of going to Hobart with her daughter. Ada Mitchell was taking Grace, and the two girls always had fun together. There was a new play at the Theatre Royal, and a natural history exhibition at the museum, all the way from London. She hoped against hope that Belle would be pleased with the plan

# CHAPTER 20

'I hate you, Mama!' Belle said, before running from the dining room in tears.

Daniel looked at his wife, silently requesting an explanation. This was an explanation Elizabeth did not feel inclined to give. She knew very well why Belle refused to go to Hobart. What were those two young fools thinking? Even without Luke's prison sentence hanging over them, there was no future for their love. Society's rules were uncompromising. Girls like Belle simply didn't marry below their station. Daniel, however, seemed blissfully unaware of their daughter's unfortunate attachment to Luke. He thought so highly of the boy. In any case, the situation wasn't really Luke's fault. It was hers, and she must rectify her mistake. Whatever it took she was determined to separate the pair.

Elizabeth smiled reassuringly at her husband and excused herself. She knew what he would do – go for a long ride into the mountains. He never fancied being at home during an argument between his wife and daughter.

Elizabeth found Belle in her room, face buried in a pillow, her chest rising and falling with heaving sobs. She sat down beside her child, gently stroking her hair until the weeping subsided. 'Belle, darling. Tell me. Is it that you have feelings for Luke?'

'Don't be stupid, Mama.'

'Your rudeness does nothing to change the facts. This is an impossible union, Belle. You must understand this right from the start. Neither myself, nor Papa, nor anybody else will ever countenance it.'

'It's got nothing to do with Luke. It's the tigers. I love them and now you mean to send me away. I can stroke Mindi now, and play with Bindi a little. Even King puts up with me. I won't go now, Mama.' Belle's face went scarlet with determination. I just won't.'

'You know as well as I do that the plan is to release the tigers high in the range. They're not pets, Belle, and, besides, you always enjoy going to Hobart with Grace.'

'Not any more. Things have changed.'

Elizabeth examined her daughter's stubborn, tear-drenched face and knew exactly how things had changed. She kissed Belle and sat for a while longer, stroking her hair.

'Very well then. You may stay.'

Belle sobbed out her thanks. Extracting herself from her daughter's grateful embrace, Elizabeth left the room. Her mood was grim. There was no alternative.

First she went to find Harrison, communicating quietly with the coachman in urgent tones. Within minutes, he was galloping out the homestead gate. Then she went looking for Luke. She found him at the killing-gallows, butchering a sheep. Ordinarily she avoided this place, but the urgency of her business left no room for squeamishness. Elizabeth drew close enough to be heard above the grinding of saw blade on bone.

'Mrs Campbell?' Luke set aside his grisly task, and washed his hands and arms at the trough. His clothes reeked and she could sense his embarrassment.

With a smile Elizabeth indicated that he should walk with her, past the greenhouses and up the little path to the orchard

As they went she confessed to Luke her fears for Belle, should she continue with her infatuation. The expression on Luke's face confirmed for Elizabeth that this unwelcome attachment was mutual. She hadn't much doubted it.

'I'm not good enough for your daughter, is that it?'

'Oh Luke, the facts of the matter speak plainly. You're on the run from the law. Any hint of a union between yourself and my daughter would ruin her. I've arranged for Belle to accompany me to Hobart but she insists she won't go. We both know that she stays for you. I dare not confide in my husband – his loyalty to you clouds his judgement. I implore you, Luke – if you have any regard for my family, and I know you do, leave here at once. I bear you no ill will. On the contrary, I'm very fond of you. But the Lord knows my wilful daughter will do as she pleases, regardless of the consequences. I doubt that even you could change her mind. So we must agree to protect her. Harrison rides to town as we speak to fetch Angus McLeod. I expect you to leave with him tonight. Tell no one, not even Belle, of your departure. Will you do this for me, Luke?'

Luke stood a minute in stunned silence, digesting her words. She was right. For the past few weeks he'd lived in a sort of fool's paradise. His status as a fugitive, his lowly birth, his shameful cowardice, Bear's dreadful secret – all forgotten in the rare glow of Belle's affection. For Belle this might be no more than a passing fancy, but for him? Luke loved her. A deep, satisfying love that caused him to smile if she smiled, be saddened by her sadness, and place her welfare paramount among his concerns. The proposition that his love in some way endangered her, horrified him.

'I'll do anything to protect Belle,' he said. 'Bear and I will leave right away.'

'No. You must leave Bear here, for his own safety.'

'He's been cleared of killing sheep.'

'Mistakenly cleared,' said Elizabeth. 'You told us yourself of his guilt.'

Guilty of more than killing sheep, thought Luke.

'Would you entirely trust him if provoked?'

Luke shook his head, lost in a haze of misery and confusion. To lose both Belle and Bear at once. Whatever he'd done, whatever mistakes he'd made in life, he didn't deserve this.

'Perhaps enough time has passed.' He was thinking aloud. 'I'll go to Hobart, see my family.'

'I thought you knew ...?'

Luke squeezed his palms against his eyes. What now?

'Your mother and sister no longer live in Hobart. After your father's death, Daniel found them work at Ruyton Girls School in Melbourne. The principal is a friend.'

Melbourne? All those times he'd daydreamed of a joyful return to his Hobart home – but he had no home. Not any more.

'Mrs Campbell, tell me. What were the circumstances of my father's death?'

She hesitated, took a moment to smooth her dress. 'Thomas and Daniel were riding for Hobart to attend your trial. His horse fell . . .' She put a hand on Luke's shoulder. He shrugged it away. 'Daniel swears he didn't suffer.'

The ground pitched beneath Luke's feet. His father. His strong, loyal, loving father. Dead, for years. Dead, because of him. It made sense now: the long years of imprisonment. losing Bear, losing Belle. He deserved every bad thing the world could throw at him. There was only one person he hated more than himself, one person even more to blame for tearing his family apart. Henry Abbott.

Elizabeth pressed a wad of pound notes into his hand. He hurled it away as if it burned his skin.

'I only thought . . .'

'What did you think?' His voice rose to a shout. 'That I was for sale?' Elizabeth shrank back. 'I'm leaving because it's best for Belle, not because of your goddamned money. No one will ever care for your daughter more than I do.'

Luke returned to the gallows, cleaving the rest of the carcass with great, angry strokes of his blade. Then he packed away, washed up and went to his little room in the cart shed. Bear wasn't there – most likely off with Sasha. Luke desperately wanted an opportunity to say goodbye.

The tigers dozed in their shed. The devils slept in their log. All had their place. All except him. He dared not think of how badly he'd miss them. Luke packed his things and lay on his bunk to wait. Knuckling back tears. Hollow with grief.

Hours later, a knock came at the door. Davey, the stableboy – no friend of his. He held the reins of a tall, dapple-grey thoroughbred. She was a new arrival at the homestead, freshly broken, still a little wild. Luke guessed Davey had deliberately chosen the mare to test him. Provisions spilled from her saddlebags.

'Bill told me to saddle Sheba for ya. Going into town?'

With a curt nod, Luke motioned him away. Strapping swag to saddle, Luke soothed the skittish horse with a low voice. He liked how her ears flicked back and forth to the rhythm of his words. An intelligent one.

A barking chorus heralded the arrival of a visitor. Luke swung into the saddle and cantered to the gate, glad to hear the dogs were back. Harrison rode in with Scruffy chasing at his heels. He stepped down from his horse, threw his reins to Davey, and strode to the house.

Angus was riding an old dun carthorse up the drive. Luke dismounted and knelt down to pat the dogs, his heart aching when Bear put a paw on his knee. Scruffy squirmed onto his favourite position on Luke's lap. When Angus reached the gate, he greeted his young friend with a broad smile on his weathered face. He looked older, thinner. Luke wondered how much he knew.

'Finally come to your senses, have you, lad? Ready to join the land of the living, 'stead of hiding out here in these here hills with mangy vermin for company?' He clambered from his horse. 'How are them wolves going? You'd make a pretty penny selling them. Zoos are paying good money for them things.'

Luke didn't know what to say. Angus clearly thought he was leaving of his own volition. He supposed he'd better play along. 'I'd be grateful if you'd maybe put me up in town for a bit. I'll not be long out of work.'

'Neither you will be, Luke, neither you will. There's plenty of jobs for willing men down the mine.' Luke flinched at the suggestion. 'That black mongrel ain't coming with you, is he? By jeepers he gives me the willies.' Luke shook his head. 'Thank God for that. Well, give an old bloke a cuppa, will you? I'm parched.'

Luke took Angus around to the shearers' quarters where a big billy sat permanently on the boil. As they drank their tea, Elizabeth came by and thanked Angus for answering her summons so promptly.

'When Luke decided to move into town, naturally we thought of you,' she said. 'Understand, Mr McLeod, that he must still be known to all as your nephew, Adam. Henry Abbott still offers a reward for his capture. There must be no slip-ups.'

'As God is my witness, ma'am, I'll protect the lad. You have my word.'

Elizabeth took hold of Angus's hand. 'Bless you, Mr McLeod. Goodbye, Luke, and good luck. You two better be off if you mean to reach Hills End before dark.'

Angus gulped down the last of his tea and smacked his lips. 'Seems like the missus here's given us our marching orders. Come on then, lad.'

Luke put Bear away in the tigers' pen, stopping briefly to fondle his massive head. When would he next see his dog? How would he manage without him?

Bear sensed Luke's sadness and paced up and down the wire, whining. Wrenching himself away, Luke mounted Sheba and joined Angus for the ride to town. What about Daniel? What about Belle? He hadn't even had the chance to say goodbye.

# CHAPTER 21

Life at Molly Swift's cottage in the dreary miners-camp end of town was very different from life at Binburra. Luke missed Daniel and Bear and beautiful Belle. He missed the elegant homestead, the well-stocked library, the nursery of native seedlings and cuttings. It was like going to prison all over again. Torn from those he loved, denied the satisfying, intellectual life he craved. Yet he never once regretted his decision to leave.

Daniel came to Molly's time and time again, begging for him to return.

'Forgive me, Luke, for keeping the circumstances of your father's death from you. In seeking to spare you, it seems I've caused you more pain.'

Each time Luke stubbornly refused to tell Daniel why he'd left. How could he return to Binburra if he was a threat to Belle?

His one remaining pleasure was to ride Sheba into the mountains. Daniel had given him the mare, who lived in a dusty little paddock behind the house. Paying for her feed swallowed up an alarming portion of Luke's small wage, but he refused to sell her as Angus suggested. She alone afforded him some freedom.

With the discovery of gold, Hills End had grown to a town of almost two thousand people, not including the prospectors and trappers living rough in the hills. It boasted a row of shops, including a blacksmith, butcher, wheelwright, post office, bakery and two general stores. There were plans to build a school on land beside the railway line. Hills End also had a police station. Luke had seen his own Wanted poster on the noticeboard outside, offering a fifty pound reward. The grainy photo taken when he first went to prison was thankfully unrecognisable. He barely knew the wild-eyed boy himself.

Molly's cottage stood in a row of overcrowded slums built on a narrow, rutted road on the bare hill above the mine. Well-heeled members of the Hills End community – tradesmen, merchants and mine managers – lived in the lower part of town. Houses were larger there, the streets broader and cleaner. Prevailing winds blew past these dwellings to the mine, sparing their residents the clouds of filthy smoke and fumes belching from the smelter chimneys.

Luke wasn't so lucky. He lived in the back room of Molly Swift's rented cottage, with a dark, depressing view over the mine. Angus had originally occupied the poky space, but had been promoted to the main bedroom. Molly was accommodating enough, but, if the truth be known, Luke felt a little jealous of her. Angus was his last remaining friend in the world and now Molly took up most of his time. However unfair it might be, she made a convenient scapegoat for what was wrong with his life.

His board was three shillings a week, a sum which Angus had covered until Luke found work. Luke struggled against it, seeking all sorts of other positions, but eventually he agreed to join Angus down the mine. Most townsfolk owed their pay packets, directly or indirectly, to Henry Abbott.


In the past few months Luke had learned more than he ever wanted to know about mining. The earth set up a great many barriers against those who sought to rob her of her riches. The men worked in huge, unstable underground chambers known as stopes. Massive staves of timber reinforced the stopes, tunnels and shafts. Penetrating these rock walls was difficult, dirty and dangerous work. Miners drilled holes with primitive augers, creating dense dust clouds. They packed the holes with dynamite, lit fuses and retreated to what they hoped would be a safe distance. Detonation followed: a moment of tearing stone, deafening shock-waves and flying rocks.

Unexploded charges could be set off by a man drilling his next round of holes, killing or crippling him with the loss of limbs or eyes. Sometimes fuses ran too quickly, allowing no time to escape the blast; sometimes too slowly, causing unexpected detonations as miners returned to the job.

The dark tunnels were death-traps of falling rocks, pools of water deep enough to drown in and pockets of poison gas. In this filthy, unforgiving environment, laden with rotting timbers and human waste, even small abrasions could develop into life-threatening infections.

Carting his tools with him, Luke negotiated the labyrinth with only an oil lamp fastened to a helmet. Each miner received three candles for his ten-hour shift underground. Careless use of lamps and candles could leave men stranded in total darkness.

Luke was started as a mucker. After rock was blasted from the stone face, teams of muckers used sledgehammers to pulverise the boulders, and shovel loose rubble into ore cars. Loaded cars were pushed manually to the main shaft, hoisted out in a cage and delivered to the smelter. Muckers were considered unskilled labour, earning even less than the miners, suffering worse privations, forced to meet brutal daily quotas or risk losing their jobs.

Luke hated everything about his new life. Descending the shaft in the clanging cage was like being buried alive – a descent into hell. Ringing shift bells sounded like death knells. Roaring machines assaulted his ears and he could barely breathe the choking air. After his months spent in the pristine beauty of a vast wilderness, the mine was pure purgatory – an unforgiving, claustrophobic world of gloom and confusion.

The darkness of the mine entered his mind, his soul. It extinguished hope and pity. Luke knew the mountain to be a live and malevolent being, resenting the presence of man. At times the ground heaved and buckled beneath his feet, as if the earth meant to spit him out. And as Luke broke his back loading cars, as he struggled to reinforce rotting timbers in the dark, as he smashed the dull ore to smithereens, his hatred for Henry Abbott grew.

Autumn was turning to winter. High in Binburra's ranges, the beech trees would be turning from green to gold, but there was no way of marking the seasons underground. Angus and Luke sat near the main shaft one afternoon, eating a meagre meal of bread and cheese. Angus slumped stiffly, back hunched against the damp tunnel wall, his body periodically racked with rasping coughs.

Lately, each surface streamed with water, and the clammy humidity sapped everyone's strength. No matter how cold it was up top, it always remained uncomfortably warm in the mine, getting hotter the deeper one went. Sweat poured from the miners' bodies. They drank gallons of water to ward off dehydration and to soothe their burning throats.

Luke peered at Angus in the dim light. The old man seemed completely spent, but his shift wouldn't finish for hours. 'Thought you said you were too old for this job?' said Luke. 'Whatever happened to opening a store with Molly?'

Luke had broached the subject before, but always received evasive answers. Right now Angus was too tired to avoid the question – and to remember not to use his young friend's real name.

'That's still the plan, Luke. Still the plan. I just need a bit more capital first. Molly thinks we'll have enough in six months or so.'

Luke's knuckles tightened around his water flask. 'Are you telling me that Molly put you up to this? She sends you down this flaming hole each day so that she can have her shop? That's more than a woman has a right to expect of a man.'

'Hold on. Don't get your back up. Fact is, I love Molly, and if we're ever going to have that store, the money's got to come from somewhere. I'll not leave her alone, to go traipsing all over the countryside trapping again, so this is me next best option. Don't you go blaming Molly. You know what they say about the men who come to this town, don't you, Luke? The mine gets them in the end, no matter what they say at the start. Just take a gander at yourself.'

A nearby miner looked curiously at them. Luke wished Angus could remember to call him Adam. On the main point he grudgingly admitted that Angus was right. They'd both been determined to avoid the job, but here they were anyway.

At the end of their shifts they rode the cage up the shaft. The crowd of weary men dressed in filthy, dripping rags emerged squinting, into the cold winter sunshine. In twelve hours they'd do it all again. Mr Dickens, the mine foreman, met the men at the gate and gestured for them to gather around.

'You lot need to look sharp tomorrow. We're expecting an important visitor. Edward Abbott, Sir Henry's son. He'll be inspecting the mine. Seems Sir Henry's keen for his boy to learn the ropes. I'll be escorting him personal, I will, and don't want any cock-ups. You blokes better be on your best behaviour. Show him what a smooth operation we run. I want your word.'

The dog-tired men murmured their assent. All except Luke. He snorted with disgust and marched away.

Angus hurried to catch him up. 'What're you trying to do? Get yourself fired?'

*There's nothing I'd like more*, he wanted to say, but kept his peace. Luke planned to go to Melbourne to see his mother and sister, bring them some money in an attempt to atone for his father's death. He needed the work as much as Angus did. They were both slaves to Abbott's paltry wage. Now he was expected to put on a happy face for the benefit of Henry's snivelling son.

Belle socialised with the Abbotts. She'd told him about her friendship with Edward, assured him that Edward was not like his father. But Luke already despised him. He strode on ahead of Angus without speaking, resentment rising in his breast like a bad case of indigestion.

. . .

That evening Luke found it difficult to be civil to Molly. He sat at the dinner table, stern-faced. Angus's dry cough punctuated the silence. What sort of woman would send an old man down a mine? Luke had lost his own father. He'd pushed Daniel away. He didn't want to lose Angus too.

Luke picked at the sinewy mutton and roast potatoes on his plate. He'd fared better living rough at the hut. Prime lamb each day of the week. Here, the humble spud in various guises formed the mainstay for every meal. He'd forgotten how often in prison, with nothing but cold, thin soup and mouldy bread night after night, he'd craved roast potatoes. Their salty, crisp skins and warm, fluffy middles.

Molly sat down and started on her own small meal. A thin woman with bright red hair, pale freckly skin and a pinched bird-like face. At thirty-one she was twenty years Angus's junior. She sat quietly eating her food and trying to ignore Luke's obvious dissatisfaction with his.

'Angus gives you all his pay, doesn't he?' said Luke. 'I'd have thought you could cook up a bit of beef now and then.'

'Don't you speak to Molly like that,' warned Angus.

'I can't eat this muck.'

Luke shoved back his chair and left the table.

Molly knotted her fingers together as Angus tried to apologise for Luke.

'Don't mind Adam. He's tired, is all.'

But the harm was done. Molly didn't like the boy. If Adam wasn't related to Angus she'd have put him out by now.

She cleared away his barely touched meal, returning it to the pot on the stove. Times were hard and she wasn't about to waste good food. The money from Angus's last trapping trip sat in a biscuit tin under her bed. Soon she'd buy a shop far, far away from the misery of Hills End.

Every Friday, Molly added half of Angus's meagre weekly wage to this nest egg. She found it difficult to run the household on the remainder. True, she now received Adam's three shillings a week, but he ate more than his board was worth. Molly scowled, recalling an argument over her hens in the coop out the back. Adam had named them, later refusing to throttle one for Sunday lunch, even when she pointed out they were old and barely laying at all. She'd had to do it herself.

Meat was a luxury. Molly worked hard in her garden to supplement the table with fresh vegetables, but the polluted air damaged her crops. Except for potatoes. She had a green thumb for growing potatoes.

On top of her financial woes, Molly worried constantly about Angus's health. She knew the mine was no place for a man his age, with or without the ever-present threat of accident. Molly always murmured a quiet prayer when he left for his shift. And, as she busied herself during the day with broom, dustpan and mop, in a constant battle against the grime from the mine, this anxiety never left her.

Molly had grown to love Angus. He was a kinder man than her husband, who'd sickened and died two years earlier. She didn't know whether it was the mine or their filthy living conditions that had killed him. Diseases were commonplace in the town: typhoid and measles, smallpox and diphtheria. Fresh milk was always suspect. As a child in a logging settlement, she'd watched her family die, one by one, from tuberculosis contracted from the milk of their own much-loved house cow. The street had no sewage system or rubbish collection. Molly dumped her rubbish in a foul culvert out front of the house. A stinking earth pit in the backyard served as a toilet.

Molly was a close friend of grief. She'd lost her babies too, all five of them. Tiny mites born months before term and buried in the children's garden at the mine's own cemetery. Miscarriage was as common as birth among miners' wives. Bereaved mothers worked miracles at their children's gravesides, coaxing swathes of foxgloves and roses to bloom in the noxious earth.

The one thing that Molly and Luke agreed upon was that the miners' camp was no place to live. There was no escaping the dust and smoke and noise. Roaring machinery and blasting never ceased.

Stamper mills below the mine on Slaughteryard Creek pounded ore and eardrums twenty-four hours a day.

The miners used copper, cyanide and mercury to extract gold from ore. Tailings washed into the creek, poisoning the fish and wildlife. The mill workers suffered too. Using mercury, known as quicksilver, led to mad hatter disease. Tremors and fatigue led to accidents. Afflicted men grew stiff and headachy and never felt properly rested. Stomach pains and dysentery plagued them. Their gums bled and their teeth fell out.

Cyanide poisoning was worse, amounting to slow suffocation, causing the skin to flush a characteristic cherry-red. Molly had seen many such men. They grew weak, confused, short of breath and dizzy. Sometimes they displayed episodes of bizarre behaviour. One man was convinced the giant stamper rams were whispering to him. He jumped in to hear what they were saying. His end at least was swift. Most victims suffered a slow slide into the grave

The cause of these illnesses was common knowledge, but the workers couldn't prove it. The mine denied all responsibility and routinely sacked men too sick to work. Thankfully Hills End drew its water supply from Black River, above its convergence with Slaughter-yard Creek. Yet the river flowed south to other towns, polluted and barely drinkable.

Sunday preachers did good trade in Hills End. Molly despised these sermons that promised people relief from their burdens in the hereafter. What use was that in the here and now? Despite all these hardships, most mine workers accepted their lot and, for better or worse, life was the mine and the mine meant life. Not everyone wanted out as badly as Molly and Luke did.

# CHAPTER 22

'Come on, lad. We don't have all day.' Angus kissed Molly goodbye.

Luke tossed Sheba an armful of hay, poured a measure of oats into her wooden bucket and gave her a last rub behind the ears. It began to rain. When he turned to go, the mare arched her neck, flared her nostrils, and uttered a long, piercing whinny. She took off at break-neck speed in a futile race around her small paddock until sweat darkened her pale coat. Cinders from the mine's chimneys clung to her, turning her silver mane to sooty grey. Sheba hated their new life as much as he did. He longed to ride her high into the mountains, far from this filthy town, and never come back. Instead, he answered Angus's second hail and joined him for the walk to the mine.

The road snaked its way downhill over pockmarked, barren land to the mine's western gate. The ear-pounding hiss and thump of steam engines grew louder as they walked. These monstrous machines squatted in fortresses of grey granite masonry crowned with red-brick chimneystacks reaching high into the smoky skies.

A desolate view, not a tree in sight. The mine consumed vast amounts of timber to shore up tunnels and burn for fuel. Teams of woodcutters operated in shifts, sweeping in relentless, ever-widening arcs to feed the ravenous machinery. Colossal log stacks, sixty feet across, piled taller than the buildings. Towering triangular frames of timber and steel, each with a sheave wheel at its apex, crouched like hangman's scaffolds over the three main shafts.

In contrast to the ugliness of their surroundings, the mine buildings were quite elegant. The facades of the pump houses, stamper batteries and smelter boasted graceful arched windows in the finest Italian neo-classical tradition. Fanlights and decorative cornices adorned their red-brick walls. Above the office entrance, ornamental masonry spelled out the words *In God We Trust*. Luke saw an obscene disparity between the beauty of the architecture and the hideous business of the mine.

The arriving miners were directed to the cobbled courtyard in front of the office. They shuffled about, turning their collars against the drizzle. Two well-dressed gentlemen stood under the verandah, chatting to the foreman, Mr Dickens. Luke froze. One of the men was Henry Abbott.

It was five years since Luke had seen the man who'd raped his sister, as good as killed his father, and stolen his life. Abbott looked smaller and older than he remembered. Beside him stood a tall, slim youth, with fair hair and a hint of the mine owner's imperious expression. He wore fine clothes – too fine for a morning down a muddy, stinking hole. That had to be Abbott's son, Edward. Belle's friend. The idea sickened him.

Dickens fawned over his guests and gave a long speech about the mine's grand vision. At the end, the crowd gave a half-hearted cheer and turned to leave. 'Hold on. I want a few of you blokes to show off your skills. Step forward if I call your name.'

To Luke's astonishment, Adam McLeod was on the list. Angus surreptitiously pushed another man forward, but Dickens wouldn't have it. He gestured for Luke to step up. Soon half-a-dozen miners stood out the front. The rest were dismissed. Angus headed for the shaft cage, all the while casting worried glances over his shoulder.

Dickens went down the row, extolling each man's virtues in turn. He came to Luke and clapped him on the back. 'Adam here's our top mucker. That means he loads the raw ore into cars.' He spoke slowly and somewhat patronisingly to Edward, who looked irritated. 'He'll not be long in that job, of course,' said Dickens. 'Adam's quick-witted and strong as a bull. A little hot-tempered at times, but we like that here. I wager he won't be shy to take some risks.'

Luke moved to face Henry Abbott, but saw no sign of recognition from him.

'I like a man who looks me in the eye,' said Henry. 'It's more than Edward does.' He cast Edward a withering look. 'I'm afraid my son lacks a backbone.'

Edward stared down at his shiny, dust-free boots.

'Why don't you show him how other young men do a real day's work, eh?' Henry chuckled as Edward's ears reddened.

Luke longed to lead Henry Abbott through the dark, treacherous tunnels below, where death might lurk around any corner. Would the mine owner venture down beside him? Would he be so foolish? Luke was ill with anticipation. But instead Henry accompanied an engineer into the office. Disappointment kicked Luke in the guts so hard he thought he'd vomit.

'Shall we get started?' said Dickens.

The men walked across the yard and stepped into the cage. Shift bells sounded, loud and discordant through the smoggy air. Dickens fitted Edward with a helmet and oil lamp. The windlass ground into action, and slowly the men disappeared underground, ears popping as they sank hundreds of feet into the gloom.

Edward had never imagined such profound darkness. It consumed the dirty yellow beam of the headlamp within an inch of his face. The scream of the hoist told him they descended still, sinking deeper and deeper into the inky void. His heart thudded and his palms grew slick, even before the mine's oppressive humidity hit him. In the lamplight,

Adam's grim face and hostile stare were an unnerving contrast to Dickens' reassuring patter. Edward gagged, fighting for breath.

The cage hit dirt and came to a shuddering halt. The infernal screech of the windlass stopped as well. Edward had expected silence, but the mine wasn't quiet. The tunnels played a song of their own. Streams trickled and bubbled through the rock walls. Water pattered like rain from the roof. Stones popped and pelted onto the path ahead, and earth trickled from fissures and flaws, giving the impression of an imminent cave-in. The walls themselves seemed eerily alive. Edward feared small spaces, but he feared his father more. So he set off with halting, echoing steps into the bowels of the mine.

A deafening blast came just as Edward was finding his nerve. He lost his footing and crashed to the ground.

'I told them to hold off while you're down here.' Dickens helped him to his feet. 'Must be an unexploded charge from yesterday. Never mind. Watch your step, sir.'

Edward couldn't believe that people worked in such cramped conditions. They passed men crouched low in narrow tunnels. One miner writhed on the floor, clutching at his legs. What was wrong with him?

'It's the cramps,' Dickens explained at Edward's expression. 'He'll be right in a moment.'

A little further on he could hear singing.

'In the sweet, sweet arms of heaven,

Around the sacred shore,

Where we shall someday gather,

And suffer here no more.'

They rounded a corner and, one by one, the voices fell silent.

'This here's a loading area,' said Dickens. 'Let's have us some fun. An ore-car filling contest between our two top muckers.'

Adam won easily, attacking the crushed rock like a madman.

As Edward moved close to congratulate him, Adam whispered in his ear. 'There's black, bottomless lakes down here, Mr Abbott, where they'd never find a man. Pockets of poison air as well. It's too easy to lose your way.'

Edward shrank back.

Luke turned to leave, but Dickens wouldn't let him go, insisting he accompany them to a blasting point. 'We have to show Master Edward the most exciting part of our operation. Come on, Adam. It won't be long until you graduate to the drills, if you play your cards right.'

Was Dickens crazy, thinking he'd welcome such a promotion? Gun drillers operated eighty-pound pneumatic hammer drills known as widow makers, all while perched on rickety ladders in near darkness. Those that survived went deaf.

They passed Angus working in the maintenance team, shoring up stopes and tunnels with stout, square-set timber. He tipped his helmet with a weary nod and trudged off.

The group moved deeper into the mine. This was the blasting zone. Walls here seemed quiet and almost dry, but the air hung stale and hot and harder to breathe. Luke stopped dead. Something wasn't right. Their lamps smoked and sputtered alarmingly. Then the sound of ten-thousand thunders ripped through the dark.

Molly stopped peeling potatoes for dinner as Scruffy barked a warning. The kitchen rattled. What was happening? The floor rippled as if a giant snake glided beneath. She screamed as the walls and furniture swayed and shuddered.

Molly ran outside, turning to see the door splinter and fall, bowing to some immense invisible force. In the paddock behind the house, Sheba raced away from the moving ground. With one powerful bound, she cleared the tea-tree fence and careered like a thing possessed into the mountains.

Molly caught her breath. All around her, women and children fled their collapsing cottages. Then, as one, they headed for the mine. Molly ran with the crowd and reached the gates as alarm bells sounded.

. . .

Deep underground, the reverberations died away. Then Luke heard a strange roar, like the bursting of a tide. Angus had told him stories about the disaster at Golden Reef a decade before. Earth tremors and careless blasting caused an underground river to burst through the mine walls, inundating the lower levels and drowning dozens.

'Run!' Luke shoved the men back along the tunnel towards the main shaft. A blast of air rushing ahead of the torrent threatened to knock them off their feet. Howling wind extinguished their lights, except for Luke's headlamp. It flickered on, against all odds, lighting their way.

Where was Angus? As they rounded a corner, rubble cascaded from the darkness, hurling Luke to the ground. He picked himself up, surprised to be standing, blood seeping from great gashes in his chest. Luke knelt down. Groping round he found an arm and took its pulse. Nothing. 'Is anyone there?'

'Here,' came a hoarse reply.

He crawled towards the voice, hoping for a miracle, hoping to find Angus. Instead he found Edward Abbott, his arm pinned to the ground by rocks. Luke freed him from the debris, and all the while the strange thunder grew louder.

He pulled Edward to his feet and they ran, stumbling, ahead of the flood. Soon they tripped over bodies. Shifting layers of earth had forced a heavy sandstone shelf from the rock wall. A group of men lay broken beneath.

Were they alive? Luke knelt down to check them These two were dead, but this one lived, and this one. Energy surged through him, allowing him to lift the slab enough for Edward to pull the living miners free. Their mangled legs wouldn't carry them. With a calmness belying his terror, Luke hauled the miners, one by one, into an empty ore car. Each bend, each cough, each breath an agony – a knife twisting in his ribs.

Closer to the main shaft something caught his eye in the shadows, draped in dust and dirt. The form of a man. A familiar pair of patched boots showed in the feeble lamplight and a primal scream ripped from Luke's throat. Angus.

Luke swept up his battered body and heaved it into the trolley. Then he and Edward raced on. Some men ahead heard the clamour of the approaching wagon and fled before it, fearful it would crush them as it tore madly through the darkness. Somehow they dodged jutting rocks and falling stones to reach the central hoist.

Up through the shaft came the wails and cries of drowning men. Luke loaded the injured into the crowded cage. Edward stood by, paralysed with fear. Luke grabbed his shoulder and shook it. 'Get in, you bastard.' Edward climbed aboard. Luke heaved Angus after him, and then climbed in himself, his strength almost gone.

The hoist roared to life with a terrible grinding sound. The cage shuddered and shook, but failed to rise.

'We're overloaded,' someone shouted. 'It won't lift us.'

'This one's past help anyway,' said another man, and hurled Angus's prone body from the cage.

Luke screamed and leaped out, wading knee-deep, trying to hoist his friend's body back to safety. A rush of bad air filled his lungs and he fell, choking, into the foul water.

The cage began to move. It was too late. He'd lost Angus, and was going to die there in the dark flood.

Then Edward was beside him, hauling him back into the cage as it began its halting journey to the surface.

Three men burst from the tunnel, too late. They climbed hand over fist up the hoist chains, dangling precariously as a wall of water swamped the space where they'd stood just moments before.

Minutes later the mountain spat the cage out into sunshine, to the cheers and tears of the expectant crowd. People rushed forward to help the injured. Luke felt strong hands lift him from the cage. He grew more and more dizzy as someone covered him with a blanket. The sun seemed to be going out. How strange.

Before his world turned fully dark, he saw Henry Abbott hurry forward to his son.

'This man saved my life,' he heard Edward say.

'Then,' Sir Henry replied, 'we are forever in his debt.'

Molly and Scruffy searched in vain for Angus among the survivors, as an assortment of horse-drawn vehicles ferried the injured from the scene. With hopes fading, they joined the crowd gathered beneath the headframe, maintaining a futile vigil for loved ones lost underground.

# CHAPTER 23

L uke woke in the softest bed, beneath the warmest quilt of the lightest eiderdown. Every bit of his body ached. Each breath hurt. Waves of dizziness forced him to squint his eyes shut. Instantly his thoughts spiralled backwards. Scenes flashed through his mind, terrifying glimpses of darkness and fear and running for his life. Where was Angus? He couldn't remember. He couldn't remember anything.

When he opened his eyes again, he was able to take in his surrounds. He lay in a luxuriously appointed bedroom: fine mahogany wardrobes, elegant chiffoniers and an ornately inlaid toilet stand. His four-poster bed was swathed in heavy crimson curtains edged in gold. A tasselled counterpane of fine, white silk covered him. The view through the casement windows was of wide lawns, dotted with elms and oaks. He hadn't a clue where he was.

A young woman dressed in maid's clothes entered the room, a warm smile on her pretty face. For one heart-stopping moment, Luke thought she was his sister. The mistake filled him with shame. What sort of man would mistake a stranger for his own flesh and blood?

She asked how he felt and then fussed about, tidying up, not waiting for a response. Luke's parched mouth and sore throat made speech difficult. He could still taste the metal from the mine. The girl leaned close, supporting his head with a cool hand, pressing a cup of water to his lips. He took great swallows.

'I'm Rose, Master Adam. You're ever so thirsty, aren't you? Why don't I fetch you some breakfast and a lovely big pot of sweet tea?'

He put his hand on her arm and tried to say thank you. Rose giggled, looking pleased. As she turned to go, Luke forced a whisper from his swollen lips. 'Miss. Where am I?'

'Canterbury Downs, of course. Sir Henry Abbott's estate. You saved his son's life and the lives of four others, so I hear. You're quite the hero Master Adam. Truthfully, the other girls are all looking to bring you in something just for an excuse. Don't be surprised if you get plenty of visitors, especially once I tell them how handsome you are.' With a smile she was gone.

Luke sat up, his head swimming, and tried to swing his legs off the mattress.

'Steady on, Adam. Where do you think you're going?'

A surge of nausea made him sink backwards. That voice. Luke opened his eyes. Two men stood at the foot of the bed. Edward Abbott, his right arm braced and bandaged, a concerned look on his face. And a portly, bespectacled man.

'Dr Lark's here to see you.'

The doctor proceeded to poke and prod him, all the while addressing his remarks to Edward as if Luke wasn't in the room. 'He's badly knocked about. Broken ribs. Sprained knee and a twisted ankle. Some nasty lacerations, and faintness brought on by concussion and exposure to poisonous gas.' He cleaned a deep gash in Luke's thigh. 'Infection is the main fear.'

A stout matronly woman joined them. Edward introduced her as Nurse Marsh. The doctor placed several apothecary jars on the bedside table and barked out a long list of orders. 'Follow my directions exactly, woman. Never once make the most trifling alteration. If my patient dies, it will be due to your failure to carry out my medical instructions fully and precisely.'

Nurse Marsh glared at him, but held her tongue.

The doctor snapped shut his black leather bag and made to leave the room. 'Give him liberal doses of laudanum at the first sign of pain, sleeplessness or nervous fever.'

Edward watched Nurse Marsh expertly dress her patient's wounds and abrasions. As Adam leaned forward, the terrible scars on his back became visible. Edward and the nurse exchanged glances.

As Adam tried to rise, gritting his teeth against the pain, Edward assisted her to push him gently back down. Then he poured a generous measure of laudanum into a medicine glass and persuaded Adam to drink it. Within a few minutes he seemed calmer and drifted off to sleep.

'I need to speak to my father,' said Edward. 'Tend this young man with the utmost care and see he takes enough laudanum to stay comfortable.' The nurse nodded and turned to tidy the assortment of ointments, salves and bandages.

Edward took a last look at the miner, both fascinated and horrified by his scars and what they might mean. It was intriguing to think that his own life had almost certainly been saved by a convict.

He found his father in the drawing room. Enormous gilt-edged paintings adorned the walls, scenes of fox-hunting, deer-shooting and falconry. An antlered stag's head hung over the marble mantel and a twelve-foot white tiger-skin, jaws frozen in a snarl, lay before the fireplace. Henry was inspecting his collection of hunting rifles. He was obsessed with guns, and always wore a loaded pearl-handled pistol at his belt, saying he didn't feel properly dressed without it.

Henry turned, took the pipe from his mouth. 'What's the word on our young friend?'

'On the improve.'

'Good, good. That boy has courage and initiative. He could be very useful to me.'

Edward's ears burned. *Unlike me*, he thought. He toyed with the idea of mentioning Adam's scarred back.

Henry took down a rifle and opened the breech. 'You took a risk, dragging Adam to safety at the last.' He smiled his close-lipped smile, which Edward rarely saw. 'It made me proud.'

Edward experienced an unfamiliar shock of pleasure. He'd been waiting all his life for his father to say those words. Now he was doubly grateful to Adam – for rescuing him from the rockfall, and for providing him with the means to impress his father. Perversely, the second more important.

'Your mother wants to know if Adam is well enough for a visit,' said Henry.

'He's yet to be told of his uncle's death. I'd wait until then.'

'Very well. I'll be guided by you on the matter.'

Edward couldn't believe what he was hearing. Since when had his father ever been guided by him on anything?

A manservant appeared at the door. 'Lady Jane requires Master Edward to have his injured arm dressed.'

Henry clapped his son on the back. 'Go on now, before your mother blames me for something.'


Ten days had passed since the mine disaster, and Luke's physical wounds were healing. Yet his grief at Angus's death had cast him into a permanent pit of despair, every bit as hellish and dark as the mine. Sixteen men had died that day. Demons of self-loathing consumed him. He'd abandoned Angus to a watery grave, yet guided an Abbott to safety. Worse still, he owed Edward for his worthless life.

On the first day at Canterbury Downs he'd resolved to kill Henry Abbott. Here was the perfect opportunity to destroy the man responsible for every cruel loss he'd suffered. But as the days wore on, Luke's mind grew increasingly muddled. When he tried to think, nothing stayed straight in his head.

One day Luke woke to find he couldn't remember his sister's name. No matter how hard he tried, it wouldn't come. Rose, concerned at his growing agitation, gave him a double dose of his morning laudanum. It tasted terrible, but was well worth forcing down. Then she gave him an extra cup at his request. Ah, there it was, that delicious drowsiness coiling through his mind. His frustration ebbed away and a precious cloud of indifference settled over him. It didn't matter if he could remember or not.

Luke shut his eyes and relaxed into his soft bed, listening to Rose prattle pleasantly on about her day. His plan to kill Henry Abbott suddenly seemed ridiculous and far too difficult to bother with. The past was losing its grip.

Hours later, through the fog of sleep, Luke heard the barking of dogs. He'd had a dog once. He struggled to remember, fighting to hold the thought . . . Bear. A flood of emotion accompanied the memory, rousing him from his stupor. Luke staggered to the window. A mounted man approached, leading a riderless horse. They looked familiar . . . a coal black stallion with a graceful, arched crest, and an elegant grey. Solomon and Sheba. Daniel had come for him.

A groomsman took the horses' reins and Daniel moved under the verandah, out of sight. Luke stumbled from his bedroom. A timber-panelled passage led to a broad staircase. He managed the stairs, and found himself in a grandly appointed front hall, punctuated by four oak doors. Luke opened them one by one. Behind the third, in a pine-panelled drawing room, he found Daniel and Henry engaged in a heated argument. He stood in the doorway, wild-eyed and unsteady in a long cotton nightgown. To his immeasurable delight, Daniel hurried to embrace him.

'Adam, collect your things. You're coming with me.'

'Return to your room, Adam. Mr Campbell and I aren't finished.'

'There's nothing here I need,' said Luke.

'Then we'll be off,' said Daniel. 'Thank you, Henry, for taking such excellent care of Adam, but we need him home.'

He took Luke's arm and guided him from the room, and out the front door to where a groom waited with the horses. Fighting waves of dizziness, Luke hitched up his nightgown and clumsily managed to mount Sheba. How good it was to feel the mare under him again.

. . .

Luke saw a curtain twitched aside at the house, and Henry Abbot in the frame of the window, a look of astonishment on his face. It would make no sense to him. Of what possible importance could Adam McLeod, the nephew of a poor miner, be to Daniel Campbell?

# CHAPTER 24

What a homecoming. Elizabeth seemed to have put aside her fears, and joined in the welcome. Belle wept with happiness. She also laughed a lot when Luke arrived in nothing but a nightshirt. This time it was his turn to blush.

Bear gambolled like a pup, refusing to leave his master's side and insisting on accompanying him into the house. He lay on Luke's bed, growling fiercely at anyone who tried to move him. The dog finally met his match in Mrs Scott, who never took any nonsense from anyone. She clouted him with a broom until he lay compliant on the floor.

For Luke it was as life after death. Elizabeth insisted he rest, but instead he dressed and followed Belle into the yard.

'I've been so worried,' she said when they were alone 'I can't believe you almost died. Why did you disappear like that? It was my mother, wasn't it? You don't have to say anything. I can tell. I wish she'd just leave us be. Come on.' She took his hand. 'I've the most wonderful surprise for you.' She led him to the stable.

There, in a bed of golden straw, lay Sasha with a wriggling pile of newborn puppies.

Bear trotted in and Sasha wagged her tail. Kneeling slowly in the straw, Luke held a puppy. So tiny. So warm and soft and sweet.

'There are five girls and five boys: Calliope, Adonis, Hercules, Apollo, Zeus, Pluto, Ariadne, Diana, Juno and Helen.' Belle picked up each puppy as she recited its name.

'But they all look the same. How can you tell them apart?'

'They are *not* all the same,' said Belle. 'They have different personalities for one thing. And Diana here? Her muzzle's a bit wider than Juno's. And Hercules is much bigger than Adonis already, and Ariadne has the cutest little ears . . .'

Luke laughed. 'All right, I believe you. But forgive me if I can't recognise them straightaway.' He hugged Bear in congratulations.

When he stood up, Belle came to him. 'Where's my hug?'

Impulsively he put his arms around her and kissed her. So much for all the firm words he'd had with himself. The moment proved irresistibly delicious to them both.

Approaching footsteps made them draw apart.

'There you are.' Daniel poked his head in the door. 'Don't overtax him, Belle. Luke still has some recovering to do.'

'At least let him see the tigers.'

The cubs had grown big in the past few months, coats streaked with burnished gold, tawny eyes bright with health. King, in particular, seemed more mature, more arrogantly wild. To Luke's delight they remembered him. The she-cubs, Bindi and Mindi, approached the wire with friendly yips, sidling along the fence for a pat. Even King deigned to be stroked. The little devils weren't so forthcoming and remained soundly asleep in their log.

'It's time for Luke to rest,' said Daniel, when Belle suggested they go riding.

As they passed the cart shed, Luke spied an emaciated black kelpie lying in the sun.

'Who's the new dog?'

'That's Rastus,' said Belle. 'Abbott's musterers found him chained to a tree at a deserted camp site. Apparently he belonged to a fur trapper, but it's a mystery what happened to his owner. The camp looked like somebody might come back at any moment . . . skins still pegged out to dry . . . but poor Rastus was nearly dead from hunger and thirst. The trapper's two horses wandered into Canterbury Downs a few days later in hobbles. Papa thinks he had some sort of accident out in the bush. Henry wanted to shoot Rastus because he was so sick, but I talked Edward into giving him to me. He's still skinny, but he's slowly getting better, aren't you, Rastus?' Belle walked over to the dog who stood briefly for a pat, then lay wearily back down. 'Come and meet him.'

Luke shook his head, horrified the kelpie would sense his complicity in its master's death. Some very unwelcome memories crowded in.

When they returned to the house, Mrs Scott saw Bear off at the door and bustled Belle away. 'You look done in, Adam. Go to bed.'

Luke didn't need to be told twice. His bones ached to their marrow and the wash of emotions had left him weak. He longed for sleep. Yet a peculiar numbness in his back and limbs kept him tossing and turning, making it impossible to lie comfortably in one position for more than a minute or two. On top of that, he was getting the headache from hell.

Mrs Scott came in with scones and tea, but Luke had no appetite. 'Could you please tell Mr Campbell that I need some laudanum. The doctor prescribed it.'

He yawned and sank back on the bed to wait. It seemed to take forever.

When Daniel finally arrived, he was accompanied by a smartly dressed young man. 'This is Dr Lovejoy, newly arrived from England and qualified in the most advanced medical theory.'

The doctor conducted an exhaustive examination. After half an hour he put down his stethoscope, moved away from the bed and began talking to Daniel in a low voice. Luke strained to hear. What was taking so long? If he didn't get that medicine soon, his head would explode.

After a minute or two, Daniel said, 'Excellent news, Adam. Your lungs are clear, and your wounds and broken ribs are healing nicely.'

'In a few weeks you'll be good as new,' added the doctor.

Instead of being pleased, Luke grew more anxious. 'Dr Lark gave me laudanum. It helps a lot. Can I have some?'

'No.' The doctor snapped his bag shut. 'I've left some soothing herbs with Mrs Scott to ease your withdrawal.'

'Laudanum's not a good idea,' said Daniel.

'But it helps.'

'My dear boy, laudanum is no medicine. It's opium dissolved in wine, effective for easing the pain of birth and death and little else. Even a short time on high doses can trigger physical dependency, so I'll forewarn you of what to expect. Sleepless nights. Aches, sweats . . . shivering, perhaps. Your stomach may cramp. However, this will pass and you'll soon feel your strength return.'

Daniel put a book on the bedside table, a copy Homer's *Odyssey*, one of Luke's favourite stories. 'Read the marked page, please. I think you'll find it interesting. We'll talk later.' Daniel patted him on the shoulder and left the room.

Curiously, Luke turned the familiar pages to the episode where Telemachus was sinking into depression, having failed to find his father, Odysseus . . . But then Helen *had a happy thought. Into the bowl in which their wine was mixed, she slipped a drug with the power to rob grief and anger of their sting and banish all painful memories. No one who swallowed this, dissolved in their wine, could shed a single tear that day, even for the death of his mother or father, or if they put his brother or own son to the sword and he were there to see it done.*

Luke put down the book in disbelief. He knew opium dens to be frequented by the desperate and criminals. As a child in Hobart, Luke had peeked into them. Strange, ragged people lying prone on filthy, foul-smelling cots. Cloying, pungent smoke in the air. Prints of naked women on the wall. These places had frightened him, as did the trembling, malnourished wrecks he sometimes saw on the streets, senseless in the grip of their addiction.

Yet the drug still held a potent allure. What did Homer say? Luke read it again . . . *the power to rob grief and anger of their sting and banish all painful memories.* How perfect, yet it was perfection tainted by

Henry Abbott's hand. Luke gritted his teeth against the pain and lost himself in tales of Odysseus, wreaking bloody revenge on those who wronged him.


Elizabeth lay in bed, wide awake, watching dawn creep in the window, listening to rain on the roof. Two months now since Luke had arrived back at Binburra. She'd tried to put her fears aside. Rescuing the miners had made him the town hero, and she too admired his bravery. But as Luke returned to health and strength, her doubts returned. Belle was more besotted with him than ever.

Elizabeth had hoped that Luke would honour her wishes and keep away from Belle. He made a show of it, for a time. Not any more. Yesterday she'd found them together in the stable, ostensibly cleaning out the puppy pen. Elizabeth did not miss their fast breathing or her daughter's flushed face. She'd spent a sleepless night, wondering how she might again separate Luke from her daughter.

Daniel stirred beside her, and Elizabeth studied his handsome face in the pale morning light: his broad, tanned forehead with barely a frown line, aquiline nose, softly parted lips and neat beard flecked with grey. She kissed him. He wrapped his arms around her without opening his eyes, as she nestled her head on his shoulder.

'What is it, Lizzie? You were restless last night.'

She wanted to, no, needed to confide in him, but she also knew he'd dismiss her concerns. His faith in Luke was too strong and his understanding of young love too weak.

'The fire made the room so hot.'

'Is that all?' He ran a finger down her cheek. 'Perhaps you're worried about me leaving for Coomalong today?'

'Riding in this rain will be an ordeal,' she said. 'Why not delay your Hobart trip?'

'You know I can't, Lizzie. The government is bringing forward the *Thylacine Bounty Scheme Bill*. That bastard Lyne is trying to push it through without debate. It's the last chance for the Royal Society to lobby for a *no* vote. They need me.'

I need you too, thought Elizabeth. She turned away, taking her head from his arm.

'But this is vital, Lizzie, as you well know. Why don't you and Belle come with me?'

If only . . . but Belle would flatly refuse such an invitation, so Elizabeth reluctantly did the same.

'As you wish.' Daniel stretched. 'But don't blame me for us being apart, when it's your choice to stay.'

Elizabeth bit her tongue. Daniel would leave for Hobart, having no clue of the emotional hot house he was leaving behind.

# CHAPTER 25

The key instigator of the thylacine bounty scheme was a man named John Lyne, independent member of the assembly for Glamorgan. A lecher by reputation, he'd earned the nickname *Leghunter*. Daniel also had him pegged as a dishonest braggart. He'd claimed his family migrated to Tasmania with letters of introduction from the renowned Earl of Bathurst, attached to the Colonial Office. A simple inquiry found this to be demonstrably false, as false as Henry Abbott's knighthood. A disregard for facts and a flair for self-congratulation also characterised Lyne's political life. He publicly dismissed reports that floggings continued in the island's prisons as fanciful.

'We are a humane society that has thankfully moved beyond barbarity,' he boasted, in line with growing popular opinion.

But eyewitness accounts contradicted him. A young station hand told Daniel he'd been assigned as a boy to Lyne's farm. 'If I didn't keep a still tongue in my head and do the master's duty, Mr Lyne gave me thirty lashes.'

Dark rumours abounded of the family's past violence against east-coast people. It was said that John Lyne personally shot Aborigines found on his land.

Now Lyne directed this considerable talent for hypocrisy to the thylacine issue. Though privately conceding that native tigers had never caused him a problem, publicly he spearheaded a campaign by rural members of parliament for their destruction. Paradoxically, it was during a discussion about the need for a closed season to *protect* native game that Lyne first proposed the government introduce a thylacine bounty. He lacked the numbers and his proposal was defeated. Undeterred, rural members waged a war of attrition against the anti-bounty MPs, never missing an opportunity to malign them. They also vastly exaggerated thylacine numbers and the damage they caused. Lyne's private member's bill soon followed, recommending *the appropriation of a sum of five hundred pounds for the destruction of tigers.* The die was cast.

The very fact that a parliamentary pro-thylacine block even existed gave hope to the Royal Society. Daniel and his colleagues spent the days before the vote furiously wining and dining the ten or so members still opposed to the bounty, shoring up their support. But they also courted the country members to gauge their opinions and change their minds.

Daniel found political lobbying to be a complicated beast. Alliances shifted like sand. He came to understand that the thylacine question was just a pawn in a much larger power struggle between urban and rural members. The average town dweller enjoyed seeing tigers on display in zoos, and thought rich farmers should pay to solve their own problems.

But to their surprise and dismay, the Royal Society found that the *Chinese question* was tangled up with the thylacine issue. Anti-Chinese feeling was strongest in the towns, so some city MP's agreed to vote for the bounty in exchange for promises from rural members to support anti-Chinese immigration legislation.

'This is outrageous! One has nothing to do with the other,' said Daniel, during dinner with a Hobart parliamentarian who was an advocate for the tigers, but an enemy of the Chinese. Here was a man who understood about habitat change and saw tigers being used as scapegoats for poor farming practices. Yet he still planned to horse-trade his vote.

'I hate Chinamen more than I love tigers,' was his response.

The members of the Royal Society grew more despondent daily. 'The standard of moral and intellectual debate in this state is a disgrace,' said Daniel. 'The bigots plan to sell out the thylacine, in spite of our facts and statistics.'

There was a murmur of agreement. The vote would take place next week and they could do little more to influence it.

The fateful day arrived. Debate commenced in Hobart's grand parliamentary chamber, before a packed public gallery. Things began well enough. Several members spoke in opposition to the bill. Mr Young said that if any group could take care of themselves, it was the large sheep-owners. Colonel St. Hill did not see that it would be a great calamity if sheep-owners were driven off crown lands anyway. Daniel felt quite optimistic when Mr Fenton ridiculed the idea of five hundred pounds doing all the good that was expected of it . . . that runs had not been given up on account of tigers, but because of wild dogs and low wool prices.

Now Lyne spoke, stating that sheep owners lost at least fifty thousand sheep each year in Glamorgan alone. Daniel could barely contain himself. He'd read the report of the Chief Inspector of Sheep. It estimated there were only forty-four thousand sheep in the whole of the district. Apparently the tigers had wiped out the entire sheep population, along with ten per cent of next year's flock!

The speeches rolled on interminably, well into the evening – some for, some against. At times Daniel was hopeful of success, next minute, certain of defeat. Everyone wanted his say.

Two more members spoke for Lyne. Mr Sutton argued that mutton would be cheaper if tigers were exterminated. So did Mr Pillinger. Then Mr Dumaresq spoke. He couldn't see how tigers could be any more numerous now than formerly. Nor could he understand why they weren't destroyed at the sheep-owners own expense. He did not support the bill. Neither did the speaker, Mr Dobson, who spoke in defence of the tigers.

The vote began at close to midnight, and remained neck and neck until the last. Daniel held his breath for the last vote, preparing a cheer. Eleven against – twelve for, and surely Dobson's vote a foregone conclusion. That meant a tie, and the motion could only be carried in the majority.

But to Daniel's horror, Dobson's courage failed him at the crucial moment. As former leader of the Opposition, he feared voting against so many of his old allies. So he refrained from voting at all.

'I think the ayes have it.'

On the basis of Dobson's missing vote, the bill had passed, twelve votes to eleven. A jeer rose from the gallery, still filled with onlookers despite the lateness of the hour. Public sentiment did not support the result, yet for Daniel it didn't matter. The thylacine was already extinct. It was now only a matter of time.

Back at Binburra and with Daniel away, Luke and Belle grew ever more reckless. Despite Elizabeth's efforts to keep them apart, they arranged secret rendezvous. Their favourite ruse was to ride out separately, on some pretext or other, and then meet at the waterfall. It became their special place, a place to explore forbidden love.

Belle, consumed by their new passion, abandoned her old friends. 'You are all the world I need, Luke.'

It thrilled him to hear it. It also thrilled him that she spent no more time with Edward Abbott. He couldn't stand the idea of her being anywhere near Canterbury Downs. With his tomboy princess by his side, all things seemed possible.

Even Elizabeth's direct pleas fell on deaf ears. Luke wouldn't give Belle up, not this time. The voice of reason faded to a whisper. Belle filled Luke's mind, banishing pain and grief more completely than laudanum ever had. When they were together, even guilt disappeared. But it crept back home when he was alone, like a soft, insistent knocking at the door. Guilt over disobeying Elizabeth. Guilt over his father's death. Guilt over Angus.

Luke hated that Scruffy remained with Molly. That woman wasn't fit to care for a cockroach. If not for her greed, Angus would never have been down that stinking pit in the first place. He would bring the little terrier home to live at Binburra. It was the last thing he could do for Angus. But not today. Today he would spend with Belle.

He slipped Sheba's bridle over her ears and opened the sliprails. He had one eye on his horse and the other on the track above the homestead. When Luke saw Belle canter Whisky up the hill, he swung on to Sheba bareback. He waited for a few minutes, watching for prying eyes. Then he gave Sheba her head and raced off in pursuit. Already tasting Belle's skin on his tongue, aching to hold her again.

Elizabeth watched him go from her bedroom window. She felt like the onlooker of an imminent train wreck, certain of looming disaster and powerless to prevent it. Both Luke and Belle denied the affair and their deceit wounded her. She wished now she'd confided in Daniel and she hoped that when her husband returned, he would somehow know what to do.

Daniel stayed on in Hobart for a few days following the disastrous vote. The decision and behaviour of the House in general had provoked significant public outrage. The wool kings were seen to be flagrantly abusing the public purse. A damning editorial in the *Tasmanian Mail* summed up popular sentiment.

*Year after year, this pampered industry wins the favours of the legislature. If any of their bills are rejected by the House, a few large landholders meet, urge their views on the accommodating Attorney-General and, hey presto, the rejected bill is reinstated. Thus the wool kings govern the House and get whatever they desire for the protection of their industry.*

*The Government puts a price upon the heads of native wolves, even though our own zoos report good specimens are rare and hard to find. They have £500 voted to them for the slaughter of rabbits on Crown Lands, even*

*though these same pastoralists brought the rabbits here in the first place . . .
there is no reason why one sixpence should come out of consolidated revenue
for the destruction of rabbits, wolves or anything else.*

Daniel took some cold comfort from a flurry of letters to the
editor, ridiculing John Lyne and his cohorts.

*Tiger Lyne, as the honourable Member for Glamorgan is now very gener-
ally called, is on the warpath, again, on the lookout for sheep killers, nay even
manslayers. If he tells us the truth, the jungles of India do not furnish
anything like the terrors that our own east coast does in the matter of wild
beasts of the most ferocious kinds. According to Tiger Lyne, these dreadful
animals may be seen in their hundreds, stealthily sneaking along, seeking
whom they may devour, and it is estimated that in less than two years they
will have swallowed up every sheep and bullock in Glamorgan.*

Daniel struggled to accept that a major extinction was happening
right under his nose, and for so little reason. Like Elizabeth, he felt
like an onlooker at a train wreck. It was just a different train wreck. A
vigorous debate began among the members of the Royal Society.
Some thought an education campaign could do some good. Others
believed zoos should try to acquire sufficient animals to support
captive breeding through a private bounty on live specimens. Maria
Island was proposed as a possible sanctuary for a remnant population.

'It's hopeless,' said Daniel. 'If a man captures a thylacine out in the
backblocks, he has only to chop its head off and claim a pound. This
does not spoil the skin, which then earns him several more. Far
simpler than lugging a live animal for miles to a train station, in the
hope of sending it to a zoo and *perhaps* gaining a greater reward.'

Glum silence greeted these words. His reasoning was faultless.

Daniel finished packing for the trip home. Checking himself in the
mirror, he snatched his tie undone and began again. He needed Lizzie.
He needed Binburra. Coomalong, his grand old house, didn't feel like
home any more. There was nothing left for him in Hobart, not now
the bounty scheme had passed.

Daniel's thoughts turned to the cubs. He hadn't told anybody from the Royal Society about his rare guests. They'd want to put them in a zoo. But he had a different plan – to release the young thylacines into the highest, most inaccessible reaches of the Binburra ranges, at a place called Tiger Pass. Let them make one final, improbable stand against extinction.

# CHAPTER 26

Elizabeth threw herself into Daniel's arms as he climbed the verandah steps. He brushed back her hair, a bemused smile playing on his lips.

'I've been gone three weeks, Lizzie – not three years.' His smile changed to an expression of tender concern. 'Lizzie? What's all this about?'

She pulled away, composed herself, then captured him with earnest eyes. 'Darling, you must listen to me.'

Lizzie confessed her suspicions about Belle and Luke in a great outpouring, the words flowing unchecked, right there on the verandah, before he'd even set foot in the door.

Daniel didn't want to believe it. He denied the possibility, even reprimanding her for allowing imagination to get the best of her. But a final, searching look at his wife's troubled face convinced him. Relocating the tigers took on a fresh urgency. It would also serve as a pretext to separate the young lovers.

Daniel planned to lead Luke, along with Bear and the tigers, into the mountain wilderness. Years ago, he'd explored deep into the ranges, guided by an old musterer named Billy. As a boy, Billy's

Aboriginal mother had taught him to navigate the remote maze of canyons, caves and undisturbed forests lying to Binburra's north.

Daniel's favourite place was a rocky pass, enclosed on either side by sheer walls of stone, which were striped and patterned with shadows, fringed with jagged sandstone battlements. This was *Loongana Warraroong* – the Pass of the Tiger, and thylacines used to be common there. Billy said that, once upon a time, the pass led to a track down the escarpment, an entrance to a vast, lost valley where families hunted abundant game and walked for weeks without reaching its limit. What was it Billy said? 'A place hidden from everything but sky.' Then an earthquake blocked the way, sealing the valley within colossal, unscalable cliffs.

'I can show you how to get down to the valley,' said Billy. The pass walls were honeycombed with caverns, filled with paintings and rock carvings. Into a cave they went. To Daniel, it had looked like all the other caves. But as they progressed into its dim recesses, it led sharply down. Ancient steps lay carved in limestone. After half an hour of climbing in near-darkness, they stood on the valley floor. Daniel had looked up, staggered by the sheer size of the cliffs rising around him, forming an impenetrable natural fortress. It was to this place that Daniel would bring the tigers.

'You must go at once, my love,' urged Elizabeth, when he told her his plan. 'Before it's too late.'

'I wonder if the cubs will follow us,' said Daniel that evening in his library, after he'd told Luke of his idea.

'Of course they will.' Luke could barely contain his excitement. 'They're completely bonded to Bear. We'd better give them time to rest up in the middle of the day and, where possible, travel with the moon at night. I wager we'll not lose them.'

Daniel's expression turned grave. 'There's one more thing, Luke. My wife tells me you're overly fond of Belle, and she of you.'

The guilt clouding Luke's face gave him away.

'This must stop, of course,' said Daniel. 'There's no future in it. Unfair it may be, but such a match is impossible.'

'I understand, sir,' said Luke, feeling like a fraud. He'd not give Belle up this time, not even for Daniel.

At midnight Luke met Belle in the stable to say goodbye. The round moon, framed in a high window, lit the space with a soft radiance. She lay wrapped in his arms, while warm, sleepy puppies pressed against them.

'I wish I could come with you to Tiger Pass.' Belle traced his lips with her finger. 'I asked Papa, but he said no. He hardly ever says no.'

'Your father suspects something between us.' Luke ran his fingers through her chestnut hair. 'He warned me off.'

'Did he?' Belle sat up. 'Don't you dare let him spoil things.' She kissed him in sweet, slow motion, stirring his blood.

'Nobody will tear us apart.' He pulled her close. 'I'll find a way to marry you, Belle. I promise.'

Luke and Daniel left on foot next day at dawn. The terrain would soon become too rugged for horses. Bear wore a pack and carried his share of provisions. Daniel half-expected the young tigers to run off on release. Instead they stayed close to Bear, slipping easily into old patterns, rippling like shadows through the foggy forest. It was only out here that the perfection of their camouflage became apparent.

Ten years had passed since Daniel had last navigated these forests, and he surprised himself with his sure memory of the land. They stopped for lunch by the banks of a stream. Luke shared some mutton with the animals. The cubs curled up for a nap in the sheltering roots of an old King Billy pine. Daniel and Luke hardly talked, each lost in private thoughts.

For three days they travelled, forging higher and higher into the ranges. As they climbed, their voices loosened, and Daniel told Luke about the bounty scheme. It mystified Luke that, for a pound, so many men wanted to destroy these rare tigers that he and Daniel sought so fervently to protect.

The animals grew more bewilderingly beautiful as they moved through the ancient forest. Playing against a backdrop of paperbarks. Slinking across moss-encrusted logs. Paddling in crystal streams. The cubs graced the elemental landscape, utterly completing it.

Daniel knew their strange journey – humans in companionship with thylacines – could never be repeated. Such extraordinary coincidences had led to this alliance. And now the thylacine stood at the very edge of the extinction precipice. Luke, too, seemed filled with melancholy. They travelled in meditative silence, experiencing a heightening of their senses: a poignant, ever-deepening connection to the land.


At mid-morning on the fourth day they reached their destination. The sun shone warm in a cloudless sky. With Bear and the tigers bounding on ahead, they entered the pass. The first thing Luke noticed was the stillness. He'd never been to a cathedral, but imagined it might feel something like this. Pale purple shadows softened the cliffs jagged edges, and the air hung heavy in the silence. Luke felt the awed reverence of a pilgrim.

A river ran through the ravine, narrow at times, then widening into a chain of dark, rocky pools. At the end of the pass it plunged, a topaz cascade, down a bottomless cliff. Tiger Pass was, in fact, a little hanging valley suspended high above a vast natural amphitheatre. For the longest time Luke simply looked, the scene one of such majesty that he couldn't absorb it all at once.

They retraced their steps, passing dozens of small caves peppering the rock walls. Daniel stopped beside a tall Huon pine. A thousand years before Christ was born, the little pine seedling had taken root beside this nameless river. Growing through the infinitely slow passage of centuries, weathering wind and sun and rain, until its twisted trunk rose sixty feet into the sky. It had served as a landmark for animals and humans alike, but the hunting parties were gone now.

The ancient tree arched its branches in supplication, trailing pendulous, feathery foliage across the rocks as if to wipe away their tears.

'This is it.' Daniel pointed to a large cave formed by an overhanging granite shelf near the base of the pine.

In they went, followed by the inquisitive animals. Looking up, Luke saw dozens of drawings on the rocks, handprints and concentric circles. People sheltering in this cave system over thousands of years had mixed ochre with their own blood to make these timeless images. As they ventured further in, the painted likeness of a thylacine gazed eerily down on them.

At the rear of the cave a fissure opened up in the floor, leading to a precipitous pathway. Daniel lit a pair of candles and gave one to Luke. King, with the keen, wide eyes of a night hunter, leapt surely down, and they all followed. Bear brought up the rear, his bulky frame almost becoming wedged in the narrow gap. With an enormous wiggle and whine he managed to squeeze after the others.

Flurries of tiny squeaking bats swarmed round their ears and vanished into the void. Water dripped from the roof. Points of cold light, furnished by a myriad of glow-worms, illuminated the clammy walls. A filigree of green and gold lichen crept over the rocks. Just as Daniel said, crude steps were carved into the steepest parts.

After a torturous descent, they emerged from the base of the cliff through a leathery curtain of gumleaves. Now they stood on the valley floor. Luke looked up. Above the cave entrance, vertical cliffs towered hundreds of feet into the sky. Stands of beech opened into protected, grassy glades. A startled mob of fat, grazing pademelons bounded into the sheltering forest. The young tigers showed a keen interest in their traditional prey. Uttering high-pitched yips and with quivering jaws, they took off after the fleeing wallabies. Only when Bear failed to join the hunt did they circle back.

Strange, beehive-shaped domes were clustered at the edge of the sandstone escarpment. 'This was once part of an ancient inland lake,' said Daniel. 'Its bed gouged from the wilderness by long-vanished glaciers. Weather eroded the soft sandstone, revealing these wind-carved towers of iron.'

Despite Daniel's explanation, Luke couldn't shake the feeling that the odd terraced towers were sculpted by an invisible human hand.

They set up camp in a cave a mile further west, at the bottom of the waterfall, beside its deep, reflective pool. It provided an ideal base for the youngsters to be reintroduced into the wild. Their plan was to keep Bear and the cubs hungry, thereby encouraging them to seek their own food.

On the first night, the animals stayed close by. Morning found them sound asleep in the ferny nest Luke had made for them at the rear of the cave. They slept the day away, while Luke explored with Bear, familiarising the dog with his new surroundings.

As afternoon wore into evening, the hungry cubs awoke. They hung around the camp for a while, unsuccessfully begging for food. Then King trotted off into the forest, followed by his sisters. Bear whined, watching them go, then gave his customary sharp bark and took off after the cubs. Luke grinned at Daniel. Now all they could do was wait and hope that Bear would bring them safely home by morning.

At first light the animals emerged from the mist, bellies distended, and snuggled down in their bed to sleep. Bear sat companionably with Luke for a few minutes. Fresh blood spattered his chest. Before long, he too curled up and slept.

This became the pattern of their days. The animals hunting nightly. Daniel and Luke exploring, collecting specimens and sketching rock paintings. Late winter sun shining in a cloudless sky. The cliffs reflected its warmth so it almost felt like spring. Luke's worries faded into the background: grief over Angus's death, guilt over his forbidden love affair with Belle – how could one worry in such a paradise? He could stay like this forever.

After an idyllic fortnight, Daniel announced it was time for him to return to Binburra. 'I'll be back in a few weeks. Once the tigers are settled, we'll dynamite the cave entrance up at Tiger Pass to seal off the valley. I want you to search for signs of other thylacines. My hope is that our cubs might mate with wild tigers to form a safe breeding stock.'

Luke nodded, thrilled to be appointed to such an important task. The prospect of living rough with the animals as his sole companions didn't daunt him. Bear was no longer the only one torn between two worlds.

# CHAPTER 27

One morning, shortly after Luke left for Tiger Pass, Belle didn't get up.

Her mother looked in on her before leaving to teach at the little mine school. 'Be lazy if you like,' she said. 'I've no time for your moods.'

But this was no mood. Belle feared she was with child.

She waited for her mother to leave, went to the library, and took a large volume off the shelf: *Advice to Mother on the Management of their Offspring*, a popular book on women's health. Then she hurried back to her room. As a curious child, Belle had often sneaked this book from the shelf. Now she turned to the section on pregnancy.

The first sign of pregnancy was *ceasing to become unwell*, which she guessed meant ceasing her periods. Horrified, Belle realised she had the second and third signs too – nausea, and painful, swollen breasts. The symptoms had bothered her for weeks now, and could no longer be dismissed as figments of the imagination. She slipped the book under her bed and hugged Sasha tightly, more certain than ever that she was in trouble.

In the coming days, anxiety ruled Belle. She couldn't eat, couldn't sleep. Her mane of auburn hair went uncombed and unwashed. She stopped bathing. The truth was, she couldn't bear to undress and reveal the body that had so betrayed her. If only she could talk to someone, but who? Sasha listened sympathetically, but offered no advice. Millie was the world's biggest gossip. Luke and her father had vanished into the ranges with Bear and the tigers. Telling Grace or Edward would cause a scandal, and it would be too humiliating to confide in her mother.

So Belle spent her days alone. Galloping Whisky at punishing speeds up the waterfall track was her only plan. She hoped it might bring on her period or that she'd discover Luke and Bear waiting for her at their special place by the falls. She was always disappointed. Sitting for hours in the mossy nest she'd shared with Luke, listening to the constant murmur of falling water. Crushingly alone. She may as well have been the last person on earth. Only that little stream, weeping beside her, brought any comfort.


Elizabeth woke one morning to find Belle had thrown up her meagre breakfast. She wasn't the only one suspicious now. Belle's *nervous condition* was becoming the talk of the household. A knot formed in Elizabeth's stomach. This could be put off no longer.

She found Belle in her room, huddled on the edge of the bed, her once rosy complexion sallow and wan. Upon seeing her mother, Belle burst out crying. Elizabeth dreaded having to ask, but the fear of the unthinkable hardened her heart. She had to know.

A pregnancy *would* be the unthinkable. In proper society, a girl could have no sexual contact prior to marriage. A hand around the waist or a stolen kiss was all young couples could hope for. Men engaged in pre-marital sex only with servants or prostitutes. Girls were virgins on their wedding night, mostly entirely ignorant and often terrified. Whether this was right or wrong did not concern Elizabeth now. It was just the way it was. She sat beside her daughter, who turned her face to the wall.

'Belle?' No response. 'Belle, what's wrong?' Elizabeth took her daughter's wrists, pulling her to her feet and forcing eye contact. The shame she saw confirmed it. 'Oh, my poor darling.'

'I'm sorry, Mama.'

Elizabeth swept her daughter up in a fierce, protective embrace. For the longest time they held each other, reconnecting. When they finally fell together on the bed, Belle began to talk. Elizabeth still held her, stroking her hair, murmuring encouragement when racking sobs interrupted the flood of words. At last Belle was spent.

'Ask Millie to run a bath and wash your hair. When she asks what is wrong, as the meddling girl is bound to do, you must complain that it's your time of the month. Then put on a day dress, not trousers, and wait in your room.'

For the first time in a long time, Belle meekly obeyed her mother.

Elizabeth dispatched Davey to town for the doctor and lay down in her room to steady her racing heart. Grimly, she held onto the hope that this was nothing more than an adolescent fit of depression. Or too much exercise? Ada Mitchell often chastised her for allowing Belle to ride out at will. Ada subscribed to the popular belief that genteel girls must be protected from activity. Too much exercise was rumoured to cause them dizzy spells and nausea, perhaps even unbalancing them permanently. Until now Elizabeth had considered this idea outdated and foolish. She hoped she was wrong.

Elizabeth reluctantly considered her options if Belle really was pregnant. There were plenty of potions on the market. Mothers of children attending her school often discussed the various efficacies of these medications – aloes, iron, cathartic powders – available from chemist shops, or by mail order though newspapers. The concoctions were advertised as *female pills* or *cures for abnormal interruptions to monthly cycles*. They were largely ineffective and sometimes dangerous, but she blanched at the prospect of her own dear daughter undergoing the horrific alternative – surgical abortion.

There was another option, of course – the most common one for girls in this sort of trouble. A hasty marriage. But Belle could never marry Luke. Even Elizabeth, with her thoroughly modern views on society, could not countenance such a thing. A convicted felon. A fugitive without money or prospects was an impossible match for her daughter. Another possibility came to mind, but for now she cast it aside. First things first.

Dr Lovejoy arrived promptly after lunch and took a glum and nervous-looking Belle off to her room for an examination. He emerged, stern-faced, some twenty minutes later.

'I believe your daughter is in the early stages of pregnancy. I'm sorry to be the bearer of such news.'

Elizabeth nodded miserably, not really surprised. 'Is she well otherwise?'

'On that matter, I can reassure you. A little thin, perhaps, but on the whole Isabelle presents as a healthy young woman.'

'Thank you, Doctor,' said Elizabeth. 'I trust I can rely on your absolute discretion?'

'Of course, ma'am. I understand that you have some difficult decisions to make. Be assured you can rely on my help.'

Elizabeth's eyes moistened as she grasped his hand. 'I pray to God it doesn't come to that.'

With a brief bow of his head, Dr Lovejoy excused himself.

Elizabeth went to see Belle. Despite the embarrassing examination and awful confirmation that she was indeed with child, a vast weight seemed to have lifted from her daughter's shoulders. Belle laid her head in her mother's lap. 'You'll know what to do, won't you, Mama? And Luke will be back soon.'

Elizabeth shushed her, squeezing her hand. 'They say a trouble shared is a trouble halved.'

Sasha's loud barking from the back verandah alerted the pair to someone's approach. They both rushed to the window. Only one man, Daniel, trudged down the hill towards the house. Belle gave a cry of utter despair.

This will simplify things, thought Elizabeth, grateful to Daniel for leaving Luke behind.

# CHAPTER 28

A tremendous calm settled on Luke in his solitude. Bear disappeared each evening with the tigers, but, in this remote place, Luke didn't fear for their safety. Men and his flocks were a world away.

Each day, Luke and Bear explored the valley's extensive limestone cave system. There were more hand stencils to be found on the rock walls. Daniel said this art was many thousands of years old. A recurring image of a pair of hands showed the outline of an elegant, long-fingered right hand, and only the stubs of fingers on the left. Luke amused himself by inventing theories to explain this. In other caves he discovered engraved symbols, lines of dots, carved domes, spirals and circles.

Luke carefully recorded and mapped each find, as Daniel had asked him to. His favourite carvings were of animal tracks, particularly those of emus. He'd heard stories of this unusual flightless bird, hunted to extinction only fifty years earlier. Apparently it stood as high as a man's shoulder. Daniel said its even larger cousin still survived in numbers on the mainland. One day he'd take Belle to see them.

It was an unseasonably warm winter. At night, the Southern Cross blazed, brightest of the numberless stars in the sky. Each day dawned more brilliant than the last. Lorikeet, magpie and butcherbird song beaded the fragrant air. Emerald rosellas flashed like flying jewels through the trees, and, at twilight, lazy flights of black cockatoos came to roost in the sheltered valley. Days melded into each other. Luke scratched notches in the wall of his home cave to mark the time. He kept a daily journal, so he could share every detail of his trip with Belle when he went home.

It became easy to imagine that he and Belle might have a future, easy to imagine that one day she'd be his wife. In this grand isolation, far from the constraints and conventions of civilisation, anything seemed possible. This wasn't like those lonely days back at Clarry's little hut. Things were different now. He belonged.

Soon he'd return to Belle and the complications their love inevitably faced. But, for now, Luke was content to just exist – exist with the animals, exist free from guilt, exist outside of the rules. Some invisible pressure lifted, allowing an exquisite appreciation of the teeming life around him. Occasionally, at dawn, he hunted with the pack, feeling at one with all creation. Luke would dearly miss this place.

Then at dusk one night, while he cooked a stew with last night's wallaby and some onions from his dwindling rations, he heard the distinct call of a tiger. Not one of his. Bear and the cubs still lounged in the cave, relaxing ahead of the night's hunt. They pricked their ears, then stole off into the twilight. Luke's skin tingled with excitement. This was what he and Daniel had hoped for – the cubs weren't alone in the valley.

Next morning, Luke scoured the nearby forest trails with a tracker's practised eye. In mud, beside a shallow upstream pool, lay the distinct tracks of a thylacine, too large to belong to the cubs. He examined the prints, memorising their appearance and location, followed them for a while, then lost them on a rocky riverbank.

'Well, mate,' he said to Bear, who seemed keen to follow the trail. 'It's up to you now.'

The dog gambolled round and round his master, pretending to

pounce. Then off he went, nose to ground, Luke close behind. They travelled for almost an hour, following the dark, swift-running stream. As the day warmed up, they sometimes stopped to play in the water. Bear, with the odd, webbed feet of the Newfoundland, was a strong, enthusiastic swimmer. Luke enjoyed holding onto his collar and being towed around the deep pools that punctuated the stream's course.

After one such swim, Luke lay back lazily in the winter sun, on clean, white river sand. Something jabbed him in the back. He sat up. There, almost buried, was a rusty gold-panning dish. Luke picked it up in disbelief. Daniel was wrong; others knew about the valley. How long might the pan have lain there? No more than a couple of years, by the look of it.

Luke re-examined everything he knew of the caves in light of this find, wondering if he'd missed something – signs of a fire or a camp. This intrusion from the outside world shattered his perfect peace. He was suddenly mindful that he didn't even have his rifle with him, so foolishly complacent had he become. Abandoning the tiger's trail, he hurried back home, keenly aware the cubs slept there unprotected.


Sleep would not come that night, although drowsy stars blinked in the sky and winds swirled in lazy play about the cliffs. The moon rose over timber-crested escarpments, coating everything in silver, and a terrible nostalgia overcame him. Thoughts of his mother and sister. Perhaps, right now, they gazed up at that same moon. Thoughts of his father, so hard-working and kind. Dead because of him. Their old rooster. Did he still crow on moonlit nights like this? But that was silly. That cock would be dead, too, the house and coop owned by strangers. His memories of home were trapped in time, frozen in childhood. Perhaps doing his journal might distract him from this terrible homesickness. Luke took it out by the falls. The bright sky was mirrored in the water's polished surface, magnifying the moonshine, turning night to day.

He tried to write, but couldn't concentrate. That voice, the murmuring voice of the waterfall, sounded a different note this evening – one of melancholy sweetness. The song of the falls was always in his ears, day and night. He heard it when he ate, when he woke, when he slept, when he dreamed . . . and now it somehow became Belle's voice, urging him home to Binburra.

From far down the valley, Bear's howl echoed, long and mournful, into the empty pit of the sky. Luke put down his journal and dived in the freezing water, swimming lengths of the glassy pool until his restless limbs trembled with fatigue. Then, his nervous energy spent, he returned to camp. Still restless, still uneasy.

He resigned himself to a wakeful night, waiting for morning to outline the cave entrance against the brightening bush. It was only when Bear and the tigers returned safely from the hunt that Luke allowed himself to sleep, rifle cocked and ready at his side.

# CHAPTER 29

Belle and Edward would marry and pass the child off as their own. This was Elizabeth's plan. It was useless approaching Jane Abbott with the truth. She possessed far too great a regard for both propriety and her husband's opinion. No, if Elizabeth was to save her daughter she must approach the young man himself, then, in circumstances of utmost privacy, confide her daughter's condition to Edward and cast them all on his mercy.

Elizabeth suspected he might be a willing conspirator, for she guessed he already loved Belle. In any case, deceitful and dangerous as this option was, the alternatives were worse. Elizabeth was damned if she'd allow her daughter to bear an illegitimate child and live a life of disgrace and public shame. But she knew full well she must guard against her own misgivings. So, a shield rose around her heart, strengthening her resolve and shutting out the sentimentality that might bring them all undone.

On the pretext of organising Belle's seventeenth birthday party, Elizabeth invited herself to Canterbury Downs. She waited until Jane became distracted with a household matter and then made her move. 'Edward, can I discuss birthday presents for Belle? You know her so well.'

'Of course, Mrs Campbell.'

'Shall we go down to the greenhouse? I can admire your mother's gorgeous orchids while we talk.'

'Why doesn't Belle visit here anymore?' Edward asked. 'It's rumoured that she's ill.'

'My dearest Edward. May I confide in you? In a sense my daughter's life depends upon it.'

Edward went white. She laid her hand on his arm, and there in the conservatory, surrounded by delicate hothouse flowers of the most exotic kind, Elizabeth confessed all. She left nothing out, not even his father's brutal attack on Luke's sister. They moved to a bench by the doorway, offering a clearer view should someone approach. Edward sat for the longest time.

'Madam,' he said at last, 'I love your daughter with all my heart and have done since we were children. Nothing would please me more than to marry her, but why would she have me, if not for love? Belle is not one to obediently accept another's counsel, I fear not even her mother's.'

'She will have no choice. Otherwise I will betray Luke to your father.'

'She is to be blackmailed into marrying me?'

'To protect her, yes. In time, Belle will thank me and come to adore you. She also has loved you since childhood, and confessed this to me more than once.'

'Perhaps, but I fear only as a cherished friend. I want a willing wife, madam, not an affectionate sister.'

'That will come, dear Edward, that will come. I beg your patience. The wedding must happen without delay, for her pregnancy will soon be obvious to all. Come to Binburra this afternoon, alone. We'll talk more and you may see Belle.'

A stunned Edward took her hand as she rose from the garden seat.

'One more thing,' said Elizabeth. 'Do *you* intend to give Luke up to your father?'

'Madam, you forget. Luke saved my life. My father can be a cold, even cruel, man. If what you say is true – that he committed a contemptible crime against an innocent girl – then Luke was within his rights to defend her. He didn't deserve to rot in prison for it. The Abbotts apparently have much to atone for, and I'll begin by guarding Luke's secret. But understand this: I'll not forgive him for defiling your daughter.'

Thank the Lord for this fine young man. Elizabeth embraced him, and they made their way back up to the house.

'Did you two work out something for Isabelle?' asked Jane.

'Yes,' they sang in unison.

Elizabeth excused herself, calling for the carriage.

'I hoped you might stay for tea?' said Jane.

Elizabeth refused the invitation. Time to go home and tackle Belle.


'But I love *Luke*. Papa must bring him home at once.'

Elizabeth girded her loins for the fight. 'The decision's been made. You'll marry Edward.'

'I won't.'

'If you don't, I'll hand Luke over to Henry Abbott.'

There it was. Belle, with her next argument primed and ready to go, lapsed into astonished silence.

'You wouldn't.'

'Oh, I most certainly would.' Elizabeth's voice was low. 'I'd cheerfully sacrifice my own life for your sake. What makes you think I wouldn't sacrifice Luke's?'

'Then you're a monster!' Belle flung herself facedown on the bed.

Elizabeth sat down beside her daughter, quietly stroking her back as loud sobs racked the girl's body. 'Not a monster, my love,' she whispered, her own heart sliced in two. 'Only a mother.'

Barking dogs announced the arrival of a visitor. Elizabeth went downstairs to find Edward at the door. Millie was also downstairs, polishing the front hall furniture, as she'd been asked.

'Welcome, Edward.' Elizabeth spoke more loudly than usual, so that the housemaid might overhear. 'Belle is still feeling poorly, and looking forward to your visit.'

Millie hurried off, no doubt keen to share this juicy piece of gossip with the other servants.

Elizabeth hesitated as they passed the double oak doors to the library. Daniel was in there, cataloguing specimens, sublimely unaware of the drama going on right under his very nose. She squeezed her eyes shut for a moment and moved on, wishing she could share this burden with her husband, certain that she could not.

Edward stood at the bedroom door, shocked to see Belle looking so thin and defeated, her face puffy from crying. She appeared entirely forlorn.

'Will you leave us please, Mrs Campbell?'

Elizabeth closed the door behind her.

Edward went to Belle. She remained silent, but did not take her gaze from him. Her full breasts spilled over her bodice.

'You must marry me.' Edward sat down and put his arm around her slim shoulders. She didn't pull away. Her vulnerability and silent acquiescence excited him. He drew her in for a kiss. Although she didn't respond, neither did she resist. With difficulty he pulled himself away.

'You know about Luke?'

'Yes.'

'And you would accept me, knowing I carry another man's child?'

'My darling, darling Belle. I would accept you if you were to live your entire life an invalid, or if you were to spend your next ten years in prison, or if you should turn mad and live in a belfry, or if you were to grow so enormously fat you couldn't even fit through the door, or if you should become a nun.'

Belle's small smile gave him hope. He knelt on the floor at her feet.

'Isabelle. If you consent to be my wife I swear I won't hold you to your vows. Once the child is born, you'll be free to go if you wish. But, at the very least, for the sake of this baby and your family, let the child be born in wedlock.'

'Do you believe Mama when she says she'll tell your father about Luke?'

'Don't test her, if you care for him. She'll do it, of that I've no doubt. She thinks she protects you.'

'Oh Edward, I can't expect you do this for me. My father will put a stop to it.' Belle fled to the door, colliding with her mother as she flung it open.

Edward watched them a moment, so very alike and both so very beautiful.

'I'm telling Papa.'

'Very well,' said Elizabeth. 'I wonder what his opinion will be when he discovers Luke has played him so false? You may risk more with him than with me.'

Belle pushed past and ran down the hall. Edward sought to follow, but Elizabeth laid a steadying hand on his arm. 'I'll get her. Wait here.'

Blood thundered in his ears. Belle loved Luke. She carried Luke's child. A marriage would be madness. Yet, against all common sense, Edward's universe had narrowed to a single, pinpoint of light – a burning desire to make Belle his wife. He would die if she rejected him.

A few minutes later Belle burst back into the room. Edward fought against taking her in his arms. 'Did you talk to your father?'

She shook her head, the picture of misery. 'I could tell Papa almost anything – but not this.'

Elizabeth came in and the argument resumed. 'Why can't I marry Luke, Mama?'

'You would be a pariah, darling.'

Edward stayed out of the way, as the war of words exploded around him. Belle raged and pleaded, but she had no foil to counter her mother's determined parries. In the end, Elizabeth wore her down.

Belle briefly buried her head in her hands. 'Fine,' she said. 'I'll marry Edward, since you give me no choice.'

Not exactly the response he'd been hoping for, but his heart sang just the same.

Elizabeth sagged with relief, clasping a hand to her cream silk bodice. 'Can I trust your word. Belle?'

'Unfortunately you can. As I must trust yours.'

'Good. We'll announce the engagement tomorrow.'

Edward loudly cleared his throat. The women looked startled, as if they'd forgotten he was there. 'Excuse me, Mrs Campbell, but shouldn't I speak to your husband? Ask for his daughter's hand?'

'No,' said Elizabeth quickly. 'I'll talk to Belle's father. But, Edward, you must tell your own parents tonight, and inform them of the need for haste . . . you understand?'

Edward nodded. What a scandal it would be . . . and a stunner like Belle. His father was bound to be impressed. Knocking up girls was a subject of pride and amusement at Henry's Hobart club. Edward had heard him say 'the boy doesn't have it in him' more than once, when asked with a sly dig to the ribs about his son's conquests. Edward couldn't help looking forward to tonight's little talk with his mother and father.

Belle sat sullenly in the corner. 'Go away, Mama. Leave me alone.'

But Elizabeth wasn't finished. 'Listen, both of you. Your engagement party will coincide with Belle's seventeenth birthday, three weeks from today. It's short notice, but if I know your mother, Edward, she'll insist on hosting the event at Canterbury Downs. Be prepared for an extravaganza, with important guests invited from Hobart and elsewhere. You're their only son, Edward, and heir to a fortune. You two will need to play the part of young lovers to quite a crowd, even if you don't feel it.'

'You can count on me,' said Edward.

Elizabeth turned to her daughter. 'And you, Belle? What will you do?'

'I'll tell your wicked lie, but not for you, Mama. For Luke.'

'A lie, my darling, can sometimes be your very best friend.'

'Mama?' Belle suddenly sounded uncertain, like a little girl. Elizabeth's expression softened. 'Don't tell Papa about the baby, not yet.'

'Of course not.' She urged Belle to her feet. 'Now you must take Edward to the front door, preferably for the whole house to see. First wash your face and put on a little powder. Your eyes are red.'

Belle did as her mother asked. Edward escorted her downstairs, and spotted Millie spying from the upstairs landing. At the door Edward pulled Belle to him. 'Is this convincing enough, do you think?' He kissed Belle on the lips. A loud gasp sounded from the stairs.

Belle managed a smile. 'You've certainly given Millie something to talk about.'

'That's the idea.'

'Thank you, Eddie, for playing this ridiculous charade. I'll think of some way out, I promise, but until then we must humour Mama. You're so good at this, I almost believe it myself. That you're in love with me, I mean.'

Edward longed to admit his true feelings, to confess he'd always loved her. 'I'm glad,' he said simply. 'Now get some rest. You're sleeping for two.' He placed his hand on Belle's midriff.

Her lips trembled. 'It's a miracle, isn't it?'

'It certainly is.'

'You're the first person to say a kind word about this baby. Mama and the doctor only frown and whisper like it's an awful, shameful thing.'

He kissed her again, this time chastely on the cheek. 'I'll see you tomorrow.'


Elizabeth watched from the top of the stairs until she was sure Edward had left, then hurried to the library.

Daniel looked up from his reference book. 'You'll never believe it, Lizzie. Two species of *Eucryphia* have been identified along the western coast of Chile. The other four occur along the east coast of Australia and, as you know, two are found right here in Tasmania. Do you see, Lizzie? This is further evidence the continents were once joined.'

'*Eucryphia?*' asked Elizabeth, at a loss.

'You know, Lizzie. *Eucryphia Lucida*? The leatherwood tree?'

'Oh, the leatherwood, how interesting . . . Daniel, I've some important news. If you could please tear yourself away from your books.'

Elizabeth took a moment to prepare herself. 'This has come as something of a shock to me, as it will to you, Daniel. I suppose there's nothing for it, but to say it. Belle and Edward are in love and wish to marry.'

'What?'

'I know you dislike the Abbotts . . .'

'That's an understatement.'

'Let me finish. This is not about you, Daniel. It's about Belle. You've said yourself you can think of nothing objectionable about the boy besides his father.'

'Isn't that enough?'

Elizabeth turned the full force of her fear for Belle on her unsuspecting husband.

'No it's not. I swear, Daniel, I'll never forgive you if you spoil this for her. Edward wanted to do the right thing, wanted to ask for Belle's hand. I wouldn't allow it, knowing your hatred for Henry. For God's sake, Daniel. The boy is not his father!'


Elizabeth stood before him, hands on hips, chest heaving. Daniel had never seen his wife so outraged. A humiliating realisation hit him. Of late, he'd been so consumed with his work that he'd neglected his family. Although he knew of Belle and Edward's friendship since childhood,, he'd never sensed any romantic attachment between the pair. But then what did he know? Nothing apparently. Lizzie must have been wrong about Belle's feelings for Luke. That was a good thing, he supposed. Of course, it was.

'Very well. I shall talk to Belle and be guided by her wishes.'

Daniel approached his daughter's room with some trepidation. Matters of the heart weren't his strong suit. He knocked softly and opened the door. Belle was lying on the bed. As he went in, she looked up and began to cry.

'My poor darling,' said Daniel. 'Whatever's the matter?' She hugged her pillow, turning her face to the wall. 'Your mother told me you wish to marry Edward. Is this truly what you want? To marry this boy?'

She turned to face him, and whispered, 'Yes, Papa.'

'And all these tears . . . are they because you fear I'll deny the match? Well, from your silence, I must assume it is so. If it's this boy you want, Belle, then it's this boy you shall have. Don't expect me to make amends with his father, though. That's beyond me.'

Belle wiped her eyes. 'Of course not, Papa.'

'Then I'll not oppose the engagement.' Daniel kissed her and left the room, almost bumping into Elizabeth, who'd been listening at the door.

'Not to worry, Lizzie,' he said. 'Belle and I had a good talk. Let me know if I can help sort anything else out.' And with that he returned to the library.

# CHAPTER 30

Next morning, Daniel set off for Tiger Pass. Weeks had passed since he'd left Luke and the cubs in the hidden valley.

'Belle's engagement party is soon,' Elizabeth said. 'What will happen if you're delayed?'

'That's exactly why I'm going now, Lizzie. Three days to get there, a couple of days to gauge how the tigers are getting on, and another three days back. I'll be home in plenty of time.'

She took hold of his hands. 'I don't want you going by yourself.'

'Lizzie, I must. The way to the pass is a secret known only to me, and now to Luke.'

'You're getting too old for traipsing around the wilderness alone. What if you have an accident on the way? I couldn't bear it. Take Davey along, otherwise I shall be sick with worry the whole time you're away.'

'Very well, if it eases your mind. With a bit of luck we'll bring Luke back with us.'

'No.'

'Why ever not? If the cubs are hunting independently and seem settled . . .'

'You know of Luke's infatuation with Belle. It might be hard for him to return on the very eve of her engagement to Edward.'

'I had a word with the boy, Lizzie. He agreed to forget about all that nonsense.'

'Maybe so,' said Elizabeth. 'But could you please keep him away for Belle's birthday weekend, just in case? I do so want it all to go well.'

'All right then, mother hen.' He kissed her on top of her head. 'Luke can remain at the pass a little longer.'

At mid-morning, Daniel and Davey started up the hill behind the house. Elizabeth waved them goodbye, but Belle was nowhere in sight. She'd begged her father to let her come.

'With your engagement so close? Your mother would never allow it.'

'Absolutely not,' said Elizabeth.

'Then bring Luke back for me. I want him here for my birthday. I must have him here.' She seemed close to tears.

'And have him abandon the cubs? No, Luke will be home soon enough. Now run along and let me finish packing.'

Daniel shot his wife a worried look. 'Perhaps you're right after all, Lizzie, to keep those two apart a while longer.'

After Daniel left, Elizabeth called for the buggy and Harrison drove her to the miners' school to brief her assistant teachers. They'd need to manage by themselves for a while. Right now Belle required her undivided attention.

Elizabeth's business there lasted until the end of the school day. As she stood on the rickety verandah with the teacher, seeing off the children, a scruffy little dog ran up to her. It looked familiar. Of course, Angus's dog. Molly, his common-law widow, earned a few shillings babysitting children while their mothers worked as servants in wealthier homes. Here she came now, trudging down the hill after the little dog. Apart from sending a hamper of goods to tide Molly over after the funeral, Elizabeth hadn't spared her a thought since. The poor woman's hollow eyes caused Elizabeth some guilt.

'How are you, Molly?'

'Well enough, thank you, ma'am.'

A little boy ran up to her and she absent-mindedly tousled his hair. A teacher led two grubby little girls over and Molly took their hands.

'I hear you've found yourself a new job, Molly,' said the teacher.

'That's right.' The children wriggled free from Molly's grasp and ran off. 'I start next week.'

Harrison drew the buggy to a halt outside the schoolhouse and Elizabeth stepped inside. 'Thank you, Harrison. Canterbury Downs.'

Molly watched the sleek buggy drive away. That's how Adam was living now, high on the hog. Yet she couldn't even afford a pittance of rent. Left Angus to die, he did, like a rat in a trap, then ingratiated himself with every bigwig in town. How she despised him. She couldn't wait to get away from this town. Perhaps at Canterbury Downs she might earn enough money for a move to Hobart. Her dream of being a shopkeeper was still very much alive. So preoccupied was she with her thoughts, that one of her small charges wandered off and was almost skittled by the wheel of a heavy cart.

'Keep your brats off the road!' The driver brandished a whip at the fallen child. 'Did you hear me, whore?'

Another woman rushed over to pluck the wailing child from the dust as the cart thundered on. Molly looked on without interest. She started to climb the hill with Scruffy and the children in tow. Tonight she'd start packing up the cottage. There was nothing left for her there.

When Elizabeth arrived at Canterbury Downs, Jane Abbott welcomed her with a warm embrace. 'Thank God you've come, Elizabeth. We've so little time and so much to do. Ada's here to help plan guest accommodation. She's kindly arranged for Isabelle and Grace to make a brief trip to Hobart for the fitting of their gowns. If that suits you, of course, dear Elizabeth.'

'That's perfect.' The further away Belle was from home the better. It might give her daughter a little perspective on things.

The women spent the day organising guest lists and menus. They decided the party should be in the style of a ball: a lavish dinner, followed by dancing. The important visitors would stay at the Abbott home, with any overflow divided between Binburra and the neighbouring Mitchell estate.

By dinnertime the invitations were dispatched to the Hobart printer. Elizabeth inspected the grand ballroom – an impressive space with a sprung oak-panelled floor and massive chandeliers of German crystal. Servants were using beeswax to polish the floorboards into a brilliant shine. Elizabeth found herself caught up in the excitement. After all, whatever the circumstances, this was Belle's one and only engagement party.

'Is the piano well tuned?' she asked. 'And we'll need a violin, a cello and at least one cornet, don't you think?'

They moved off to the dining room. Belle's pregnancy remained the great unmentioned.

# CHAPTER 31

Whsen Daniel and Davey reached Tiger Pass, they found Luke camped in the entrance cave marked by the towering pine tree.

'Whatever are you doing up here, Adam? What of the cubs?' asked Daniel, as Davey helped him off with his pack.

'There's good news, Mr Campbell. They've hunted each night without fail for the last week, even independently of Bear. I've been keeping this lazy bloke well fed on wallaby meat, haven't I, Bear?' Luke ruffled the dog's coat. 'Bear's been camping up here with me. We go down in the morning to check on the cubs. Each time we've found them sleepy and content with full bellies. I've seen their tracks around fresh kills, proving it's our tigers that are responsible.'

'Why, that's wonderful. Better than we could have hoped for. But you say the evidence points to *our* tigers? Are you saying what I think you're saying?'

Luke grinned. 'I am, Mr Campbell. There are others in the valley.'

Davey failed to see what all the excitement was about. His grandfather had achieved some renown as the first official *tiger man* to be employed by the Van Diemen's Land Company back in the thirties, paid to guard farmers' flocks. The snaring of each thylacine had reaped a rich reward, and the title of *tiger man* conferred a romantic, heroic status.

As a child, Davey had dreamed of this sort of fame, and he did not embrace his employer's strange love of the pests. Yet all talk now seemed to be of the damned tigers. On top of that, Davey had enjoyed the undivided attention of Mr Campbell during the trip to the pass. Now he'd been relegated to second place. From the very first, Davey had envied Luke his favoured position in the household. All the old resentments came flooding back.

In the morning Luke and Daniel made the climb down to the valley floor. The cubs now disapproved of Daniel, hissing at his approach. They were becoming truly wild.

'Show me where you found the gold-panning dish,' Daniel said.

They set off along the creek.

'How are things at home?' asked Luke. 'I hate that we can't really talk when Davey's around.'

Daniel bent down and fossicked around in the creek bed. When he stood up, a bright golden nugget the size of a thumbnail sat in his silty palm. 'I warrant this is what our visitor was after.'

Exciting though this find was, Luke was desperate for news of home, news of Belle. Daniel did not seem inclined to talk. Luke kept pressing, and was finally rewarded with a progress report on the devils and pups. 'And Mrs Campbell . . . Belle. How are they?'

'Ah . . . Mrs Campbell sends her love. Plans for Belle's seventeenth birthday consume most of her time.' Daniel strode on again, apparently unwilling for the conversation to continue.

'Shall I return with you? The cubs don't need me now.'

Daniel shook his head. 'The time isn't right.'

There was a puzzling finality to his tone. Luke felt utterly rejected. 'When are you leaving?'

'In the morning. You'll come home next time. It won't be too long.'

A wall had risen between them and Luke didn't know why. He'd done all Daniel had asked of him, hadn't he?

They spent a strained day searching for more evidence of intruders in the valley. A little further upstream, Daniel found a piece of charred timber, the remains of a campfire.

'No more than a year or so old, I'd guess. What do you think?'

Luke nodded, uninterested. All that mattered was that Daniel was excluding him.

The next morning Daniel and Davey left. Until the very moment Luke waved them goodbye, he believed Daniel would change his mind and ask him to come home. Or at least provide him with a satisfactory explanation as to why he must remain up at the pass. Daniel did neither.

Luke stood forlornly in the shade of the old pine tree and watched the men head off. He considered walking along with them for a while, but changed his mind. It felt lonelier now to be with Daniel than to be alone. Bear whined and pushed his head into Luke's hand.

'Come on, boy. Let's do some prospecting. If I make my fortune in gold, nobody will stop me from marrying Belle.'

A shiver of longing ran through him. Tiger Pass was no longer his haven. It was a place of banishment.

# CHAPTER 32

**M**olly took the lid off the battered blue biscuit tin she'd found under Adam's bed. Since Angus died she'd had no energy to clean and the formerly spotless little cottage was thick with grime and littered with waste. Mine management always wanted widows out to make room for new workers. On Monday she'd begin her new job as a scullery maid in the Abbott household.

Such work was easily come by. The assortment of servants at Canterbury Downs amounted to a small army, and harsh conditions combined with low pay ensured a swift staff turnover. Molly had a sixteen-hour workday to look forward to and wages of but a pound a month, but with bed and board provided she could still add to her nest egg. But she couldn't take Scruffy. She'd have to leave him with Adam. The boy had been by twice already, demanding the terrier, saying he'd be better off at Binburra. It grated to admit he was right.

Scruffy whined and Molly bent down to stroke him. What a comfort he'd been, this little dog, in the dark days since Angus died. At night she drew his warm body close, burying her tears in his wiry fur, trying to recapture something of the essence of Angus. She'd lost so much, and now Adam would have the only important thing she had left. Who was Adam anyway? Molly had met Angus's brother at the memorial service for the drowned miners. He said Angus never even had a nephew.

Adam hadn't bothered to attend the service. He was too busy *recuperating*, first as some sort of a hero at the Abbotts' stately mansion, then at Binburra. Hero? Traitor more like it. Molly seethed, her heart a ball of bitterness and grief. She resented Angus for lying to her. She hated the prospect of losing Scruffy. Worst of all, she blamed Adam for leaving her poor Angus to drown. Something sharp lodged in her throat, making it hard to draw breath. Somehow, someday, he would pay.

The task of cleaning house could be put off no longer. Molly dreaded discarding the bits and pieces of her life, so she'd started in Adam's room. There was less of Angus there.

Curiously, she examined the contents of the biscuit tin. Letters. Dozens of them, all addressed to *My dearest mother* in Adam's distinctive copperplate hand. How extraordinary. According to Angus, Adam's mother was dead, but if Angus had lied about Adam being his nephew, she wasn't sure what was true. The lie still hurt.

Molly took the tin into the kitchen and sat down. Reading was a slow and laborious task, but she persevered. Perspiration beaded her forehead. Time slipped away. Hours later she put down the last letter, trying to absorb what she'd learned. That Adam was certainly not Adam. He'd signed the letters *Luke*. That he'd escaped from jail. That he bore a bitter hatred for Sir Henry Abbott.

In spite of herself, Molly was moved by these heartfelt letters of a son to his mother. Written, but for some reason not sent. Clearly he loved his family and missed them terribly. Molly understood this – how one could so terribly miss loved ones. Just as she missed her own family, her dead babies, her departed husband . . . just as she missed Angus. That thought hardened her heart. She reinspected the tin.

Beneath a ragged square of linen at the bottom of the tin, she found what she was looking for. A neatly addressed envelope bore the name *Mrs Alice Tyler* at a Melbourne address. The surname rang a bell. It was the surname of that escaped prisoner, the one Sir Henry had posted such a large reward for, the talk of the whole town for months. Luke Tyler.

None of it made any sense. Why would Angus deceive her, bring an escaped convict and danger into her home. Harbouring a felon was a crime. She lay down on her bed and wept.

# CHAPTER 33

Luke whiled away his days in the wilderness, pressing the rusty gold-panning tin into service. Angus had taught him the technique. Scoop up some earth, hold the dish on a slant and swirl it in the creek. Water carried away light grains of sand. Heavier gold particles sank to the bottom. He soon had a measurable quantity of bright gold dust in a little pouch, together with a few tiny nuggets.

Now and then, the young tigers accompanied Luke up the river on his expeditions. Through the calm, early stillness, scattering after fish in the shallows and playing hide-and-seek with Bear. As the sun rose higher, a yawning Mindi and Bindi always shook themselves dry and retreated to their cave for sleep.

Sometimes King stayed on longer, intent on securing a plump spotted trout for breakfast. One such morning, Luke was fossicking where the stream flowed close to the cliff-face. Baffled by the quick-silver swiftness of his prey, King splashed out of the stream in disgust, flinging himself down in the entrance of an arching cave.

'I reckon he's got the right idea, eh, Bear?'

Luke flopped down beside the grumpy tiger. He poked King in the ribs, hoping to provoke a play fight, one of their favourite games. King gave an impatient growl and raised himself up, kangaroo-like, on hind legs. His ears were cocked beyond Luke to the rocks behind. Without warning, King launched himself right over Luke, landing on a boulder and flushing out a spotted quoll hiding behind it.

The quoll fled, bounding up the wall and shooting into a granite fissure above Luke's head. King rocketed after it, slamming into the narrow space with such force that his head and forequarters became firmly wedged in the gap. He let out a series of piercing cries, while his hind legs scrabbled vainly for purchase on the smooth stone wall.

Luke stopped laughing and tried to help. Grasping King's flailing back legs, he tugged with increasing force. This produced a fresh chorus of yelping, but the tiger remained stuck fast. Luke picked up a sharp stone and painstakingly chipped away at the ledge, gradually widening the gap. Eventually he managed to extract the tiger. King licked his bruises for a while in an embarrassed sort of way, touched noses with Bear and slunk off home.

Luke stood on his toes and peered into the crumbling breach in the wall, hoping to spot the quoll. Something half-hidden in the gloom caught his eye. An odd shape with contours too soft to belong to the rocky hollow. Luke reached in. His fingers closed on a coarse hessian sack. Another lay behind it. He dragged the bags from their hiding place: one large and weighty, one small and light, both coated in inches of dust.

Luke moved out into daylight and opened the larger bag. He couldn't believe his eyes. A treasure trove of coins and gold nuggets, some as big as hen's eggs. Luke opened the second sack. Bundles of pound notes spilled to the ground. Stunned, he carefully replaced the money and fastened both sacks with their frayed ties. Angus's words came to him: *Clarry had a fortune hidden away somewhere . . . Stashed in the bush, he told me.*

A sudden fear of being observed made him raise his eyes to the cliffs. He saw nothing but their rugged outline against the sky, heard nothing but the desolate cawing of crows.

Luke put the bags in his swag and whistled Bear. As he turned to go, a thought struck him. What if there was more? He returned to the cave and inspected it more thoroughly. Right at the back, where it was hard to see, he found pick-axe marks in the walls. He narrowed his eyes and poured a little water from his flask onto the scored rock, rubbed the moist surface with his sleeve. A vein of gold gleamed in the faint light.

Back at the entrance, Luke made a makeshift footstool of rocks, which allowed him to get a better look inside the hollow. Another bag lay in a shadowy nook. He pulled it out and looked inside.

What he found made him spring back in alarm. Dynamite, perhaps ten sticks. And blasting caps too. Old explosives and detonators could be highly unstable and blow up at the slightest disturbance. Judging from the dust, this bag must have lain hidden in the rock for years. With the careless way he'd hauled it out, he was lucky not to have been blown to kingdom come.

Luke inspected the dynamite. A crystalline substance coated the sticks – nitro-glycerine leached out over time. Some of it had pooled and hardened in the bottom of the bag. With exaggerated care, Luke lifted the sack, positioning it as safely as he could at the back of the cave. Then he surrounded it with a protective ring of rocks. The last thing he wanted was for some unfortunate animal, particularly one of his tigers, to inadvertently trigger an explosion.

Luke picked up his swag and headed back to the home cave. A kaleidoscope of possibilities whirled through his mind. He was rich, very rich, for surely it was no crime to take a dead man's gold. Rich enough to do whatever he wanted. Rich enough to marry Belle. Their wild dream of a future together would come true after all. For a short, painful moment, he wished Angus was alive to share this good fortune. He could have bought Molly a dozen shops.

Luke couldn't stop thinking about Clarry, while walking the same track he'd walked. The old bloke had lived like a hermit, when he could have led a privileged life in Hobart or anywhere else for that matter. What could drive a man to embrace that sort of deliberate isolation? Luke reflected on his own circumstances. If not for Belle and Daniel, he might have ended up the same way.

Luke looked at his watch. Two-thirty in the afternoon. He could be gone by three, with hours of light left. What day was it? He'd lost track. He went to the carved notches on the wall that served as his calendar. Wednesday. With luck, he'd be home by Saturday night. A few days early, maybe, but what difference could a few days possibly make?

# CHAPTER 34

The celebration was in full swing. Sideboards groaned with lobsters. Guests feasted on truffles and oysters, foie gras and squab, while speculating on whether or not this was more than a birthday party. Their idle curiosity was soon laid to rest. A short speech by Daniel, proposing a toast on the occasion of his daughter's seventeenth birthday. Then a long speech by Henry, announcing his only son's engagement to Miss Isabelle Campbell. Much polite applause, accompanied by knowing nods. The odds had always been in favour of this union.

Elizabeth knew it was asking for trouble, seating Henry and Daniel at the same table, but convention demanded it. Tensions ran high between the two men during the cock-a-leekie soup. By the time the beef wellington arrived, their voices were raised. Jane looked across the table at Elizabeth in alarm. There were still eight courses to come.

With agonising slowness, the procession of dishes marched on: venison, loin of lamb, chartreuse of duck, quail eggs in aspic, baked trout. The diners washed their food down with copious quantities of champagne and claret, sherry and port. Henry seemed well on the way to drunkenness. A dangerously long break until dessert allowed for much sniping across the table. Afterwards, the orchestra would strike up to introduce the main event of the evening – the ball. It couldn't come quickly enough for Elizabeth. Belle quietly appealed to her father to ignore Sir Henry, but not quietly enough.

'So, my soon-to-be daughter-in-law thinks to ignore me,' said Henry. 'Once married, she'll change her tune and become as obedient as my own son.'

Edward went red, and Daniel opened his mouth to reply.

'Hold your tongues,' scolded Jane. 'Both of you.'

Henry and Daniel lapsed into glowering silence. The timely arrival of desserts defused the situation: pineapple-cream cake, ginger pudding, wine and walnut trifle, colourful ices and fresh fruit salad in glittering crystal punchbowls. A truce settled on the table.

At long last the orchestra struck up, signalling the conclusion of the meal. Elizabeth breathed a sigh of relief, and followed Belle and Edward to the ballroom, her arm through Daniel's. As guests of honour, Belle and Edward led off in a minuet. He was an ideal part-ner, his steps perfect. The next dance was a lively polka. Edward spun Belle around the floor in a flurry of giddy twirls, leaving her flushed-faced and shining. Elizabeth looked on approvingly. There was no hiding it, Belle was enjoying herself.


Ignoring Elizabeth's protests, Daniel retreated to the verandah. He gazed across the valley to the remains of an orange sunset. No breeze stirred the birches, yet above him high winds tore the clouds to shreds. A logging burn-off smouldered in the ranges, causing the rising moon to glow a dramatic bushfire red. Thin ribbons of pink-satin smoke scudded sullenly across its face. What an unusual sky. Ominous too. Like a beautiful stage curtain shielding an audience from the shocking scenes being prepared behind it.


Luke paid no attention to the strange moon as he and Bear hurried down the waterfall track to Binburra. All he could think of was Belle.

A barking chorus greeted him as he headed for his room at the end of the cart shed. The double-brougham was missing. Damn, the family was out.

Sasha bounced out to greet them. Bear trotted off with her, no doubt to reacquaint himself with his puppies.

Another dog dashed from the shadows. 'Scruffy?' Luke picked up the little terrier, who squirmed with delight and licked Luke's face. 'What are you doing here?'

Davey hopped out of the shearing shed, trying to put his boots on at the same time. 'I could ask you the same question. You're supposed to be up at the pass.'

'Where is everybody? Where's Belle?'

Davey's lips curled in a leer. '*Belle*, is it? I suppose you don't know then. They're all at Canterbury Downs for the engagement party. Miss Isabelle and Edward Abbott. Getting married, they are.'

'You're lying.'

'Ask anyone,' said Davey. 'Anyway, what's it to you?'

It made no sense. Luke ran to the tack room, stowed his precious swag, grabbed a bridle and headed for the stockhorse night paddock. The herd raised their heads at his approach. Sheba reared, her silver coat burned bronze by the blood-red moon. With a low nicker, she came to him with a proud, high-stepping walk. Luke whispered to her, kissed her nose, stroked her neck. The mare nuzzled him and consented to the bridle. Luke looked around for Bear, thinking to lock him up should he try to follow. The dog was nowhere in sight. Unwilling to waste another moment, Luke swung into the saddle and took off down the hill at a gallop.

By road, a carriage might take upwards of an hour to complete the trip to Canterbury Downs. But with a swift horse and a full moon Luke could halve that time, cutting across country by way of Murderer's Hill. Sheba sensed her rider's reckless urgency and raced on, trusting Luke to steer her course.

With flying hooves they cleared a fallen tree, half-seen in moonlight. Luke checked his mare as they neared the summit. Flanks heaving, Sheba gulped down great lungfuls of air. Careful now. The ground ahead was rocky and he wouldn't risk laming her. The mare cocked back one ear as Bear caught up with them. Luke swore and yelled for him to go home, but nothing could convince the dog to turn back. Luke started down the other side of the hill, holding Sheba to a canter until he cleared the steepest slope of loose stones. Then they took off in earnest, thundering down the dim hillside with the shadow of Bear at their heels.

# CHAPTER 35

E dward finished a waltz with Grace. The whole affair was becoming tedious. It would be different if he could have each dance with Belle. Where was she anyway? He longed to search her out, but he'd promised to join his mother in the quadrille, the last dance before supper. Edward's irritation grew. Burning wax dripped onto his neck from overhead candelabra and small talk left him cold. Perhaps mother had forgotten? But no, she caught his eye as the band struck up and dutifully he went to her side.

Rosy moonbeams striped the grass on their way to the conservatory. Such a beautiful night. They barely needed the lantern. Belle paused, glanced back over her shoulder towards the house. 'We should let Edward know.'

Henry touched a finger to his lips. 'He must think I chose this engagement present myself, without advice from you.' Too much brandy caused his words to slur together. A prickle of unease nipped at her spine.

'You don't need me,' said Belle. 'Edward will love your gift, whatever it is.'

'No, Isabelle, I want your opinion. You know my son better than anyone.' Henry smiled, perhaps for the first time that evening. 'He's a lucky man to have found such a lovely wife.'

Belle felt a small rush of gratitude. This was the first time she'd heard Henry say a positive word about their engagement.

He reached for her hand, patting it in a fatherly fashion before releasing it. 'Shall we?' He gestured to the moonlit path. Her apprehension melted away.

The conservatory was dark, even with the lantern. Henry led her past palms and orchids, their exotic leaves casting mysterious silhouettes against the glass. Belle's steps faltered as her disquiet returned.

Henry turned to face her, the fixed smile on his lips no longer kind. Belle's stomach tightened. She willed herself to stay calm, though the knowledge of Becky's rape was looming larger and larger in her mind. Surely Henry offered no threat? Not on her engagement day. Not with a house full of people.

'Where is it?' she asked. 'What have you brought me to see?'

He seemed closer now, too close, though she hadn't noticed him move.

The lantern went out – no accident, of that she was certain. Every instinct screamed *run* but her feet were frozen, like in a nightmare. By the time her legs would move, Henry was upon her, tearing at her bodice, grabbing at her breasts. She tried to shove him away, and he struck her in the face.

She tasted blood in her mouth when she screamed.


Luke had approached the homestead from the rear. An assortment of carriages, large and small, littered the grounds. Coach drivers and footmen lounged against their vehicles, smoking and playing cards to wile away the time. Luke tethered his heaving mare to a rail. Crowds and darkness would work to his advantage. He might not be noticed, at least until he entered the house.

Suddenly, Bear took off across the garden. Why had he ever let that damned dog come? Luke gave chase, heading for the conservatory.

Nobody paid much attention to the pair as they raced across the shadowy lawn. Nobody except Molly. She was carting two buckets of perfectly good food to the pigsty. *Those pigs eat better than most people,* she thought. Then she spotted him. Adam or Luke, or whatever his name was. There was a big reward on that boy's head. Molly returned to the house, wondering who to tell.

Bear crashed through the conservatory door, with Luke close behind. What the hell? Luke surveyed the scene inside with shock and rising fury. The dog was heading straight for Belle, where she struggled with Henry Abbott in the shadows.

Tearing free from Henry's grip, Belle rushed to Bear and crouched behind him. Luke took in the missing buttons from Belle's bodice, the torn sleeve and bloody lip. She buried her face in Bear's fur. The dog stood stock still, eyes trained on Henry, a menacing growl in his throat.

Henry turned to Luke. 'Get out, Adam,' he said in a drunken drawl. 'This has nothing to do with you.'

Time stood still.

'My name's Luke Tyler, you bastard, and this time I'm going to kill you.'

'Luke Tyler?' A stunned recognition dawned on Henry's face as he straightened his waistcoat 'And to think I paid your wages, welcomed you into my home, nursed you back to health, lauded you as a hero. What a fool you've made of me.'

Henry reached for his pistol.

Bear was upon him before the firearm cleared his belt. Crushing fangs choked the scream from Henry's throat as the dog took a death grip. Luke put his hands on Belle's shoulders, guiding her outside, shielding her eyes. He knew what was coming

'Sir Henry said he had something to show me,' sobbed Belle, while Luke rocked her in his arms.

Moments later, Bear emerged from the conservatory. He went over to Belle, smearing blood on her lilac gown.

Her face contorted in horror. 'Bear, what have you done? Luke, do something.'

'It's too late. Abbott's dead.'

'No!'

Luke stroked her hair, hating himself for what he was thinking. It was no use. He needed to know. 'Is it true, Belle? You're to marry Edward?'

Belle confessed everything in a great outpouring of emotion. She told him of her terrible loneliness, of the weeks worrying about pregnancy. She told him about the baby and about her mother. 'Mama threatened to expose you if I didn't agree. She thinks she's saving my reputation.'

Luke felt himself burning with shame. He'd made Belle pregnant, and now she was entering into a loveless marriage – sacrificing herself to protect him and their child. How utterly selfish he'd been. Putting the girl he loved in an impossible position, deceiving Daniel, allowing Edward to stand up in his place. To be the man he couldn't be. It was unforgivable, nothing a bag of gold could atone for. And, now, having as good as murdered Henry, he was more of a liability than ever.

Voices called from the darkness. Luke pulled her further into the garden, crouching down behind a swathe of lavender.

'We can run away together,' said Belle. 'Right now.'

'No, listen to me. I love you. I'll always love you, but what future would you have with me? A fugitive who has dishonoured you and your family. Who's as good as killed a man.'

'You've done nothing wrong,' said Belle. 'It was Bear. It wasn't you.'

'It's the same thing. Do you think I'd let them shoot Bear for saving us both? Abbott's dead and I did nothing to stop it. We're equally guilty, Bear and I.'

'Do you expect me just to let you go?'

'You'll do it for our child,' said Luke fiercely. 'I'm not like you, Belle, however we might fool ourselves. I might have been once, but now I'm changed. I'm like Bear, not truly civilised. Abbott attacked you and still you wished to save him. I stood by, my heart a cold stone in my chest. You deserve better than me.'

For a minute that felt like a lifetime, Luke clung to Belle, kissing her, holding her, absorbing her. 'I love you,' she cried. Then he ran with Bear to the horse lines, mounted Sheba, and sped away towards Murderer's Hill.

# CHAPTER 36

Molly felt faint, head throbbing, legs so weary she could hardly stand. This party had been a nightmare for the kitchen staff, who'd worked nonstop since before dawn. Molly pulled her cracked, aching hands from the washtub full of soiled pans and dabbed them on her apron. She'd had enough. It was time to tell somebody about Adam and claim that reward. To the astonishment of the other scullery maids, she marched upstairs right under the head cook's nose.

Molly almost collided with Edward on the porch. 'Sir, I must speak with you.'

'Get out of my way.'

'Sir, it's important.' She blocked his path. 'I saw that escaped convict Luke Tyler here tonight in these very grounds, along with his big brute of a dog.'

'What are you talking about, woman?'

Molly trembled but stood her ground. 'With respect, sir, Luke Tyler is passing himself of as Adam McLeod, that young miner who had the run of the house a while back.'

. . .

Edward stepped back. Luke was here? That man had Belle under a spell. He could ruin everything, snatch her away in the blink of an eye. 'Have you told anybody else about this?'

'No, sir,' said Molly, her voice quaking. 'Not a soul. I'll claim that reward if I may, sir. It's to start a little shop.'

Edward's mind raced. It wasn't too late. He could simply pay this woman off, send her away and nobody would be the wiser. He owed Luke that, surely. Yet a small voice whispered in his other ear that this was the perfect opportunity to dispose of his rival. Even though Luke had saved his life, even though he'd promised Belle and Elizabeth never to betray him.

Belle. In his mind's eye he saw her lovely face, her sweet mouth swearing that she loved Luke, not him. A love that would destroy her reputation and break her heart.

'What is your name, woman?'

'Molly, sir. Molly Swift.'

'Well, Molly, you shall have your reward,' said Edward, keeping his voice low. 'But first you must find Mr Cornish, the house steward. Tell him what you told me.' She mumbled her thanks. 'And Molly . . .'

'Yes, sir?'

'There's thirty pounds more if you keep my name out of it. Don't tell Mr Cornish who sent you to him.'

Molly clutched his hand. 'Of course, sir. Thank you, sir. I'll never tell a soul.'

Edward watched her go, torn between guilt and elation. Cornish would undoubtedly send for Sergeant Murray. It was out of his hands now.

A cry came from the garden and he hurried off to find Belle.


When Edward reached the conservatory, Tom Howard, the station manager, beckoned him inside. A dreadful scene greeted him. His father lay on the floor, drenched in blood, a gaping hole where his throat should be. What in hell's name had happened here? It seemed more like the attack of some monstrous animal than that of a man.

Edward turned away from his father's blank eyes and the frozen look of horror on his face. A movement caught his attention – someone lurked in the shadows. 'Who's there? Show yourself.'

An ashen-faced figure emerged from behind the palms.

'Belle, oh my Lord.'

Her golden hair was down and tangled, her gown torn and blood-stained. Edward ran to her, and she fell to her knees. He knelt too, taking Belle's trembling hands in his as she confessed every last appalling detail.


Elizabeth sat beside her daughter in Jane's upstairs parlour, while Belle finished her story.

Daniel touched her cheek. 'Abbott didn't . . . he didn't violate you?'

'No, Papa. He tore my buttons and put his hand up my skirts. Then Bear arrived.'

'Thank God.' Daniel marched around the room, grim-faced, finding it hard to think clearly through his anger and hurt. 'We must go to the police at once and report that Abbott assaulted our daughter.'

'Edward hopes to spare his mother that shameful fact,' said Elizabeth.

'What? And whitewash that monster even in death? Do you care nothing for the truth, Lizzie?' Daniel stopped at the curtains, took the satin fabric in his hand. 'I can hear the accusation now. They'll say Luke deliberately set the dog on Henry. How can we defend him if we can't raise that he acted in Belle's defence?'

'Belle is with child,' said Elizabeth softly, 'and Luke is the father.'

Belle gasped like she'd been struck, but she didn't deny it.

Daniel looked down at his hand, white-knuckled against the rich red drapery. He let go. 'I don't understand, Lizzie. Luke promised me there was nothing between them.'

'Then he lied.' Edward entered the room, his face ghostly-white. 'There's no protecting him now, sir. I've just come from the conservatory. Luke has been recognised.'

'But how? All here know him as Adam.'

'That I don't know,' said Edward. 'But I do know he'll face the gallows. His only hope is to escape.'

'Please, Daniel,' said Elizabeth. 'Please. The truth will further humiliate our daughter. Have you no regard for her?'

Daniel looked at Belle. She'd changed into a plain gown and sat beside her mother, looking like a frightened child. 'What would you have us do?'

'I'll tell my story to save Luke,' she said. 'Of course I will.'

The fear in her eyes tore at his heart. What was the point? With Luke unmasked there was no saving him if caught.

'Very well,' he said. 'I'll hold my tongue. But if Luke stands trial the truth must be told. Not that the truth seems to stand for very much around here.' Elizabeth heaved a relieved sigh. 'So, this marriage? A pretence all along to salvage Belle's reputation?'

'No pretence for me, sir,' said Edward. 'I love Belle and will cherish her child as my own.'

'Very good,' said Daniel stiffly, so used to disparaging Edward that anything else felt odd indeed. 'Right, then. I'll go downstairs to keep an eye on things. Ah . . . I would offer my sympathies, Edward, but I think there've been quite enough lies told for now, don't you?'

'Father was a complete bastard, to me perhaps more than to anyone,' said Edward. 'And after what he did to Belle? It's hard to summon grief through so much anger.'

Daniel went downstairs and stood on the verandah overlooking the courtyard. A few carriages were leaving. It was a good night for travelling, clear and bright. Luke could go far. The boy had betrayed him, lied to him, deceived him, but he didn't deserve this.

Daniel prayed Luke would have enough sense to avoid Binburra. It was the first place they'd look for him.

# CHAPTER 37

The bloodshot moon guided Luke and Bear surely back to Binburra. He was oddly blank. Not sad exactly, but stripped of hope. The homestead lay asleep. He collected his swag from the tack shed, feeling insubstantial, like a ghost. Like he was already dead. Then he rode north, cantering up ungrazed slopes, which were swiftly reverting to forest.

When the going became too rough, he turned Sheba loose. She followed him for a few minutes, until spooked by a high gust of wind in the trees. Then she whirled and galloped down the mountain. Luke trudged on. Perhaps up at Tiger Pass, Bear would be safe.

Hour after hour, they forged into the wild uplands. When Luke lost his way in the dark, Bear set him on the right course. When the moon burned out, they paused for a brief sleep. When dawn broke they were already on their way.

Sunrise saw a group of riders set off from Canterbury Downs for Binburra – Sergeant Murray, two constables, three men from town, and Edward Abbott.

Edward was a reluctant conscript. It was bad enough he'd put Luke in this predicament, and he was already sick with guilt. He'd wanted his rival out of the picture, that was all – not to hang. In truth he wished Luke all the best: wished he might escape and start a new life far from Hills End. The last thing Edward wanted was to hunt him down like an animal.

'I'm no bushman,' Edward had told Sergeant Murray. 'I'd slow you down.'

'You'll do fine,' said the sergeant. 'And we could use the extra man. I had trouble raising a posse in town.'

Edward knew why. His father was widely hated, and his death considered a well-earned one. The folk of Hills End would be more inclined to cheer his killer than hunt him down.

Sergeant Murray shot him a shrewd look. 'I assumed a man would want to help track down his father's killer.'

Edward had managed a half-hearted nod. It would look suspicious if he didn't go.


When they arrived at Binburra, Daniel was waiting for them on the verandah. 'Adam McLeod? Shot through last night and took his things. You're welcome to take a look around.'

Murray gave him a knowing smile. Daniel was bound to have sworn the servants to secrecy. He doubted he'd uncover any leads.

Davey was shaving in a bucket outside the shearers' quarters when Sergeant Murray found him. 'Morning, son. Did you happen to see Adam McLeod around here last night? Or maybe this morning?'

Loyalty demanded his silence, but jealousy made him speak. Davey didn't know what Adam had done, but the chance to get him into trouble proved irresistible. 'He was here. Last night. Him and his dog took off for the Abbott place. Haven't seen him since.'

It was the truth, wasn't it? What right did Mr Campbell have to make him lie?

'Any idea where he might go if he didn't want to be found?'

Davey clammed up. He'd probably said too much already.

'We think this bloke murdered Sir Henry Abbott last night. You didn't know that, did you, son? You'll be in a lot of trouble if you don't cooperate. Getting in the way of a murder investigation. Are you sure you don't know anything?'

Davey's mouth was dry, and a combination of fear and malice loosened his tongue. He told Murray of his trip to the valley in the ranges with Adam and Mr Campbell.

Sergeant Murray marched him around to the front of the house. 'Young Davey here thinks he knows where Tyler is. It might mean a few days of bushwhacking. I'd appreciate some provisions for the trip, Mr Campbell.'

Daniel glared at Davey, who was glad to have the burly police sergeant standing between him and his boss.

'Any chance of you joining us yourself, sir? Nobody knows this land like you do.'

'I'm afraid not, Sergeant.' Daniel turned on his heel and marched inside.


An hour later the men were ready to go. Davey was keeping out of the way in the cart shed. Old Bill came by and dropped rations and a waterskin at his feet. 'Your horse is ready in the yard.'

'Thanks Bill.'

'And one more thing. Once you're back, pack your bags and get out.'

Davey shouldered his swag and walked glumly to the yards. He looked around for his horse, but saw only Baringa: a barely broken, flaxen-maned chestnut with a wild streak.

'That's a fine colt, son.' Sergeant Murray grinned. 'Got a bit of go in 'im.'

Davey tried to mount. It took two people to hold the restless horse still. He hung on grimly as Baringa reared. Whatever had he got himself into?

· · ·

215

Luke had been on the move for hours. He couldn't be sure he was being followed, but it was a fair bet. If so, he had a fair start on them. His first trip to Tiger Pass had taken four days, but that was travelling at the pace of the cubs, and without the advantage of a horse for those first few miles. With luck he could cut that almost in half.

They travelled steadily, making good time, barely resting. They drank from mountain pools. Bear caught rabbits and shared them with Luke, who was loath to use his rifle. They ate raw meat so no smoke betrayed them. Sometimes Luke crept onto a rocky ledge or ridge top with a view down the range, but saw no sign of pursuers. They seemed utterly alone. Even so, he tied bundles of grass and bracken to their feet to obscure their footprints. Bear kept chewing his off.

By Tuesday morning they reached Tiger Pass. It felt like coming home. The canyon walls stretched into the blue. Shimmered light blended cliff tops with sky. It was hard to decide where earth ended and heaven began. He thought of the rock paintings. Had the first people known it, too, this hallowed feeling?

A certain calm came over him. Since the night of Becky's rape, he'd seethed against something. Injustice, Abbott . . . himself. Now he surrendered to the idea that none of it mattered. Neither he, nor Bear, nor the tigers. They were all insignificant specks in a vast universe, and would soon be forgotten. It was a strangely welcome notion.

Luke and Bear climbed down to the valley floor, and found the tigers safe and sound. The sleepy cubs greeted their visitors and curled back up again. The cave contained some spare rations and Luke sat a while, glad for a meal of biscuits and raisins. The raw meat had made his stomach churn. Bear rose from his place beside the cubs, padded to the cave mouth and snarled, sensing the coming storm. Wearily, Luke shouldered his rifle. He'd set himself a difficult and dangerous task for the day and there was no sense putting it off.


That night, Bear hunted once more with the tigers. Luke stayed behind and, like in the old days, waited for the dog to return. Under cover of darkness he allowed himself a fire to cook the last rabbit, but his appetite failed him. Clouds rolled in on a high wind, snuffing out the stars. A curtain of rain swept up the gorge and closed over the cave mouth. The fire's glow served only to darken the night beyond. Never before had Luke been so conscious of his own frailty, of hanging onto life by a fragile thread, and yet never before had he felt so protected.

Bear and the cubs trotted in after midnight, seeking shelter from the worsening weather. The animals sat companionably around the fire, regarding Luke with interested eyes. Thought and mind were there, and he suddenly wished they could talk to him. Well, maybe they couldn't, but there was nothing to stop him talking to them. So he told them a story he'd heard from Daniel as a boy, one in keeping with the odd spirituality of the occasion.

'Once upon a time there was a prince called Siddhartha Gautama. He lived a life with everything he ever wanted. He didn't know that outside his palace, the world was a tough place. One day he rode out among the people and saw so much sadness. Cruelty and disease and hunger, not just for humans but for animals too. So he decided to leave his old life and just wander about, searching for the secret of happiness.

'He went walkabout for seven years, studying and asking questions, but couldn't find the answer. In the end he sat down under a big old tree. For forty-nine days he just sat there, until one night, known as the sacred night, a bit like this night maybe, he realised that wisdom wasn't out *there* somewhere, but inside him. Now he wasn't called Siddhartha Gautama any more, but Buddha, the Enlightened One.'

Bear came and laid his great head on Luke's knee.

'Buddha told people that suffering is caused by desire.' An image of Belle's lovely face flashed before him. 'Desire creates endless miseries. If you can stop wanting things to be different, you can stop suffering.'

Luke used a stick to trace a circle in the sand.

'So then Buddha invented a kind of wheel, with each spoke a rule for happiness'

He racked his brains to remember this bit. Somewhere nearby, a mopoke owl began its rhythmic calling. Bear and the cubs watched him expectantly.

'One . . . I've forgotten one. Two is be kind. Three, don't lie or condemn or judge. I'm not too good with that.' As he said each number he drew a line on the circle in the sand. 'Four, don't kill or steal or harm. Five, don't get rich off the misery of others. Six, keep your self-control. Seven, don't think evil thoughts. Eight . . . I've forgotten eight as well.'

Nevertheless he traced in the last line. An eight-spoked wheel lay in the sand.

'Then Buddha said, there is no you or me, because we're all parts of this one big whole. Even Abbott is, I suppose. Nothing is good or bad, because everything is the same and can't be divided. He said we might all need to live thousands of lives before we understand. That's called Karma. When Buddha died, he passed into everything. He's even right here, with us, in this mountain. What do you think of that?' he asked Bear.

But Bear was either meditating or asleep. Luke lay close beside him, trading comfort and warmth as night tiptoed towards morning.


Sergeant Murray's party broke camp at first light. Davey wasn't being much help, but at least he'd got them started on the right track. By noon, the way became impassable for horses. Someone had to take their mounts back to Binburra, which meant he'd lose a man.

With numbers reduced from eight to seven, the men pressed forward on foot. They barely needed Davey's uncertain navigation skills. Edward had been talked into bringing his father's pair of bloodhounds. They stood a yard high at the shoulder and were consummate, relentless hunters. Their forefathers had been imported from England to hunt down Aborigines during the Black War. Not once did the dogs falter on the trail. By Wednesday night the party found themselves, according to Davey, only half a day's travel from Tiger Pass.

· · ·

They set off early Thursday morning under pale, rain-washed skies. The country curved up to a rim of rocky battlements, bare-sided, and crowned with trees. Sergeant Murray gazed at the cliffs rising stark and forbidding in the distance.

A sudden thunderclap echoed around the range. The men peered skywards, where streamers of cloud scattered before a light wind. How was there thunder? Minutes later the same thing, like gunshot, but much louder. Twice more that morning, the mysterious retort rang out. The rained-out trail made it difficult for the bloodhounds to find the scent, but they were close enough now for Davey to remember the way. By noon, the party reached the entrance to the pass.

They stopped for a briefing.

'Don't shoot till he has the chance to surrender,' said Murray. 'I plan to bring this boy home alive.'

'We'll be sitting ducks,' said Davey. 'That bastard's armed and a crack shot. He could pick us off, one by one, from the cliffs.'

'I reckon Tyler's no killer.' Sergeant Murray shouldered his pack and they headed up the canyon.


Luke had spent the morning in target practice. He'd made the precarious climb up from the valley to Tiger Pass, cradling five sticks of dynamite and a dozen blasting caps. If they came for him, he'd finish what he and Daniel had started – blast out the rear of the cave and seal Bear and the tigers safely in their secret valley.

Without fuses, he needed to find a way to detonate the explosives. Luke positioned a blasting cap in a clearing away from the cave. He took aim and shot. To his delight, it detonated, causing a feeding flock of cockatoos to take flight, bright yellow crests raised in alarm. Three more times Luke repeated his test. Spot on every time. Satisfied, he arranged the remaining caps and dynamite at the back of the cave.

Bear prowled around, gazing up the pass. He came to crouch at Luke's feet, a growl rumbling low in his throat.

Luke sensed it too, this approaching menace. They'd be here soon.

He rechecked the cache of explosives, loaded and primed his rifle, strapped his swag on his back. He tied new grass bundles to Bear's feet. Then he sat down under the ageless Huon pine and waited, mouth dry, scarcely breathing, alert to the slightest sound.

The sun had passed its peak and was slipping away to the west when there came the excited howl of a dog. For hours now, Bear had heard boots crunching on sand, the rustle of clothes, whispered conversations, even laboured breath as men climbed.

Luke called a snarling Bear inside the cave and urged him down the tunnel leading to the hidden valley. The dog obeyed and waited for Luke to follow. Instead Luke wedged rock after rock into the narrow space between them, walling him off. Bear whined, scrabbling away at the heavy stones with powerful forepaws. He stopped at a sharp word from Luke and sat, disconsolate, as the rocky barrier grew.

Content that Bear was out of harm's way, Luke took up a position at the cave entrance offering a clear view down the pass. How surreal it seemed, like a play acted by another. A bloodhound trotted into sight, not two hundred yards away. There was no hiding from dogs. After a moment's hesitation, Luke shot it between the eyes. A second came into view and met the same fate as his companion. Then, a man. Luke drew back into the shadows.

Sergeant Murray, rifle at the ready, surveyed the towering walls of the gorge. Cautiously, he moved forward, motioning for the others to follow. Luke spotted Edward among them . . . and Davey. This was a surprise. He'd expected to die at the hands of strangers.

Murray examined the dead dogs. His practised eye judged the bullets had come from somewhere in front of them, but where? Dozens of caverns peppered the cliffs.

'I don't want any trouble, son.' His voice echoed round the ranges.

'Lay down your weapon and come out where we can see you, hands high.'

Murray scanned the dozens of caverns peppering the cliffs, then ordered his men to fan out in a line and inspect the ground. It was no easy task. Luke had covered his tracks well.

Hours later, Murray found what he was looking for, the faint paw prints of a dog in the damp earth. They led to a cave at the base of a tall pine tree. He motioned his men to vantage points around the entrance and once more urged Luke to surrender. Then Murray marched into the cave, deeper and deeper again. Passing from light to darkness, he moved as a blind man until his eyes adjusted. Dim shapes emerged from what had been a sea of black. Was that a pillar of stone ahead or the form of a man? He meant to call out but a sudden dread stole his words.


Luke peered into the depths of the cave, searching. There, to the right. The tarnished gleam of a detonator cap caught the faint light. Luke swung his rifle barrel.


Murray saw the motion and shook off his unexpected fright. He could just make out the figure of someone standing with his back to him. Odd. Why wouldn't a man face his pursuer? Slowly, Murray raised his rifle.

A snarl of unearthly savagery reverberated around the stone chamber. He looked wildly about as his terror returned. Then a fast-moving shadow, darker than its surroundings, launched itself at him from out of the very walls. Murray took swift aim. A deafening shot rang out and the huge black form fell motionless at the sergeant's feet.

He heard Luke scream out, 'No!' then another rifle shot.

With a thundering boom, the roof rained down rock. Murray ran for his life towards the light. When he turned around, an immense curtain of stone had descended, shielding the boy and his dog from the sergeant's horrified eyes.

# CHAPTER 38

E dward took off his hat and held it to his chest. 'I'm sorry, Belle.'
Belle's face crumpled, her features clouded by tears. 'No.'
She rammed her hands against her ears, rocking from side to side.
'No, no, no.'

He moved to take her in his arms, but she slapped him away.

'You were there,' she said, her eyes wide and accusing. 'Why didn't
you protect Luke? You should have protected him.'

Edward braced himself as Belle rained down blows on his arms,
his chest. The pain went straight to his heart.

Daniel sprang forward and wrapped his daughter in a tight
embrace. 'Shush, my darling, shhh.' He held her tighter, his own eyes
filled with tears. 'Edward did what he could for Luke – I'm sure of it.'

Daniel looked to him and Edward's mouth went dry. He licked his
parched lips. 'Of course I did, sir.'

The lie choked his throat. He could have stopped this. He could
have shielded Luke, but instead he'd urged Molly to betray him. Urged
her to tell her story, reveal Luke's true identity – even promised her a
reward. He'd caused the man who saved his life to flee like a hunted
animal, even providing the hounds. He'd killed Luke as surely as the
rockfall had. If he could take it back, he would.

Another part of him felt a shameful liberation – free of his father's shadow and with Belle all to himself. Everything he'd ever wanted, and he bore no public blame for any part of it. Private guilt over Luke's death? That was another thing. It had stalked him during the long trek home from the ranges. It ambushed him at every turn, making him doubt his worth as a man as efficiently as his father ever had.

Elizabeth sat Belle down, dabbing her brow with a damp handkerchief and insisting she take some brandy. Edward's eyes shifted to Belle's waist. A little thicker than before, perhaps, evidence of the child she carried – not his child. At times he'd struggled with this knowledge, wondering if he could truly care for another man's baby. Then it came to him; a way to atone for his guilt and make up for his own loveless childhood at the same time. He would raise Luke's child to know nothing but approval and affection. For every insult his father had given him, Edward would give encouragement. For every criticism, praise. For every frown, a smile. The child would flourish in the warm glow of his affection. This would be his tribute to Luke. This would be his atonement.

He looked at Belle, at her tear-drenched face and stricken eyes, and felt a surge of hope so powerful it made him tremble. In time her grief would pass. In time they would build a future together, a bright future filled with love.

# CHAPTER 39

Luke lay across Bear's body in total darkness. Numb. Drifting in and out of consciousness. The young tigers were safely sealed inside the hidden valley, and this knowledge brought with it a deep comfort. He stroked Bear's head, praying for a miracle, a resurrection. No, his best friend was dead. Being alive himself came as a surprise, but it wouldn't last. Soon the air would run out and he'd slip away to wherever Bear was. Perhaps meet his father? At this sweet prospect he let his eyelids fall. He was done with life. Summoning the memory of Belle's beautiful face, he waited for the end.

Hours later, Luke woke and opened his eyes. He'd been wrong. This was no peaceful hereafter. He was buried alive. The numbness had fled, and each fibre of his body screamed with pain. His gashed legs burned like fire, and broken ribs made each breath a torture. The swag on his back, wedged between Bear and a fallen boulder, anchored him in place. He struggled to extract the pocketknife at his belt, hacking at the straps until they gave way.

Luke writhed sideways, dragging the pack free and seeking to relieve the agony of cramped and contorted limbs. In blind panic he scrabbled at the stones above him. Pebbles rained down. He stiffened, resisting the urge to tear at his smothering prison. The roof was a jumble of jagged, precariously balanced rocks, jammed together, miraculously supporting each other. Any one might be the keystone that could bring tons of rubble crashing down.

Luke forced himself to be calm. Air was reaching the cavity, so there must be an opening somewhere. He inched forward. Then slowly and methodically he began to dig away at the rocks in front , moving them to an empty space behind him Impossible to judge time or direction in the featureless dark. Was it day or night? Was he digging towards the cave mouth or to the rear? Would he reach freedom or find himself trapped with the tigers in the hidden valley? Luke could think of worse outcomes.

Digging, digging, digging, passing out, pissing where he lay – and repeat. Memories filtered back. He'd been hurled into the air by the blast. Bear had cushioned his fall, protecting him even in death. The dog had wanted him to live, and he had a duty to honour that courage. A duty to survive, to escape this black hole. To somehow make his worthless life count. Luke pushed aside the hollow thought that without Bear and without Belle there was no point in living.

Time dragged by. So thirsty he couldn't piss any more, yet still he dug. Relentless. Moving each stone with the care and precision of a surgeon. Burying Bear as he went. He licked moisture from the rocks, and rationed strips of dried rabbit and wild berries from his swag. The treasure he'd been so proud of, the pouches crammed with gold and cash, lay inside his swag, discarded in the dust. All the wealth in the world would not help him now.

Days must have passed. How many, it was impossible to tell in the cramped gloom. But at last his painstaking labour bore fruit. On moving yet another rock, a chink of light appeared ahead of him. Luke blinked, trying to focus. After living in inky blackness for so long, the faint glow hurt his eyes. A sudden energy pumped through his body, and he longed to scramble forward and heave the rocks aside. Instead, he took two steadying breaths and maintained his measured progress.

Inch by inch, stone by stone, he moved towards the light, dragging his swag after him. When Luke at last unearthed himself from his living grave and saw a bright sunset framed in the mouth of the cave, he gave thanks for the miracle of life. Never again would he wish it away.

It took a long time for Luke to recover his health. It took even longer to come to terms with how profoundly life had changed. He slept a lot, thought a lot, ate a lot. Wild food was abundant at Tiger Pass. At night, he lay pressed up to the rockfall, as close to Bear's final resting place as he could get.

Gradually, reality sank in. Bear was gone. Belle was lost to him – at least for now. She would think him dead, Daniel too. Edward, the police – everyone. Nobody should have survived that cave collapse. Perhaps it was for the best. However painful it may be, Belle needed to marry Edward to protect her reputation and make the child legitimate. It would be easier for her to go through with the charade if she believed Luke was dead. Later on, after the baby was born . . .

One sparkling morning, Luke examined the money bags. He emptied out wads of notes and counted them. A fortune in cash, and there was the gold as well. Nobody would be looking for him now. He had a chance to start over, really start over this time. No longer hunted. No longer a fugitive. He would go away for a while, reinvent himself. Visit his mother and sister in Melbourne to share his newfound wealth. When enough time had passed, he'd return for Belle and his child. Return to reclaim his life.

# CHAPTER 40

Melbourne – Ruyton Girls School.

It was an unseasonably cold day, even for mid-December, yet the wind and rain could not penetrate Luke's new woollen coat. He straightened the strangling collar of his fine linen shirt. Luke still felt like a worthless outsider. Like any moment now, the world would see through his expensively tailored disguise. He half-expected to be given short shrift when he mounted the imposing stone steps and rang the school's brass bell. But apparently Shakespeare wasn't wrong when he said clothes maketh the man. A prim lady, wearing a beribboned cap too large for her head, gave him an approving glance and beckoned him inside.

Luke gave the little speech he'd prepared. He was a distant relative, with some confidential news for Mrs Alice Tyler regarding a deceased estate. 'I believe she's a housekeeper here at Ruyton.'

'She is indeed, and a most wonderful find. We don't know what we'd do without her.' She smiled through uneven teeth. 'Sir, if you would remain here in the parlour, I shall send Mrs Tyler to you. Let me take your coat.'

Luke put down his valise and ran a finger down the crease of his trousers, his heart hammering against his ribs. Would Mama know him after all this time? He'd gone to prison a boy and returned a man. It would be a terrible shock, him turning up alive, without any warning, but this was the only way he could think of to contact her safely. A letter falling into the wrong hands could doom them both.

The grandfather clock in the corner ticked away, yet time stood still. Surreal, to think that any second he would be face-to-face with his mother. Luke strained to hear footsteps in the hall. There, a brisk trip-trap, growing louder. Was this her? He stiffened as the doorknob turned, held his breath, fighting an urge to hide and leap forward at the same time. Alice opened the door.

Luke had tried to prepare himself for the flood of emotion when he saw her. But he hadn't prepared for the instant flash of recognition and astonishment on his mother's face. Her hand flew to her mouth as she spun to shut the door. On turning around, she wore an expression so tender, so full of love, it almost brought Luke to his knees.

'A miracle,' Alice said. 'God has brought me a miracle.'

Luke held her oh-so-familiar hands, drank in her sweet smell, closed his eyes – and he was a little boy again. Creeping into bed beside her warm, soft body on a freezing winter's morning. Snacking on apple slices while she cut them up for pie. Collecting eggs together, and Mama's musical laughter at the discovery of a newly hatched clutch of chicks. The warmth of her hug. The kindness of her smile. A rush of memories so vivid, so precious, that he dared not open his eyes in case she would be gone.

Alice stroked his cheek as she used to when he was small. 'You're real. You're my Luke.'

She made his name sound like a prayer. He was suddenly ashamed for having so often abandoned it.

Luke ventured a closer look at her. She didn't seem any older, though it had been five years. Sheer joy had stripped time and worry away, leaving her girlish. Papa had always called her a beauty. Luke saw what his father must have seen – no weary, careworn drudge in a housekeeper's apron, but a vibrant woman.

His parents had been very romantic, very affectionate. Holding hands on High Street like young lovers, kissing in the kitchen. Luke used to tease them about it, but what had a foolish child known about love? Now he understood how a pulse could pound with desire, how a heart could dance with passion, how a soul could ache with wanting, and break with loss. He knew what it must have cost her when Father died. Because of him. The knowing moved him to tears. That surprised him. He thought he'd used up his lifetime supply.

Luke turned away, unable to face her. 'I know about Papa . . . Can you ever forgive me?'

His mother wrapped him in a crushing embrace, and whispered in his ear. 'What should I forgive you for, my brave, brave son? Defending your sister? Sacrificing yourself to protect her reputation? Papa died in an accident that could have happened at any time, on any road, on any day. If there's blame, it lies with Henry Abbott, fair and square.' She took his shoulders and spun him round. 'Look at me, Luke.' Her eyes filled with a fierce pride. 'To Becky, to me – you're a hero. And now, this miracle?' Her eyes smiled and cried all at once. A sun shower. 'Come, my darling . . . sit with me. Explain how God has returned you to us.'


The sun was going down on the best day of Luke's life. Becky flicked a switch on the wall and twin wall lamps flickered briefly, and then glowed with a steady warmth. 'We have electricity. The whole school does.'

Luke gave an admiring nod, stifling a burp. Mama's trifle was fit for a king, and he'd had two serves. He tried to clear away the dessert dishes, but Becky wouldn't let him. She wouldn't let him do much of anything, other than eat and drink and tell stories. When he stood to stretch his legs, she stood with her back to the door, as if he might try to escape. No chance. He could cheerfully spend the rest of his life in this place, basking in the glow of his family's affections.

Becky and Alice lived in two downstairs rooms at the rear of the main house, with views of the kitchen garden. Their tiny bedroom opened onto a pretty parlour with an overflowing bookcase, writing bureau and small dining table. Potted palms lined the wide windowsills. A pair of wingback armchairs flanked the fireplace. Mama seemed to have the run of the school kitchen, where she cooked a tasty mutton stew and brought it back to their rooms for dinner. Its rich aroma conjured up yet more childhood memories.

A toilet and laundry lay a little way along the timber verandah, but Alice had provided Luke with a jug and basin for washing – and a chamber pot. He had strict instructions to remain inside. A man staying the night at Ruyton was against the rules, and his appearance would cause a scandal.

Luke watched his mother take the kettle from a hook over the fire and make a pot of tea. Her cheeks must be tired from smiling. Becky came to sit beside him at the table, taking his rough hands in hers. How proud he was of his sister. She'd changed so, grown into a tall, graceful young woman with dark, glossy ringlets and a keen, intelligent gaze. However some things hadn't changed; she was still a chatterbox.

'We couldn't believe it when we heard Sir Henry was dead, could we, Mama? I'm glad, of course. Does that make me a terrible person? Tell me again about how you found the treasure.'

'Who told you about Abbott?'

Alice gave him a cup of tea and sat down. 'Mr Campbell wrote us a letter.'

'He thinks you're dead,' said Becky. 'Everybody does, even Belle—'

Alice's lips pursed and she shook her head a fraction. 'Dear, would you put some biscuits on a plate, please?'

Becky hesitated for a moment, before going to the fireplace and taking a tin down from the mantelpiece.

Luke hadn't told them about his love for Belle, or about their child, or his plan to one day have a life with her. One shock at a time. So why had Belle's name even come up? He glanced enquiringly at his mother and saw a tinge of concern behind her smile. What was he missing?

Becky offered him a biscuit.

'Thank you. I have something for you too.' Luke pulled his valise from under the table and took out a jewellery box. 'You always said how you loved opals.'

Becky opened the box. Inside lay a star-pendant gold necklace set with fire opals.

Her face lit up. 'I've never seen anything so lovely!'

'Put it on.'

Becky laughed and lifted her hair while he fastened the chain. She ran to the mantle mirror, turning this way and that, admiring how the brilliant stones flashed against her skin.

'And for you, Mama.'

Alice opened the box he gave her. 'My God, Luke. How much did this cost?'

He pinned the ruby and diamond brooch to her dress. It was shaped like a butterfly. 'We passed a jewellers in Hobart once, Mama, remember? You pointed to a brooch like this one and said how much you loved it.'

Alice shook her head in disbelief. 'You couldn't have been more than nine or ten. And that brooch was paste. Is this a real diamond?'

His mother's delight made Luke's heart burst with pleasure. But the brooch was nothing compared to the ring he'd bought for Belle. The blinding rose-cut diamond set in a platinum band had cost him a fair slice of his fortune.

'There's so much I want to do for you both.' He took his wallet from the case and counted out two hundred pounds. 'Here, Mama. Plenty more where that came from. Gold, too. I'm a rich man, with money in the bank.'

The eager manager had barely glanced at his forged birth certificate when he opened the Collins Street Colonial Bank account. It had been Luke's first sweet taste of money opening doors.

Alice picked up the cash and spread it playfully out like a fan. There was that girlish grin again. It made his heart sing.

'Almost enough for one of those cottages outside the school grounds,' she said. 'Imagine having a kitchen, and a garden, and chooks. You'd have your own room, Beck. No putting up with me snoring. If we save hard enough...'

'I'll buy you a cottage for Christmas,' said Luke. 'Who do I need to see?'

It was past midnight when Alice and Becky smothered Luke in good-night kisses and retired to their bedroom. They'd moved the table back against the wall, and made up a makeshift bed on the carpet. Charming, how his mother fussed about, worrying if he was warm enough and comfortable enough. Stoking up the fire. Adding last-minute layers of cushions. How horrified she'd have been at the prison camp's lice-ridden bunks or the old hut's bracken bed on the ground.

Lying restless on the floor, staring into the flames, inevitably brought back memories. Waiting for Bear to return from the nightly hunt. Wishing he was with his family. Wishing he was with Belle. Life was cruel, giving with one hand and taking with another.

His family could never be intact again, not without Papa. Yet reconnecting with his mother and sister, receiving their forgiveness, being in a position to support them financially? That was a blessing he hadn't expected. He'd never see brave Bear again, a heartache his newfound wealth could not cure, but he would have Belle. Somehow he would retrieve her from her loveless marriage, atone for his self-ishness, and together they'd build a life for their child.

He threw off the blankets and got up. No point trying to sleep with his mind abuzz. He turned on the lamp, poured himself a glass of water from the pitcher on the table, and wandered around the cosy room.

Daniel had done the right thing by Alice and Becky. Finding his mother this live-in housekeeping job, and his sister work as a teaching assistant. Poor widows and their children could easily find themselves in far more dire circumstances. Becky was such a clever girl. How she must love working at a school, surrounded by books. He longed to thank Daniel for his kindness. One day he would. One day, when he and Belle were reunited.

Perhaps reading would calm his racing thoughts. Luke took a

novel from the shelf and sat by the fire, but he couldn't concentrate on the story. All he could think of was Belle, and how she thought him dead, and how he should get word to her. But it wasn't fair to burden her with the secret of his existence when there was no way to fix things. No way to be together.

Luke tossed his book aside. What an appalling situation he'd left Belle in. How was she coping? What was she feeling? His mind drew pictures. Belle, red-eyed from weeping, sick with grief. Edward, helpless to comfort her. Or was she putting on a brave show, swallowing her sadness, only giving into sorrow at night when she was alone?

Luke hurled a log on the fire with such force that it erupted in burning embers. Was Belle alone at night? She'd be married by now. Would Edward do the honourable thing? Respect the fact that his marriage was a sham? A deplorable but necessary pretence? Luke groaned and marched around the small parlour. Not knowing was killing him.

What about the letter? Mama said Daniel had written to say Abbott was dead, and Luke too. He refused to think of her heartbreak on reading it. What else was in that letter? Had it mentioned Belle? He went to the corner bureau, opened the top drawer and rummaged around. Nothing. In the bottom drawer he found it in an envelope addressed to his mother.

Luke sat down in one of the arm chairs to read. The rawness of Daniel's grief dripped from the page. He apologised to Alice for having kept Luke's whereabouts from her. *I believed that keeping the secret would protect us all. Instead it has led to tragedy.* He told of his despair at having to convey such terrible news to a mother, his rage at Henry Abbott, his grief at failing to shield Luke from harm. And, most moving of all, considering how Luke had so compromised his daughter, he wrote of the depth of his affection for *a young man that I loved like a son.* Nothing about Belle, though. Not a word. Luke's disappointment was palpable.

He idly flicked through the drawer. Some invoices and receipts. An invitation to a music recital. Some more letters. Luke's heart stopped. He pulled one out and held it up to the lamp. No mistake. His mother's address was written on the envelope in Belle's flourishing script. With trembling fingers he unfolded the letter contained within.

*My dear Mrs Tyler,*

*Please accept my deepest condolences on the tragic death of Luke, your only son. I cannot imagine your pain. Please also extend my sympathy to Rebecca. He loved you both very much, and often told me so. I hope your belief in heaven brings you some comfort, because that is where Luke is, sitting at the right hand of God, the brightest star in the sky.*

*I have a confession to make. I also loved Luke. We wanted to marry, but circumstances conspired against us. I trust this news does not come as too much of a shock, because there is more. I am carrying Luke's child. You are to become a grandmother.*

*Please do not worry, Mrs Tyler, because I am recently married to a dear childhood friend of mine, Edward Abbott. He is a good man who swears he will cherish this child as his own. Edward will never replace your son in my heart, but I confess I am learning to love him. He is kind and makes me happy, and there is no doubt he will be an excellent father. We are both so excited about the upcoming birth, as I hope are you. Edward and I plan to raise this baby, your grandchild, in a house filled with joy and love.*

*You and Rebecca will always be welcome guests in our home. However, I do ask that you keep the contents of this letter private. It must never be revealed that Luke is the father of my child. Such a scandal would tear our fledgling family apart, and my dearest wish is for the baby to grow up in a loving, stable home. Please understand this is no reflection on the affection I bore your son, nor the depth of my sadness at his death. I pray it is a comfort knowing your grandchild's future is secure.*

*Most affectionately yours,*
*Isabelle Abbott*

Luke's hand trembled as he re-read the letter once, twice, three times. A slow tear fell on the paper. Certain phrases stood out: *He is kind and makes me happy, and there is no doubt he will be an excellent father . . . We are both so excited about the upcoming birth* and *I confess I am learning to love him.* And the one that burned most deeply: *It must never be revealed that Luke is the father of my child.*

His eyes brimmed over. When would he ever learn? Belle wasn't broken-hearted and pining over him, crying herself to sleep. That wasn't who she was. She was embracing her new life, excited about the baby, planning a future with Edward. She was happy. His dreams of sweeping back into her life after the child was born were just that – dreams.

Luke felt a touch on his shoulder. His mother.

He scrubbed a hand over his eyes. 'All day, Mama? All this day you've known about me and Belle and the baby. Yet you said nothing.'

'I wanted you to tell me yourself, when you were ready.'

Luke waved the letter in her face. 'She's happy, Mama. She's happy with Edward. Happy with Henry Abbott's son.'

He gave an anguished cry, like the howl of a stricken animal. Alice hugged his shoulders and kissed him. 'Belle still loves you, my darling. I don't doubt it for a second. It shows in each line, in her shaky hand. In the fact that she cared enough to write me that letter at all, confessing a truth that could bring her undone. But Belle thinks you're gone, Luke. She's making the best of things, and bravely too.'

Luke bowed his head 'What does Becky know?'

'She's read the letter.'

'I haven't abandoned Belle, Mama. I'm going back for her. Once the child is born, once I establish a new identity . . .'

'No,' said Alice, her voice low and urgent. 'You'll be recognised. Not only will you expose the shameful truth about who fathered her child, but you'll hang for Abbott's murder. That won't help Belle. That will destroy her.'

'I have money now. We'll go away.'

Alice put a hand on his arm. 'And tear that sweet girl from everything she knows? A young woman with a first baby needs her family round her, not to be isolated and on the run.'

'I'll be her family.'

'You'll be a poor substitute for Belle's mother when the child has colic, or her breasts throb and swell.'

Luke shrugged his mother aside and paced round the room, but Alice would not be silenced. 'This cannot be, Luke. If you love Belle, as I know you do, you'll let her go. Let her get on with her life, as you must get on with yours.'

It could just as easily have been Mrs Campbell speaking. Mrs Campbell at the killing gallows, imploring him to leave for Belle's sake. Luke stopped pacing and re-read the letter one last time. Then he hurled it into the flames. 'All right, Mama. Nobody will learn the truth from me.'

Alice breathed a big sigh. 'You could come and live with Becky and me in our cottage. Use your money to set up as a carpenter like your father. It's a good, honest trade, Luke, and you were always handy with a hammer.'

'I can't stay here in Melbourne, knowing that Belle and my child are living just across Bass Strait. I couldn't bear it.'

'My poor darling Luke. What will you do?'

'I'll spend Christmas here, Mama, see you and Becky right. After that, in the new year, I'm going as far away from Tasmania as I possibly can.'

# CHAPTER 41

'Won't be a jiffy, miss.' Millie collected up the washing. 'It's absolutely wonderful to have you home, Miss Belle, even if only for a little while.' She backed out of the door, beaming broadly.

Sweet Millie. How she'd missed her. Belle arched her back and exhaled, glad for a moment to herself. She looked around her old bedroom. It was achingly familiar. Ruffled bedspread. Pretty French provincial dressing table. The sunset through the lace curtains was shades of rose and gold.

An Indian summer had lingered into March. Belle threw open the windows to watch the sun go down. A warm wind kissed her cheek, fragrant with native mint and sassafras. She gazed out to the forests beyond. Wild, unchanging – a view she loved. It reminded her of another sunset that seemed like a lifetime ago. She'd gazed out on this same view, wondering about Adam and where he'd gone. Made up her mind to find him. Had it really been six months since Luke died? It still didn't seem real. She missed him as fiercely as ever. A sudden surge of energy took hold of her. Perhaps if she walked off through the forest to that little shack in the clearing, she just might find Luke waiting for her.

Sasha pressed her nose into her mistress's hand. Concern shone in

237

her big brown eyes. 'All right.' She took hold of the dog's collar. 'I'll stay here. Stop worrying about me. You're as bad as Eddie.'

Edward was insisting she travel to Hobart for the birth in a few weeks' time, and her mother had teamed up with him. Belle had reluctantly agreed, but begged for these last few days at home before she left. Edward had gently chided her. 'Canterbury Downs is your home now, sweetheart. Not Binburra.' But the Abbott mansion didn't feel like home. Henry's ghost roamed its manicured gardens and velvet-draped halls, sucking out the joy.

A sudden twinge took her mind off the view. She rubbed her belly, still surprised by how large it had grown. Ah . . . there was another one, stronger and low in her back. Sasha whined and led Belle over to the bed. She lay back on the pillows and waited for the strange pain to pass. But although its intensity waned, a nagging ache at her spine remained.

Millie returned with an untidy vase of native hyacinth orchids, yard-high sprays of spectacular speckled-pink blooms. A golden stag beetle roamed along one stem. Millie placed the vase down on the dressing table, then prattled on as she always did while putting away clothes. Belle didn't hear a word. Her gaze was fixed on the flowers. Their simple beauty symbolised all that was right with Binburra and all that was wrong with Canterbury Downs.

Belle had not settled into life at the Abbott estate since the wedding, a low-key affair after the death of Edward's father She hated the red roses that appeared like magic on her chiffonier each morning, artfully arranged by some nameless servant, each bloom perfect and beetle-free. She hated the wrought-iron chandeliers, the gothic statutes and ivory figurines. The massive Georgian furniture. Her carved four-poster bed of black oak looked like a coffin. It gave her nightmares.

Edward had tried his best to make her feel at home. Giving Whisky pride of place in the beautiful stables. Giving Belle free rein to update the artwork in their private wing. She'd replaced portraits of stuffy old men with paintings by modern artists such as Arthur Streeton and Tom Roberts: living depictions of rural and outback

Australia that looked out of place on the gloomy wood-panelled walls. He'd allowed Sasha to sleep in her bedroom, much to his mother's chagrin.

Edward's room adjoined Belle's, connected by an internal door. There were a few raised eyebrows at the young couple's separate sleeping arrangements. However, it wasn't unusual for husbands and wives to occupy different bedrooms, and Belle's swift pregnancy put paid to any gossip.

Jane Abbott indulged her new daughter-in-law in any way she knew how, even withdrawing her opposition to dogs in the house, but it was no use. Belle had been raised with the kind of physical and intellectual freedom that was outside Jane's understanding. She felt as bored and trapped in the stuffy Abbott mansion as Whisky did in the grand bluestone stables. Each longed for the freedom of Binburra's mountains.

The stag beetle reached the top of the stem and waved his iridescent green antlers in the air. Belle wanted a closer look. She tried to stand, but another stab of pain floored her. She fell back on the pillows, this spasm painful enough to make her eyes water. 'Rescue that beetle, Millie. Put it out the window for me.'

'Yes, Miss, but I'll never know why you're so fond of creepy-crawlies.' Millie turned round, took one look at Belle, then stopped in her tracks. 'Miss Belle, what's wrong? You've gone all pale.'

'I'm having a few pains,' she admitted.

'Oh lordy, Miss Belle.' Millie's hand flew to her mouth. 'What can that mean?'

'How should I know?' said Belle. 'When you've put the beetle out, you'd better fetch Mama.'

Millie squealed in alarm, hurled the unfortunate insect through the window, and ran from the room.

Five hours later, Belle's bedroom held quite a crowd. Elizabeth sat on the bed, holding her daughter's hand. Millie passed around a tray of biscuits and barley sugars, and was taking orders for cups of tea. Mrs

Scott fussed about: tidying the already tidy room, piling up fresh towels and disinfecting the washstand and basin with kettles of boiling water.

A prim nurse sat in the corner and a midwife, whom Belle had not met before, stood at the foot of the bed, complaining about Sasha. Mrs Goetz was an old woman with thinning grey hair, a hooked nose and a German accent. Belle took an instant dislike to her and wished that cheerful Mrs Potter could be there instead. Apparently she was away on a call, and Dr Lovejoy couldn't be found. Harrison had left to fetch Dr Lark, a physician Belle had little faith in. Nobody was ready. Nobody had expected her to go into labour this early.

Edward and her father stood muttering together by the door. They fell silent as Belle cried out, another cramp gripping her body.

Elizabeth put a damp flannel to her daughter's brow. 'For Christ's sake, Daniel. Where's the doctor?'

'We don't need a doctor,' said Mrs Goetz. 'We just need to clear this room and let Miss Isabelle get on with it.' She shooed everybody out, except for Elizabeth and the nurse. 'And take that dog with you.'

Somebody had closed the window, and the room was insufferably close. Belle lay on a sheet, damp with perspiration. When each contraction came, she moaned and twisted, clamping down on her mother's hand so hard she feared she'd break it. Her body was out of control, consumed by the baby's need to be born.

Time wore on. There would never again be a night as long as this one. She was a twig running rapids on a river of pain. Where was the doctor? Why would this baby not come? Belle had never listened to the gossip of matrons on the subject of childbirth. She'd always found it boring, but she should have paid attention. Then she'd know if there was something seriously wrong, if she was taking too long to have this child. She couldn't rely on her mother or the midwife. They were treating her like a child herself. One minute they were making soothing noises, reassuring her. Next, they were huddled in the corner, whispering and casting worried glances her way.

Belle twisted and screamed as another spasm racked her exhausted frame. She seemed to have been in this tortured, sweating nightmare all her life. Belle had once seen a heifer in labour for two days who died without ever having her calf. She couldn't stand two days of this pain. She'd perish first.

'Thank the Lord.' Her mother's voice reached Belle through the fog of pain.

Dr Lovejoy was suddenly at her side, whispering words of encouragement and placing some kind of mask over her face. She caught the whiff of a familiar smell from her father's specimen studio. Chloroform. 'Deep breaths, Belle,' he whispered. 'Deep breaths.' There came a respite from the worst of the contraction, a blessed moment of relief. The next moment it felt like someone was wrenching her insides out. She clawed at the mask as it was dragged from her face.

Gradually, the quality of her pain changed.

'It's up to you now, Belle,' said the doctor. 'You must bear down. The baby's coming.'

This was better. This she could do.

Dr Lovejoy offered her the mask between pushes, but she barely needed it. 'One more,' he urged.

She heard an animal scream torn from her own throat and, with a final mighty effort, Belle's son was born. She lapsed into an exhausted sleep before she heard the child's cry.


Belle woke with morning light streaming through the window. Her mother dozed in a chair beside the bed. Yesterday's ordeal seemed like a dream. She tried to sit up, and the truth of what she'd been through came to her. Her body ached as though it had been run over by a steam train. Wait, where was her baby?

Elizabeth stirred beside her. 'Mama.' Belle grabbed her arm and shook it, filled with a sudden dread. 'Mama, my baby? Is it all right?'

'You have a lovely little boy.'

Belle sank back, dizzy with wonder. A boy. She would call it Luke. 'Where is he?'

Elizabeth offered her a drink of lemon barley water and Belle gulped it down. 'I'll bring him to you.'

. . .

Belle gazed down at the tiny cherub that her mother laid in her arms. So quiet, so good. How could something this small have caused so much trouble. Dimpled cheeks. A delicate rosebud mouth that pursed sometimes, then yawned. Downy copper-coloured hair. What colour were his eyes? If only he'd open them. Perhaps he was hungry?

'Should I feed him, Mama?' Belle fumbled with the ribbon at the front of her gown.

A knock came at the door, and Edward entered, wearing the proudest smile she'd ever seen. 'My sweet Belle.' He kissed her tenderly on the cheek, then did the same to the baby.

'Your wife wants to feed her son,' said Elizabeth. 'We should let her try.'

Edward frowned. 'Belle must regain her strength, you heard what the doctor said. And with the baby so weak . . .' He took hold of Belle's hand. 'I have an experienced wet nurse waiting downstairs, darling. She comes highly recommended.'

'Wet nurse? I don't understand,' said Belle. 'Why is my baby weak?'

Belle took a closer look at her sleeping child. So beautiful, so flaw-less – yet she still hadn't heard him cry, not even a whimper. 'Is there something wrong with my baby, Mama? Did I hurt him?'

'Of course not,' said Elizabeth. 'You were wonderful and strong, and braver than I could have been. However, he is early and there was a complication.'

Belle did not miss the slight shake of Edward's head. 'Tell me, Mama.'

'She has a right to know,' said Elizabeth. 'The child was born with the cord round his neck. Thank God for the doctor and Mrs Goetz. They worked together to free him, but baby took longer than normal to breathe.'

'But he's all right now, isn't he?'

Edward took the baby, Luke's baby, from her reluctant arms, murmuring soft nothings. 'He's more than all right. He's absolutely perfect.' He kissed Belle on the forehead. 'Now rest, my angel.' And with that, he disappeared from the room with her son.

'No, come back.' Belle tried to get out of bed, but was too sore and dizzy to stand. 'I want my baby.' She turned to her mother. 'Why did Edward take him?'

Elizabeth urged her to lie back down. 'The baby was breech, and had to be turned. The truth is that both you and the child nearly died,' she said. 'And you lost a great deal of blood. Edward's right to say you must rest.'

'Is he right to engage a wet nurse without consulting me? It's positively mediaeval.'

'I'm not defending Edward.' Elizabeth offered Belle another drink. 'However, the harrowing birth has left Robert extra sleepy, slow at feeding. And you need time to recover.'

'Robert? Why did you call him that?'

'Edward said . . .'

'I don't give a damn what Edward said. The baby's name is Luke.'

'Belle, you can't.'

A soft knock came at the door. Edward came in with a vase of red roses.

'Take those away.' What energy Belle had left was knotted in a tight ball of rage. 'How dare you name my baby. He's going to be Luke, not Robert.'

Belle would have welcomed an argument, was ready for a fight. Edward merely smiled and nodded, as if he was humouring a child. 'We both want to honour Luke.' He infuriated her further by putting the vase down in front of the orchids. 'However, the Abbotts name first-born sons in a particular way. Mother would be suspicious if we departed from this tradition. Especially since the baby came so early.'

'What tradition?'

'First-borns are named after their great-grandfathers, in this case, Robert Hiram Abbott.' Edward's lips formed a tight line. 'They inherit their middle name from their grandfather. I'm sorry, Belle, but it must be this way.'

Belle's woozy brain tried to process what she was hearing. The baby's grandfather . . . 'So by your theory his middle name will be Daniel? I like that.'

Edward shook his head. 'I mean his paternal grandfather.'

It took a moment to sink in. Not Henry. Her anger glowed white-hot. Surely Edward wasn't proposing that Henry's name be in any way attached to Luke's son?

'The birth registration is already on its way to Hobart.'

'Exactly what have you named our baby?'

'Robert,' said Edward. 'Robert Henry Abbott.'

# CHAPTER 42

**N**othing in sleepy Tasmania had prepared Luke for the melting pot that was Cape Town. So many nationalities, so many clashing cultures. The colony was a hotbed of tension, and the recent discovery of gold and diamonds only heightened this unrest.

War broke out soon after his arrival. If it had been a native uprising, Luke would have gladly fought for the Africans. Nothing angered him more than the appalling exploitation they suffered at the hands of their colonial rulers. In a battle between the Boers and the British, however, Luke felt no sympathy for either side. He spent his time in restless wandering, avoiding conflict zones and discovering all he could about his astonishing new country.

Luke roamed from the spectacular Drakensberg ranges in the east, to the endless scrublands of the Great Karoo. From the Kalahari Desert in the north, to the beaches of the dramatic Elephant Coast. He lived the life of a pioneering naturalist and adventurer. Climbing mountains. Canoeing the courses of wild rivers. Exploring the country's vast underground cave systems – caves he'd read about in Binburra's library. They contained bones of early humans. Daniel had called Africa the *cradle of mankind*, and Luke was thrilled to see it for himself. But however far-flung the mountain or remote the river, it was never far enough to escape his memories of home or his restless yearning for Belle.

Five years of lonely travels brought him to the little town of Nisopho, in the Transvaal. How Belle would love these wide plains, teeming with wildlife. Daniel, too. Though they wouldn't like to see the farmers encroaching on the grasslands. Fencing in the waterholes. Fencing out the great herds. Slaughtering lions, leopards, cheetahs and wild dogs along the way.

At twenty-five years old, Luke finally knew what he wanted to do with his life. How often had Daniel said that the best way to protect the forest was to own the forest? These plains were as unlike Tasmania's forests as they could possibly be, but the principal remained. Luke would buy up farms surrounding Nisopho, and dedicate his life to protecting this savannah, just as Daniel had protected Binburra.

Luke drew rein at a rocky ridge atop of a hill. He breathed in the view. To the west lay an endless expanse of grassland, dotted with umbrella-shaped thorn trees. In the foreground lay the Zola River, a peacock-blue ribbon, winding its way through the shaly terrain. The midday sun burned hot in a cloudless sky, and the air shimmered with its heat. He could see forever.

Luke had grown to love this corner of the savannah. Its primal landscapes and the immense canopy of stars at night. The massive slate-grey thunderstorms that rolled in across the plains, bringing life-giving rains. The unique wildlife. Before him, a family of elephants bathed in the river. Herds of gemsbok, giraffe and zebra dotted the scene and, directly below, in the shadow of the knoll, dozed Dark Mane's pride. It was always a relief to find these lions safe and well.

When he first came, two families of lions had lived here at Themba. Poachers slaughtered the river pride shortly after, even the cubs. Skins fetched high prices in Cape Town.

Then Dark Mane had arrived from the north, single-handedly deposing and killing the bad-tempered twin kings of the plains pride. He bore the trademark black mane and large body of a Kalahari lion. Luke had spent weeks tracking him, accustoming him to his presence, studying his behaviour. The new king was a fierce but fair leader, whose wives liked and respected him. Luke liked and respected him too. Spending time with the lions was one of his greatest joys. He had a special fondness for these mighty hunters, the apex predators of the African veldt, just as thylacines were the apex predators of Tasmania's wilderness. A memory of the tiger cubs flashed across his mind's eye: their bright eyes and whiskery noses. Were they alive, he wondered, living safely in their secret valley?

His chestnut colt shied when he caught the lions' scent. Luke soothed him with his voice. Caesar snorted and pricked his ears towards the east, where a desperate scene was unfolding. A tall black man was running for the shelter of the stony knoll, racing like his life depended on it, strides swift and sure as a cheetah's. In the distance, a group of mounted men rode in pursuit. It would be a matter of minutes before they caught him.

The posse wasn't the only danger confronting the man. He was heading straight for the pride, who lay camouflaged behind a screen of low acacia trees. Luke spurred Caesar up and over the rocky embankment and down the other side, shouting as he went. The lions leaped to their feet, snarling and lashing their tails. The man stopped running when he spotted them, and glanced back over his shoulder. Then he kept on coming, more ready apparently to take his chances with the lions than with his pursuers. It took a brave man to face a pride on foot, whatever the reason.

Luke unslung his rifle and fired shots in the air. The lionesses and cubs turned tail and ran, scrambling into the scrub. Dark Mane stood his ground. He wasn't afraid of Luke, but Luke was afraid. The armed men were almost upon them. Dark Mane was in as much danger as the fleeing man.

Luke shot over the lion's head. Dark Mane still didn't flinch, but it was too much for Caesar. The combination of lion and gunfire sent the colt into a rearing, plunging panic. Damn. It was all Luke could do to stay mounted, and he was losing precious seconds.

Luke regained control just as the man cannoned into the scrub. He stopped in front of Luke, chest heaving, coal-black skin slick with sweat. Luke sized him up: about his age, tall and thin, limbs lined with ropes of muscle. He carried a Zulu axe, its half-moon blade designed to hook an opponent's shield. Luke knew now why he'd braved the lions. With courage and a weapon, he'd have half a chance.

Dark Mane roared and tossed his head about. Luke raised his rifle as the thunder of hooves grew louder. He shot at the ground beside the lion, but he still didn't budge. Damn. If he was to chase Dark Mane off before the riders arrived, nothing but a full charge would do. Luke spurred Caesar forward, but the colt reared again, mad with fear. Luke leaped from his back.

Caesar galloped off, hooves raising puffs of dust as he tore away. Luke ran at Dark Mane, waving his rifle, shouting and whooping. At such close quarters, the king of the veldt was a terrifying sight. Half as big again as his lionesses, ten feet from tip to tail, four-feet tall at the shoulder and with teeth like ivory daggers. Dark Mane backed off a few feet and then propped, a defiant snarl on his lips.

Luke was rooted to the spot. There was something paralysing in the lion's stare. He roared, and Luke could feel the blast of his breath. Dark Mane crouched low, grinding the ground. Bracing, balancing. The black tassel on his tail twitched. Everything screamed attack, yet Luke was frozen, captive in the lion's golden gaze. He couldn't raise his rifle to shoot, even if he wanted to.

With a blood-curdling yell, the other man ran in, his axe raised. The spell was broken, and Luke joined in the charge. This was too much for the lion. He loped away, melting into the bush. Luke sagged with relief and shot his unlikely friend a grateful glance. There was no time for more. The mounted men were upon them.

As they drew their heaving horses to a halt, Luke recognised the lead rider. Herman Smit owned the Nisopho diamond mine. Grandly named the Superior Mine, it was an ugly assortment of pits and tailing dumps on the town's eastern edge: mongrel diggings where half-starved workers scratched for small, flawed diamonds, poisoning the air and water in the process.

Herman unslung his rifle from the saddle and peered short-sightedly at Luke. 'Who the fuck are you?'

Luke stepped forward so Herman could see him.

'My apologies, Colonel Buchanan.' Herman said as he lowered his weapon, doffed his hat, and changed from Afrikaans to English.

Luke acknowledged this courtesy with a nod. He knew firsthand the bitterness born by the Boers against the British, and vice versa. On arriving in Cape Town, he'd been mistaken for an Englishman, a hated *rooinek*, and was beaten half to death in a putrid laneway behind an Afrikaans-speaking bar. So he'd invented an alter ego – Colonel Lucas Buchanan from New South Wales. Inventing a title had worked for Henry Abbott. It had worked for him too.

Luke told the Boers he'd volunteered on their side in the war. For the British, he was a decorated officer who'd fought with them. His wealth was sufficient to ward off questions, and to garner admiration and acceptance wherever he went. It never ceased to amaze him how gullible people were.

Herman wiped droplets of sweat from his florid face with a handkerchief. A brilliant diamond shone beside the gold wedding band on his finger. 'I caught this thieving Kaffir stealing rations.' He gestured to his men. One rode forward, uncoiling a rope.

Luke raised his hand for the rider to stop. He glanced sideways at his companion, who was holding his ground, clutching the axe and glaring at the mine owner with murderous intent. Anyone who tried to take him would feel the bite of that axe, Luke had no doubt. He addressed the fugitive in Zulu.

'These men pursue you with rifles for a few loaves of mealie-bread?'

The man grinned. 'Not a few loaves, baas. I emptied the whole storehouse and shared out the food, rotten as it was. We are meant to get board and five shillings a week, but we haven't been paid in months. Men are starving at that fucking mine.'

Luke turned back to Herman, seeing instead a sneering Henry

Abbott standing before him. 'What do you intend to do with this man?'

'Flog him, chain him. If he's stolen a diamond, I'll shoot him. He's always been a troublemaker, this one.'

From the look on the black man's face, there was little doubt he understood English. He raised his axe and the horsemen raised their rifles.

'This is nothing to concern you, Colonel. Hand him over, we'll be on our way and you can get on with your hunting.'

'I will have this man for myself,' said Luke. 'If he's such a trouble-maker, you'll be well rid of him.'

'A troublemaker he may be, Colonel, but Tau is strong, and cost me a pound at a labour auction not two months ago.'

'I'll pay you four pounds for his contract. Come and collect it this evening.'

'That is generous, Colonel, but I'm running out of men. How will I work my mine? Six have deserted this month. I can't afford to let him go.'

'Five pounds then.' Luke gestured for Tau to follow him.

'He may have stolen a diamond,' called Herman. 'We must search him.'

'I shall search him myself,' said Luke, wary of Tau's flexing axe hand. 'If I find a diamond, you may have both the man and stone back, and keep my five pounds.' His tone brooked no argument. 'And, for the record, I am not hunting. My lands are game reserves. I'd have you remember it. Now, if you'll excuse me, I'm busy.'

The mine owner looked around in wonder. Luke was miles from nowhere, without horse, or men, or tools of any kind. If he wasn't hunting, what on earth was he busy doing?

'Good day to you, sir. I shall call upon you later.' Herman saluted, wheeled his horse, and led the riders away.


Luke and Tau trudged in through the compound gate. Luke had purchased a dozen farms around Nisopho, choosing the largest property, Themba, as his home. The historic gabled homestead was built by Dutch settlers who farmed the land in the 1700s. It boasted thick whitewashed walls and small shuttered windows designed to keep out the scorching summer heat.

A useful assortment of outbuildings surrounded the homestead, including a dozen mudbrick rondavels with thatched roofs. These traditional round huts once provided accommodation for bustling crowds of servants and farm workers. Now they stood almost empty. Luke had hired only two people: Lwazi, an elderly man who looked after the horses, and Sizani, a round, cheerful young woman who could read and write and who ran the house. She peered through the kitchen window as Luke showed Tau into one of the humbly furnished huts. It had sleeping mats, timber headrests, and a few wooden cups and bowls on a bench.

Tau made a show of putting down his axe, a sign of trust. Luke filled a cup with bore water from the hand-pump outside and offered it to Tau. He gulped it down and fetched himself another.

'Come up to the house when you're ready,' said Luke. 'I'll find you clothes and blankets and whatever else you need. If you want to leave, that's up to you, but I could use a good man.' He smiled in open admiration. 'Somebody who isn't afraid of lions.'

Tau returned the smile and Luke's heart lifted.

'I offer good wages, better than that fat *kont* wasn't paying you.'

They held each other's gaze for a long moment. Something passed between them: a common understanding transcending race and culture, a yearning for companionship between two lost young men.

'I'll stay, baas.'

'Good. When you come to the house we'll eat and discuss your duties.'

'Yes, baas.'

'Don't call me baas. My name is Luke.'

Doubt flared in Tau's eyes, the same doubt Luke himself had felt when Mr Campbell said 'Call me Daniel', all those years ago. An unheard of presumption, and here in South Africa a thousand times more so. It was a lot to ask of Tau. Blacks had been shot for less, but it suddenly meant the world to have this man address him as an equal. 'Please, Tau. Call me Luke.'

The answer came clear and proud, although it rolled awkwardly off Tau's tongue. 'Yes, Luke.'

The pair grinned at each other and shook hands, then clasped thumbs over thumbs in a traditional expression of respect and friendship. For the first time since Bear died, Luke didn't feel alone.

# CHAPTER 43

The two men ate, drank and talked the afternoon away. Tau wolfed his food like a man starved. Sizani could barely keep up, refilling his bowl again and again with scoops of *bobotie*, a spicy minced-meat dish with baked custard topping. She served it with steaming plates of roast pumpkin, sweet potato mash and wilted spinach. A large calabash of cool, fermented milk sat on the table, and Luke found a bottle of Cape wine. Afterwards, they moved on to Sizani's home-brew.

Tau had grown up with his sister, Nandi, on a missionary settlement in the Transkei. They were too young to remember their parents dying of cholera. A Scottish pastor took them in. They attended the mission school and learned how to read and write English. Later on, Tau helped teach local people blacksmith and carpentry skills. 'When Father Mackenzie died, the settlement closed and I went searching for work.'

'And your sister?'

Tau frowned and sculled his beer. 'She married.' His expression warned against pursuing the topic.

'I also have a sister.' Luke found himself opening up to Tau, sharing things he hadn't talked about since leaving Tasmania. He told him about Becky, and Daniel and Bear. About being in prison and Henry Abbott's death. He told him about Belle.

Tau looked askance at him. 'You are wealthy now. You love this girl and she has your child? Yet you abandon your country and let another man have her? That is not the Zulu way.'

'You don't understand —' Luke stopped mid-sentence. The explanation he was about to give suddenly seemed absurd. A surge of missing Belle crashed in. 'Tell me about the mine,' he said instead. 'I worked down a goldmine once. The place was a fucking deathtrap.'

'It's no different here. Baas Smit works us like dogs, sunrise to sundown. When the reef walls crack, they can smash down and bury us. Two men died last month, and many more were injured. All for spotty pebbles . . .' Tau retrieved something from his ear and held it out to Luke. 'Like this one.' The pale stone shone faintly against his skin.

Luke grinned and plucked it from Tau's palm, rolling it between his thumb and forefinger. The little gem was muddy yellow, pitted and flawed – not much of a diamond, but still worth many months wages to a poor miner like Tau.

'Why not sell it and, I don't know, start a shop or something?' Luke regretted the words the moment they were out. He didn't want Tau going anywhere.

Tau burst out laughing. 'Start a shop? What should I sell, Luke? Beads and ladies' dresses?' He finished off the last piece of pumpkin. 'No, I will work for you.'

Luke exhaled. 'What if you had enough money for whatever you wanted? What would you do?'

Tau's smile turned fierce. 'I'd buy out the other men's labour contracts, as you have done for me. Nobody should have to work for Smit.' He poured himself another beer. 'There are stories that he owned gold and copper mines in the remote north, when he was a young man. Some say he kidnapped bands of San people, the small brown bushmen of the Kalahari, and entombed them alive. Casting them down narrow holes, never again to see daylight. Men, women, children – it didn't matter, as long as they could dig ore and send it up in a basket to the surface. There was no way out. Some survived for a few years, eating what was thrown them, until one by one they perished. When the last one died, Smit would take a new lot.'

Bile rose in Luke's throat. 'Surely these are just rumours?'

Tau shrugged. 'A man told me he once worked Smit's old diggings in the desert. Said he found nine little dried-up bodies down one mine, all curled together, including two tiny children.'

They sat in silence. Luke, with the bitter taste of bile in his mouth. He tried to swallow it away.

'It might not be true.' Tau ran his finger along the table's smooth surface. 'This man might have lied to cause trouble. Smit had flogged him.'

Sizani came in with a coffeepot. She'd changed from her house-maid's shift and apron into a colourful wraparound *kanga*, showing off her ample curves. Amber beads shimmered against the sleek swell of her breasts. Tau couldn't stop staring.

'Mr Eli is here, Colonel,' she said. 'In the parlour.'

Eli Goldsmith was a solicitor and the manager of the town's only bank. When Luke first arrived in Nisopho, he'd rescued Eli from a brutal street mugging and the two men had since become friends. Once a week, Eli came over to play cards.

'There's someone else here, too,' said Sizani. 'Mr Smit. Should I show him in?'

So Herman was here to sell him Tau. 'Let the fucker wait.' Luke was thinking hard. Liberating Tau wasn't enough. He could no longer stomach the idea of Smit and his foul mine. 'How many men work at the diggings?'

Tau gave him a curious look. 'Maybe sixty? The baas loses more each week. If he doesn't start paying wages soon, he'll have none left.'

Luke made up his mind. 'Sizani, show Mr Smit into the parlour. Bring brandy and three glasses. Then take Tau to the storeroom. Give him clothes, blankets, candles, soap – anything he needs.'

. . .

Luke and Eli sat side by side in the white-walled parlour, while Herman Smit regaled them with stories of mining glory. Eli was a small, lively man with a curly moustache of which he was inordinately proud. He tweaked it when bored. He was tweaking it now.

Herman certainly loved to talk. Luke let him go, making the odd flattering comment and sizing up his guest. Finally, he held up his hand, peeled five pounds from his wallet and handed them to Herman. 'For Tau.'

Herman took the money, ashed his cigar on the carpet, and leered at Sizani's chest as she topped up his brandy balloon. 'You're a grand fellow, Colonel,' he said. 'A grand fellow. I should have made your acquaintance sooner.'

'I've always been fascinated by diamonds,' said Luke.

'Then you're in fine company, Colonel. The Romans believed they were splinters of fallen stars.'

'And the Greeks believed they were tears of the gods.'

'Ah . . . an educated man.' Herman sighed and wiped his moist brow. 'You've no idea how I miss intelligent conversation in this land of savages.'

'Know what I miss?' Luke opened the drawer of the side table and took out a deck of cards. 'Playing poker. Gentlemen?'

Eli nodded. 'That's what I'm here for.'

Herman slapped his thigh and rubbed his pale palms together. 'You're on, Colonel. Deal away.'

Herman kept on talking as they played, speaking openly of the mines he once owned in the north. 'Poor concerns that brought me little profit.'

'How did you manage for workers?' Luke asked. 'It's hard enough finding men here, let alone in the desert.'

'I used the little brown people. Just the right size to fit down mines.'

Luke felt sick. He couldn't bear to hear more. Instead, he poured Herman another brandy and changed the subject.

As the evening wore on, Herman proved himself an expert player.

Luke made sure not to win. He also made sure the mine owner drank up and won big.

Eli, a novice of the game, was surprised at Luke's bad luck. 'It's certainly not your night, Colonel.' He gathered up the few notes left in front of him. 'Nor mine, it seems. I'll sit out the rest of the game.'

The pile of cash in front of Herman grew, as did his confidence. 'Don't feel too bad, Colonel.' He tapped his balding skull. 'A photographic memory, you see. And no disrespect' – this time he tapped his nose – 'but I can read you like a book.'

'You're good, Herman, I'll give you that.' Luke opened his wallet and frowned. 'Cleaned me right out. Probably for the best, eh?'

Herman's eyes narrowed in disappointment. 'The night is young, Colonel. Perhaps we can come to another arrangement?'

'I don't think so, Herman. The game has lost its appeal.'

'There's only one thing that makes two-handed poker interesting, and that's high stakes.' Herman pointed to the grandfather clock in the corner. 'A fine piece of furniture. My Henny has always wanted one like it.' He pushed his pile of cash into the middle of the table. 'My winnings, against your clock.' He leaned closer, and Luke could smell his stinking breath. 'Or what about your house girl? She a good fuck?'

Luke resisted the urge to smash his face in. He studied Herman's heavy jowls and sunken eyes. The lumpy jaw half-buried in his bulbous neck. More toad than man.

Luke walked over to the grandfather clock as it chimed the hour. It had come with the homestead, and the agent had considered it quite a selling point. Dark mahogany, with intricate devotional carvings of saints and pilgrims, the case standing on ball and claw feet.

To Luke it looked like an upended sarcophagus, but what did he know? The case was Queen Anne and it bore on its face the mechanically animated lunar and tidal dials that were so popular. Luke ran his fingers down the polished wood. 'Beautiful, isn't it? Built in 1750 and still in perfect working order. I'm told it's of Dutch design.'

'The maker?'

'Gerrit Knip.'

'Ah . . . Knip,' said Eli. 'Once the most fashionable clockmaker in all Amsterdam.'

'My good lady wife comes from Holland,' said Herman. 'The match arranged by our parents. Henny arrived in the Cape forty years ago as a blushing bride of sixteen. We'd never set eyes on each other until the week before our wedding.' He sighed. 'Henny has never been happy in Africa. The climate doesn't suit her, but a wife's place is beside her husband, is it not?'

Luke refilled Herman's glass. He doubted the climate was the true cause of Henny's unhappiness. It was rumoured that Herman beat her, and flaunted native mistresses right under her nose. 'Maybe now is the time to take Mrs Smit back to her home country,' he said. 'Fact is, I'm interested in buying your diamond mine.'

Herman's fleshy mouth turned down. He clearly did not welcome Luke's offer, and would need persuading.

'You want high stakes?' said Luke. 'Win the next hand and the clock's yours. If I win, I get an option to buy your mine. I'll pay a fair price. Eli, here, can give us an independent valuation.'

'I can indeed.' The banker was enjoying himself far more now he wasn't losing money. Luke recalled the promise Eli had made him the day they met. 'I'm eternally in your debt. If I can ever be of assistance, in any way at all, it will be my honour.' He might need to call in that favour.

'No, no my friend. Not possible.' Herman's voice grew husky with emotion. 'Mining is more than a business for me. It is in my blood, it's my life. As you can see, Colonel, I have the heart of a risk-taker, a gambler. I've finally dug deep enough to reach blue ground. Tomorrow could be the day I stop turning up *kak* and find the kind of stones Cecil Rhodes himself would envy.'

'What, like this one?' Luke took a jewellery box from his pocket and snapped it open. Belle's diamond ring shone with such brilliance, it lit up the room. Herman's eyes bulged as Luke handed him the box. 'Perhaps you'll reconsider the wager? An option on your mine against my clock . . . and I'll throw in the ring.'

Herman swallowed, a struggle showing on his face. Lips twisting, pursing, puckering, scowling. Luke held his breath. Would he take the bait?

At last Herman extended an arm. 'You have a deal.' They shook hands. 'Hope you're not too fond of this gem.'

Luke tried not to grin. He didn't intend to lose Belle's ring. Herman had been cheating all evening. Nothing very elaborate, simply hiding cards in his hand, but skillfully done. He had the two aces – hearts and clubs – up his sleeve right now. But two could play that game. Luke surreptitiously opened the side-table drawer, confirming it contained paper and a fountain pen. Then he indicated for his guest to give the jewellery case back.

Herman did so grudgingly, and Luke picked up the cards.

'Not so fast, Colonel.' Herman held up his palms. 'I've no doubt you're an honourable person, but we're men of the world, are we not? We must set down our agreement before we play.'

The last piece of the plan was falling into place. Luke feigned offence. 'Surely a handshake is enough between gentlemen?'

'Perfectly sufficient for me, Colonel, but if your luck should change and you win the bet, Eli may require proof of the wager before transferring the mine. Isn't that right, Eli? I'm trying to protect you, my friend.'

Luke ummed and aahed for an appropriate period of time, before retrieving the pen and paper from the drawer. 'You do the honours.'

Herman went to sit at the leather roll-top desk in the corner, a look of eager concentration on his face. 'The diamond. I must make an accurate description.'

'Of course.' Luke handed him the ring.

Herman extracted a jeweller's loupe from his pocket and examined it with an expert eye. 'How many carats? Three and a half? Four?'

'I bought it as a four-and-a-half-carat stone.'

Herman sighed like a man in love. 'Such symmetry, such clarity . . .' It was plain his passion for diamonds was real. 'This gem will have lost much of its weight in the cutting, you know. The Koh-i-Noor from India was 793 carats in its raw state, yet cut out at only 186.' He chortled. 'Listen to me – *only* 186 carats. I should find such a stone.'

Herman examined the ring a final time, then snapped the loupe shut. He gave Luke a searching look. 'There is a story behind this beauty, eh?'

Luke shrugged. 'A girl, years ago . . .'

'And you still keep the ring? Ah, my friend, she is not worth it.' Herman put on his reading glasses and began to write. 'Time to move on. I will do you a favour by taking this sad memory off your hands.'

Luke excused himself and went to fetch Tau. If things went according to plan, it might help to have backup.

When he returned from the fresh night air, it was to the stale stink of brandy and cigars. Luke read the agreement Herman had drawn up, re-read it, and signed it with a flourish. Eli witnessed it, then Luke closed the roll-top over the document and locked the desk.

He sat back down at the table and toyed with the mine owner. 'Do you wish me to count the cards?'

Fear flashed across Herman's face and his forehead beaded with sweat. A card count would reveal the missing aces.

'No, Colonel. I have complete faith in your honesty.'

More fool him. Herman thoroughly shuffled the pack. Then it was Luke's turn. 'Not overhand,' said Herman. 'Riffle.' He flicked his thumbs together.

It was almost impossible to stack the deck with a riffle shuffle. Almost. Luke had mastered the art as a starving boy back in the prison camp, when winning meant extra food, and being caught cheating could cost your life. Luke shuffled precisely six times and prepared to deal.

'Wait.' Herman indicated for him to lay down the deck. Luke would have preferred Herman didn't cut the cards, but this was only a small obstacle for an expert sharp. He swept the top half of the deck from the table into his left hand, then appeared to sweep the bottom half on top in the same manner. In reality he slid the second half underneath, with his right hand covering the move. The cards remained in the same order as before.

Tension filled the room, along with the smoke from Herman's cigar. Luke dealt, checked his hand and frowned. A disparate collection: jack of diamonds, three of spades, four of clubs, plus the five and two of hearts.

Herman stole a glance at Luke's face, and his mouth turned up in satisfaction. 'I'll take two.' When Herman picked up the new cards he made the switch. The two aces formerly up his sleeve were now in the palm of his hand. He'd given up all attempts at keeping a poker face.

'Four,' said Luke.

'Four?' Herman could not conceal his glee. 'Bad luck, my friend.'

Luke shrugged and drew the cards.

Herman took a cigar, snapped the seal with his thumbnail and put it between his lips without lighting it. Then he laid down his hand with a flourish: three aces and a pair of jacks. 'Full house.'

Luke paused, drawing out the moment, savouring Herman's impatience. Finally he showed his hand, all those diamonds. A straight flush.

The cigar slipped from Herman's lips as the colour drained from his face. He blinked stupidly at the cards on the table, struggling to process what they meant. He would not be going home with the grandfather clock and the beautiful diamond – and he'd lost the mine to boot.

'My god, Colonel,' said Eli. 'You've won.'

Luke kept a keen eye on Herman's right hand, ready to act should he foolishly reach for the pistol concealed in his belt. Herman glanced around the room. Searching, no doubt, for the letter of agreement he'd pressed so hard for, the letter that lay safely locked in the desk. How he must be kicking himself.

'Come now, Colonel,' said Herman in a wheedling tone. 'You can't possibly believe I'd bet my mine on a single hand? A device designed to spice up the game – nothing more.' His eyes darted to and fro like a cornered jackal.

'I won fair and square,' Luke said. 'You will honour our wager.'

Herman sat for a while, digesting Luke's words. Then he jumped drunkenly to his feet, overturning the table and roaring like an animal. 'You're a fucking cheat, Colonel – your fingers too fast and your palms too sticky. Nobody swindles me.' Stumbling to the desk, he tried to force the roll-top open. When that didn't work, he reached for his gun.

Luke leaped to Herman's side, seizing his wrist, disarming him, and emptying the bullets from the pistol. Herman swore and swung at him wildly. Luke easily countered the punch with one of his own. Herman crashed to the floor with a thud.

The ruckus brought Tau running. Herman clambered to his feet, wearing a mask of hatred and baffled rage. 'What's that filthy Kaffir doing here? Should have shot him when I had the chance.'

Luke grinned at Tau. 'Will you do the honours, please?'

Tau gripped Herman by the back of his belt and his collar, half-strangling him in the process, and propelled him from the room, down the hall and out the front door. Luke and Eli followed, enjoying the spectacle.

Herman sprawled on the front verandah, a string of vile curses escaping his lips. Tau planted his bare foot on the man's backside and shoved hard. Herman rolled down the steps, landing at the bottom in a heap, quivering like a blancmange.

Luke shook with laughter. 'Goodbye, Herman. It's been a pleasure doing business.'

He slammed the door shut, went back to the parlour, unlocked the desk, and re-read the letter of agreement. He passed it to Eli. 'Is this enforceable?'

'It most certainly is. You have a guaranteed option to buy based on my valuation. Do you intend to exercise it?'

'I most certainly do.'

Eli shook Luke's hand. 'Congratulations, Colonel. You're the proud new owner of the Superior Diamond Mine.'

# CHAPTER 44

A cold April sun streamed through the bedroom window. Belle idly rubbed her belly, once again big with child. Why did she have to be so damned fertile? Why couldn't she be like Whisky? Six years of running with Eddie's Arabian stallion and her palomino mare had only produced one foal. Belle wished she knew Whisky's secret. After six years of marriage, she would soon give birth to her third baby. She loved her children, of course she did, but Belle wanted more from life than just being a mother.

Eddie was thrilled, of course. He saw six-year-old Robbie and three-year-old Clara as just the beginning of the big family he wanted so badly. Belle smiled when she thought of Clara. Such a bright little thing, and the apple of her grandparents' eye. Daniel was always calling by to steal her and whisk her away to Binburra.

Eddie didn't seem to mind. He knew Clara had a special relationship with her grandfather and loved their visits. It would be different, Belle knew, if Daniel had wanted to borrow Robbie. Eddie was completely devoted to that little boy and didn't like sharing. Not even, it sometimes seemed, with his own wife.

Sarah finished filling the tub in the adjoining bathroom. Belle pulled off her lace nightgown, slipped in and closed her eyes. The scented water was deep enough to float a little. Deep enough to lift the weight from her weary bones. She almost felt like a girl again. Her mind floated too, drifting back. Back to a fern-fringed mountain pool, ringing with birdsong. To a shining waterfall, fresh with snowmelt. To Luke's strong arms round her waist, as they made love in the shallows. To whispered words of love. Her body responded to the memory, as it always did.

Belle sat up with a guilty jolt. She was trying to make this marriage work, she really was, and she did love Eddie in a way. In a way. How he would hate to hear that qualification. Just as well he couldn't read her mind.

Edward was a good man. He'd never once thrown the circumstances of their wedding in her face. He was caring and respectful. A wonderful father, accepting Luke's child as his own in spite of everything.

Robbie was different from other boys his age. Belle hadn't noticed at first, having no other children to compare him with. But since Clara, she knew. Robbie had been slow to walk and slow to talk, and he still wasn't good at dressing himself. He tantrummed like a two-year-old. He spent endless hours marching battalions of toy soldiers and ships into war. He preferred playing alone, although sometimes Clara was allowed to join in, on his terms. He knew the rank of each little metal figure, the dates of each English battle, and could replicate those battle plans in elaborate detail. Yet when Belle brushed his hair or read him stories, he remained unengaged, in another world. It made him difficult to love.

After Belle's second child, she'd tearfully spoken to her mother. 'What's wrong with me, Mama? Why don't I love Robbie like I do Clara?'

Elizabeth soothed and reassured her. 'There's nothing wrong with you, darling, and it's not a competition. I blame Edward. Snatching Robbie away to a wet nurse like that, preventing you from properly bonding with your baby. It was sad for you both. And that terrible birth, the cord around his neck . . . It affected Robbie, made life harder for him than for other children.'

'If I was a proper mother, that would make me love him more.'

Elizabeth hugged her tight, like she had when Belle was little. 'There's no right or wrong way to love, Belle. Don't be so hard on yourself. That little boy is very lucky to have you.'

Maybe. Luckier, perhaps, to have Edward. With him, there was no holding back. That man loved Robbie with every fibre of his heart, loved him with a fierceness that put Belle's imperfect affection to shame. He spent every moment he could with the boy. Tolerating his tantrums. Teaching him how to ride a bicycle, make slingshots and play marbles. He took Robbie to the mine to see what gold-bearing ore looked like. He took him to the wool sales to see the difference between a Corriedale and Merino fleece. He took him to the sawmill to see raw logs turned into timber. Robbie was his father's shadow. Perhaps she should make a greater effort with her son before this new baby stole away her time.

Belle climbed from the tub with a soft sigh, and wrapped herself in a robe. The water was growing cold and there was an oily slick on its surface. She couldn't relax anyway. Too much tangled thinking.

Sarah came in with Belle's clothes, looking more worried than usual. 'You're out of your bath already, ma'am. Is there something wrong?'

'Why do you always imagine there's something wrong? It makes me cross.'

Sarah's face crumpled, and she made a clumsy curtsey. 'I'm very sorry, ma'am.' She looked as if she was going to cry.

'And stop apologising all the time.'

'Yes, ma'am. Sorry, ma'am . . . Should I help you dress?'

'For God's sake, Sarah, I'm not helpless.'

Another curtsey. 'No, ma'am. Sorry, ma'am.' Sarah put the clothes down and fled the room.

Belle sat on the bed, feeling ashamed. Why had she spoken so harshly? The girl always seemed half-terrified of her as it was. Belle didn't like the person she became around Sarah. The truth was that she blamed poor Sarah for not being Millie. She wanted to be called 'Miss Belle' again. She wanted to laugh and joke. She missed Millie's smile, her funny comments, her cheeky disrespect. She missed Millie's friendship.

Staff weren't friends at Canterbury Downs. At Binburra, they'd been part of the family. Not here. Here they knew their place. A yawning divide existed between them and the Abbotts. Belle hated it. Sometimes she saw the servants looking at her with a veiled hostility.

Sarah's tentative knock came at the door. 'Miss Clara wants to see you.'

The little girl ran in, clutching her favourite panda toy. She leaped onto Belle's lap, tipping her backwards onto the bed.

'Mind your mother, Miss Clara.'

'It's all right, Sarah,' said Belle, her tone kinder now. 'I'm just having a little lie down.' She shut her eyes.

Clara burst out giggling and shook her. 'Mama . . . wake up. Wake up! You shouldn't be in bed. You should be dressed, it's lunchtime.'

Belle opened her eyes and shushed her daughter with a finger to her lips. 'I can't get up,' she whispered. 'The baby's asleep.'

Clara's eyes widened and she put her ear to Belle's stomach. 'I can hear it snoring.'

It was Belle's turn to laugh. She pulled Clara in for a hug, breathing in her sweet smell, finger-combing her shiny chestnut hair. It was getting so long, long enough to plait.

Clara began jumping on the bed. 'I'm all packed, Mama.'

Packed? Of course. Clara was off to Binburra after lunch.

'Knock, knock?' Edward pushed in the door. 'Can we join you or is this party just for girls?' Robbie followed him into the room – a handsome, fair-haired boy, with Luke's melting brown eyes. He clutched a tin soldier in his hand.

Clara squealed with delight. 'Papa.' She bounced off the bed into her father's arms.

'How are my two best girls doing?' Edward kissed Clara and then his wife.

Belle called her son onto the bed, but he stayed by his father. 'Robbie, Clara is going to Grandma's house. How about we spend this afternoon together? Just the two of us? We can do whatever you —'

'Robbie's coming with me to the sheep sales today,' said Edward. 'We're going to buy some new rams, aren't we, son?'

Belle glared at her husband, but he didn't seem to notice. 'Maybe Robbie doesn't want to go look at a lot of smelly sheep,' she said. 'Maybe he'd rather spend some time with his mother.'

'Smelly sheep? We're talking about top stud rams. They'll have been primped and preened within an inch of their lives. I probably smell worse than they do.'

Clara burst into giggles. Even Robbie managed a smile.

Belle couldn't see the funny side. 'Come here, Robbie.' He jammed his hands into his pockets. Belle went over and knelt down awkwardly beside him on the carpet.

'Careful,' said Edward.

Belle waved his concern away. 'Robbie, darling, stay with me. We'll have lots of fun.'

His father put an affectionate hand on the little boy's shoulder. 'You're spoilt for choice today, son. What will it be?'

Robbie slipped his hand into Edward's. 'Papa's buying me my own ram.'

That was cheating. Why couldn't she have Robbie for one bloody afternoon? It was ridiculous, the way her husband monopolised him. To think she'd been worried he might not accept another man's son.

'All right, Robbie,' said Belle as Edward helped her to her feet. 'I'll come to the sales too. You can tell me all about those rams.'

Robbie's face lit up. 'We're buying Saxon Merinos, Mama. They grow extra fine, soft wool.' He stepped out from behind Edward and went to his mother. She reached out and stroked his hair. 'Papa wants some Lincoln and Southdown ewes too.'

'Does he?' said Belle, well-pleased with the compromise she'd proposed. 'That's settled then.'

Edward frowned. 'What would people think of me dragging my pregnant wife around a muddy sales ground?'

'Who gives a hoot what people think?'

'Sorry, Belle, I'm afraid I can't allow it.'

'You can't allow it?' Her voice rose a notch. Robbie edged away from his mother. 'Since when do I need your permission?' Eddie had never spoken to her in such a way before.

'That came out all wrong.' Edward's tone softened to one of careful contrition. 'What I meant was that I'm not comfortable jolting you about on those rough roads. It's up to you, of course, but with only a few weeks to go I wish you'd stay home and rest.'

A wave of weariness washed over her. She was tired. Tired of being pregnant. Tired of living in this stuffy house. Tired of her lingering grief at Luke's death. She started to cry, quietly at first, then in great, heaving sobs.

Robbie bolted from the room. Clara's face creased with concern. She rushed to Belle and wrapped chubby arms around her as far as they would reach. 'Please don't cry, Mama. It makes me sad.'

Edward guided Belle over to the bed and gently sat her down. Then he kissed his daughter. 'It makes me sad too, honey. What can we do to cheer Mama up?'

'I know.' The little girl put Panda in Belle's lap. Clara adored that toy, despite it being threadbare and with stuffing coming out. Nobody could ever prise it away for long enough to mend it. 'You keep Panda while I'm at Grandma's,' she said solemnly. 'So you won't be lonely.'

Belle's tears subsided. She and Edward exchanged proud glances. What a special, loving, generous daughter they were blessed with.

'That's a lovely idea, Clara, but I think you'd better take her with you. Panda might find it hard to sleep without you.'

Clara hugged Panda tight, clearly relieved that her mother had not taken up the offer.

Edward took Belle's hand. 'See how very loved you are?'

'Why don't you two get on with things and let me rest. Ask Sarah to get my novel from the parlour. *The Jungle Book*, on the table by the window. And tell her not to lose my place.'

'I'll get it for you myself,' said Edward as the dogs began barking. 'That will be Grandpa wanting his princess. Kiss Mama goodbye.' He hoisted Clara onto his shoulders and they left the room, smiling and blowing kisses.

At least they were happy. Belle herself remained on the edge of tears. She padded to the window and watched her father climb down from the seat of the brougham. Her favourite carriage had been repainted a lovely claret colour, and she didn't recognise the in-hand pair of matched bays drawing it. With a wrench, she realised Papa must have bought them without consulting her. There was a time, not so long ago, when he wouldn't have dreamed of doing such a thing. Buying horses had always been a family affair. Belle loved the excitement of visiting stables, trialling new teams, comparing and researching pedigrees. Loved having the final say, as she invariably did.

Not any more. Papa loaded Clara's case, and then Clara herself into the elegant little coach. His princess. They looked up at her window and waved. Belle's heart lurched with loneliness – and something more, something shameful. Envy. Envy of her own daughter. What was wrong with her?

She hadn't paid much attention when her mother said marriage wasn't enough. When she said a woman needed to fill her life with something more meaningful than domesticity. That's why Mama had started the school at the mining camp. How often, as a girl, had Belle teased her? 'You want to appear charitable, Mama. That is your goal.' Since Belle had started her own family, she'd regretted those unkind words. Where would the poor of Hills End be without that school? It had grown from half-a-dozen children in an old miner's cottage, to over fifty pupils in a building designed for the purpose.

Well-loved by the townsfolk, the school not only offered an affordable education, but also held evening classes for women on subjects such as childbirth, health and hygiene. Belle was no longer a carefree, thoughtless girl. She understood the importance of these things. Perhaps, when the baby was born, she would volunteer there. It would please Mama and be an escape from the tedium of Canterbury Downs.

The matched pair took off for Binburra at a spanking trot. Eddie's phaeton swung into the driveway and drew to a halt at the front door. He emerged from under the bluestone verandah. Robbie followed close behind him, clutching a small leather case, which contained the sheep stud books. They climbed in and drove away.

Belle arched her aching spine. Another empty afternoon stretched before her. What was the point of even getting dressed? She climbed under the covers, eager to dive into her Indian jungle adventure. Belle made herself comfortable, and looked across at the bedside table. Eddie had forgotten to bring up her book.

# CHAPTER 45

S ettlement day. The Superior Mine had officially changed hands. Luke and Tau drew their horses to a halt on high ground over-looking the deserted diggings. Spread out before them lay a rambling open-cut quarry of ten acres or more. The sides had been dug out first, and the excavation had taken on the shape of a vast wheel, with tall blocks of standing ground in the middle and piles of tailings round the edge. A ramshackle collection of yards, sheds and huts ran along the river on the eastern flank. A dozen draught horses, their ribs protruding, hung their heads over rails, and a few half-starved bullocks crowded together in the spindly shade of some thorn trees.

Luke clapped his companion on the back. 'Lead on, Tau. I want the full tour.'

When Luke cheated Herman Smit out of his mine, he'd never intended to operate it. He'd meant to shut it down, free the workers from their labour contracts and send them on their way. However, when he arrived at the bank to execute the agreement, Eli had delivered some unwelcome news.

'Are you sure you want to go through with this? Buying the mine will leave you perilously short of funds, Colonel. Even if I undervalue it, as of course I will . . .'

'Do you speak as my banker or my friend?'

'As both.'

Luke had stared at him, blankly. For years he'd been living off old Clarry's fortune, careless of how he spent it. Travelling where he wanted, buying what he wanted. Sending his mother and sister generous monthly allowances. To a poor boy like him, it had seemed an inexhaustible amount. Yet, here was Eli saying he was running out of money.

'How much is left?'

'Enough to live comfortably for a year or so.'

'No more than that?'

'Not without an additional source of revenue. You've purchased a great many farms recently, but none will give a quick return. Can you call on family money? Or perhaps you have investments I'm unaware of?'

Luke shook his head. He had no investments. Not growing up with money meant never learning how to manage it. Putting it in the bank had been the extent of his financial plan. Still, a year was plenty of time. He could work a couple of his farms instead of turning them back to bush. Generate an income that way.

'If you're determined to go ahead, why not operate the mine?' said Eli. 'It's foolish to close it down. Now Smit's hit blue ground, it has potential.'

Luke turned the idea over in his mind. Playing safe and turning farmer wouldn't complete the humiliation of Herman Smit. Finding diamonds would.

'Execute the deed, Eli,' he'd said at last. 'Looks like I'm in the mining business.'


'I've learned a bit about goldmines in my time,' said Luke as Tau showed him round the open cut. 'But I haven't a clue about all this. I bloody well hope you do.'

'What would I know?' said Tau. 'Hauling rocks all day like a donkey.'

Yet for a donkey he seemed surprisingly knowledgeable.

'Why are the diggings shaped like a circle?' asked Luke.

'We dig out the sides first, because hauling is easiest from the edges.'

'What's this *blue ground* people talk about?'

Tau took him to the edge of an eighty-foot pit. 'See how the earth changes colour down there?' Luke peered over the cliff. The reef walls consisted of streaky yellow shale, but at the base the rocks turned a bluish-black. 'That dark rock is blue ground. Holds the best diamonds, but it's hard as iron.'

'So . . . ?'

Tau grinned and threw his arms wide. 'Kaboom! We need dynamite. Baas Smit is an idiot. Sends us to dig out solid rock with picks and shovels, then rages and beats us when we can't.'

Since the cave collapse that killed Bear, dynamite scared the hell out of Luke. Here, it would be an everyday tool of trade. He gazed out over the ruined landscape of craters and cliffs and mullock heaps. He intended to discover all there was to know about diamonds. He intended to turn this rundown, unproductive mine into a profitable business, but he would not spend his days in the noise and dust and heat. He'd had his fill of pits and explosions. What he needed was a manager he could trust, someone to run the mine while he established the game reserves.

'Tau,' he said. 'I have a proposition for you.'


Luke checked the provisions in his saddlebags one last time, then tightened Caesar's girth. 'Choose two good men as your foremen,' said Luke. 'Buy new bullocks and horses, and turn out the old ones while I'm away.'

'The storehouse is empty,' said Tau.

'And whose fault is that?' Luke grinned. 'Go into town and stock up. No stinting on quality, I want my workers well fed. You're authorised to put things on my account.' He turned to Sizani, who was stroking Caesar's soft nose. 'Go with him. Make sure he's not robbed.'

Sizani and Tau exchanged broad smiles. They were sweet on each other and looked for any excuse to be together.

Luke hadn't owned the mine for long, but things were moving quickly. He'd already renegotiated the workers' labour contacts and offered to re-employ them. To a man, they'd signed on. Full board and thirty shillings a week was six times what Smit had been paying them – or, more to the point, not paying them.

Tau had a reasonable working knowledge of the mine, and had thrown himself into the manager's role with enthusiasm. Sizani was also proving useful, organising accounts, supplies and pay. So much so that she had little time for the house. 'Find someone to take over your duties,' Luke told her. 'You're worth more in the office.'

Leaving Tau in charge, Luke was heading off for a few weeks on a mission to learn all he could about modernising the mine. He thought back to the massive steam pumps and stamper rams of the Hills End mine. Henry Abbott might have been a monster, but he was a shrewd businessman. He'd understood the value of mechanisation. There must be a better way than picks and shovels and bullock carts.

Luke had spent the last few weeks identifying problems. The collapse of reef walls was a constant threat, and excavations were haphazard. Dirt was piled on adjacent ground for sorting, obstructing the digging of productive land. Diamond-bearing soil was carted out for washing in wagons: twelve-hundred-weight loads drawn by six oxen, and as many drivers and assistants. Getting those wagons from the bottom of the mine to the top was a nightmare, especially when it rained.

On his travels, Luke had made many friends, some of whom owed him favours. One such friend worked as a supervisor at the famous De Beers diamond mine at Kimberley in the Northern Cape Province. Luke planned to visit him and learn all he could.

Luke clasped Tau's hand, then mounted Caesar. 'Keep thing's running, brother. I'll be back.'

# CHAPTER 46

Belle waited until after dinner, after the three children had gone to bed. After Eddie had finished his first glass of cognac before the fire and poured himself a second.

She studied him while he read the paper and sipped his drink. A handsome man, the picture of sartorial elegance, though that moustache made him look older than he was. Forehead high and straight. Sandy hair cut short these days. She preferred it when it was longer, long enough to move in a breeze. And those steel blue eyes. Eddie couldn't help it, of course, it was just . . . every year there was more of his father about him. She rubbed the goosebumps from her arms.

He glanced up from his reading and caught her watching him. His eyes crinkled with warmth, and the resemblance to Henry vanished. Eddie patted the Chesterfield couch. She sat beside him, the cold leather chilling her legs through her dress.

'Can we talk, Eddie. Anne is two years old now, and I've made a decision. I'm going to help Mama teach children at the mine school.'

Edward put down his drink and took his time rolling a cigarette. Belle shifted in her seat. She hated the suspense, the feeling that she was waiting for permission.

'Will you delay a while longer?' he said at last. 'Our sweet baby girl is still so young. Surely your place is here, with us. With your own children.'

Belle pressed her lips together.

'Don't be like that,' he said.

Her eyes flashed. 'Tell me then, Eddie, how should I be?' She sprang to her feet, prepared for an argument. 'It's different for you. You actually do things. I can't drop a handkerchief without some servant rushing to pick it up for me. Robbie and Clara are busy all day with tutors and governesses. You don't approve of me going with Papa into the mountains any more. Grace is married and moved to Hobart . . .'

He stood up and took her hands in his. 'Belle, sweetheart, I understand, I do. The girl I fell in love with wasn't one to sit around.' His smile, one of infinite affection, disarmed her. 'I propose a compromise?' She watched him, wary yet curious. 'Remember how you loved to draw when we first met? I shall build a studio in the garden, and engage an art teacher – the best I can find. Would that amuse you until Anne is a little older?'

Belle was after a lot more than amusement. She was after fulfilment. But Eddie was right about one thing: she had loved to draw, and the idea of studying art intrigued her. A favourite childhood memory was sitting with Luke and her father, painting animals and birds. Later, when she moved to Binburra, it was landscapes that had captivated her. The mountains and forest casting their spell, colours transforming, making her see with different eyes.

Leaves weren't green any more. They were apple and olive and mistletoe. Sage-green, sea-green and the green of sprouting wheat. Willow-green, pine-green and the green of alpine moss. Shadows were no longer grey or black. They were cobalt and indigo and midnight blue. Charcoal, iron-grey, driftwood-brown and every shade in between.

'Well?' His hand brushed her hair. 'What do you say?'

She was touched he'd remembered her old passion for painting. It helped close the space between them. 'I would love my own studio.' He squeezed her hand. 'But I do intend to teach, sooner or later.'

He put his arm round her waist. 'Who knows? There may soon be a new baby to keep you busy.'

A twinge of guilt made her shift away. Belle didn't want a new baby to keep her busy. She'd learned Whisky's simple trick. To avoid pregnancy, avoid sex. On the occasions when Eddie persuaded her, she used a thin sponge soaked in quinine as a contraceptive.

The art teacher duly arrived, having been lured away from a Sydney girls school by Edward's deep pockets and the promise of a talented student. Miss Emily Durant was a woman of indeterminate age, neither old nor young, who boasted of French heritage. She moved into the ivy-covered guesthouse nestled in a corner of the garden.

Everything about Emily fascinated Belle. Her self-assurance and flaming red hair. The fact she'd travelled the world on her own. 'Men have no right to rule our lives,' she said when Belle asked why she'd never married. Her wonderful collection of books and magazines, especially those featuring modern art. When Emily showed her a colour plate of Arthur Streeton's *Still glides the stream, and shall for ever glide*, Belle had burst into tears. She wanted her own brush to embrace the sun, sky, water and hills that way. She wanted to celebrate Tasmania's diverse landscape with a rainbow palette.

Emily, however, had other ideas. She made Belle sketch vases and coffeepots in black and white, saying, 'Still-life drawing is the best school, the very best exercise for artists.' When Belle complained, Emily wagged a finger. 'This is how to learn light and perspective. It gives you the tools to paint everything else.'

One morning, Belle was sitting in her teacher's little parlour. Emily had taken down the curtains and converted it to a makeshift studio. Autumn light streamed in, casting the room in shades of soft gold. Belle wished she could swap homes. The cottage was a far more cheerful place than the main house. Belle studied her half-completed sketch of a fruit bowl and frowned. Drawing bananas wasn't her idea of art.

Emily looked up from her own work. 'Let me try to convince you once more about the importance of practising object drawing.' Emily took a book from the shelf, bookmarked a few pages and handed it over.

Belle studied the three prints by William Harnett: *Secretary's Table*, *A Study Table*, *The Banker's Table*. Tabletops crammed with eclectic collections of objects. And suddenly she understood what Emily meant. Harnett was less painter than illusionist, the coins and quills and books so real she wanted to pluck them from the page.

Emily smiled as comprehension dawned on Belle's face. 'Streeton, Tom Roberts, McCubbin – all these modern impressionists you admire so much? To master the art of impressionism, first you must master realism.'

Belle tackled her sketch with renewed enthusiasm.

Everything was so much better, so much happier now. Belle had become consumed with her art. Emily wasn't only an inspiring teacher, but also an excellent companion. Eddie was touchingly happy to have pleased her. He threw himself into planning her studio, his designs growing grander by the day. Belle wasn't impatient. She was free to escape to the sunny cottage whenever she wanted.

Even her relationship with Robbie was improving. Her baffling little boy was seven years old now. Simple children's games like skittles and hopscotch confused him, yet he could name the elements of the periodic table and recite generations of ram pedigrees. He also had a fascination with art. At last, Belle had a way to connect with her son.

Mornings saw Robbie trotting down to the cottage, as often as going to work with his father. Emily would set him up with paper and pencils, or sometimes an easel and palette of paints. He had a talent for detailed depictions of buildings.

'You're stealing my boy away from me, Miss Durant,' Edward said over dinner one evening. 'I might get jealous.'

Eddie's eyes smiled, but there was a toughness behind his joking tone. When his mouth took on that hard twist, Belle was glad he was on her side.

. . .

Emily's teaching moved on apace, and she seemed well-pleased with her student's aptitude and commitment. She introduced the new topic of portraits by referring Belle to a beautiful set of da Vinci reproduction notebooks.

'Although renowned for his portrait painting, I admire some of these informal sketches more than his popular pieces.'

'These are in my father's library,' said Belle as she turned the pages. 'When we were children, he'd have us copy the animal sketches. My favourites were the horses.'

'Leonardo had a great love of horses,' said Emily. 'Even his rough sketches possess an almost magical, lifelike quality.' She glanced up from the book. 'You said *we*. Aren't you an only child?'

'I meant Luke and me.' Emily's eyebrows asked the question. 'He was my . . . my best friend.' Belle knew how odd that sounded. Little girls didn't have boys as best friends. 'He died.'

'I'm sorry.' Emily tilted her head, pushing her glasses up her nose. For a moment it looked like she might pursue the subject. 'Da Vinci believed artists must not only know the rules of perspective, but also the laws of nature. He dissected corpses to understand the structure of the body. He made thousands of notes and drawings.' Emily turned to a marked page of a gloriously detailed sketch of a girl in profile. 'Da Vinci grouped facial features into three major types: those that lie flat along a baseline, those that rise, and those that fall from the baseline. He urged his students to study these variations until they could confidently paint a portrait from life, or even from memory.'

'From memory?' Belle had never heard of such a thing.

'I confess it's beyond me,' said Emily. 'But I know of those who can. It requires great skill, and depends on how well the artist can recall a particular face.'

An image exploded inside Belle's mind, an image recorded years ago in exquisite, heart-breaking detail. One she'd struggled to forget. Luke's face, bronzed by wind and sun. Lips, warm and sweet. Dark eyes, kind eyes, filled with a wild sensuality that stirred her blood. A portrait of intelligence and strength. How many times had she longed for a photograph of that dear face? Belle's cheeks flamed, her mind alive with possibilities.

Emily gave her a curious look. 'You seem quite taken by the concept. However, let's leave advanced portraiture until later, shall we?'

Belle pushed back her chair, and started gathering up her art materials.

'What are you doing?' asked Emily. 'We've barely begun.'

'I'm checking on the new studio.' Belle could hardly contain her excitement. 'Eddie said it might be finished today.'

'Excellent,' said Emily. 'We shall move our lessons there, and I can reclaim my parlour.'

'Sorry.' Belle headed for the door. 'The studio is mine.'

## CHAPTER 47

L uke returned from his time in Kimberley, head spinning with information and eager to apply what he'd learned.

'How did you fare while I was away?'

Tau took a leather pouch from his belt and poured out a quantity of diamonds. 'These are our best.'

Luke examined them in the light of his new knowledge. Nothing special, the biggest barely a carat. All of them marked and off-colour. Weight was important, but transparency and flawlessness defined a stone's value. 'What's the yield?'

Tau grinned at him. 'At least you sound like you know what you're talking about.'

Luke playfully punched his arm. 'Well?'

'Not even quarter of a carat.'

Luke frowned. The yield was calculated from the number of carats found in sixteen cubic feet of broken blue ground. The average yield at the Kimberley mine was more than two carats. Stones weighing seventeen carats and more were common.

'We've had problems. Reef cave-ins,' said Tau. 'And when we dig down forty feet or so, the pits fill with water.'

'What happens then?'

Tau shrugged. 'We dig somewhere else. That's what Baas Smit did.'

Madness. Digging a series of shallow forty-foot holes was a waste of time. True diamond-bearing breccia was found at more than twice that depth. They'd need pumps to drain the water.

The cave-ins on the open cut couldn't be so easily fixed. Some mine owners excavated the reef in stepped terraces, but that was only delaying the inevitable. Sooner or later there'd be an avalanche of weathered, unstable ground threatening worker safety and halting production. The only permanent solution was to take the mine underground.

Luke was so lost in thought, he didn't notice someone coming out of the house with a tray. Only when the drinks were on the table did he look up. This young woman must be Sizani's replacement. Wild hair. No maid's uniform or colourful kanga. Instead, she wore men's trousers and a bush shirt that pulled tight across her breasts.

'Meet my sister,' said Tau. 'Nandi.'

Her oval face and chiselled cheekbones framed large eyes, flecked with gold. She was tall and lean with narrow hips and long, long legs. She moved with the grace of a cheetah. Luke sucked in a quick breath. Tau's sister was strikingly beautiful.

Nandi didn't smile, as most maids would. She didn't curtsey or say, 'Pleased to meet you, baas.' Instead she regarded him with a cool, haughty expression. Then, with head held high, she swept from the porch without a word.

Tau was watching Luke. 'She's a pretty girl, eh?'

'Why yes.' Luke still felt a little mesmerised 'Very pretty. But I don't think she likes me.'

'Nandi doesn't like any man.' Tau swigged his beer. 'Except for me, of course.'

'Why not?'

Shouting and clattering came from the kitchen. Then a scream. Sizani came running out holding a wooden spoon. 'Lions, baas. There's lions.'

Surely not. But Luke snatched his rifle, which was never far away.

Tau raised his hand. 'No, Luke. It's all right.'

'All right?' cried Sizani. 'How is lions in the kitchen all right? They're eating your sister.'

Luke rushed inside, where an astonishing scene awaited him: Nandi, with a lion attached to each leg.

'Umfazi, Baby,' she said, 'get down.'

A third lion emerged from behind the door, and grabbed the seat of her pants.

The lions tore at the cotton, shaking their heads and growling. Nandi's legs and shapely rear emerged progressively through the rips.

Luke lowered his rifle. He knew lions. These were just cubs, though well-grown ones, and this was play, not aggression. He guessed they were between four and five months old. Their coats retained the dark rosettes of youth, and the tufts on their tails were only just starting to grow. Still, each cub must have weighed fifty pounds. Nandi had sunk to the floor beneath their weight. Where on earth had these gorgeous lions come from?

Luke and Tau went to Nandi's aid, wrestling the cubs off her, though she seemed curiously calm and largely unharmed. Her assailants directed their mischief elsewhere, standing on hind legs to swat things from the benchtops. One of them made off with a loaf of bread. A chopping board went flying, followed by a decorative soup tureen. It smashed into a thousand pieces, splashing its contents all over the floor. The youngsters greedily lapped up the spill.

Sizani, standing in the doorway, yelled her displeasure. She seized a broom and advanced on the cubs, keeping up a nonstop tirade of abuse. The youngsters yowled in protest as she beat them over their heads. Luke fought off a painful pang of remembrance – Mrs Scott laying into Bear, driving him from the bed as Luke lay recovering from the mine accident that killed Angus.

Nandi jumped to her feet and snatched the broom from Sizani. 'Leave them alone. You're hurting them.'

Tau roared with laughter as the cubs escaped out the back door. 'Come, sister. Time to explain your children to the Colonel.'

. . .

Encouraged by her brother, and several cups of Cape wine, Nandi told her story.

'Tau and I grew up on a mission. When I was very little, I believed Father Mackenzie was my father. When I was older I learned this was not true, and that the Boers and British had stolen our country. I felt betrayed. Then I met a man. He was very handsome.' She lowered her eyes. 'Khosan said he loved me. I wanted a man to love me very much.'

Luke noticed a pulse starting in Tau's throat. 'I tried to warn you—'

Nandi silenced him with a look. 'Yes, brother, you did, yet I chose not to listen. I thought Khosan was a hero, fighting to reclaim our country. In truth, he was no better than a bandit, using the cause of freedom to excuse his thuggery. He slaughtered our wildlife, selling trophies and skins to the very men he professed to hate. He misused our own people. When I tried to leave, he threatened me. When my son was stillborn, he called me cursed.'

Luke was struck by the fundamental unfairness women faced regarding sex and children. Taking the blame for bearing dead babies. Forced into loveless marriages. The fear of rape. Becky, Nandi, even his beloved Belle had suffered from a double standard that left women wholly burdened and men barely burdened at all.

Tau moved to stand behind Nandi's chair and wrapped his strong arms about her.

'After my baby died, Khosan brought me three newborn lion cubs: Baby, Umfazi and Girl. I raised them with goat's milk; I loved them like my children. He said a man would come and buy them for a zoo. We waited and waited, but the man did not come. Khosan grew impatient. He said they were growing too big and eating too much meat. One night he said he would kill them, so we ran away.'

'Where have you come from?' asked Luke.

'The bush, outside Isanti.'

'Isanti? That's a hundred miles away. How did you bring the cubs through the towns?'

'I didn't. Someone would have shot them or stolen them.'

Luke stared at her in disbelief and open admiration. 'You came cross-country in mid-summer?' It was a miracle any of them had survived. 'One day you must tell me of your adventure.'

Another crash came from the kitchen, followed by Sizani's scream. Nandi rushed out.

Luke turned to Tau. 'Ask Lwazi to butcher a goat for the cubs. And, Tau, Nandi will not do as Sizani's replacement. She's entirely unsuitable. You must engage somebody else.'

Tau's nostrils flared. 'Nandi is my sister. She needs a job, somewhere safe to stay. If she goes, I go.'

'Oh, I have a position in mind for her,' said Luke. 'Just not the position of maid. A woman like that is wasted serving drinks.'

'Nandi is no fucking *loskind*.' Tau's face was a storm cloud. 'You will respect her.'

'Calm down, big brother. Your sister's honour is safe enough. I want Nandi to work with me to establish the game reserve. I want her for my head ranger.'

Tau's mouth fell open. 'Head ranger? But she is a woman.'

'Now who isn't respecting Nandi?' Tau looked confused. 'Your little sister made it across a hundred miles of savannah in high summer, on foot and by herself. Risked her life to save three lion cubs. Can you imagine anyone more qualified to protect Themba's animals?'

A slow smile of understanding spread across Tau's face. 'You are right, Luke. Nandi is strong, like a man.'

'And braver than most. Can she handle a rifle?'

'As well as me,' said Tau.

'It's settled then. Go tell her the good news.'


To say that Nandi was thrilled with her new job would have been a serious understatement. She threw herself into her duties with such pride and enthusiasm, Luke could barely keep up. Her understanding of local wildlife proved a bonus.

'We will teach your cubs to hunt, and release them right here at Themba.'

'Are there not lions here already? Yes? Then we cannot release them,' she said. 'Lionesses in a pride are all related and outside females will not tolerated.'

'I don't intend for your cubs to join the plains pride. Two families of lions once lived at Themba. One pride was killed by poachers. I want your cubs to take their place.'

Nandi frowned. 'Most prides contain at least five females, their cubs, and one or two males. Three lions is not enough. It's too dangerous. I won't allow it.'

Luke's brows lifted in amusement. 'I guess we should find you some more cubs then, and quickly, while your babies are young enough to accept them. Will you allow that?' Nandi's frown slipped. 'It will be your job to care for all of them, Nandi. Help teach them about the wild.'

Her expression changed to one of pure joy, stirring something in Luke's breast, a feeling he'd thought long dead. An excitement about the future, and about sharing it with someone. Luke returned her smile, almost shyly. Nandi was exactly what Themba needed.


The new lions duly arrived. A pair of sisters, Honey and Sal, purchased from a private game park, where they were destined for canned hunting. A pair of brothers, Cain and Abel, orphaned after their man-eater mother was shot – all younger than Nandi's cubs.

Luke had converted two of the rondavels into lion dens, complete with spacious runs. Baby, Umfazi and Girl already occupied one enclosure. The new cubs moved into the run next door.

Nandi wasn't the only one devoted to the lions. Luke couldn't stay away. He hired more staff. A housekeeper, house boy and cook. Men to build paddocks and enclosures. Men to patrol the park borders, freeing up time for him to spend with Nandi and her young charges. Although conscious of the expense, he had little choice. Themba was growing fast, acquiring not only new people, but new animals as well.

Luke planned to restock the savannah with species that had been hunted out locally. He was especially interested in predators – cheetahs, caracals and Cape wild dogs. But he also hoped to re-establish herbivores. Eland and kudu were missing at Themba. Rhinos, too. They had presented easy targets for poachers.

Luke put out the call, and the wildlife trickled in. He only paid for rare animals that would otherwise be killed for their hides and horns. Yet he was determined to accept any creatures who could rightfully claim a home on South Africa's plains. Baboons that had grown too big and dangerous to keep as pets. An orphaned litter of aardwolves. A mangy, half-starved buffalo calf. All were welcome at Themba.

Twelve months later, Luke sat in Eli Goldsmith's office, a poky space off the main building of the Nisopho Bank. Sluggish dust motes floated in the dull light. Even the fierce African sun struggled to shine through Eli's grimy window. Sweat trickled down Luke's forehead, and not just from the heat. Luke was here for more money, and going by his friend's furrowed brow he wouldn't be keen to hand it over.

Agonising minutes ticked by as Eli pored over the pile of accounts and ledgers. Luke stood up and paced the floor. The room was stifling. He tried to open the window, but it wouldn't budge.

At last Eli looked up. 'Sit down. You've spent a lot of money in the past year, Colonel. These sums make my eyes water.'

'Not *spent*,' said Luke, toying with a pencil. 'Invested. I've gone underground. It will soon be the twentieth century and I need a twentieth-century mine. Modern machinery that is far more efficient and spares the men. Tramways to replace bullock teams. Pulverising engines to break down the blue ground, instead of picks and shovels.' The pencil snapped. 'Rotary washing machines can process six hundred loads of dig a day, and find diamonds missed by dry sorting. They'll pay for themselves in no time.'

'I hope so,' said Eli. 'Because, at present, your expense-to-profit ratio is a catastrophe.' He shuffled the papers before him. 'Look at this.' He pointed to an item on the page. 'A fortune for ladders, when your Kaffirs could knock some together for a fraction of the cost.'

'Timber rots. We need iron ladders down the shafts.'

'Three hundred pounds worth?'

'Better that than a man's life.'

Eli handed Luke a wages record. 'And this? Even accounting for the fact that you pay your miners like kings, how is this possible? You said mechanising the mine meant a smaller workforce. According to this, you're employing and supporting thirty more Africans than you did before.'

Luke glanced at the document. 'These people aren't all miners. Some work for me at Themba.'

Eli stared in disbelief. 'You need such a large staff?'

Luke didn't feel like explaining the concept of rangers and wildlife sanctuaries to the banker. Didn't feel like explaining about the school he'd set up for children in the village. He fought vainly with the dingy window one more time, then sank back down in the chair. 'Steam is dead, Eli. I'm importing internal combustion engines and electric motors from England. I need more money.'

'Colonel, I hate to be blunt, but you don't *have* any more money.'

The words hurled Luke back to the time when poverty forced him and Angus down Henry Abbott's deadly mine. Yet, here he was, begging for the chance to invest in the same dirty business. Luke tried to swallow but his mouth was dry with doubt. He had to believe there was a difference between him and the Abbotts of this world. He paid his workers well, didn't he? Was committed to their safety.

'A loan then.' Luke set his jaw. 'I must have this money. We've hit a deep pipe of diamond-bearing ore. Any day now . . .'

'Listen to yourself. You sound like Herman.'

'Please, Eli.'

Eli shoved the ledgers aside, sweat beading his brow. 'All right, Colonel. The bank will extend credit for six more months. After that, well . . .'

Luke leaned over the desk and shook his hand. 'Thank you, Eli.'

'In return, I'd like a tour of the mine. Your modernisation process sounds most intriguing.'

Minutes later, Luke escaped the suffocating office, still struggling to nail down the difference between himself and Abbott, or Smit, or dozens like them. Then it came to him. He was ploughing his profits into protecting Nisopho's unique wildlife. Trying to stay true to Daniel's vision. Trying to be a man who, in another lifetime, Belle could have loved.

# CHAPTER 48

'Happy birthday, my darling.' Elizabeth kissed Anne and gave her a small beribboned box. The little girl's green eyes widened.

'What beautiful wrapping,' Belle said to her mother.

'I want Clara to watch me open it.' Anne dashed from the verandah to where the other children were playing *Ring a ring a Rosie* with Emily on the lawn.

Daniel leaned back in his chair, stretched his legs and reached for his tobacco pipe, a recently acquired vice. 'Where has the time gone, Lizzie? Seems like only yesterday when our own beautiful daughter had her third birthday party.'

Belle sat down beside her mother. 'What did you give Anne?'

'A carved wish fairy.'

'Stop filling the girl's head with unscientific nonsense,' said Daniel. 'What will you have her believe in next? Leprechauns?'

'It's just a bit of fun.' Elizabeth poured herself a lemonade from the jug on the table. 'Belle had one when she was little, and it did her no harm.'

Belle smiled. 'You rub the fairy three times and make a wish from the heart.'

'That's right,' said Elizabeth. 'You couldn't think of a wish when I first gave it to you, so I made one for you.'

'Do you remember the wish, Mama?'

Elizabeth reached for her daughter's hand. 'I wished for you to be happy.' A cloud of concern passed over her face. 'Has my wish come true, darling?'

How to answer? She was as happy as she could possibly be – with Luke dead, and this growing distance between her and Eddie, and the vague feeling there was something more she should do with her life. Belle tried to force a smile, but it wouldn't come.

What an ungrateful wretch she was. A loving family. Children. Health, wealth and privilege. Everything most people strived so hard for had been handed her on a platter. Perhaps that's why painting meant so much. You couldn't buy the patience and practice it required, or pay the servants to paint for you. Hard work and talent weren't for sale. Art was the great equaliser.

'Belle? You seem a world away.'

'Of course I'm happy, Mama.'

Elizabeth put down her glass. 'I'm going to Hobart next week. Why not come with me? Leave the children at home. We could do the rounds of the galleries.'

Belle usually resisted such invitations. These days, she found the hustle and bustle of Hobart jarring. Her spirit belonged to the bush, to the rugged wilderness that dominated the scenery beyond the mansion's manicured grounds. Riding Whisky along lonely forest trails. Capturing the ever-changing mountains with her paintbrush. Here was the wild landscape of her heart, of her happiest memories. The place where she could still feel Luke.

But Elizabeth seemed unusually determined. 'There's an operetta on at the Royal, Victor Herbert's new one. And isn't it about time you visited Grace?'

It had been two years since Grace moved to Hobart. The two friends had hardly seen each other since and Belle missed her.

Elizabeth seemed to sense that, for once, her daughter was open to persuasion. 'You should stay with me, of course, at Coomalong.' Her mother knew how much Belle hated Abbott House. The scene of Becky's rape. The beginning of the end for Luke.

'All right, Mama. I'll talk to Eddie.'

Where was he anyway? Belle hadn't seen him for a while. She scanned the garden. The party games were over. Emily had set up easels on the lawn for the children to paint, but he wasn't there. It wasn't like him to miss the party fun.

'Have you seen him?' she asked her parents.

'He and Robbie went to look for something,' said Daniel.

A worm of worry squirmed in Belle's stomach. 'Where did they go?'

'Down to that studio of yours. Robbie drew a picture of Anne for her birthday and needed help finding it.'

The worm flipped right over. How could that be? She always left the place locked. 'I'd better go see.'

Belle hurried from the verandah and down the garden path. She met Robbie coming back up, clutching his drawing. 'Where's your father?'

'He won't come,' said Robbie. 'He's still looking at your paintings.'

'I'll fetch him,' said Belle. 'You go back to the party.'

She broke into a run. How dare Eddie go through her studio? That was her private place, her sanctuary from the world, the one place at Canterbury Downs where she could truly be herself.

As she drew near, Belle could see Eddie through the window, hunched over a table. She burst in the door. 'How did you get in here?'

He didn't look up. 'Did you really think I wouldn't have a key?'

It was as she feared – dozens of paintings and drawings strewn over the tabletop. All of Luke: Luke and Bear, Luke at the old shack, Luke riding Sheba. Luke magically brought back to life.

Belle steadied her breathing. She tried to view the images objectively, through Eddie's eyes. The first thing she saw was that she'd done a good job. Each detail of Luke's youthful face was recreated with astonishing accuracy. Not a crime in itself. Edward couldn't object to her talent as an artist.

'What does it matter?' she said.

He held up a drawing in black and white, exquisite in its simplicity. 'Oh, it matters to me.'

Belle drew in a quick breath. It was Luke, shirtless by the waterfall, their waterfall. Arm extended as if to take her hand, gazing from the picture. Beckoning for her to join him in the crystal stream. She knew now why Eddie's eyes brimmed with hurt. Each line, each shadow, each loving sweep of the pencil betrayed her passion for the man. Even now she longed to step inside the drawing.

'For Christ's sake, Belle, it's been ten years. Will he always come between us?'

Eddie's cry came from the heart. How betrayed he must feel. She opened her mouth to say sorry.

'Burn them.'

The apology died on her lips.

'Burn them, Belle.' His voice trembled. 'And we'll never speak of this again.'

She blinked hard. Could she? For the sake of her marriage, her family. Could she destroy these drawings of her lost love?

Belle moved forward, one halting step at a time. She picked up a charcoal sketch – Luke cradling a pair of Sasha's puppies in his arms.

Edward took a matchbox from the mantle and pointed to the fire-place. 'Do it. For us.'

Belle stared at the picture awhile, then clutched it to her breast. 'I can't, Eddie. I won't.'

Anger replaced the pain in his eyes. 'Then I will.' He picked up a small sketch – a man gazing out across a forested valley, which was purple with sunset. Although drawn from behind, there was no doubt the man was Luke. The narrow hips and broad shoulders. The supple stance. The way his hair grew in a peak at the nape of the neck.

Edward set fire to the corner of the paper.

A cry erupted from Belle's throat. She launched herself at him, snatching at the sketch, scarlet with desperation and rage. The flame blew out, and the singed piece of paper fluttered to the floor. Belle dived for it, but Edward was quicker. He seized the sketch and tore it in two. Then he grabbed Belle, roughly pinning her arms to her side, propelling her towards the door. With a shove, he pushed her from the studio.

Belle landed hard on her knees. Behind her, the sound of a key turning in the lock.

She climbed to her feet, screaming and pounding on the door. Through the window, a terrible sight greeted her. Edward, ripping up her paintings and drawings. Sacrificing them to a hungry flame that lurked in the hearth. It was like losing Luke all over again.

She picked up a rock from the edge of the path and smashed the window, reaching through to fumble with the lock. The jagged glass sliced her arm, but she didn't feel it. Blood stained the pale green satin of her dress. By the time she managed to open the door, it was too late. What was left of Luke lay in the grate, a pile of dying embers. Silent tears slid down her face.

Edward stepped towards her. 'Your arm. Let me see.'

Belle pulled back. She couldn't bear to look at him. 'I'll never forgive you, Eddie. Never.'

'Yes, you will. Just as I'll forgive you.' He kicked at the cinders, stirring up a twist of smoke. 'I blame this place.' He gestured wildly around him. 'This house, these hills, the very air we breathe. Luke haunts the whole damn lot.'

'Oh my God.' Her mother's shocked voice sounded from the doorway. 'Belle, whatever's happened?'

'She tripped into the window,' said Edward.

Elizabeth grabbed a clean smock from a hook and tied up the wound, which was still bleeding. 'She's shivering. Let's get her to the house.'

Edward offered his arm, but Belle shrugged him away. She tried to avoid her mother's searching eyes, but as usual Elizabeth missed nothing. Not the shrug, nor the knot of tension in the room. Not the rock on the floor in a bed of broken glass. She stepped in to help her daughter up the garden path. Edward trailed behind them.

Belle grimaced. The pain was setting in.

. . .

Belle sat in her bedroom opposite her mother, confessing everything. No point holding back. She had neither the strength nor the will to withstand Elizabeth's interrogation.

'Whatever were you thinking, Belle? I can understand one drawing, as a keepsake, perhaps, or to test your talent. Maybe even two. But . . . how many were there?'

'Dozens.'

'So that's what you've been doing all this time, locked away in that studio of yours.'

'And now Eddie's burnt them, every one.'

'Can you blame him.'

'Yes, I can.' Belle's eyes blazed. 'He had no right. Those pictures were for me, Mama, just for me. I didn't show people, not even Emily. They couldn't hurt anyone.'

'Don't fool yourself, Belle. They could hurt Edward, and they did.'

She couldn't deny it.

'Things will be difficult between you two for a while. Be patient with your husband, darling.'

'What's the point? We're almost like strangers. Eddie works all the time.'

'And you paint all the time.'

'What else should I do?'

'Other than paint portraits of dead lovers, you mean? Perhaps take an interest in your husband's business.'

'Which one of the family businesses should I show an interest in, Mama? Squeezing out small-holders and clearing virgin bush to run sheep? Cutting down the forests I love for timber? Or paying men a pittance to risk their lives down the mine? Emily says it's wrong. She says the mine workers should form a union to fight for better conditions. I never used to think about where our money came from, but now I do.'

'Emily should mind her own business. It's not as simple as that. Wool growing, the timber mill, the mine – they mean jobs for Hills End. The Abbotts have always done these things, Belle. Nothing's changed.'

'I've changed, Mama, and so has Eddie.'

Elizabeth made a face. She nodded towards the door and silently mouthed '*He's coming.*'

'I don't care if he hears.' Belle's voice rose a notch. 'Sometimes I think Eddie's turning into his father, only worried about making a profit. Teaching Robbie to be the same way.' Belle turned to her husband with a defiant glare as he appeared in the doorway. 'I hate how you earn a living. I hate being here in this gloomy house. Sometimes I think I even hate you.'

Edward sat down in the corner chair. His furious expression had been replaced with one of stony indifference. 'It's good to get some honesty for once, to hear how my wife truly feels.'

'Belle's overwrought,' said Elizabeth. 'She didn't mean it.'

'On the contrary, I believe she meant every word.' The new hardness in Edward's eyes gave Belle a chill. 'Did she tell you about the pictures? Yes? They were finely executed, by the way. Strange, to be cuckolded by a ghost.'

'That's nonsense, Edward. Those paintings were mere flights of fancy. You know how imaginative Belle can be.'

Edward remained unmoved. Elizabeth tried once more to smooth things over. 'Your wife feels cooped up here. She needs a break for her health, and for both your sakes. I'll take her with me to Hobart, if that suits you, of course. I feel sure a week or two apart will change both of your perspectives.'

Edward's cold gaze fell on Belle. 'Do you want to go to Hobart, darling?'

She nodded, sensing a trap.

'What an excellent idea. However, I have a better one. Let's not talk of one or two weeks. Let's make the stay permanent.'

Belle blanched. 'Whatever do you mean?'

'I mean I'm moving the family to Abbott House in Hobart. We pack immediately.'

'But why?' said Belle. 'In Hills End you are close to your work.'

'A fact that you seem to despise.' For a moment his mask slipped, and Belle caught a glimpse of real pain. 'I'll appoint local managers.

Our companies are growing too large for me to continue in my current role. It will be more efficient to administer them centrally.'

'What about the children? They're so happy here.' Belle struggled to keep the cry from her voice. 'They'll miss their grandparents terribly, and Robbie loves painting with me in the studio. It's the way I connect with him.'

'He's too old now for home tutors and playing around with paints. It's time he had a first-class education, one befitting an Abbott.'

'But Robbie's not like other boys,' said Belle. 'He learns best by doing. Look at how his arithmetic has improved since going to the wool sales. The best education for him is being out and about with you.'

'That won't be possible in Hobart, I'm afraid, not when I'm working from my office. I'm thinking of Scotch College.'

'But that's in Melbourne.' Elizabeth couldn't help herself. 'Robbie won't cope with boarding school.'

'Why not? I did,' said Edward. 'And if you don't mind, this is between me and my wife.' He gestured towards the door.

For a moment it looked like Elizabeth was going to argue. 'Very well. I'll speak to you later, Belle. Don't say anything you'll regret.' She turned to Edward as she left. 'That advice applies to you too.'

'Stop all this, Eddie,' said Belle when the door closed. 'Please. You've punished me enough.'

The pain of losing the paintings of Luke paled beside this new threat. She simply couldn't live in the city. Her heart, her very soul, belonged to the wild mountains of Hills End.

She watched for the hard line of his mouth to relax. Waited for the warmth to return to his eyes, signalling forgiveness. They'd had arguments before and Edward always came round. But this time his expression didn't soften.

'My mind is made up.'

'*Your* mind. I have a mind as well, Eddie, or have you forgotten? You can't dictate the terms of our marriage merely because you're the man.'

'Did Emily tell you that?'

'She didn't have to. Marriage is supposed to be an equal part-nership.'

'Not this time.' He turned his back, moved to the door, paused once. 'Oh, and Emily is dismissed.'

# CHAPTER 49

L uke looked up at the towering headframe and took a deep
breath. The stink of dynamite. The shattering roar of the blast-
hole drills. It all conspired to take him back to that terrible day at Hills
End when Angus died. Normally he avoided visiting the mine at all
costs, but Tau was away on his honeymoon with Sizani, and somebody had to inspect the new works.

Luke had decided to sink a third shaft in a last-ditch attempt to
make the operation more profitable. With only a trickle of small,
substandard diamonds coming in, he'd been barely breaking even. He
certainly wasn't making enough for Eli to extend him more credit,
and more credit was exactly what he needed. When they discovered a
new pipe of diamond-bearing blue ground, he'd put the last of his
borrowed funds into it.

The engineer started the motor and the windlass ground into
action. Fighting the inevitable claustrophobia, he stepped into the
cage and began his halting journey underground. The new shaft
wasn't finished, only extending one level down, but so far the men
had done a good job. The reef walls were dry, tiered for stability and
the pumping equipment was operational.

The cage hit dirt. Luke started off down the short tunnel, glad it was so shallow. It meant some natural light from the surface still penetrated the gloom. Not enough though. He switched on his new patent-pending battery-powered lamp, the very latest in mine safety. Electric lamps were odourless, smokeless, and emitted less heat than combustion-powered lighting. They could be instantly turned on and off, and avoided fire risk. He'd provided one for each of his miners.

Everything looked good. The modern tram trolley system was in place. It removed ore for crushing, speeding up production and lightening his workers' load. The rock walls looked promising. Pure Kimberlite, the name given to such coarse blue ground after rich finds were made at Kimberley. Everything was in place to make this mine a success. Everything except the diamonds.

Luke turned to go, well-satisfied with the inspection and eager to return to daylight. He'd almost reached the cage when something caught his eye: a glint reflecting in lamplight on the tunnel wall a few feet above his head. He found a ladder and used his pocketknife to prise the shiny object out. This wasn't possible. A diamond? Or was somebody fooling him with a piece of glass?

Heart racing, Luke returned to the surface to inspect his find. It looked real enough, except for its improbable size. Luke took it to Scotty in the mine office, whose job it was to weigh and assess every diamond.

Scotty whistled through his teeth and cleaned the stone. Released from its grimy prison, it shimmered with the light of a thousand stars. 'This came from the new shaft?' He examined the crystal with a jeweller's loupe more slowly than Luke had ever seen. 'No detectable flaws, exceptional clarity, and it has that rare blue-white quality, so treasured by buyers.'

Luke swallowed hard. The year before, a large diamond had been discovered at the struggling Toti Mine, after many years of fruitless operation. The Pietersen Diamond weighed in at over six ounces, or more than eight hundred and fifty carats. Thomas Pietersen became an overnight millionaire.

'Now for the weight.' When Scotty looked up from the scales, his eyes shone with tears. 'Fifteen ounces. Fifteen fucking ounces. That's two thousand, one hundred and twenty-five carats.'

What?

Two years of digging up spotty little pebbles, as Tau called them. Two years of worrying about Themba's animals, and people's jobs, and when the money would run out. And now this? He would be rich again. Not just rich – wealthy beyond measure. He hadn't been able to send his family much money lately. He pictured Mama and Becky in the little cottage behind the school. He could buy them a mansion now. Hell, he could buy them the whole school. And to think Herman Smit had lost this miracle of a mine for the sake of a four-carat stone.

Luke exhaled. The engagement ring that would never grace Belle's finger lay at home, in the darkness of his desk drawer. He would take it out tonight, let its light shine. In a very real way, Belle and that ring were responsible for his change of fortune. How he longed to share this news with her. But that was impossible. She didn't even know he was alive. For her sake, and the sake of their son, it had to stay that way. A wave of emptiness washed over him, and he closed his eyes. Strange, how all the money in the world couldn't buy him what he most wanted.

'Congratulations, Colonel.' Scotty kissed the stone. 'You have just unearthed the biggest diamond in the world.'


Expert analysis in Cape Town confirmed it – the Buchanan Diamond was the largest, rough gem-quality stone ever found. The papers were full of the discovery. It was front page international news.

'See how perfectly smooth it is on one side?' The buyer from Rothschild's bank ran his finger down the diamond's shining surface. 'Sheared off from a much larger stone by natural forces deep underground. It is only a fragment, Colonel, probably less than half of an octahedral crystal. The other portion, and more stones like them, still await discovery in your mine. Cecil Rhodes himself will be green with envy.'

The buyer was right. Shaft three produced gem after gem of exceptional size and quality, though none equalled the sheer grandeur of that first find. The price of diamonds increased exponentially according to their weight. With stones of over one hundred carats, Luke could ask what he liked. For princes and potentates, price proved no object.

At just twenty-seven years of age, Colonel Lucas Buchanan had become a household name, and joined the illustrious ranks of South Africa's richest men.

# CHAPTER 50

'There's trouble brewing in Europe,' said Edward, his head buried in *The Mercury*. 'Germany is building a high seas fleet to compete with our British navy.'

Belle buttered her toast. 'I'm going away for a few days, Eddie. With Grace. To see Robbie and do some shopping.' She refilled Edward's coffee cup. 'We sail on the *Pateena* this Thursday.'

'You'll miss the Premier's Ball. I was counting on you to rescue me from Neil's insufferable stories.' He lowered his newspaper. 'Robbie will be home in a few weeks.'

'I don't want to wait that long.'

He sighed. 'Always the impatient one. You know I miss our boy too, Belle. The holidays can't come soon enough for me.'

*Then why did you send him away?* she wanted to ask. *Why did you tear him from his home and family, from all that was familiar? Was it to punish me for the paintings?* But she knew she'd get no sensible answers. Just platitudes about building character and learning to be a man. Eddie loved their son, she knew that, and in his own misguided way was trying to do the best for him. But Robbie didn't cope well with change, and boarding school had been an unnecessary ordeal. He was different, vulnerable, and children were cruel.

Almost thirteen now, growing tall and handsome, with a heart-wrenching likeness to Luke. Robbie had the physical strength to stand up for himself, yet he seemed more than ever like a lost soul. Especially lost without his father. In some ways, Eddie was equally lost without his son. Those two shared such a special bond. They'd both be so much happier if Robbie could come home. It was maddening, this Abbott tradition of squeezing each male child into the same box.

'The weather's turning, Belle. Spring sailings can be rough. I'd rather you didn't go.'

'Sorry, Eddie, but I simply must. I've promised Grace.'

'Oh, very well, I suppose the girls and I will manage. '

Belle escaped the breakfast room before Edward could think up any more objections. She hadn't been entirely honest. The main purpose of her trip to Melbourne wasn't shopping, or even seeing Robbie. It was to visit Emily, who'd secured a teaching position at Ruyton Girls School.

Since Edward had summarily dismissed Emily three years ago, they'd secretly kept in touch through letters, exchanged via Elizabeth. For Belle, receiving those letters opened a wonderful window on the world, a world beyond insular Hobart society. Emily led a bold, charmed life. She travelled, had adventures, experienced things Belle herself had once dreamed of. Camel journeys across Zanzibar. Gondola rides through Venice. Women's suffrage protests in London's Hyde Park. All as a single woman, with neither the protection nor governance of a man. Belle longed for a similar freedom.

By contrast, she'd never been further than Melbourne. Eddie seemed perfectly happy to stay in Hobart, and expected Belle to do the same, even jealously opposing her spending time at Binburra. Accusing her of seeking out Luke's memory. When was the last time she'd ridden alone into the mountains, or spent time with her parents? She had to wait until they came to Hobart. Papa had been unwell lately with a lung complaint, so even these brief visits had stopped.

The truth was that Eddie had no spirit of adventure. It frustrated Belle beyond measure. Whatever happened to his youthful dreams of exploring the world? He'd once wanted to explore the coasts of Africa and India. Now, he was disinclined to let others oversee his local business interests, and in the last year had turned down invitations to London and New York. Not that she really wished to travel with Eddie by her side any more. The gulf between them yawned too wide. He spent more and more time away from home. Neglecting his daughters. Working late. Evenings at the club. Sometimes he didn't come home at all. Impossible to believe that he'd once been her best friend. Marriage had become a boring, lonely trap.

It was the year nineteen hundred, a brand new millennium. So much she wanted to see and experience. The World's Fair in Paris, showcasing the art, inventions, and architecture of the future. Puccini's acclaimed opera *Tosca* was playing in Rome. The Olympic Games had opened in France and someone had invented a ship that could fly. This coming century was one of magical possibilities. Yet here she was, already thirty years old, and life was passing her by.

There was more. Hateful gossip had reached her ears. Rumours that Eddie was gambling and drinking too much, although he didn't bring it home. Rumours of other women. Perhaps it was her fault. How long was it since she'd welcomed him to her bed? So long that he'd ceased asking.

As Belle went upstairs to pack, she heard the front door close. Eddie wouldn't be home until late that night, perhaps not at all. Though she told herself she didn't care, a surprise tear rolled down her cheek.

She roughly wiped it away. No sense feeling sorry for herself. Not when she had something to look forward to for once. Something more than garden parties and croquet and vacuous talk. Emily was as different from the stuffy Hobart set as night was from day, and it wasn't only Emily who Belle was excited about seeing. Luke's mother and sister also lived in Melbourne. Edward had insisted she not make any contact, and she understood why. The world must not suspect Robbie was Luke's son.

But it had been long enough. Becky taught with Emily at Ruyton. The universe was conspiring to bring them together. A shiver ran up her spine. Seeing Becky and Alice Tyler would, in some small way, reconnect her with Luke. Her breath caught in her throat. Damn that man. Dead thirteen long years. Why, oh why, couldn't she let him go?

'How lovely to see you, Mrs Abbott. Won't you sit down?'

Luke's mother was a tall woman, about sixty, with warm hazel eyes and cheeks that dimpled when she smiled. Still handsome, despite greying hair and a careworn face. She wore an elegant blue afternoon gown of textured satin with turquoise accents.

'Please, Mrs Tyler, call me Belle.'

'And you must call me Alice.'

Belle took a seat in the French wingback chair. She wasn't sure what she'd expected, but it wasn't this beautifully appointed drawing room, handsome enough for the wealthiest banker. The floor boasted carpet of a rose pattern design. Curtains of shot silk hung at the windows. Bouquets of lilies graced sparkling crystal vases on the marble mantle. Papa must still be helping them, and most generously. She hadn't realised.

'I'll pour us some tea. Becky and Emily should be here any minute. They finish teaching at four.'

'What a beautiful pin,' said Belle.

Alice's fingers felt for the butterfly brooch at her neck. 'Isn't it?' Her voice swelled with pride. 'Luke gave this to me.'

Luke? The diamond looked real enough, but it was hard to tell these days. The more interesting question was, when had he given it to Alice? As far as Belle knew, Luke had never travelled home to Hobart after he escaped the prison camp. He'd been concerned about putting his family in danger. Before he went to jail then? No. The brooch was a quality piece, and even as costume jewellery it would have been pricey. How could a poor boy have afforded it?

A murmur of excited voices echoed down the hallway, growing louder, until two people burst into the room. Belle was breathless with anticipation.

Emily hadn't changed, hadn't aged at all. She could have just walked in from the porch at Canterbury Downs. Belle recognised the other woman as well, although they'd never met. Belle greeted Becky a little shyly. She was a female version of Luke. The same brown eyes, with a hint of challenge in them. The same thick, dark hair and even features. Classically beautiful. A woman like Becky would not have lacked for suitors, yet apparently she'd never married.

Emily strode forward and gave her a heartfelt hug. 'So, you've finally escaped your husband's clutches. Don't look so surprised, dear. Your letters betray your true feelings. I know how things are. He doesn't even know you're here, does he?'

Belle had forgotten how blunt Emily could be. She'd been like that herself once: outspoken, unafraid to state her opinion. Yet here she was, shocked to hear a truth so boldly stated. She wasn't used to it. Years of living within the confining rules of polite society had stripped her of directness.

'We haven't known Emily for long,' said Alice. 'But we love her already.'

A maid came in with a silver tray, groaning with pastries and other goodies.

'Thank you, Sylvie. Now sit down, everyone, and try something. Essie bakes the most wonderful cakes, far better than mine.' Becky nodded in an exaggerated way. 'There's no need to agree with me,' scolded her mother.

Servants, too? Belle took an éclair and gazed around the magnificent room. 'You have a lovely home here, Alice.' A harmless enough comment on the face of it, yet she regretted the words as soon as they were out.

'Mama came into an inheritance. She's a wealthy woman.'

It seemed Becky was as straightforward as Emily. There was more than a hint of challenge in her eyes now.

'Oh, I didn't mean . . .' But she had. She might as well have said, *You've come up in the world*.

Alice reached over and patted Belle's hand. 'It's all right, my dear. You're not the first person to wonder where the money comes from.'

An odd choice of words. Perhaps Alice was the beneficiary of a perpetual trust.

'This calls for more than tea,' said Emily. 'It's a celebration, a reunion. Alice, shall I bring out the sherry?'

'Oh yes, dear, and there's champagne in the icebox. I think we could all use a drink.'


Wine flowed freely as the afternoon wore on. With Emily in her element, and Alice the perfect hostess, Belle and Becky had the chance to get to know each other.

'What was Luke like as a child?'

'A real scallywag,' said Becky. 'Got into all sorts of strife, and me with him just as often. Stealing apples from trees for fruit fights. Popping acorns in Mr Wigg's mouth while he sat snoring on his porch. Unhitching horses from overloaded carts when nobody was looking. When the driver came back and raised his whip, the horses just trotted off, leaving the cart behind.'

Belle giggled. She could see Luke doing that. 'He loved horses.'

Becky topped up her glass 'There was a Catholic orphanage near us. The priest used to make the boys stand in the blazing sun for hours while he stood in the shade of an oak tree and preached his sermons. Small kiddies and all. We'd see them faint sometimes. Luke decided to do something about it.'

Alice stopped chatting to Emily and paid attention to the conversation.

'How old was he?' asked Belle.

'Eleven, maybe twelve.'

'What on earth could a child do?'

Becky paused for dramatic effect. 'One night he chopped down the tree.'

Alice gasped. 'You never told me that.'

'He made me swear, Mama.'

'What a scandal at the time. And you're saying it was our Luke?' A grin split Alice's face. 'I've never been prouder of my boy than I am right now.' Alice turned to Belle. 'Oh, he was a wag. Once he turned all my little china pigs a tiny bit each day until they faced the wall. He had me thinking our house was haunted.'

A warm rush of emotion left Belle weak. 'Thank you, Alice, and you too, Becky, for sharing these wonderful stories. I feel so much happier, so much closer to Luke.' Belle felt the first stirring of tears.

Becky's hand flew to her mouth. 'You still love him?'

Emily pulled a chair close and stroked Belle's hair. 'Why don't you tell us all about it.'

With a sob, the dam burst. Belle poured her heart out to these people who had no connection with her life back in Hobart. Free to tell them everything, with no recriminations, no repercussions. Things she'd bottled up for years. Things she couldn't tell Grace or even her own mother. She talked of her crushing loneliness. Of Eddie, and the burnt paintings and the terrible rumours. Of Robbie, and his traumatic birth and how it had made him different from other children. Of her stubborn, impossible love for Luke.

'Luke is Robbie's father?' said Emily. 'That explains a lot. You married Edward under sufferance.'

'You don't understand. Eddie wasn't like this at the start. We were friends; he was kind. I was grateful.'

'My dear girl, gratitude is no basis for marriage.' Emily looked up at the roof, with a small huff. 'It's completely unfair. Pregnant girls are forced to marry or be ruined, though the fathers face no such diabolical choice. An innocent girl like Becky was brutally attacked, yet she's the one who was blamed and shamed and lost her job. Meanwhile Henry Abbott, who it seems was a serial rapist, got off scot-free.'

'Not in the end.' Becky smiled in satisfaction. 'Luke killed Henry.'

'No, not Luke,' said Belle. 'His dog. There's a difference.'

'You're splitting hairs. What if the dog hadn't done the deed?' Becky's steady gaze dared Belle to think it through. 'Luke would have killed Henry to protect you.'

Belle shivered, recalling his words at the end, words burned into her brain. 'I'm like Bear. Not truly civilised.'

'Goodness.' Emily raised her eyebrows. 'I'm liking the sound of this Luke. No wonder Belle is still madly in love with him.'

'Well, of course she is,' said Alice. 'Why wouldn't she be? Luke is simply the finest, most generous, most wonderful man in the world.'

*Is.* Belle fiddled with her hair as the old, familiar pain closed in. It hurt to hear Alice speak of her son in the present tense, like he might walk into the room at any moment.

Becky frowned. It must have upset her as well. 'Mama, can I see you in the parlour please?'

Becky and Alice left the room.

'How does your painting go?' asked Emily. 'My most talented student ever. No, really.'

'I don't paint much now.' Belle lowered her eyes. 'Edward makes it difficult.'

It was true. She couldn't paint a simple landscape without him imagining some connection to Luke. In Hobart it had been easier to give up her art than to bear her husband's simmering jealousy. Yet here in front of Emily, it seemed the confession of a coward who'd sold her soul for a little peace.

'You worry far too much about what Edward thinks. What are you doing tomorrow?'

'Taking Robbie to the zoo.'

'And Sunday?'

'I'm going home on Sunday.'

'No, you're not. You're coming with me to an exhibition of the Heidelberg School.'

'I'm not sure . . .'

'Let me think who's on offer. Tom Roberts, Charles Conder, Arthur Streeton, Frederick McCubbin . . .'

Belle listened, transfixed, as Emily rattled off the names of her artistic heroes. Something stirred inside her, a sense of who she once was and would be again.

'When should we meet?'

# CHAPTER 51

The old bull lay like a great grey boulder on the riverbank. Inkosi had not died easily. The ground around was soaked in blood, and churned from the thrashing of giant limbs as he'd struggled to stand on wounded knees. Bullets had ripped open the heavy folds of his flank, and one great tusk ploughed into the ground to half its length. The other arched over Nandi's head, where she crouched beside the body. She ran a hand along its smooth surface, then glanced back at Luke, her expression full of sorrow.

Inkosi had not been killed for his ivory, although no doubt men would risk venturing onto Themba land to claim the tusks. He'd been killed for rampaging through the local farmers' fields once too often, and was the fourth elephant to die for this crime in a month.

Luke slid down the bank to join Nandi, hollow with sadness. Stroking the great lifeless trunk, still warm. He loved all Themba's elephants, but this old bull had a special place in his heart. He remembered the day they'd first met with vivid clarity, not far from this very spot. Inkosi bathing in the river, allowing Luke the best view of an elephant he'd ever had. Vast upturned tusks, as thick as a man's body at the base. They must have weighed two hundred pounds each. Bullet holes in his huge flapping ears. The strange prehensile trunk with its soft, fleshy tip, searching the air.

Luke had moved nearer, and nearer again, drawn by the tusker's ancient eyes, eyes that stared straight into his soul. Overcome with a feeling of such majesty that he could not turn away. It was dangerous to approach an elephant so closely, especially a bull, yet something told him not to be afraid. When Inkosi moved off upriver, Luke went with him.

That began an odd alliance between the elephant and the man. They would disappear together for days at a time. Why Inkosi tolerated him, Luke never knew. Sometimes young bulls would join old ones to learn the laws of the savannah from the patriarch. Where to find choice seasonal fruit and seed pods. How to find water in the desert. When to seek out females in oestrus. Perhaps Inkosi accepted him in this time-honoured role. Whatever the reason, the bull seemed to enjoy his companionship and Luke became well-versed in elephant lore.

He would have risked his life to stand between his old friend and the guns. Yet now he faced the dreadful task of hacking Inkosi's tusks from his skull and burying them. He'd be damned if others would profit from the bull's death. After that, he'd lead Cain and Abel's pride to the riverbank. The brothers were seven years old now, and in their prime. They had many young cubs, and the carcass would provide them with weeks of meat.

Luke offered Nandi his hand and pulled her to her feet.

'We must not let this happen again,' she said. 'We must keep the elephants from the farms.'

'How? The season is dry,' said Luke. 'They're hungry.'

'Hungry for maize, yes. Hungry for beans. But not hungry for chillies.'

'Not hungry for chillies . . . why do women talk in riddles?'

'When I was a child at the mission, elephants sometimes came through the compound at night, trampling fences and hurting people. We made a brick of chilli mixed with elephant dung and put hot coals on top. The smoke kept them away.'

'We can't do that all the way along our boundaries.'

'No, we can do better. Elephants hate chillies. You are a rich man. Pay our neighbours to grow chillies instead.'

Luke turned the concept over in his mind. Nandi was famous for coming up with unusual solutions and he'd learned not to dismiss her ideas without proper consideration.

'Chillies won't feed people's families.'

'But they bring a high price,' said Nandi. 'If you can support farmers until their harvest is ready, they will earn more money than with maize and beans. And buffer rows of chilli plants will protect their own food crops.'

The more Luke thought about it, the more he liked it. It would keep Themba's elephants out of conflict with man, and improve the lot of local farmers at the same time. Everyone would win.

'Nandi, you're a genius.' He picked her up, and spun her around until they were both dizzy. When he set her back down, she was breathless and glowing. She looked very beautiful, with her laughing face and polished skin. He fought a sudden urge to take her in his arms again.

'You are pleased?'

'You know I am, Nandi. Everything about you pleases me.'

She held his gaze. There was an invitation in those dark, lustrous eyes. He reached out to touch her cheek. Nandi was a strong, intelligent, desirable woman who shared his passion for the animals of Africa. She had feelings for him – he didn't need Tau to tell him. He cared for her too, loved her in his own way.

But she wasn't Belle.

Luke took one last look at Inkosi, wishing his friend a silent goodbye. 'Time to go, Nandi. We must fetch the river pride before the hyenas come.'


That night Luke lay awake, listening to the distant roar of lions and the barking of jackals. Thinking about how much his life had changed, and how much it had stayed the same.

The fortune of a king, yet he slept in the same humble room as before. Money to travel the world, yet he spent each day working for the animals of Themba alongside his staff. Famous enough to woo and win the world's most beautiful women, yet his heart remained stubbornly true to a girl he hadn't seen for fifteen years. A girl he didn't deserve, could never have, and who was married to another man. What was wrong with him? No wonder Tau thought he was crazy. Put so bluntly, it sounded insane, even to him.

The last two letters from Becky lay unopened on the table beside his bed. The life she talked about back in Australia seemed more and more unreal to him. He refused to return, even briefly. It would open up old wounds. Instead he worked on convincing his mother and sister to come and live in South Africa.

They'd been over for visits, however Mama complained the climate didn't suit, and Becky remained wedded to her teaching. Even the promise of an estate in Constantia couldn't sway them. It didn't help that the damn war still raged in some provinces, although it didn't touch Themba's little corner of the veldt.

Small feet pattered on the roof above and something buzzed near his face, hopefully outside the mosquito net. Luke waved it away, then sat up, reaching in the dark for the bottle of tonic water beside his bed.

Problem was, he didn't feel any different today than when he was eighteen and running from the law. If Belle was with him right now, he still wouldn't feel worthy. He'd failed her, and Daniel, and Bear. Failed the son he'd never known. Nothing could ever change that.

Luke lay back again and closed his eyes. Images of the old life in Tasmania danced inside his lids. Cool, rugged ranges clothed in eucalypts and ancient rainforests. Wildlife that seemed strange and exotic to him now. Kangaroos and devils and platypus. Animals that hopped and had pouches and laid eggs. The dazzlingly beautiful tiger cubs. It felt like a different world, another lifetime.

He had to stop living in the past. Time to let go of his old life, to really let go. Time, perhaps, to explore his feelings for Nandi. As Luke drifted into sleep, Belle's face appeared at the edge of dreaming.

# CHAPTER 52

The telegram arrived at noon on Friday to say that Papa was in bed with a chest complaint. It didn't sound urgent, but Belle planned to leave for Binburra in the morning, just in case. The influenza had been bad this year.

Eddie insisted on coming along. He'd been unpredictable lately: one day charming and the next, a grump. This was one of his charming days. He'd imported a car from America, a shiny red Oldsmobile Runabout, and she guessed he wanted to test out his new toy.

'Top speed is over twenty miles per hour,' he said. 'Quicker than waiting for the train tomorrow. We could leave after lunch and be there by tonight.' His face was eager, expectant. This was the first time all year he'd offered to return with her to Hills End.

Belle wasn't sure. The Runabout's leather roof, which came as a separate accessory, had not yet arrived. However, the weather looked fine and she was curious herself to try out the new car, the first they'd ever owned.

'All right then, Eddie. I'll pack two bags.'

An hour later she was ready. Eddie stood in the driveway beside his new car, waiting for her. He looked quite dashing. Peaked hat.

Goggles pushed high on his forehead. Stylish driving coat of the finest tweed, hanging a little loosely perhaps. He'd lost some weight, and it suited him.

Belle climbed in beside him. He turned the side crank a few times and the motor roared to life. With a loud bang they were off through the streets of Battery Point. People turned to stare as they went by, and Eddie tooted the horn and doffed his hat. She felt sorry for horses sharing the road. They shied, or even bolted away. Eddie took to stopping the car so they could pass by safely.

He gave her a turn at driving once they left Hobart. She loved the spring sunshine on her face, the wind in her hair, and how the car magically powered along at a steady speed, as fast as a horse could gallop. It took a while for her to master the steering, which was via a central tiller. When she ran into a ditch, they laughed and worked together to push the car back onto the road. He took over the driving again, and Belle settled back for the ride. It was hard to believe they were actually having fun. She snatched glimpses of the old Eddie, her best friend from years ago.

Their relationship had improved over the last year, and it was all thanks to that day in Melbourne at Alice Tyler's house. The day Belle had vowed to reclaim her power. On returning to Hobart she'd begun teaching at Campbell College next door to Coomalong, her family's Hobart home. Where she and Luke met as children twenty-five years earlier. Now she was principal. Teaching provided her with the purpose she'd been so desperately craving.

Edward had forbidden it, of course, and refused to help, but she forged ahead despite his resistance. The first teacher she hired was Becky Tyler, shamelessly poached from Ruyton and a willing truant. They'd become friends, although she kept their relationship from her husband. These days Belle had more in common with Becky than with Grace, whom she'd known all her life. They shared so many interests, but she still couldn't penetrate a certain reserve Becky showed when talking about Luke.

Although Eddie had railed against the school in the beginning, times were changing and he'd eventually come round. Society was becoming more tolerant of working wives, especially when their work involved charitable pursuits, which were viewed as fashionable. Belle also liked to think that Eddie respected her for standing up to him.

He still worked too hard. Often he came home dog-tired and went straight to his room. He still spent nights at the club, but he vehemently denied the rumours about other women. In the absence of firm evidence, Belle had decided to give him the benefit of the doubt. Sometimes he came home full of energy and enthusiasm for his family. Clara and Anne loved those times. If Belle was honest, she loved them too. Intimacy was returning to their marriage.

Eddie swerved wildly to dodge a sow and piglets dashing across the road, and they both shrieked with laughter. He laid a proprietorial hand on her knee and she let it stay. Why couldn't he be like this all the time?

Three hours into their journey and the sun disappeared. The breeze stiffened and shifted southerly. Belle shivered and pulled her wrap around her shoulders. Clouds were scudding in from the west.

As the day grew darker, so did Eddie's mood. He cursed as bone-jarring corrugations rattled the car. He swore as they slid into potholes. When they hit an especially deep rut in the road, he slammed on the brake and jumped out. 'I need a piss.'

Belle needed a toilet stop too, but not here. They should have stopped in New Norfolk. Here there was nothing but bare sheep paddocks. No trees to hide behind. She wished she was a man. How very convenient were trousers and standing up to pee.

It started to rain. Belle reached for her jacket on the seat beside her. Something fell from the folds, a small cut-glass bottle with a silver top, full of a dark liquid. She picked it up. No label. She unscrewed the lid and wrinkled her nose in distaste at the distinct, pungent smell of laudanum. Belle's breathing grew shallow. It was as if someone was tightening a vice in her chest. She could see her husband standing with his back to the road, searching through his coat.

Eddie was chasing the dragon.

It explained so much. His frequent tiredness and lack of appetite. The mood swings and erratic behaviour. What a fool she'd been. Mistaking his bouts of energy and enthusiasm for a renewed interest in their marriage. It cast everything she believed about him into doubt.

Belle stared at the pretty little bottle, remembering Luke's brief brush with laudanum after the mine accident. He'd once begged her to bring him some, lying about Dr Lovejoy prescribing it. Her father's words echoed in her ears. 'Drug-takers are all liars and cheats, Belle, without exception. While in the grip of their addiction they may never be trusted, no matter who they are or what they say.'

Eddie was swearing again, and turning out his pockets. Kicking at a fence post. A sudden fear rippled through her, a fear of what he might do if she confronted him in this lonely place. Belle tossed the bottle into the long grass beside the road.

Eddie got back in the car and they drove on without a word. The rain pelted harder. Belle pulled her hat down and fastened the veil across her eyes. Nothing for it but to endure the ride. When she reached Binburra, Papa would know what to do.


Belle stood in the parlour, her chin trembling. She covered her ears. 'Oh, Mama, no. Don't tell me. I don't believe you.'

The rawness of Papa's death was etched into her mother's face, a face haggard and contorted with grief. It showed in her eyes, red from weeping, set in dark hollows that hadn't been there before. Sounded in her tremulous voice, so hoarse and weak that Belle could barely hear her. She seemed to have aged a lifetime.

Dr Lovejoy led Belle over to a chair and sat her down. 'If it's any comfort, your father's death was painless. When the pneumonia really took hold he lapsed into unconsciousness and slipped peacefully away in his sleep.' His voice broke with emotion. 'A dignified end to a remarkable life.'

Belle opened her mouth to speak, but no words came. Edward moved to comfort her and she ducked away. Her feelings didn't make sense; they made her ashamed. Anger instead of sorrow. Anger that Papa had left her so unexpectedly, without a word. Resentment instead of sympathy for her mother. Mama had lived a charmed life with the cleverest, kindest, most generous man in the world, a man who'd loved her wholeheartedly and beyond measure. Nothing to pity there. Belle wanted that too. The contrast with her marriage had never been more stark.

'I want to see Papa.'

The doctor glanced over at Elizabeth, then he led Belle upstairs to the main bedroom. Her father might have been asleep. She shook his shoulder to be sure. Kissed his cheek and touched his hair, startled by how stiff and cold he was. She pulled the blanket higher to keep him warm. Perversely, he looked more peaceful now than the last time she'd seen him. Death had smoothed all the care from his face.

'Papa?' Belle blinked back tears as the truth hit home. The body in the bed looked like her father, but it wasn't him. The character and spirit that made him was gone, lost forever.

She turned to find Eddie beside her. 'I'm sorry, Belle. He was a good man and a fine father. I used to secretly wish he was my father. I envied you.'

A few hours ago, his heartfelt words would have meant a lot. They would have had the power to comfort, but now they left her numb. She'd needed Papa to help her decide what to do about Eddie. She'd needed to talk to him. There was nobody else in the world that she trusted as much, not even her mother.

For one terrible moment she wished she hadn't thrown the pretty little bottle away.

# CHAPTER 53

Luke was eating dinner on the porch with Nandi, Tau and Sizani when Becky's telegram arrived. He read the brief message over and over with a sense of disbelief. How could it be? Daniel Campbell and his wife, Elizabeth, dead, departing this world within a few days of each other. The implications were immense. Belle had lost her father and mother in one savage blow. His son had lost his grandparents. And Luke had lost the most profound influence of his life.

Memories of Daniel flooded in: days on Mount Wellington, walking to Tiger Pass, cataloguing specimens in Binburra's library. Could his mentor be dead when he still lived so vividly inside Luke's heart? Daniel's compassion and wisdom and burning thirst for knowledge continued to guide Luke every single day.

Luke dropped the telegram on the table and Tau picked it up. 'You have told me of this man. Your teacher and friend – like a father.'

'He was more than that.'

Tau passed the telegram to Nandi. 'What will you do?' she asked.

Luke felt helpless, full of emotions with nowhere to go. 'I can't go back. Everybody in Tasmania thinks I'm dead.'

Nandi placed her hand on his. 'You are the famous Colonel

Buchanan, King of Diamonds. You can do whatever you wish, go wherever you please.'

She was right, as usual. He could return if he wanted, pay his respects. The question was, did he want to?

It was barely a month since he'd vowed to let go of his past. Could he bear to revisit the landscape of a long-vanished life? Luke squeezed his eyes shut, felt the sun on his lids. Could he bear not to? Daniel had been his roadmap. When in doubt he always asked himself, *What would Daniel do?* This vast sanctuary of Themba only existed because of Daniel. He deserved to be properly honoured.

Luke squeezed Nandi's hand. 'You're in charge while I'm away.'

He left the next morning. As the train rattled towards Cape Town, Luke read Becky's letters, which were full of news of the far-flung island that he'd once called home. About how, since Federation, Tasmania was a full state of the Commonwealth of Australia. About how the new parliament was close to giving women voting rights. About the spectacular success of the revitalised Campbell College.

Although she taught at the college, side by side with Belle, Becky didn't mention her once. Deliberately so, he guessed.

Luke stared out the window, briefly startled by his own reflection. Nandi had insisted on lightening his hair to disguise him. She'd done a good job. He barely recognised himself. The featureless veldt flashed by as the train brought Luke ever closer to a past he'd strived very hard to forget.

# CHAPTER 54

'Bye, Mama. Bye, Papa.'

'Goodbye, girls. Be good today.' Edward kissed his daughters warmly on the cheek. He loved their breakfasts together; it was the only time of the day when he could pretend they were a happy family.

'Bye, my darlings,' said Belle. 'Good luck on your spelling test, Clara.'

Edward went back to his newspaper 'Listen to this.' He folded the pages in half to more easily read the article.

> Millionaire mining magnate Colonel Lucas Buchanan has arrived in Hobart on private business. The Colonel is a Boer War hero, and famous for discovering the largest diamond in the world. Two gems, cut from that immense stone, grace the Crown Jewels on display at the Tower of London. He arrived without fanfare, and the length and purpose of his visit is unknown.

Private business, eh. Wonder what that means?'

Belle nibbled at her toast. Hetty tried to serve her from the silver warmer of scrambled eggs and was waved away. Two months now since her parents were laid to rest, and she still had no appetite. It seemed disrespectful somehow to eat a hearty breakfast when they couldn't.

'I wager the Colonel's looking for investment opportunities. He's an important man. We should host a welcome gathering for him.'

'Not here, Eddie. I'm in no mood for parties. Hold it at the club if you must.'

'You're not interested in meeting him? Some say the Colonel's fortune rivals that of Cecil Rhodes himself.'

'That's hardly a glowing endorsement. Rhodes is from all accounts a greedy, ignorant man who treats the native Africans worse than animals. No doubt Buchanan is the same.' Belle finished her cup of tea. 'I must go, Eddie, or I'll be late for work.'

Edward nodded and rolled a cigarette. He lit his smoke and watched Belle leave the room. Her trim figure needed no corset to cinch in the waist, even after three children. Disappointing that their family had never grown larger. Despite his great affection for Robbie, he would still love a son of his own blood, but Belle didn't want more children. She'd made that plain enough.

He'd resented Belle's teaching at first, but had come to be proud of her. She was a thoroughly modern woman – a respected educator and accomplished artist. Her impressionist landscapes and animal drawings were attracting attention from Hobart's cultural crowd and she would soon hold her first exhibition.

Belle was also an understanding wife. She'd stuck with him through everything, even when she'd discovered his taste for laudanum. He'd promised to stop, but he was weak and unable to keep his word. He wasn't the best husband. Sometimes her loyalty surprised him.

Edward took a drag on his cigarette. He was ashamed to know that loyalty was not his strong suit. His mind travelled back, for the millionth time, to the fateful night of his father's death. When he'd paid a kitchen maid to betray the man who'd saved his life. The man Belle loved. His treachery still haunted him. He'd sacrificed his humanity to dispose of his rival, and for what? Belle's heart had never truly belonged to him.

Hetty began clearing away the breakfast dishes. 'Have you time for another coffee, sir?'

'Why not?' He wasn't looking forward to his day in the office. A meeting with an accountant who would no doubt confirm what he already knew – the Hills End mine hadn't turned a profit for months. He'd been hoping to avoid the expense of sinking more shafts. With wool and timber prices down, the last thing he needed was another major capital cost. Hills End Resources was still recovering from the collapse of the state's main bank a decade earlier. Edward had been a director of the Bank of Van Diemen's Land, having succeeded his father to the position.

For seventy years the bank had enjoyed a reputation for probity and stability. Edward's directorship coincided with a period of high-risk lending and business gambles. A Royal Commission concluded that one hundred thousand pounds of cash and bullion, listed as bank assets, had existed only in the fertile imaginations of the directors. Edward was lucky to have escaped charges.

The bank closure heralded a difficult decade, though he'd managed to shield Belle from his financial problems. Drought and depression slashed profits. Class conflict led to state-wide unrest, with the timber, pastoral and mining industries embroiled in bitter industrial action. Edward faced protracted strikes on all sides as his workers formed unions.

Of course it didn't help that he'd also lost a fortune from gambling. It was his chief recreation, along with laudanum, drinking at the club and discreetly entertaining other women. He'd formed a special attachment to a ravishing young creature named Fanny Catchpole, and installed her in rooms not far from the club. Edward loved his wife, but he had needs, and Belle had banned him from her bed. Fanny was only eighteen, a dark-haired beauty who accepted him for who he was. She didn't try to make him a better man.

Edward picked up the paper and re-read the article. To hell with the whining accountant and his gloomy forecasts. Edward would set up a meeting with this Colonel fellow instead. He might very well be the answer to his prayers.

# CHAPTER 55

'Do you understand your assignment?'

'Yes, sir. Leave this here hotel by that fancy carriage.' He pointed out the window. 'To distract them newsboys.'

'That's right.' The concierge had done an excellent job of finding him a double. A bit shorter and the nose wasn't quite right, but with his bleached hair and dark beard, and without close inspection, he would pass as Colonel Buchanan well enough.

'After an hour you should return to the hotel. Within reason you may charge items to my account, but only by ringing down to reception. Do not speak to anybody in person, do not go out and do not get drunk. I may be gone a few days.'

'Yes, sir, Colonel. Easiest job I ever done.'

Luke and Becky alighted from the train at Hills End station. He filled his lungs with mountain air. It felt as though he'd been away for a lifetime and yet had never left. Ever since he'd arrived in Tasmania, the feeling of *coming home* was growing stronger. The cool eucalypt-scented air, the crystal clarity of light, even the noise and grime of

Hobart's back streets struck an achingly familiar chord. But here, in the shadow of the ranges? He hadn't expected the sense of belonging to be so complete.

'Well,' said Becky. 'Where do we go first?'


It seemed like he was always visiting graves. His father's and Uncle Hiram's in Hobart, and now he stood before the twin marble tombstones of Daniel and Elizabeth Campbell. It didn't seem possible. Memories tumbled in. His first nervous day at Campbell College. How warm and welcoming they'd been. Their courage and kindness in giving a fugitive youth shelter. Elizabeth begging him to leave for the sake of her daughter, yet still caring enough to send for Angus so he would be safe. That magical trip he'd taken with Daniel, Bear and the tigers to Tiger Pass. What a proud young fool he'd been back then.

He knelt to lay the flowers and murmured a prayer.

A cloud passed over the sun. 'Can we leave now, please?' said Becky. 'I hate grave-yards.'

'Go back to the buggy. I have one more wreath to lay.'

Luke made his way past the old oak tree ringed with iron stakes, to the far side of the cemetery. Here the graves were humbler, some marked simply with crosses or engraved metal plates. Some were not marked at all. Luke stopped at a plot by the edge of the cemetery. A figure knelt before it, pulling out weeds. A small bouquet of wildflowers graced the headstone.

'Excuse me, madam.'

She turned around. For a moment he didn't recognise the frail woman with greying hair. Molly Swift.

Life had not been kind to Molly. She couldn't have been much more than fifty, but looked years older. Her thin face had grown thinner, almost skeletal, and deep black circles ringed her eyes.

Luke crouched down beside her to lay his wreath.

Her eyes brightened with pleasure. 'Why, thank you, sir. Did you know my Angus then?'

'I did.' He was surprised, after all these years, to find tears of sadness and shame welling in his eyes.

Molly lost her balance trying to stand. Luke caught her arm and helped her to her feet. She stumbled, racked by a series of hacking coughs, and pulled her threadbare coat tight around her.

'You're ill, Molly.'

'How should you know my name, sir?'

He felt her forehead; it was burning up. 'Never mind that. You're coming with me.'

Molly lay on the bed at the Railway Hotel, barely conscious. The doctor snapped his bag shut. 'This woman has a fever of one hundred and four, congested lungs and is suffering from malnutrition. It's amazing she was still standing.'

'Can she be moved?'

'Certainly not.' He scribbled out a prescription and gave it to Becky. 'Get this filled. Give Mrs Swift a tepid bath, burn those filthy rags she's wearing, brush her teeth and put her to bed in a clean nightgown.' He put a bottle of eucalyptus oil and cough syrup on the night stand. 'Four drops of the oil in a teaspoon of sugar, every four hours. She may have doses of the syrup and medicinal brandy as required. Feed her as much tea, toast and chicken soup as she will take. I'll be back in the morning.'

'Oh, but I can't,' said Becky. 'I have to be at work tomorrow.'

'We will need to engage a nurse,' said Luke. 'A qualified nurse. Cost is no object. Mrs Swift's welfare is important to me.'

'A nurse can be arranged.' The doctor tipped his hat. 'I shall send you someone.'

Luke watched Becky put a blanket over Molly and make her pillows more comfortable. It still seemed strange to him that beds here weren't draped with mosquito nets.

'She's asleep,' Becky said. 'Now I want to know what this is about.'

In hushed tones, Luke told her of his history with Molly, and how unkind he'd been. 'I blamed her for everything. For Angus not taking me prospecting. For us having to work down the mine. I even tried to take her little dog away when she was grieving. I misjudged her, Beck. Angus loved her and she did her best for him, and for me. He'd turn over in his grave to see her like this.'

Becky laid her hand on his arm. 'You were young. We all make mistakes.'

'Well, this is one mistake I intend to put right. If she lives, Molly Swift will never want for anything again.' It felt good to know he could do this last thing for Angus.


A nurse arrived within the hour. She examined her charge, who was confused but conscious. 'Molly's fever has broken. With rest and nourishing food, she has a fair chance.'

'I'm staying here in Hills End,' Luke told Becky. 'Shall I book you a room?'

'No. I'll take the train home this afternoon.' She frowned and took him aside. 'Come back with me, Luke. What if Molly recognises you?'

'I'm not leaving her.'

Becky pressed her lips together. 'Well, I need to go. The children have an excursion to the museum tomorrow. Belle will need all hands on deck.'

Belle.

Luke started at the mention of her name. 'Is she happy, do you think?' He'd deliberately not asked about her until now.

'Belle finds teaching very rewarding.'

'I didn't ask you that. I asked if she was happy.'

'Yes, of course she is.'

Becky's smile seemed forced, and there was something about the way she said it.

'What aren't you telling me?' His sister looked away. 'What of my son? How is he?'

'Robbie is at Scotch College, the finest school in Melbourne. His father is devoted to him.'

Luke did not miss the censure in her tone.

'Luke, leave it alone. You have a good life in South Africa. Belle thinks you dead, all these years. For both your sakes it needs to stay that way.'

Luke put on his hat. 'I'll walk you to the station.'

Becky pulled at his arm. 'Listen to me. You're still wanted for murder in Tasmania. Money can't change that. Pay your respects and go home.'

He handed Becky her coat. 'You don't want to miss that train.'

She sighed and threw her arms around his neck. 'You haven't changed one bit. Still as stubborn as ever.'

Molly coughed and stirred on the bed.

Luke drew Becky in for a long, heartfelt hug, breathed in her sweet scent. How good to hold his sister close. How would he bear to leave her?

When he let Becky go, her eyes shone with tears. 'You're a good man, Luke Tyler.' She blew her nose. 'Please be careful.'

He kissed her forehead. 'Always, little sister. Now let's get you to that station.'

That night, Luke sat out on the hotel verandah with a beer, watching the sun set over the ridges, the rugged heartland of his youth. The highest peaks glowed gold in the lingering rays, while shadows cast the valleys and slopes in mysterious shades of purple and pink. The longer he gazed at the mountains, the more powerful their hold on him grew.

Luke's fingers trembled where he held his glass. He loved Themba's vast savannah, but not like this. This powerful, remembered love threatened to overwhelm him. Somewhere out there lay Bear, enfolded in the rocky arms of the ranges. Somewhere out there roamed his magnificent tigers, at least in his imagination. Had they survived in their hidden valley? Did they or their offspring still hunt wallaby there?

He needed to know.

The hotel owner came by. He didn't know Luke was the famous Colonel Buchanan, but he did know his guest had bottomless pockets. 'Could you use another beer, mate?'

Luke nodded. 'And arrange a good horse and provisions to be ready at first light. I'm going bush for a few days.'

The sun was barely up when Luke said goodbye to Molly. 'You look better this morning. Stronger.'

Molly pointed to the brandy and he gave her a small cup. She gulped it down. 'Oh, that's good, that is. Warms the cockles of my heart.'

'I'll be gone for a few days,' he said. 'Nurse Kendall will stay with you until I get back.'

She took his hand in hers. 'God bless you, sir. You're an angel. Sent from heaven.'

'None of that, Molly. If you want to thank someone, thank Angus.'

'How did you know my Angus?'

'Let's just say we were friends.' He surprised her by kissing her cheek. 'Goodbye, Molly, and go easy on the brandy.'

Luke trotted the bay mare out of town. When they reached the road to Binburra, she bucked and broke into a gallop. He let her have her head. A thrill ran through him as the familiar blue gums rushed past. He was going home.

Luke cantered up the drive and dismounted to open the gate. The deserted house looked the same. Only the trees had changed. Snow gums and stringybarks he remembered as saplings, now towered twenty-feet high. A rainforest understorey of waratah, correa and leatherwood was returning.

Luke unsaddled the mare and turned her into the paddock where Sheba and Whisky used to graze. He hefted his pack up to the house. It was locked, but the cart shed where he'd once slept wasn't. He lay on his lumpy old bed, staring up at cobwebs on the tin roof. A far cry from the luxury he could afford now. Luke closed his eyes. He would give his entire fortune to open them and find himself transported back sixteen years.

Luke went back outside and did a tour: the killing gallows, the stables, the devil and tiger pens. Sasha's grave. Most of the plants in the greenhouse were dead. He gathered those still clinging to life, took them outside and watered them from the hand pump. His heart thumped harder; he almost expected Belle to creep up behind him for a kiss, so strong was her presence there.

Luke cast one last look around Binburra's homestead, then shouldered his swag and marched up the waterfall track.


He reached the cave at dusk of the third day. It took him a long while to venture in. This wasn't what he remembered. A tunnel ran through the wall of stone that had killed Bear and so nearly killed him. Neat piles of rocks stood either side of the entrance, and timber shored up the central passage. Did he have the wrong cave? No, there on the roof above him, the familiar collection of rock paintings: hand prints and circles and the image of a thylacine.

What had happened here? He spun the lamp in a slow circle, illuminating the walls. First up high, then lower, and lower again. Bats whirled past his face. He hardly noticed. A dark shape on the ground caught his eye.

He lowered the lamp. The square brass plate was set in stone. *In loving memory of Luke Tyler and his loyal dog Bear. My heart is forever yours. Bluebell.*

He stared at the words in wonder, remembering the day he'd given Belle her nickname. She'd done this? He examined the timbers under lamplight. They were clean and free of rot. Bat droppings weren't piled in the tunnel as they were in the cave corners. Glow worms had barely begun to colonise its walls. The plaque had been placed there recently.

*My heart is forever yours.* Could Belle still love him after all this time?

Something was shifting inside him. He'd camp here tonight with Bear, keep him company. Then he'd return to Hobart, but not to say goodbye as he'd originally planned. An unfamiliar surge of hope filled Luke's heart. Maybe, just maybe, he had a chance to reclaim his life.

# CHAPTER 56

'I'm telling you, Belle, the Colonel's a bloody hermit.' Edward drained his coffee cup. 'Where's Hetty?' He swore under his breath and then poured himself another. 'Must I do everything myself around here?'

'I don't understand, Eddie. Why is it so important that you meet this man?'

'A man like the Colonel doesn't come to an end-of-the-world outpost like Hobart for nothing. He has business here, I'm sure of it. Trouble is, he's been holed up in his hotel ever since he arrived. Nobody's seen him. I can't even reach him on the phone.'

'Perhaps he's having a holiday and wants some peace and quiet.'

'Don't be so naïve, Belle. He'll be taking somebody's calls. There's a profit to be had here. I wish I knew how to find it.'

'Let it go, Eddie. It's not like you need his money.' Belle finished her tea and wiped her mouth. 'Our companies are doing perfectly well on their own.' She stood up and smoothed her skirt. 'I'm off to work. Will I see you tonight?'

'I'm staying at the club.'

Belle shot him a swift accusing glance before she swept from the room. To hell with her. He'd long since stopped feeling guilty about

Fanny. If he came home, Belle would have gone to bed anyway – gone to her bed, in her wing of the house, where he wasn't welcome.

Edward took a sip from his hipflask of laudanum, and waited for it to chase the anger away. He'd once seen the concoction as the secret to happiness. Yet the longer he used it, the lesser its stimulus and the greater its side effects. Shaky hands, cloudy thinking, insomnia. His sleep had been peppered lately with nightmarish visions: being buried alive with mummies and skeletons or kissing beautiful girls who transformed into slimy things. Once, half-awake, he'd imagined Fanny was attacking him and had struck her in the face. It was time to wean himself off the drug, he knew that. But not yet. Not today.

Edward jumped as his chauffeur entered the room. His nerves were getting the better of him. 'Your car is ready, sir.'

'The Imperial Hotel.'

Maybe a personal visit would coax the Colonel from his hotel room and into a meeting.

Edward shifted from foot to foot. How dare this character keep him waiting so long? He'd been standing at the hotel's grand reception desk for half an hour, feeling like a fool. Part of him wanted to leave. However, the concierge kept insisting the Colonel would be down soon. Perhaps he was testing Edward's patience. Or his persistence. A good business partner required both those qualities.

Edward slipped his hand into the pocket of his newly tailored three-button sack coat. Teamed with a contrasting waistcoat, club-collar dress shirt and bowler hat, he epitomised the latest in London fashion. Edward viewed his reflection approvingly in the large gilt-edged wall mirror, just as the concierge nodded towards the stairs. 'Here's the Colonel now.'

Buchanan was an imposing figure. Half-a-head taller than Edward again, an erect bearing, impeccably dressed – a most distinguished-looking person, indeed. But it was his eyes that made the biggest impression: piercing, intelligent eyes, the kind that had seen a lot of life. The kind that could see right through a man.

'Good morning, sir. Welcome to Tasmania.' Edward extended his hand. The Colonel's grip was like a vice. 'I'm Edward Abbott.'

'I know who you are.' There was only a faint trace of the clipped Boer accent in his voice. 'Your reputation precedes you.'

'In a good way, I hope?' The Colonel inclined his head. 'How long do you expect to be in Hobart?'

'I have not decided.'

'In that case, Colonel, perhaps you'll give me the pleasure of your company at my club tonight. Over dinner.'

The answer was a long time coming. 'Of course, and, please, call me Lucas.'

'Excellent. Shall I call for you at seven?'


Edward left the lobby with an unfamiliar lightness in his step. From what he knew, Colonel Buchanan had barely stepped outside his hotel room since arriving. Yet now the man wanted to spend an entire evening with him. Was this as strategic a move on the Colonel's part as it was on his own? Hills End Resources was the largest mining company in Tasmania, the natural choice if Buchanan Diamonds wanted to partner with a local outfit.

Did Lucas have a proposition for him? Perhaps he'd had agents on the ground all along. If so, he'd kept that very quiet. Edward couldn't think of anybody unusual making enquiries, or stories of mineral exploration teams. No matter, he'd find out soon enough.

Edward grinned at the doorman and tipped his hat on the way out. How long had it been since he'd felt this kind of excited anticipation? His hand hesitated as he reached for the little bottle in his pocket. For once he barely needed it, but his fingers closed on the smooth silver flask of their own accord.

# CHAPTER 57

L uke glanced at the clock, then gazed out the window to the
evening scenes on the road below. Life was strange. Once, as a
brash young boy, he'd foolishly felt like he owned these streets. Now,
as the fabulously wealthy Colonel Buchanan, he did. He could buy and
sell any man in Hobart ten times over.

The town had changed since he'd been gone, entered the modern
century. Street-lighting and motor cars. Bustling crowds of pedestri-
ans. Electric tramcars, the first in the Southern Hemisphere. Yet it was
still recognisably the town where he'd grown up, and he was thrilled
to be back. Thrilled to be rid of the vague, background homesickness
that he'd been suffering these many years without even knowing it.

The telephone rang. 'That's good to hear,' said Luke. 'I'll come by
to see her now.'

Molly and Nurse Kendall had travelled back to Hobart with him,
and shared the next door suite. Luke knocked and went in. Molly sat
in a chair by the window, with a rug across her knee. Colour had
returned to her face, and it lit up when he entered the room. She
looked happier than he could remember, even when she and Angus
were together. As if, for the first time in her life, she hadn't a care in
the world.

'How are you feeling, Molly?'

'On top of the world, thank you, sir.' Her eyes had recovered their keen, bird-like quality.

The nurse seemed a little flustered that Molly sounded so chipper. 'It will be weeks before Molly is fully restored to health. She will need me for some time yet . . .'

'Oh, yes, do keep Evie on,' said Molly. 'She's right good company, is Evie.'

Luke smiled. 'I hope you'll stay here with us, Nurse Kendall, until your patient is entirely well.'

The nurse beamed. Luke pulled up a chair opposite Molly. 'Is there anything you need?'

'Yes, sir. Some yarn, knitting needles and a pattern book. I feel so useless sitting here. And a magazine would be nice.'

'See to it, please, nurse, but don't let her overdo it.' He patted Molly's hand and stood up.

'Sir?'

'How often have I said it, Molly? My name is Lucas.'

'Oh, I can't call you that, sir. It don't seem right, considering.'

'Considering what?'

'Considering there's something I haven't told you.'

Luke checked his watch, almost seven. 'Tell me in the morning, Molly. I must go.'

'But sir . . .'

'In the morning, Molly. In the morning.'


Edward led the way up the imposing bluestone steps of Hobart's exclusive Mountbatten Club. 'Must you always dodge the press at your hotel like that, Colonel?'

'Vultures, the lot of them. Just you wait. By tomorrow there'll be wild speculation in the paper about our dining together.'

The doorman greeted Edward by name, as did the maître d'. He escorted them past Chesterfield lounges and an elephant-foot umbrella-stand to a table in the restaurant. 'Your usual, sir?'

'You must try this brandy, Colonel. An Armenian variety. It won the Grand-Prix award in Paris last year.' Edward sank back in his chair with a sigh. 'Welcome to my home away from home. Privacy, comfort and an escape from domestic bliss.'

'Escape? You don't receive privacy and comfort at home? Does your wife not please you?'

'Oh, Isabelle pleases me well enough.' Edward lit a cigar. 'You're not married, Colonel, no? A wise man. Living with women is not easy.'

'What makes you think I don't live with women?'

'Forgive me.' Edward flushed. 'I meant no disrespect. African customs are, no doubt, ah . . . very different.'

'How is business?' asked Luke as the drinks arrived. 'Your goldmine?'

Edward hesitated, his eyes flicking sideways. 'Production has never been better. Of course, my company has other irons in the fire. Wool. Timber.' Edward leaned forward. 'Though the fact is, Colonel, I'm keen to expand my mining interests.'

'Lucas, please.' Luke downed his drink in two gulps. 'You're right, it's an excellent drop.' He signalled to a waiter. 'Bring us a bottle of this brandy.' He selected a cigar from the box on the table. 'Is your good lady wife expecting you home early tonight, Ed?'

Edward snorted. 'My good lady wife is not expecting me home at all.'

'Then shall we make a night of it? It's been nothing but business since I arrived.'

'Capital. How about a game of poker after dinner?'


By midnight, Luke knew a great deal more about his companion's character, none of it good. Edward Abbott was an inept gambler, who had a loose tongue when he drank too much. There was a girl stashed away somewhere, and on top of that, Edward was addicted to laudanum. He barely tried to hide the little silver hipflask with its distinctive, pungent odour. How could a man with everything, including Belle, have sunk so low?

Edward kept angling for information about the purpose of Luke's visit. He seemed a bit too keen to get in on any commercial deal that might be afoot. Luke wasn't sure what to make of it. Should he add greed to the list of Edward's vices? Or was Hills End Resources not as profitable as he pretended? It wouldn't be hard to find out.

When Edward's losses grew too large, Luke insisted they leave the gaming table. 'I'm doing you a favour, mate. It's not your night.'

'It never is.' Edward slurred his words. 'But you did all right. Let's have a drink to celebrate.'

'Not for me. I'm heading back to my hotel. Shall we share a cab?'


They pulled up at a double-storey terrace house a few minutes' drive from the club. Luke shook Edward awake. 'Is this where your . . . your lady lives?'

'Fanny? Yes, Fanny's a great girl. A real goer. Always up for it.'

*She'll be disappointed tonight*, thought Luke.

Edward stumbled out onto the street, forgetting his hat, and almost fell.

The driver tapped on the hatch. 'Shall I help the gentleman to his door, sir?'

'No, drive on.'

Edward could rot in the gutter for all he cared. Luke felt sick. What had he done? Leaving Belle and his son to the mercy of that pathetic excuse for a man. More importantly, what was he going to do about it?

# CHAPTER 58

That night, Luke dreamed he was back in the depths of Abbott's mine, rushing blindly ahead of the flood. More of a vision than a dream. When the noxious air cast him choking to the ground, he rose above the flood and witnessed what happened next – Edward, dragging him to safety.

Luke woke up in a sweat, with the morning light streaming in. He relived the dream, seeing the fear in Edward's eyes as he leaped from the cage. It was an act of bravery, and Luke owed Belle's husband his life, damn him. It complicated things.

A knock came at the door, and a waiter rolled in the breakfast trolley. Devilled kidneys, kippers, bacon, boiled eggs, poached cod – a fine spread that should have been welcome after a night of drinking. But a cold stone lay in Luke's stomach where his appetite should have been.

Maybe he'd ask Molly to join him. He didn't know what it was. Perhaps because she was a living link to a remarkable time in his life. Perhaps because he was channelling Angus these days. But for some reason she always made him feel better.

. . .

'Did I wake you Molly?'

Snores came from the nurse's room.

'Oh no, sir. I always was in the habit of rising early.'

He wanted to say how he remembered. How when he was young and ungrateful, it had annoyed him when she rose at dawn to beat rugs and chop wood on his one day off. Instead he said, 'Good, because I'm inviting you to breakfast.'

Luke smiled as Molly piled her plate high with eggs and kippers back in his suite. Watching her tuck in revived his own appetite, and he helped himself to the poached cod.

Molly's appetite did not match her ambition, and before long she put the plate aside.

'You're too good to me. It's more than I deserve.'

'Nonsense.' He picked up the pot to pour her some tea.

'I need to talk, sir.'

There was something about her tone and the way her eyes held his – a certain gravitas. He put down the pot.

'I won't blame you two hoots if you turf me out on the street afterwards. Still, it needs saying.' She cleared her throat. 'I know who you are. You're Adam.'

Becky had warned him of the danger, but Molly hadn't seemed to know him and he'd reckoned himself to be safe. He should have prepared for this moment, thought of what to say. There was no point denying it. She knew him as surely as he knew her.

'When?'

'I supposed you was Adam as soon as I saw you, but I put it down to the fever. Once I was in my right mind, well, there were no doubt.'

'And what do you plan to do now?'

'Clear my conscience.' Her voice was strong and clear. 'I did you a terrible wrong, sir. A wrong I thought could never be put right. It's been eating me up, all these years, and now God has sent me a miracle. You, back here, alive, so I can apologise for my sins.'

Where was this going?

'It were me that turned you in to the coppers. I'd found your letters in the cottage, signed as Luke, and put two and two together. When I

341

saw you that night at the party, well . . . there were a reward for Luke Tyler, and I blamed you for not rescuing my Angus.'

He reached for her hand. 'If I could have, Molly . . .'

'Oh, I know that now, sir, but back then I were bitter and angry and blind with grief. It tore my heart out, though, when I heard you'd died. It were all my fault. Angus loved you, that's the truth, and I should have protected you. He would have wanted that. My worthless life hasn't been worth living since I took young Abbott's blood money.'

'Young Abbott.' Luke stiffened. 'You mean Edward? What's he got to do with this?'

'It were him I told, sir. He sent me straight to Mr Cornish who fetched the sergeant. Paid me thirty pounds on top of the reward money. Thirty pieces of silver, more like it, and I've been cursed ever since. I want you to know how sorry I am.'

Luke released Molly's hand and tried to make sense of her words.

So . . . it was Edward Abbott who'd betrayed him. Who'd wanted him hanged for the *crime* of protecting Belle, the girl he'd professed to love and went on to marry. Luke's heart hammered against his ribs so hard it hurt. Why? Not to avenge his father, surely? Edward hated Henry. Luke had done him a favour, he'd as much as said so. No, this was about Belle. The one way Edward could ensure Luke was out of her life forever. Or so he'd thought. Luke's hands clenched into fists. Big mistake.

Molly stood up. 'I should go.'

'No.' Luke sat her gently back down. 'It's my turn to apologise. I was an ungrateful young fool back then. You took me in, looked after me . . . It was unforgiveable the way I treated you. By disrespecting you, I hurt Angus as well. He didn't deserve that.' Luke couldn't meet her eyes. 'Angus loved you very much, Molly, he told me all the time. I think I was jealous of that love. Can you forgive me?'

When he looked up, her eyes were streaming with silent tears. He knew now what Angus had loved about this woman: her courage, her generosity, her strong moral compass. Molly could have gone to the papers, earned a fortune for the story of the year. The famous

Colonel Lucas Buchanan, war hero and millionaire, exposed as a poor boy from Hobart, an escaped murderer, destined for the gallows. Or she could have kept quiet, accepting his patronage and hoping it continued. Instead, she'd risked everything to tell him the truth.

'*A peace above all earthly dignities,*' he murmured. '*A still and quiet conscience.*'

'What's that, sir?'

'Shakespeare, Molly. You embody that quote far better than Thomas Wolsey ever did. It would be my honour if you'd remain here as my guest.'

Molly flushed with pleasure and relief. 'I won't be no burden. Once I'm well I'll get a job and pay me own way.'

'As you wish.' He stood up, wiped his face with a napkin and kissed her. 'From now on, you should suit yourself in all things.'


Becky glanced around and closed the classroom door behind her. 'Luke, what on earth are you doing here?' Her voice an angry whisper. 'Belle is just down the corridor.'

'I've rented a house.'

'Where? You don't mean in Hobart?'

'Not far from here, actually.'

Becky took Luke's arm, hurried him down the hall and out the front door. 'You have to go.'

He took an address from his pocket and pressed it into her hand. 'Come round tonight. I'll cook you dinner.'

'You will?'

Luke grinned. 'See you at six. Housewarming.'


Becky arrived early at the thoroughly modern single-storey home of red brick. It had a rambling garden and gables carved with kangaroos and kookaburras. Becky loved it. Luke showed her through its charming rooms, which were more cosy than grand, with window seats, chimney corners and arched leadlight windows sporting wattle and waratah designs.

'Nobody knows about this place.' Luke stoked the fire in the front room. 'It will be my haven, my bolthole. A chance to escape the spotlight. Do you know it's been six weeks, and newsmen are still camped outside my hotel?'

'Luke...'

'I've made your favourite, Beck. At least, it used to be your favourite: corned beef and cabbage followed by apple pie. The pie's from the hotel kitchen, but I cooked the rest myself.'

Becky frowned. 'What are you doing?'

He poured her a large glass of wine. 'Drink this and I'll tell you a story.'

Becky held out her glass to be refilled. 'It was Edward who betrayed you? I can't believe it.'

'Do you think Belle knows?' Luke could barely look at his sister as he asked. The pain if Belle did ...

'Absolutely not. We've often talked about that night. Belle thinks that Edward did everything he could to protect you.'

'By paying Molly thirty pounds to turn me in?'

Becky went pale. 'Believe me, Belle has no idea.'

'Perhaps it's time she did.'

'It would devastate her, Luke, and to what end? To make her marriage more torturous than it already is?'

'So her marriage is torturous?'

'I spoke out of turn.' Becky gulped her wine. 'Can we eat now? I'm starving.'


After dinner, they sat before the fire, drinking hot cocoa, lost in thought. It could have been the old days. Lamplight and shadow-flames dancing on the wall. Becky's face in the glow of the firelight, turning back the clock. Her profile like that of a young girl.

They used teaspoons to scoop up the last of the sweet, chocolatey froth.

At last Becky spoke. 'You've made up your mind then – to stay?'

'Yes.'

'Despite the danger?'

'Yes.'

'You can't have Belle.'

'Can't I?'

'You're dead, remember? And even if you weren't . . .' Becky came over, knelt down in front of Luke's chair and laid her head on his knee. 'Before Elizabeth Campbell died, she asked Belle to promise her something. *"Whatever happens, stay with Edward and make the marriage work. Be the strong one, for the sake of Robbie and the girls."* Belle made that solemn promise to her mother. She won't resile from it. Edward would have to hit rock bottom before she would abandon him.' She yawned. 'Let's not talk about it any more.'

Luke stroked Becky's hair for the longest time, digesting what she'd told him. A deathbed vow. It was almost funny, Elizabeth still managing to keep them apart.

Half an hour later, when he looked down, Becky was asleep.

'So Edward would have to hit rock bottom,' he murmured. 'That could be arranged.'

# CHAPTER 59

'I'm dining with the Colonel at my club tonight.'

'Again?' Belle dropped a sugar lump into her tea. 'That's three times this week. Why not bring him here instead?'

'I thought you couldn't bear him? That you believed him greedy and ignorant.'

'Perhaps I misjudged him. I've heard he has a clever wit.'

'You'd be bored stupid, Belle. All that business talk.'

She did not look convinced. 'Is anything coming of all that talk?'

'Nothing definite, but he's hinted at an investment opportunity in the works. I have to be patient. He's not a man to be hurried.' His wife's cool gaze unsettled him. 'In any case, there's more to life than business. I like him. We have a great deal in common.'

Belle's faintly raised eyebrow said it all. She didn't believe an important and successful man like the Colonel would want to socialise with someone like him. To hell with her. 'Think what you want. I'm going to the office.'

'Before you go . . . Yesterday I asked Benny to harness my greys, and he said they'd gone. Have you turned them out to spell?'

'No, I sold them.'

Belle's mouth fell open. 'They weren't yours to sell. Papa gave them to me. He paid a hundred pounds for Martini and almost as much for Sultan.'

'Then he'd be pleased to know I more than doubled his money.'

'Who would pay double what they're worth? We don't need the money, Eddie. My father gave them to me . . . You must bring them back or I'll never speak to you again.' She shoved her chair back from the table, spilling her tea. He watched the liquid soak into the table-cloth as she slammed the door behind her.

They did need the money, actually. With timber and wool prices still in the doldrums, he'd ploughed their dividends back into the mine to pay for excavating new shafts. Things would be tight for a while. He'd already sold off a few farms and forestry coupes. If she reacted this badly to losing a couple of horses, what would she do when she learned Binburra was on the market? *I'll never speak to you again.* An empty threat. She barely spoke to him anyway.

Edward had been lonely for a long time. Robbie at school. No real connection with Belle. And, as his fortunes had fallen, old friends dropped away. There was Fanny, of course, but their relationship had its limitations. It didn't help that booze and laudanum had rendered him mostly useless in bed. Apart from the physical side of things, there wasn't much companionship to be found with an ignorant eighteen-year-old girl, however beautiful.

The Colonel had come along at a time when he could really use a friend . . . and what a friend! The once-reclusive millionaire had spread his wings. He was guest of honour at business banquets, charity galas and society balls. Dazzling Hobart's upper crust with his good looks, charm and charisma. Edward helped to arrange these functions, and it did not go unnoticed that he was often at the Colonel's side. In the eyes of his peers, Edward's stocks were rising fast.

However, reflected glory wasn't enough to keep it that way. He needed substance as well as style. It had been more than two months now since they'd met. Time to draw Lucas out, to discover what he was really doing in Hobart.

. . .

The Mountbatten Club was busy that night. Lucas insisted they sit at a separate alcove for pre-dinner drinks, beneath an out-sized portrait of Tasmania's first Lieutenant-Governor. This private seating arrangement seemed promising enough, but then the Colonel avoided all talk of business.

'I haven't met your good wife, Ed. We must remedy that.'

'My wife?'

'You do have one, don't you? I fear we've raised some eyebrows along the way: me without a lady on my arm, and you without your wife at these soirées.'

Edward forced a smile. Great. First Belle and now Lucas. Theirs was an encounter he intended to put off for as long as possible. The Colonel was a man of the world. As such, he understood about the seedier side of Edward's life: the booze, the drugs, the gambling. Fanny.

Belle, on the other hand? If she did know of his excesses, she had turned a blind eye. No doubt she'd drawn her own conclusions from his overnight absences, but so far she'd never been confronted by the bald facts. The outspoken Colonel might well let something slip.

If Edward was honest, there was another reason why he didn't want the two of them to meet. He valued his new alliance, cherished it even. Of all the people Lucas could have befriended in Hobart, he'd chosen Edward. It was hugely flattering. Lucas was also a handsome charmer, popular with the ladies, although he never favoured anyone in particular. He was sure to be impressed by Edward's beautiful, intelligent wife. And vice versa. Perversely, he wanted to keep Lucas to himself.

'My wife has no heart for frivolous parties. She prefers books, philosophy and art. And a secluded life.'

'You are ill-matched then.'

Edward flinched. Innocent remark or insult? He couldn't tell. That lack of tact was precisely why he didn't want Lucas anywhere near Belle.

Their venison soup arrived, interrupting the moment. By the time the roast beef came, Lucas seemed to have forgotten his campaign to meet Belle. He'd relaxed, had a few drinks. It was time to bring up the topic of investment. However, just as Edward was planning his move, the Colonel beat him to it.

'I received my geologist's report today, Ed. On a potential diamond field in the state's north-west. Turns out it's quite promising.'

'You kept that quiet. I had no idea you had a team on the ground.'

'Which is precisely the way I wanted it.' Lucas returned to his meal. 'This Yorkshire pudding is damn good.'

Edward waited on tenterhooks. How could the man drop a bombshell like that and then change the subject? It was maddening. Time ticked by.

Lucas looked up. 'Something wrong with your meal?'

'No. No, it's just . . . I'd like to hear more about that report.'

Lucas put down his cutlery and wiped his chin. 'Truth is, Ed, I'm looking for an investor. Tasmania's a long way from South Africa. I need someone local on the ground to oversee the operation. Someone I can trust.'

Edward wet his lips and tried to stay calm. This was it. This was what he'd been waiting for.

Lucas looked him straight in the eye. 'Would you be interested, Ed?'

'Why yes, I might be.'

Lucas reached over and slapped him on the back. 'Good man. I'll send the preliminary report over tomorrow, but in the meantime . . .' He took a small kidskin pouch from his coat pocket and poured a glittering cascade of stones onto the table. 'Samples from the site. You'll find a few garnets and zircons among them, which, as you'll know, are diamond indicators. All from an unusually rich placer deposit, with the probability of underground kimberlite pipes.' He plucked a blue-white gem from the pile. 'That's a two-carat stone right there.' Lucas dropped it in the palm of Edward's hand.

Edward stared at the rough diamond, rubbed its shining surface between his fingertips. He'd never understood gold fever, the kind that sent men into the unforgiving wilderness, prepared to risk their lives, to bear any hardship in the hope they'd one day find a golden flash in their pan. But diamonds were altogether more seductive.

It was a wrench to hand back the stone. Already he missed touching it. 'Fragments of stars,' said Lucas. 'Tears of the gods.' He trailed his finger through the gems.

Edward glanced around the room, jealous someone might see. He angled his chair between the diamonds and the rest of the room. 'When can I have the report?'

'First thing in the morning.'

'I'll need to send my own engineers to evaluate the site.'

'Of course.'

Now for the big question. 'How much are we talking?'

Lucas returned the diamonds to their pouch. 'Ninety thousand pounds for a third share.'

Edward turned the figure over in his mind. Difficult to come up with that sort of money, especially now, but not impossible. He could sell some more properties, his shares in the shipyard . . . borrow the rest. A craving hit him hard, whether for the future diamond mine or the silver flask in his pocket, he couldn't tell.

'I'll throw these in to sweeten the deal.' Lucas tossed him the pouch.

'It could take a while to raise the capital.'

'You have until the end of the month.' Lucas lit a cigarette as a waiter cleared the table. 'In the meantime, I'm in the market for a country retreat, a place where I can escape the press. Cost is no object.'

Edward thought of the extravagant price Lucas had paid for Belle's pair in hand. This was too good an opportunity to miss. 'I can help you there. A lovely estate of mine at Hills End is for sale. Elegant homestead, magnificent scenery. Out of the way. It belonged to my late father-in-law.'

'Excellent. I'll take it.'

'Surely you want to see the property . . .'

Lucas held up his hand. 'I trust your recommendation.'

Edward couldn't believe his good fortune. 'Some champagne to celebrate?'

'I'm afraid not, Ed.' Lucas stood up. 'Have the contract of sale ready for me by tomorrow afternoon, with a fourteen-day settlement period. I'm anxious to get out of town.' He stubbed his cigarette. 'And keep our deal under your hat.' With that he marched from the club.

Edward ordered the champagne anyway, his mind a whirl. In the space of one evening his life had entirely changed. A shiny new investment opportunity. A means to climb out of the financial hole he'd dug for himself.

He'd never had the business acumen or ruthlessness of his father, no matter how hard he worked at it. Yet now? A partnership with one of the wealthiest men in the world. Edward longed to shout it from the rooftops, longed to watch his former friends come crawling back.

This change in fortune, wonderful as it was, seemed hollow without someone to share it with. It might be weeks before he could make any public announcement. He wished Robbie was home from school. His son would be thrilled with the news, proud of his father. They shared a bond that meant the world to Edward. In Robbie's eyes he could do no wrong.

What about Belle? Would this stunning coup be enough to make her think well of him again? Possibly, if it wasn't for the small matter of him selling Binburra. She still didn't know about that, and he couldn't put off telling her for much longer. He'd have to give her some time to get over it, but then, who knew? This could be the beginning of a new chapter in their lives, a resurrection of their love. They were both well rid of the place. Too many memories. One day she'd understand, but he didn't have the fortitude to face her tonight. He resisted the urge to reach for his hipflask. Time to clean up his act, become a man his wife could be proud of again.

The Premier came across to his table. 'You look like the cat that ate the cream, Ed.' He nodded at the bottle of French champagne. 'What's this in honour of? You dined with the Colonel tonight. Anything you want to tell me?'

'All in good time, Neil. All in good time.'

The Premier gave him a shrewd look. 'I'm having a pheasant shoot at my Glenorchy estate next week. Just a few close friends. Why not join us? Bring the Colonel if you like.'

'I'll see what I can do.'

Edward watched the Premier leave the dining room with immense satisfaction. It was happening already. By the time this deal became public, he'd be the talk of the town.

To hell with celebrating alone. He'd spend the night with Fanny, the one person he could rely on for a warm reception, if only because he paid her bills. Then tomorrow he would go home and tackle Belle.

It was near midnight when a cab dropped him off at the Lillie Street terrace. Edward used his key to get in, then went upstairs to Fanny's rooms, trying to decide how much to tell her. Bursting to share at least some part of his news.

He knocked on her door. 'Fanny?' Knocking louder this time.

The door on the opposite side of the landing swung open, and a hard-faced young woman in a dressing-gown stepped out. 'That won't do you no good, sir. Fanny's gone.'

'What do you mean, gone?'

'I mean she up and left two days ago. Didn't tell me why or where, and we've been friends a year and all.'

Edward unlocked the door and went inside. It was just as the woman said. He searched every room. There was no sign of Fanny, not even a stray stocking. It was as if she'd never lived there.

# CHAPTER 60

Edward didn't talk to Belle the next morning – about the
diamond mine or Binburra or anything else. Fanny's mysterious
vanishing act had thrown him too much. For all he knew, Belle was
the one behind it.

He'd been making an effort to moderate his alcohol and laudanum
intake; spending more time with his family in three weeks than he
had in six months. The girls loved it. If he was to be honest, he loved it
too. He didn't miss Fanny nearly as much as he'd expected to.

If Belle had anything to do with Fanny's disappearance, she was
hiding it well. Edward watched his wife for signs of added resentment, feeling a little paranoid. Yet he detected no change, no crack in
her cool, aloof exterior.

The longer it took him to talk to her, the harder it became. Especially since he'd hit a legal snag concerning the sale of Binburra. Belle
had inherited the estate upon the death of her parents, and Edward
had assumed, therefore, that it belonged to him. Any assets accruing
to a married woman, whether through wage, investment, gift, or
inheritance, automatically became the property of her husband. That's
how it had always been.

However, according to his lawyer, recent legislation had changed all that. *The Married Women's Property Act* of 1900 allowed such women to own and control property in their own right. In principle he agreed with women's equality, but in this case it had some unfortunate consequences. Belle would never agree to sell Binburra.

His lawyer had suggested a deception to work around the problem. Present Belle with some papers requiring her signature. Tell her they related to the grant of probate for her parents' estate. Slip in a *transfer of land* document, making Edward the proprietor of Binburra. Have her sign it along with the rest.

The plan worked. The contract of sale was duly executed, with the shortest possible settlement period, as the Colonel had requested. And in time, Edward told himself, Belle would thank him.

But this was time he did not have. Robbie was coming home for a few days next week, and Belle planned to take the children back to Binburra for a visit. Yet Lucas had already taken legal possession of the property, and had left Hobart for Hills End. Edward would have to pluck up the courage soon or risk an embarrassing encounter between his family and the good Colonel.

Soon after, he surprised Belle by inviting her for a picnic. He did it over breakfast, ensuring the girls were present for added leverage.

'I planned on finishing a painting,' Belle said.

'You still can. Picnics don't take all day.'

Nine-year-old Anne, always the cheeky one, perched on her mother's knee and pinched her cheeks. 'Please, Mama. Pleeeease!'

The corners of Belle's mouth turned up a fraction. She was weakening. It occurred to him that it was a long time since he'd seen his wife smile.

'Come on, Belle,' he coaxed. 'It's a lovely day. When did we last spend a family Sunday together?'

'And whose fault is that?'

He put his hand against his heart. 'Mea culpa. Let me make it up to you and the girls. What do you say, Clara?'

Clara was twelve now, a serious child who could generally be found in the garden with her head buried in a book. 'Can we take the Oldsmobile?' she asked. 'I want to ride in the rumble seat.'

'Henry Roberts has a zoo in his grounds not far from here. We could have our picnic there.' Edward's association with Colonel Buchanan had resulted in a recent flurry of invitations from Hobart's gentry. Roberts owned a successful wool-broking and stock-agency company. His socialite wife, Mary, had a collection of exotic animals. 'You and Mary would get on.'

'My friend's been there,' said Clara. 'She says they have a real lion. I've never seen a real lion.'

'Me either,' said Anne.

Belle sighed. 'Very well. I'll ask Hetty to pack us a basket.'


The spacious grounds of the Roberts' mansion had been turned into a menagerie of creatures great and small. Aviaries of brightly coloured birds. A monkey house. The promised lion.

Clara and Anne ran from one enclosure to another as Mary Roberts gave them the grand tour. She was a tall, dignified woman of about sixty, with the passion and energy of someone half her age. Belle seemed almost as excited as the girls.

'I knew your father, my dear,' said Mary. 'A wonderful man who worked tirelessly to protect our wildlife. Such a dreadful loss.'

'Thank you, Mary.' Belle pointed to some small kangaroos roaming free on the lawn, along with a flock of geese. 'Bennett's wallabies and Cape Barren geese. Oh, and are those pademelons at the back?'

'Quite right.' Mary beamed. 'You are indeed your father's child. So lovely to meet somebody who appreciates our natives. Most people are only interested in the exotic species.'

Edward grinned. He'd been right about Belle and Mary getting on. They hadn't stopped talking since they met. Belle threw her head back, laughing at some remark or other. Bright eyes brimming with delight. Shining chestnut hair as thick and full as ever. Her simple white lawn-dress of Irish lace showed off her trim figure to great advantage. This was the girl he'd married. A sudden rush of love left him weak.

'Come and see the devils,' said Mary.

'You have devils?' asked Belle.

'Oh, yes, and native tigers, although the devils are my favourites. I'm the first to have bred them in captivity, you know. People have such exaggerated opinions about them being ugly and fierce. When visitors see my babies, lively and happy, running to my call, they realise the devil is not so black as he's been painted.'

Even Edward was curious to see the living tigers, having only ever seen skins. His father had helped engineer a controversial bounty scheme that had seen the rare animal become even rarer. So rare, Belle had once told him, their population would probably never recover.

The tigers were in the next enclosure, crouched at the back of a shallow shed full of straw. A pair, one larger and heavier than the other. Photos and skins hadn't prepared him for the living animals. Apart from the distinct dark stripes across their backs, they bore no resemblance to tigers. These were wolves, with large jaws and powerful streamlined bodies. Pouched wolves. Simply magnificent. Edward felt a catch in his throat. What had his father done?

'This pair is destined for the Bronx Zoo in New York City,' said Mary. 'International zoological societies place far more importance on these animals than Tasmanians do. I know, my dear.' She touched Belle's shoulder. 'Such fools. We won't know what we have until it's gone.'

Clara ran over. 'Don't cry, Mama.'

Tears were streaming down Belle's face, and Edward didn't know why. Instinctively, he gathered her to him and for once she didn't push him away. 'Come on, sweetheart . . . girls.' He smiled his most encouraging smile. 'Let's have that picnic.'

The zoo and park-like grounds were a popular weekend destination for families. Edward found a free spot under a spreading chestnut tree, put down the blanket, and fetched the basket from the car. Hetty had outdone herself. Melt-in-the-mouth sandwiches which

Clara insisted on feeding to the geese. Egg and bacon pie, salmon patties, strawberries with lashings of whipped cream. Anne made herself sick on lemonade and gingerbread. Belle cheered up and ate three little fruit flans in a row. A sea breeze tempered the early summer sunshine, and though the silver flask lay snug and safe in his pocket he did not touch it.

'Can we do this every Sunday, Mama?' asked Anne.

'Not every Sunday.' Belle caught Edward's eye and moved a fraction closer to him. 'I think every second Sunday would do, don't you?'

Edward poured her a glass of chilled lemonade from the icebox, and she thanked him with her eyes. The delicious prickle of a connection was in the air. If only Robbie was here, it would be as perfect a day as he'd known.

'Thank you for today, Eddie. I feel so alive here. And meeting Mary has reminded me of where my real passion lies. Not in teaching, but in conservation.' He didn't like where this was going. 'I've made a decision. I want to join the Royal Society. I want to continue Papa's work at Binburra, restoring habitats and protecting native species. Mary said she'll help me. What do you think?'

Oh. He should have spoken to her sooner. Still, he couldn't let the sale stand between them. She deserved to know. However, there was something he needed to do first.

Edward took the silver flask from his pocket and handed it to Belle. Concern clouded her face, and at first she wouldn't touch it.

'Why is Papa giving you his medicine?' asked Clara. 'Are you sick, Mama?'

Edward froze with shame. He didn't know that the girls knew, or that Belle had invented an innocent explanation for the flask.

'I don't need my medicine any more,' he said, not taking his gaze from Belle's face. 'I think I'm well again.'

She wrapped some leftovers in two napkins and handed one to each child. 'Go and feed the swans on the lake for me. See if you can count how many black ones and how many white ones.'

'It won't be that easy,' said Belle when the girls had run off. 'Opium creates a physical addiction. When Luke came home after the mine accident, he craved laudanum so fiercely it made him ill. Papa gave him herbs to ease the pain.'

'What sort?'

Belle reached across to take his hand. 'You're really serious about this, aren't you? I remember a few: ginseng, chamomile, valerian . . . and golden root, I think. Shall I try to find out more?'

'We'll find out together.' He squeezed her hand. 'You have my solemn promise that this will not beat me. I want a fresh start, Belle. I want my family back. But first, there's something you should know.' He wished he could have a swig of Dutch courage. 'I sold Binburra, sweetheart. To Colonel Buchanan.'

Belle's hand crept out of his. 'You couldn't,' she said. 'Papa left it to me.'

His mouth went dry. 'What's yours is mine,' he said. 'As your husband.'

'Not any more. That's all changed. Married women have the right to own property.'

'Perhaps, but see, the thing is . . .' He rubbed the back of his neck. 'You signed the title deed over.'

'I did not.'

'You did, sweetheart.'

He could see her mind ticking over. 'Are you telling me, those documents you said were for probate . . . ?'

'I thought you knew . . .'

'No, you didn't.' Her voice was rising. The people under the next tree looked over at them. 'You tricked me. That's fraud. The sale isn't legal.'

'I'm afraid it is. In fact, it's already gone through. Just because you don't read what you're signing . . .'

'Don't put this on me. I trusted you.'

'Of course you did, and you had every reason to. We still have Canterbury Downs if you fancy a weekend in the country. I did this for us, Belle, to bury the memories that have torn us apart in the past.'

Belle jumped to her feet, face flushed, hands clenched tight. 'How could you? she shouted. 'I'll never forgive you.' She spun around and marched away.

'Belle, come back. Please.'

He held his breath as her steps slowed, then stopped. She turned on her heel and, with halting steps, walked to him.

'Thank God, Belle. Sit down, sweetheart. We can talk this through. I'll try to get Binburra back, if that's what you want.'

A blinding pain exploded in his face. The silver flask bounced off the bridge of his nose and landed in his lap. He squinted up at her through half-closed eyes.

'Damn you, Eddie.'

Edward's fingers closed over the flask. When he next looked up, he saw Clara standing over him with wide eyes. 'What's wrong, Papa? Are you sick again? And why is Mama running away?'

# CHAPTER 61

The girls stood by the bannister. Clara, hollow-eyed and blank. Anne's lips trembling, as if she was fighting back tears.

'Take the children upstairs, Mrs Blair.'

'No, please, Eddie. Let me spend some time with them.'

He shook his head. 'Mrs Blair?'

The governess started to shepherd the girls upstairs.

Belle forced a smile and waved. 'Goodbye, my darlings. Mama loves you.' Her voice cracked with emotion. 'Be good and I'll see you tomorrow.'

Edward crossed his arms and stepped in front of Belle, blocking her view of the staircase. 'Don't tell them that. It's not happening.'

Today was the first time he'd spoken to his wife since the disastrous picnic. Becky had called by later that same afternoon to say that Belle was staying at Coomalong, the Campbell's old home next door to the school. When he'd gone round there, she wouldn't talk to him. However, she did have the nerve to send him a letter demanding he send her the girls. She should never have thought leaving him would be so simple.

The two faced each other across the empty entrance hall. In the space of ten days his wife looked smaller, thinner, older, with her

360

lovely hair pulled back tightly and secured in a low bun. A few stray strands escaped and clung to her face, which was red and puffy from crying. Even her spine seemed bowed. He almost felt sorry for her, for the desperation in her eyes.

Then he thought of how she'd humiliated him publicly at the very time he wanted to avoid a scandal. It was no secret that Belle had left him. Edward's friendship with the Colonel had raised his profile, but it could not protect him from gossip. Perhaps it made things worse. Separation was unheard of among Hobart's polite society. Now, all knew Edward Abbott as the man who could not hold onto his wife.

'Look at you. You're a wreck, Belle. It's clear you can't look after yourself.' He managed a faint smile. 'Come home, and we'll try to put this behind us.'

'Apologise for your deceit, Eddie. Return Binburra to my rightful hands, and I might consider it.' The silence yawned between them. 'Where's Robbie?'

'Upstairs.'

'I want to see him.' A tremor in her voice belied the calm request.

'Robert doesn't want to see you. Can you blame him, after you abandoned him and his sisters?'

She drew herself up to her full height and, in an instant, all her fire and beauty returned. 'I did not abandon my children.' She fixed him with burning, reproachful eyes. 'I abandoned you.'

Edward breached the space between them in a bound, and pulled her roughly to him. She twisted in his arms, arching her body to get free. He gripped her tighter, not caring if he hurt her, and pressed a savage kiss on her lips. Her mouth remained unyielding, her open eyes as hard as flint.

'Arrgh.' He shoved her away. 'Go then. Go if you must, but don't expect to see your children again.'

For a moment her eyes softened and he saw what looked like pity there. 'You don't mean that, Eddie. I shall call again tomorrow.' Belle turned and left the house with a dignity he couldn't help but admire.

The unfamiliar sting of tears pricked his eyes, and he wanted to chase after her. Explain how he'd travelled to Hills End to redress the wrong he'd done, and tried to buy Binburra back. That was despite the Colonel having paid twice what it was worth.

Lucas had been unmoved by his pleas. 'This place is perfect for me, Ed. Your wife is, of course, most welcome to visit.'

Damn that man. Edward went to the library and sank into a chair. He should never have sold Binburra to begin with. Although, perversely, that neglected estate was the one property for which he'd received a good price. All round, he'd had the most terrible luck raising money at short notice for the new diamond mine.

He'd put several prime landholdings on the market, but buyer after buyer had pulled out on the brink of purchase. With time of the essence, he'd been forced to accept offers well below market value.

Recent wool sales hadn't been what he'd hoped for either. A newly-formed collective of graziers was undercutting him, losing him buyers altogether or forcing him to take a loss. How they could afford to sell at such prices was beyond him. Bales produced by his low-paid farmers couldn't match those of the Midland Woolgrowers Cooperative, in either weight or quality. Belle had often urged him to improve pay and conditions on his farms. It seemed she'd been right.

And then there was the trouble at Hills End Mine. The new shafts were weeks behind schedule, with so many holdups and accidents he almost suspected sabotage. On top of that, he had labour problems. Some of his best engineers had been poached by a South African consortium. Rabble-rousers were stirring up the workforce, organising unions and causing strife. Their demands for improved safety and higher wages couldn't have come at a worse time. Strikes and go-slows were slashing production.

If only there wasn't such a tight timeline. He was still thirty thousand pounds short of the amount needed to seal the deal, and the deadline was looming. The pouch of gems from Lucas had passed muster. Tiffany's agent in Melbourne had pronounced them stones of the highest quality. An independent valuer's report on the diamond field was due on his desk this morning. If it came up trumps, he'd have no choice but to borrow the additional funds.

Edward took a swig from his silver flask, having replaced its former contents with whisky. He was trying to honour the promise he'd made to Belle at the zoo, countering the clenching pains in his gut with aspirin and some kind of hideous concoction from his doctor. Nothing really helped. He couldn't eat, couldn't sleep, couldn't work. Yet he was determined to fight the addiction. For the sake of his family. For the sake of himself. This whole mess could still turn around. If Belle forgave him, as she always had before. If the diamond deal went through. Well, he'd be sitting pretty.

He stood up, clutching his stomach as a spasm ripped through him. Better have a strong black coffee or two before heading into the office for the assayer's evaluation. With any luck it would confirm the Colonel's preliminary report and he'd be drinking champagne by lunchtime.

As his driver dropped him off, Edward caught the glimpse of a familiar figure walking away down Macquarie Street.

'Fanny?' He ran after her. 'Fanny, stop!'

She increased her speed.

Edward reached her, spun her round by the arm. Had he made a mistake? On first sight, this demure, smartly-dressed young woman bore little resemblance to the scantily-clad little strumpet who'd once pranced around his rented Lillie Street rooms. Her shining ebony hair was fastened in an elegant chignon. She wore a high lace collar, an elegant pleated blouse, a satin skirt, flared from hip to ground.

But when they locked eyes he knew. 'Whatever happened to you?'

She wrenched her arm away. 'A gentleman, that's what happened. A proper gentleman, this time.'

'Where did you go, Fanny?'

'None of your bloody business, and it's Francine now.'

'Where are you off to?'

'If you must know, I'm going to work.'

He stifled a laugh.

Fanny thumped Edward hard enough to make him wince. A smart dress and pretty sun bonnet hadn't weakened her right arm. 'Don't s'pose you think I can do a respectable job. All she's good for is opening her legs, is that it?' Her eyes blazed with resentment. 'I'm training to be a nurse, like Florence Nightingale. Matron says I'm right clever, she does.'

What had happened to his brazen coquette? Edward was flabbergasted. 'A gentleman, you say. What gentleman?'

She delivered one last punch, adjusted her hat and turned her back.

As Edward watched her hurry down the street, he was hit by a sharp pang of loss. He could understand a rival stealing Fanny away. She was a rare beauty, after all, but any man who could afford Fanny could surely afford to keep her. Why send her off to be a nurse? That wasn't where her talents lay.

No matter. Probably best that Fanny was out of the way, though he'd still like to thrash the man who'd robbed him.

Edward continued on to his office. As soon as he'd hung up his coat and hat, George Bentley, his senior mining engineer, tapped him on the shoulder. He held up his valise with a flourish and grinned. 'The assessment report. It's a good read.'

Good was an understatement. This was better than he could have dreamed of. Gem-quality diamonds had been found in profusion at the site, along with garnets and zircons. The author was wildly enthusiastic. His report concluded that the proposed one hundred thousand shares of stock were easily worth fifty pounds each.

'What do you think?' asked Edward. 'What's your advice?'

'The consulting engineer has staked out the adjoining hundred acres himself,' said George.

Edward cheered. 'That says it all, right?'

'Perhaps, but I do have one concern . . .' George hesitated, as if he couldn't find the words.

'For God's sake, man, spit it out.'

'The proposed mine is on land that belonged to a farming family. The husband recently came home from the Boer War, a hero apparently. Awarded the Victoria Cross for retrieving wounded soldiers under fire. He also came back a cripple, unable to work his farm.' George lowered his voice. 'It's rumoured the Colonel paid him a pittance, barely what the land was worth as mongrel sheep country. I fear there'll be a backlash when the details hit the press.'

'That's nothing to do with me.'

'Perhaps you could talk to Buchanan,' said George. 'If the two of you, as co-directors, were to make recompense, it could avoid a public outcry.' He sat down on the desk and slipped his spectacles further down his nose. 'I confess I'm uncomfortable about how this man has been dealt with. Aren't you?'

'Hell, George, this is business. I'm not about to make waves.' Edward called in his assistant. 'Make an appointment with my bank manager. Tell him it's urgent.'

'Hold on, Ed. This report is good, maybe too good. We need our own geologists to take a look before we move.'

'There's no time. I only have a few days.'

George looked unconvinced, disapproving even. 'You asked for my advice, Ed.'

'More fool me.' He felt his temper rise. 'Get out, George. Get out of my sight.'

Edward slumped back in his chair, weak with anticipation. He was about to make an unimaginable amount of money. If his father could only see him now.

# CHAPTER 62

Belle lay down on the old four-poster bed she'd slept in as a girl, listening to a scrabbling in the roof. Papa said the name Coomalong meant *plenty of possums*, and that hadn't changed. The room had changed, though, thanks to her mother's fondness for updating the décor. Pretty oil lamps replaced with electric ones. Dust-collecting damask drapes replaced with airy curtains of linen and lace to let in the light. Despite these changes, it was still the easiest thing in the world to imagine herself back in the carefree days of childhood.

A painted sunset faded in the window. Strange to be here alone, to be anywhere alone. Thirty-three years old, and she'd barely spent a night by herself in her life. Here in her old home, there wasn't even a servant. She liked it, fending for herself. The time to think. The time to remember who she was. In some ways, this was the happiest she'd been since Luke had died.

Except for the children. Eddie would never let them go. It would be Christmas soon, and she couldn't allow her feelings to ruin their happiness. She would return to Eddie, try for the umpteenth time to make it work, honour the promise she'd made to her mother – but not yet. She needed this time alone to regroup and gather strength.

Belle snuggled fully clothed into the embrace of the old feather mattress. Perhaps she'd rest here for a while. Not sleep. She didn't want to sleep. In the fortnight since she'd left Eddie, her sleep had been haunted by ghosts: Mama and Papa. Sasha and Bear. Luke – a recurring dream of them making that long-wished-for journey to Tiger Pass together. Of finding tigers thriving in their hidden valley. Luke forever nineteen, in the full vigour and bloom of youth.

She should get up and light the fire, but instead she pulled up the counterpane. She wanted to rest a little longer. Rest, but not visit that land of dreams where her loved ones lived. Each waking was like losing them all over again. As she closed her eyes and drifted into sleep, Luke held out his hand.


When Belle woke, the sun streamed in the window. After days of snatching snippets of sleep here and there, she'd enjoyed a full, refreshing twelve hours and, for once, the shock of waking didn't come with such a heavy dose of grief.

She might be furious with Eddie, but she had to thank him for one thing. That Sunday at the zoo had been an epiphany. Mothering, painting, teaching – these things were important, satisfying, but there was something else she needed to fulfil her life.

Taking up the conservation fight where her father had left off – that's what really mattered. And that fight would begin with Binburra. The precious land that Papa had spent a lifetime restoring and protecting was in the hands of a mining tycoon. Why was she waiting in the wings? If Eddie wouldn't or couldn't fix this, she would. Time to tackle the problem head on. She would go to the Colonel and state her case. He couldn't possibly be more pigheaded than Eddie. She'd take the train to Binburra today and reclaim her birthright.


'Sorry, the rest are out,' said the man at Hills End Livery. 'This jinker's all I've got.'

Belle frowned. Paint flaked from the dilapidated little cart; its gnawed leather seat a nest for rats, the spokes of its wheels more rust than steel. The too-large harness hung on the old pony's skinny frame down to his knees. Belle stroked his soft nose. He closed his eyes and went to sleep.

'Have you any saddle horses for hire?'

'Only Rebel, miss.' He pointed to a ribby chestnut gelding, pacing restlessly around the yard. 'But he's green broke, a little wild.' The man stepped close and Belle could smell rum on his breath. 'Truth is, miss, I won him in a card game after he bucked three blokes off in a row. No good for a lady such as yourself.'

'He'll do. Tack him up please.'

The livery man scratched his head. 'I'll have to catch him first.'

After much shouting and swearing, he cornered the chestnut and wrestled him into the stable. When they emerged, a ridiculous little side-saddle was perched on the horse's back, looking like the proverbial pimple on a pumpkin. 'Put a regular stock saddle on him,' said Belle. 'And show me where I can stow my case and change.'

Belle emerged from the shed dressed in denim trousers. She tucked her blouse in and, on an impulse, let down her hair. It fell free of its ribbons and pins, and she pushed it back behind her ears, feeling like a girl again.

The livery man held the prancing horse still while she mounted. Then they were off under a blazing summer sky. After a few exuberant pigroots, she held tight to a fistful of tangled mane and gave her horse his head. Rebel was a dream ride, as captivated to be heading out of town as she was. He snatched at the reins, stretched his neck and settled into a rhythmic, pounding canter. Belle drew in the pure mountain air. Not a soul knew where she was or where she was going – an overwhelming liberation. She stood in her stirrups and yelled to the watching trees. 'I'm back!'

Hobart's stuffy streets seemed a world away. How long had it been since she'd ridden like this?

The noonday sun beat down. By the time they reached Binburra's rutted driveway, Rebel was soaked in sweat, but keen as ever. He tackled the steep driveway at a canter and she reined him in. 'Pace yourself, boy,' she whispered. 'It's a long way back.'

She rode through the oh-so-familiar front gate, dismounted and put Rebel in the front yard. He took long, greedy draughts from the trough. Belle wished she could do the same, but the water was a little too green. Her throat was tight and dry from dust and apprehension. Nerves were getting the better of her now. She hadn't thought this through. Far better to have arrived in a smart buggy drawn by a matched pair, or even a motor car. To have been dressed like a lady. Instead, she'd arrived on a skinny, scruffy horse, looking like a hobo.

Speaking of matched pairs, the two dapple-grey carriage horses dozing in the shade looked strangely familiar. Belle moved closer and gave a cry of surprise. No wonder. They were her own horses, Martini and Sultan. So the mysterious Colonel had bought them too. Did he covet everything she owned?

He'd been in possession of Binburra for several weeks now, and she'd been worried that clearing might have started in the overgrown paddocks. It was a relief to see nothing had changed, apart from a line of newly planted seedlings along the fence line. Blue gums. She nodded approval. They could stay.

Belle unsaddled Rebel and turned him loose in the paddock. Having to catch him again and tack him up could prove a good delaying tactic, if she needed extra time to argue her case. She washed her face in the trough, damped down her hair and combed it roughly with her fingers. That would have to do. Time to tackle the Colonel.

Belle marched to the verandah in case he was watching through an upstairs window, hoping she looked more determined than she felt. She'd imagined such a famous man would travel with an entire entourage. Yet there was nobody around, no car, and only her two horses in the paddock. Maybe he wasn't here at all?

She resented having to knock on her own front door, but knock she did, expecting some butler or other to open it. No response. She turned the handle and pushed open the door. The hall was empty. She wiped her boots and went inside.

Belle had underestimated the gut-wrenching heartache of being here again, the first time since her parents died. Nothing had changed. The John Gould prints on the wall. The butterfly tapestry by the stairs. If she went to the library - she felt her feet already taking her there - Papa would be standing at his desk cataloguing spiders or combing through the latest *American Museum Journal*.

Belle opened the door. She'd left the library tidy, yet the books and pamphlets strewn over the table were some of Papa's favourites. *Honeyeaters of Australia*. *Tasmanian Ferns*. Belle picked up a guide to forest fungi. How extraordinary. Was the Colonel a naturalist? It seemed improbable, but it was more likely than Papa's ghost haunting the library.

Belle explored downstairs. The parlour was a mess, with dirty plates on the side-board, a pair of men's argyle socks on the floor, and an empty beer bottle at the bar. In the kitchen, a box of groceries sat on the bench. Eggs, bread, half a round of cheese with a wedge cut out. Apples spilling from a hessian bag. She poured herself a glass of water from the big willow-pattern jug, as she'd done a hundred times before. Nothing had been put away, and a trail of ants led from an opened tin of raspberry jam to the window. She smiled, imagining how horrified Mama would be. Didn't this man have servants?

The ring of axe on timber sounded from somewhere close by. She hurried out the back door and down to the woodshed. A man with his shirt off was chopping timber, facing away from her towards the encroaching forest, cleaving logs with great strokes of his blade. It was highly inappropriate for her to be here like this, alone with a half-naked man, but what choice did she have? In any case, nobody was here to see. Nobody except the man himself.

Belle drew nearer, admiring his powerful build. Cords of muscle rippled beneath a dark tan and sheen of sweat. Could this possibly be the Colonel himself? He still hadn't seen her. Good, she would have the element of surprise.

Suddenly Belle stopped short, her heart stilled in her chest. No, it couldn't be. The man's back was crisscrossed with a pattern of raised scars. A pattern she knew by heart: every weal, every angle, every silvery stripe.

She barely dared say the name, her breath all gummed up in her throat.

'Luke?'

He spun around at the sound of her voice.

Belle's legs went weak, and she retreated a few steps. Older, of course, with a full moustache and beard that mostly hid his face. Fairer hair. But there was no mistaking the eyes, or the recognition they held. Luke's eyes. Luke's beautiful brown eyes, which she'd thought were closed forever.

This must be some kind of vision, some sort of waking dream, but whatever it was, she'd take it. She wanted him to speak, wanted to hear his dear voice again.

'Belle.'

Ah, there it was. She laughed in delight, and moved forward one halting step at a time, until she was within arm's length. Then closer again. He seemed so real, she could feel his breath. She reached out her hand and touched a flesh and blood man.

Confusion engulfed her and Belle staggered back. He had her, and in an instant she was in the circle of his arms. Solid, warm, living arms. A miracle was happening, right here in her own life.

She touched his face, delirious with joy. 'It's really you?'

'It's really me.'

Luke picked her up and carried her to the house. He took her into the cool parlour, laid her on the chaise lounge, stroked her tangled hair. 'You haven't changed, Belle.'

'Haven't changed?' She laughed aloud. 'If you only knew.' A cloud of concern crossed his face. Her fingertips touched his cheek. 'The past doesn't matter,' she said. 'All that matters is that somehow, some way, we've found each other again.'

He kissed the tip of her nose, then her eyelids, then her mouth. She responded like it was the first time, drinking in the sweetness, sure she'd soon wake from this magical encounter. Belle closed her eyes, but when she opened them, there he was, large as life. She would never stop smiling.

'I've got a million questions. Where have you been all this time? I thought you were dead. My poor Luke, I grieved so much for you. What about the Colonel? Where is he? Do you work for him?'

Luke knelt beside her and took both her hands in his. He looked so serious. Why wasn't he as happy as she was?'

'Listen to me.' He licked his lips and a pulse started in his cheek. Whatever it was, he was struggling to get it out. 'Colonel Buchanan is right here, Belle. I am the Colonel.'

At first it didn't register. 'What do you mean?'

'I am Colonel Lucas Buchanan. I'm the one who bought Binburra. I bought it for you.'

She shook her head. 'I don't understand.'

'Bear died in the cave collapse, but I survived. You were pregnant, Belle, and Edward seemed to love you. What could I offer? A murderer on the run, facing the gallows . . .'

A swift intake of breath. The impossible truth was starting to dawn. For a long time neither of them spoke.

'I had to stay dead, Belle, disappear. I did it for you . . . so you could live your life in peace and forget my name.'

'Forget your name?' Her own voice sounded bitter and hollow in her ears, as her happiness leaked away. 'Are you mad? Your name has haunted me for sixteen years, my constant companion. I have called it in the dead of night, murmured it by our waterfall, cursed it when I could find no pleasure or comfort in the arms of my husband. And now I find the man I've mourned all this time is alive and well and masquerading as a stranger? You may be able to forget your name, Luke. I have not found it so easy.'

Tears filled his eyes. 'I thought you could be happy with Edward, you and our son.'

'Happy? Your death ruined me. So many years of grieving. Years of days when I could feel no joy, and nights when I closed my eyes and could see nothing but your poor broken body. Just last year my father searched, dug through the rockfall to bury you properly, to help banish that dreadful image from my mind. He didn't find you – of course not. You were off making your fortune while I was dying of grief.'

Luke put his hands to his ears. 'Stop it, Belle. I can't bear it.'

She hated the pain in his eyes, but she couldn't stop. 'And Becky, who pretends to be my friend. Does she know too . . . ? I see she does. Who else has played me so false. Mama? Edward?'

'No, Belle, I swear. No one knows except Becky, my mother, and Molly, Angus's widow. We met some weeks ago as I put flowers on his grave. She recognised me.'

'And what of Edward? He admires you, counts you as a friend. Did he not recognise you?'

'He did not.'

Belle couldn't speak, her throat too dry, her heart too sore.

'It tore me apart to leave, Belle, but I believed Edward would provide a good life for you and our son. Since coming to know him, I've realised my mistake. He is a weak man, who has used you most ill. Forgive me.'

'Was I ever to know?' A mere whisper.

'Yes, Belle. Yes, of course. I just wanted the time to be right.'

She closed her eyes. Luke was alive. It should feel like a dream come true. Why, then, did it feel like a nightmare?

'I have to go.'

'I won't let you.'

She stood up, rather shakily. 'Now you sound like Eddie.'

He buried his head in his hands. The hair peaked at the nape of his neck, just as she remembered. She wanted to kiss it. Instead, she turned and headed for the door.

'Wait,' he called. 'I have a great deal to explain.'

'I am in no mood to hear it.'

He looked so crestfallen she almost relented. If he'd been the one who'd come to her . . . but as it was . . . ? Luke had been in Tasmania for months. What game was he playing?

'Goodbye, Colonel.'

Luke followed her down to the paddock in silence. When she tried to catch Rebel, the horse had other ideas. Binburra's lush pastures were a far cry from his regular diet of dusty chaff and coarse hay. The big chestnut wanted a belly full of green grass and was playing hard to get.

'Leave him,' said Luke, as Rebel cantered off up the hill. 'I'll harness the greys and take you into town myself.' He clapped his hands. Sultan and Martini trotted straight to him.

'They're actually my greys,' said Belle. 'A present from Papa. Eddie had no right to sell them.'

'Your greys then.' Luke rubbed their ears. 'Binburra is all yours, Belle. Lock, stock and barrel. I'll sign the transfer whenever you want.'

Despite her shock and anger, it was a thrill to have Binburra back again. A smile slipped out unawares. Who'd have thought the Colonel would just hand the place over?

Rebel was keeping a wary eye on them from the far side of the paddock, snatching up mouthfuls of grass. 'I can't leave him. He belongs to Mr Chapman at the livery stable.'

'That old rogue.' Luke whistled loudly, and Rebel pricked his ears. 'He's a nice type, but he needs a good feed.'

'I know,' said Belle. 'Poor thing.'

'Let him stay. I'll buy him when we get to Hills End.'

Luke headed for the yards, with the greys following meekly behind. He still had a way with animals; that hadn't changed.

Whatever was she going to do? A wild, reckless part of her wanted to run after Luke; wanted to forgive him and offer to run away together. But where would that leave her pride? Where would that leave her children?

The law set a very different moral standard for men and women. A man could get a divorce by proving his wife had committed a single act of adultery. Even being here alone with Luke was risky. Whereas wives needed to show both unfaithfulness and cruelty on the part of their husbands. With a bit of digging, she might be able to prove Eddie's infidelity, and what could be crueler than him tricking her out of her birthright? But the courts might not see it her way, and she couldn't risk losing her children. Luke was alive. It was a miracle. Yet she was as trapped in her marriage as ever.

Belle moved down the hill in slow motion, trying to make each moment last. Luke was harnessing Martini and Sultan to the claret-coloured brougham, her favourite carriage. He was moving slowly too. Was it for the same reason? There was so much she didn't know.

At last, the brougham was ready. Luke climbed into the driver's seat, fixed her with a steady gaze and held out his hand. 'My lady.'

She blushed as fiercely as on that first day. Belle had meant to ride inside, but she was so flustered she let him pull her up beside him.

'Yah.' He shook the reins and the horses moved off.

Belle looked at her hand, her fingers tingling where he'd touched them. A jolt went through her when Luke brushed against her thigh, sending a shock of love to her heart. How could she ever go home to Eddie now, knowing what she knew, feeling what she did? She had regained Binburra, but would never know peace in her life again.

# CHAPTER 63

After Belle returned from Hills End she shut herself away at Coomalong. Existing in a fog of confusion, where nothing was clear and the ground moved beneath her feet. Luke lived, and the foundations of life had unalterably shifted.

For more than a week Belle kept the windows closed and shuttered. She ignored knocks on the door. The ringing phone went unanswered. Letters slipped through the mail-slot went unread. She had no wish to engage with a treacherous world.

The reality of Luke's existence side-tracked every thought. He'd been gone for years. Now that she'd found him, she was paradoxically crippled by an overwhelming sense of loss. As if all her griefs had been focused through a magnifying glass.

Her entire adult life had been based on a lie, and she didn't know who or what to believe. Not Luke certainly, the chief instigator of her misery. Not Becky, her best friend. Not Alice Tyler, Robbie's grandmother. These people, whom she loved, had played a cruel trick on her.

What about her parents? Luke had sworn they knew nothing. She examined her own memories of them in the light of this new information. She could think of nothing in Mama's or Papa's behaviour to suggest that they knew Luke lived. Papa had been devastated by the rockfall. That, at least, was a relief. She couldn't bear to believe they'd been in on the deception.

Eddie. Was it conceivable he'd spent so much time with the Colonel and not recognised him? Perhaps. She'd had the advantage of seeing Luke as she'd always seen him. At Binburra, at a task she'd seen him perform countless times before. She'd seen his scarred back. She'd looked into his face as they moved together under the waterfall. She'd loved him.

Eddie had barely known him, and it was as a poor miner, a farm labourer, a common fugitive. He'd met Luke again in an entirely different context. At the club, impeccably dressed, with everyone hailing him as the famous Colonel Buchanan, war hero and diamond king.

It was possible, even probable, that he'd been fooled. The bigger mystery was why? Why had Luke returned after all this time? Why had he acted out this charade of friendship with Eddie? Why hadn't he come to her and revealed himself? These unanswerable questions went round and round in her head. She needed a crystal ball.

In the afternoon, Belle opened up the glass door onto the balcony, the final renovation her mother had made at Coomalong before she died. Such a change from the former small-paned window and heavy drapes. The summer sun burst in her face. Mama had been updating the house, combining its old-world charm with an open-air lightness in the latest style.

Her mother had been intrigued and enthusiastic about the advances of this new century: motor cars, electric lighting, telephones. A relaxation of the rigid Victorian moral code. Federation. King Edward on the throne: a modern monarch, patron of the arts and science. Mama loved that interior décor was evolving too: simpler themes, brighter colours, less clutter. She talked about it all the time. Belle never took much notice. It had seemed almost quaint, how excited Mama had been by current fashions.

Belle watched sunbeams glance off the stained-glass sundial set into the window. Something stirred inside her as she grasped her mother's vision. What a condescending fool she'd been. The joy Mama had found in these contemporary styles was the same joy Belle herself found in the play of sunlight on a waterfall, or the gleam and quiver of gumleaves after rain. It was the joy of life itself.

A sudden realisation hit her. Mama would hate how she'd locked herself away. Mama would hate how she'd locked up Coomalong, excluding air and light, shutting out the world. It was an insult to her memory.

Belle ran through the house, unfastening shutters, opening curtains and windows. A summer breeze blew in, room by room, chasing away the staleness. Sunshine flooded dark corners and the scent of boronia and honeysuckle wafted on the air. The house was coming alive.

From Papa's study she saw Becky come through the side gate from the school. Moments later, a knock came.

Belle went to the front hall and opened the door.

Becky took off her hat. 'Thank God. You know I've come by every day.'

'I saw Luke.'

'He told me.' Becky looked past her into the hall.

Belle managed a half-smile. 'Come in.'

Becky took a seat in the parlour and Belle perched herself on the sofa opposite. They sat a while in awkward silence. Belle had a hundred questions that she couldn't bring herself to ask.

Becky moistened her lips and adjusted her trumpet skirt 'I know what you must be thinking.'

'I doubt that. Did Luke send you?'

'He has no idea I'm here.' A tear glistened in the corner of Becky's eye. 'You deserve an explanation, only I'm not sure where to begin.'

Belle fought a surge of impatience. 'How about starting with why Luke let me think he was dead all these years?'

'Luke came to Mama and me in Melbourne, in the December after the cave collapse. Until then we'd believed him dead too. He'd found a stash of money and gold in the hills, enough to set him up for years. He wanted to go back for you. I tried my best to talk him out of it.'

'Why?'

'Luke went to jail once for my sake. Next time he'll hang. He's a wanted man in Tasmania, even now. You'd do well to remember that.' Belle did not miss the note of censure in her friend's voice. 'But I couldn't convince him. He was determined to return to you, even at the risk of execution. Then he found your letter . . .'

'Letter?'

'The one you wrote my mother. It said you were happy, looking forward to the baby, falling in love with Edward. Luke did not want to ruin that happiness.'

Oh. For the first time Belle tried to put away her own hurt and see things from the other side.

'His whole life in South Africa has been dedicated to you and your father. He's set up game reserves that protect thousands of animals. He's built village schools, not only providing poor black children with an education, but also teaching locals about the importance of wildlife.' Becky stopped for a long, shuddering breath. 'He's never married.'

Belle looked down at her hands, ran her thumb along the skin where Luke had touched her. Twisted her wedding band. 'Even so, now he's back. A rich and powerful man, a great success. Why not reveal himself to me?'

Becky threw up her hands. 'For someone who professes to love my brother, you don't understand him very well.'

Belle leaned forward. 'Help me then. Help me understand.'

'All the money in the world won't change how Luke feels on the inside.'

'How does he feel?'

'Like he's not worthy. Think about it. Thrown into prison at fourteen. Flogged and treated like dirt. Then he's on the run, unable to claim even his own name. Our father's dead, leaving Mama a widow, and Luke thinks it's his fault. You're pregnant. He's let everyone down. Then Edward steps up to take his place.'

'Edward's not a fraction of the man Luke is.'

'Luke didn't know that. He thought that you and Robbie were

happy, so he stayed away. And when you discovered the truth, that he's alive, you blamed and rejected him. You confirmed what he's feared all along – that he's not good enough.'

Belle sat in silence, digesting Becky's words and what they meant. Unable to look at her friend. Her white-hot anger had died down to embers. How selfish she'd been, how full of self-pity and entitlement.

'If he believed Eddie and I were happy, why did he come back?'

'I wrote to tell him your parents were dead. He loved them, Belle, and wanted to pay his private respects. That's why he came back. He intended to return to South Africa, however circumstances changed his mind.' Becky cleared her throat and glanced over at the liquor cabinet. 'Perhaps a glass of sherry?'

In a daze, Belle fetched the bottle and two glasses, poured them both a generous serve. 'Go on.'

'At the cemetery he met Molly, Angus's common-law wife. She has since confessed that she recognised him at Canterbury Downs on the night Henry Abbott died. Molly was the one who caused the Sergeant to come.'

'I suppose it had to be someone . . .'

'On Edward's instructions.'

Belle's heart stopped beating. 'No, Eddie tried to protect Luke.'

Becky sculled her drink and poured herself another. 'Your Edward paid Molly thirty pounds to betray my brother. We have the proof. Molly was so scared she'd be accused of stealing, she asked for an acknowledgement note. She still has it, signed in Edward's own hand.'

Belle tasted bile in her throat. This was monstrous. Luke had risked his life for Eddie down that mine, and was repaid with treachery. She ripped off her wedding ring with a savage twist and hurled it across the room. She could not return to Eddie now, not even if it meant losing her children. She'd rather die.

'Why are you telling me this?'

Becky reached across and took her hand. 'Luke has a score to settle, but that's not why he stays. There's no use me fighting him any more on this. He stays for you, Belle, whatever the risk. He stays for you.'

# CHAPTER 64

'It's not possible. What about the preliminary report? What about the independent valuation? The site samples alone were worth thousands.' Edward used a handkerchief to wipe his face. The office was stifling, but there was more to his sweating brow than a stuffy room and a warm day.

At George Bentley's insistence, their own engineers had completed a survey of the new mine site. The chief geologist stood before them, wringing his hat in his hands.

'Cut to the chase, man.' Edward threw the report on the desk. 'Did you find diamonds?'

'We did, sir. Yet, wherever we found them, we also found garnets and zircons in too neat an arrangement for a natural deposit. In addition, the stones were found only in disturbed ground. We spent three days doing tests, which included digging ten deep trenches in a dry creek bed, where diamonds should have been distributed well below the surface. Yet there were no diamonds found at depths greater than three feet.'

'What is your explanation?'

'My explanation?' The geologist squirmed like a bug on a pin. He looked imploringly at George for help and received only a shrug. 'My explanation is that someone has been pushing diamonds into the ground with a stick.'

Edward steadied himself with a hand on the desk, then dropped into a chair. 'Get out,' he said. 'Both of you.'

The two men glanced at each other.

'Get out!' He sprang to his feet, fists clenched, and the others hurried from the room. Edward sank back down, weak with shock and confusion. He'd been had. The Colonel's doing? But why? He and Lucas were co-directors of the new mining company, and between them owned one hundred per cent of the shares. Only they would profit by its success. Only they had everything to lose if it failed. There must be another explanation.

Edward retrieved the report and read it again, this time more thoroughly. Hoping to find a flaw in its reasoning. It was a false hope; he couldn't fault it. The diamond field was utterly worthless and he was the victim of a massive fraud.

Edward felt sick. On top of selling half his assets, he'd borrowed to the hilt to make this deal. He'd have to sell what was left at fire-sale prices to repay the loan. The prospect of being left penniless filled him with dread; the prospect of public humiliation even more so. He could see the headline now. *The Great Diamond Hoax: How a Gullible Son Lost His Father's Fortune.* The papers would have a field day with how easily he'd been duped.

# CHAPTER 65

A crystal clear Sunday morning, its peace broken only by carolling magpies and the occasional clip-clop of hooves. After a sleepless night, Belle had been up since dawn, staring out an upstairs window to the quiet street below. She was as nervous as a schoolgirl waiting for her secret beau.

This would be a very different meeting to their last. Belle was possessed of the facts. She'd had time to adjust. She'd made up her mind.

Shortly before ten o'clock, she heard the hum of an engine. It grew louder. She could see it now, a shiny green motor car, slowing down outside her house, stopping.

She ran to the mirror, smoothed her dress, inspected her face, her hair. She'd changed three times already, settling on a tailored white blouse and skirt of pearl-grey satin. A simple silver chain with a cameo pendant. Now she wished she'd dressed up more. Her hair, swept into a top-knot, looked too severe. With unsteady hands she teased it out a little so a few soft curls fell round her face. She used powder to hide the feverish colour in her cheeks.

The knock came. Belle couldn't move; her legs were like lead. It came again, harder this time. With a wrench she turned from the mirror and went downstairs, her heart thumping in her chest, blood rushing in her ears. She grasped the doorknob, took a steadying breath, and opened the front door.

There he stood. What a difference. No wonder Eddie hadn't recognised him. She barely recognised him herself. Luke was dressed in a dark tailored blazer, pin-striped shirt and contrasting waistcoat of the palest dove-grey. Its hand-painted enamel buttons featured native tigers in different poses. His beard was neatly clipped and fair hair trimmed close. He cut a debonair figure, yet something suggested his polished veneer ran only skin-deep.

Luke doffed his kettle-edged homburg hat. 'M'lady.'

Belle offered her hand. Luke took it, kissed it. Had he noticed her wedding band was missing?

A car came down the street and stopped. A man jumped out and began taking photographs. A reporter, or perhaps a private investigator hired by her husband?

Luke swiftly stepped in and closed the door behind him. She'd worry about the photographer later. Right now, her mind was too full for any other thoughts.

'You look lovely,' he said. 'All grown up.' They shared a smile. 'When you surprised me at Binburra, you looked like a young girl.'

Belle was far more flattered than she should have been. 'Let's sit out in the sunshine,' she said. 'I'm not used to being inside with you.'

She led him into the parlour, through the French doors and out to the garden. Luke looked around in wonder. He hadn't been at Coomalong since he was a child. They sat side by side on a cast-iron bench, beneath a dappled canopy of scarlet roses. He took her hand and Belle swallowed hard, overcome by the romance of the moment. Her body felt tight and loose all at once, the strangest of sensations.

Perhaps if she filled the space between them with words? 'Becky said you came back to pay your respects to my parents.'

'I did. Your father was a great man. Just knowing that he lived was a comfort to me in exile.'

'In exile? Is that how it felt?'

'That's how it was.'

'I'm glad you're back.' Belle leaned over to kiss his cheek.

He stiffened into a splendid statue. In the back of her mind she heard Becky say *... what he's feared all along – that he's not good enough.* It seemed impossible that this magnificent man could suffer even a moment of self-doubt, but then again, Becky knew her brother.

'I understand why you stayed away.'

'If I'd known you were married to such a cad—'

She squeezed his hand. 'Eddie told me about the salted diamond field. I now know my husband betrayed you all those years ago. Is that why you wanted to ruin him? For revenge.'

Luke's eyes blazed. 'I held no gun to his head, Belle. At every stage he could have stepped back, but weakness and greed led him on. Edward has been the master of his own destruction.'

'Eddie won't be the only one to suffer, though, will he? The Hills End mine will close, throwing hundreds out of work. His wool-growers will lose their farms.' She moved a fraction closer to him. 'Eddie is so distraught, I think he's forgotten he banned me from my children. In any case he tolerates my visits, confides in me even. The girls are too young to understand, but Robbie is fifteen now, a young man. Against my advice, Eddie told him about the bogus diamond mine. Robbie is furious at you for engineering his father's misfortune.'

'I am his father.'

She gave him her kindest smile. 'No, you're not Luke. Eddie has been the best father he knew how to be to our son. For that I cannot fault him. When his humiliation becomes public, it will devastate Robbie.'

Luke lit a cigarette. 'So, what, you want me to let that bastard off the hook?'

'I don't want innocent people to be hurt, especially our son.' She took the cigarette from between his lips and took a deep drag. 'Mama never did like me smoking.'

Luke took the cigarette back and tossed it away. 'Your mother never liked you doing this either.' He drew her to him, wrapped her in his arms, pressed his lips to hers. She savoured the tremor where he touched her, the eagerness of his mouth, the wanting in his body. She wanted him too. His kiss sang through her veins.

He pulled her down on the grass, ran his hand down her spine, traced the soft swell of her breast. And there, in the sunshine beneath the roses, they explored a love long overdue.

# CHAPTER 66

'Show Mr Abbott up, please.' Luke put down the telephone. Bright sunshine lit the hotel suite. It was a fine day for a reckoning.

Luke nodded to Molly, Francine and Nurse Kendall, who were playing cards by the window. 'If you three wouldn't mind waiting next door?'

'Come on, girls,' said Molly. 'But don't think we won't be listening through the wall.'


Edward strode in without a word, clutching a copy of *The Mercury*. His face was puffy and florid from drinking, though it was but ten in the morning. He folded the newspaper and thrust it forward.

The headline read *The Millionaire and the Magnate's Wife* and the article itself was no less salacious.

*Wealthy South African diamond tycoon and war hero Colonel Lucas Buchanan has scandalised Hobart society by courting the wife of local mining magnate, Edward Abbott. Mrs Isabelle Abbott, mother of three, has abandoned her husband and children, moving out of Abbott House, the family home.*

A grainy photograph of Luke's car outside Coomalong, and another of Belle opening the door, accompanied the article.'

'Well?' Edward thundered. 'Do you deny it?'

'Not at all.' Luke folded the newspaper and put it on the desk. 'I'm in love with your wife, Ed. I'm going to marry her.'

At first Edward seemed more astonished than angry. The whites of his eyes showed, like those of a startled horse. 'Damn you, sir.' He extracted some crumpled sheets of paper from his pocket and hurled them in Luke's face. 'My own engineer's report on the diamond field. Apparently it's worthless.'

'Apparently so. It seems the mine's initial promise did not pan out.'

'Don't give me that. You're a swindler, Colonel, and I'll sue for fraud. You salted that mine.'

Luke settled in his chair with exaggerated slowness. 'Why would I do that, Ed? My shares are as worthless as yours.'

'I haven't figured that out yet.' Edward jabbed a forefinger in Luke's direction. 'But I know you're responsible.'

'Careful, Ed. You're sounding a little unhinged.'

Edward whirled on him. 'What's left of my assets will go to repay the bank. I'm ruined. My family's ruined.' Luke shrugged one shoulder. 'I don't understand. I thought we were friends.'

'Painful, isn't it, Ed, to be betrayed by somebody you trust? To be brought to your knees.'

Edward gave him a searching look. 'Why did you really come here, Colonel? To destroy me? It almost seems personal.'

'Oh, it always has been, Eddie boy.' Luke leaned back, stretching his arms. 'It always has been.'

Edward's eyes narrowed, bored into Luke's until they pierced right through him.

Luke waited. Aah, there it was, as clear as a perfectly-cut diamond. The delicious shock of recognition.

'Good Lord, can it be? Luke?'

Luke pulled a chair up to the desk. 'Take a seat, Ed. We need to talk.'

Edward sat down in a daze, rubbing his forehead like he was

getting a headache.

Luke opened the drawer, took out a sheaf of papers and spread them out on the desk. 'These four documents require your signature. Number one is an agreement with your tenant farmers, setting a minimum floor price for their wool. Number two is a proposal to the miners' union, offering wage rises of fifty percent. Number three – you'll submit to an independent safety audit of the Hills End mine, and act on the recommendations within two months.'

Edward grimaced. Already he seemed smaller, his suit a size too big. 'Back from the grave, and behind all my misfortune. I suppose there was no impoverished farmer either, no war hero cheated out of his land?'

'A moral test, Ed, one you failed.'

Edward started to laugh, an empty, hollow sound. 'What's number four? Sell my daughters?'

'Very close. You'll give custody and guardianship of the children to Belle, and agree not to fight the divorce petition. In return for signing these four documents . . .' Luke pulled out a valise from under the desk and flipped it open. It was filled with wads of banknotes. 'One hundred thousand pounds, and clearance of all your debts. In addition, details of our unfortunate joint mining venture will never reach the press. Edward Abbott will emerge from this whole sordid business with his reputation intact.'

'Or I could give you up to the police.'

Luke inclined his head. 'It is your style, of course.' He lit a cigarette. 'Years ago you paid a woman thirty pounds to turn me in. Knowing my dog acted only to protect Belle. Knowing I'd hang.'

Edward's face went white. 'That was before father died. I believed you faced no more than prison.'

'No more than prison? You should try it, Ed.'

Edward sank down on the chair beside Luke's. 'How could you know this?' He helped himself to a cigarette. 'I've never told a soul.'

Luke gave him a light. 'You knew Henry was dead when you released the bloodhounds.'

'I had no choice.' Edward ran a hand over his face. 'Damn it, I saw you die. What have you done, Colonel? Made some kind of Faustian pact?'

'That does not concern you.'

Luke handed him a pen. Edward rolled its smooth barrel between his fingers, and then put it down. 'I don't want a divorce.'

'It's not up to you, Ed. Belle can show infidelity, and a pattern of drinking, gambling and opium abuse on your part that amounts to cruelty.'

'That might be hard to prove.'

'I have witnesses and the best attorneys money can buy. You, more than anybody, should know that money and power trump everything. Belle will win, with or without your cooperation.'

'I'll get the children. The husband always does.'

'Ed, Ed, Ed . . . times are changing. Women have rights. Ask Emily Durant, she'll tell you about it.' At the mention of Belle's suffragette friend, Edward's nostrils flared. 'There's a new legal presumption that, all things being equal, children belong with their mother.' Luke took a long puff and exhaled in Edward's direction. 'But all things won't be equal, will they? Not after my lawyers finish dragging your name through the mud.'

Luke stubbed out his cigarette. For a long time neither spoke. The tick of the wall clock counted out the seconds.

'I wanted Belle,' said Edward at last. 'With you out of the way . . .' He threw his hands in the air. 'I was fooling myself. Belle was always yours, even when she thought you dead. I sacrificed my honour, my humanity. Betrayed a sacred trust, and in return? A loveless marriage and a life of self-loathing.' He picked up the pen. 'You're doing me a favour.'

Luke pushed forward the documents and Edward began to sign.

When he'd finished, Luke handed over the valise. 'Have the children at Coomalong by five o'clock Sunday.' He locked the papers away in the drawer. 'You can see yourself out.'

Francine and Molly were waiting in the hall outside. Edward stopped short when he saw them.

'Surprised to see me?' asked Francine with a defiant tilt of her chin.

'I suppose I shouldn't be. So the Colonel . . . he's the gentleman?'

'You ain't fit to speak his name, you ain't.'

Molly stepped forward. 'You might not remember me, sir, but I'm ashamed to say that years ago I took your blood money. You should be ashamed as well.'

'My dear lady, be assured that I always have been.'


'Here they come.' Belle ran to Coomalong's front hall.

Luke hovered in the library entrance. His customary self-assurance had completely deserted him. Until now, he'd only seen photographs of his son.

Belle flung open the door. 'Clara, Anne . . . my darlings, I'm so very happy you're here.'

They threw their arms around each other, chattering away in great excitement. Where was Robbie?

Nine-year-old Anne looked like a picture-book princess, with pale golden ringlets and roses in her cheeks. Twelve-year-old Clara was taller than he'd imagined, with hair the warm colour of a golden chestnut horse. She looked so much like her mother. Clara cast him a curious glance: serious green eyes beneath arched brows, eyes that seemed too large for her face. 'Is that him, Mama?'

Belle heaved a big breath. 'Yes, that's him. Come and meet the Colonel.'

The girls came over with shy smiles and he shook their hands.

'Are you going to live with us now, instead of Papa?' asked Anne.

Belle put a hand on her shoulder. 'Shush, Anne.'

'Why shouldn't she ask?' said Clara.

Luke dropped down on one knee. 'Anne, Clara . . . You'll still see your father as much as you want, but I love your mother and we are going to be married. When that happens, I'd be honoured if you'd let me stay.'

'Will you take me riding?' asked Anne. 'And will you let me climb trees? Papa never lets me climb trees.'

Luke grinned. 'So, the princess is a tomboy, like her mother.'

'And will you take me fishing?'

A voice came from behind him. 'No, he won't take you fishing, and we're not staying here, ever.'

Luke turned round. He'd been so intent on the girls, he hadn't seen his son come in. Lanky and well-built, halfway between a boy and a man, with clear brown eyes and dark hair that brushed his forehead. The boy's resemblance to Luke was obvious, except for a certain naivety in his expression.

Robbie grabbed Clara's arm and pulled her towards the front door.

'Let her go,' said Belle

Clara tried to shake him off, but he was too strong. 'Stop it, you're hurting me.'

Luke stepped between them and the door. 'You heard your mother.'

Clara squirmed free and ran to Belle.

'Get out of my way,' said Robbie. 'I know what you did to my father. He told me, and I hate you.'

Belle moved towards him. 'Robbie, please.'

Robbie retreated a few steps, his eyes accusing. 'And you, Mama, how could you betray us like this? You've destroyed our family.' He eyed the front door, but Luke still blocked his escape.

Belle kissed the girls on their cheeks. 'Go upstairs to your rooms. They've been redecorated. See if you like them.'

Anne and Clara glanced at each other, then retreated upstairs.

'Your father has agreed to this, Robbie,' said Belle. 'He and the Colonel have come to an arrangement.'

'Papa's been tricked. He would never send me away.' Robbie's eyes clouded with tears. 'I'm going home.'

Robbie shoved his way past Luke and flung open the front door. He kicked aside the bags on the porch and ran to the car, which was still parked in the road. Edward sat in the driver's seat. Robbie climbed up beside him.

Belle followed her son down the front steps.

'Wait,' said Luke. 'Let me try.'

392

Belle hesitated, and cast him a tortured look. 'You can't tell him,' she said. 'Not yet. Not like this.'

A painful knot in his gut twisted tight. Today was a day he'd thought might never come. He'd waited sixteen years to meet his son, imagined dozens of ways it might happen. This wasn't one of them.

As Luke approached the car, Robbie inched away from him and turned to Edward. 'I won't go with that man, Papa. Please don't make me.'

Edward's gaze met his, and Luke saw something he hadn't expected to see. A tender expression of love and compassion for his son. A plea to not push him. A plea to let him go.

'You're no longer a child, Robbie.' Luke felt hollow with the knowledge he was losing something he'd never had. 'You can do what you want.'

Robbie glared at him. 'I want my father. I'll always want my father. I'll never trust you.'

A wild desire gripped Luke, a longing to claim his son. To say: *I am your father. Come with me. Let me know you.* Fearing those words were years too late. The look on Edward's face confirmed this wasn't about him. This was about Robbie, and what he needed. And right now he needed the only father he'd ever known.

Luke wrung his hands, as if to scrub away the disappointment. 'You can pick the girls up on Saturday.'

Edward nodded and put an arm around his son's shoulder. Robbie slumped against him. 'I'll tell him if you like, Colonel. He deserves to know who his father is. It will be better coming from me.'

Robbie shot him a puzzled look.

Luke nodded a silent thank you, trying to swallow the lump lodged in his throat. 'Goodbye, Robbie.'

The boy looked into the distance as Edward started the car and drove away.

Belle ran down the steps and took his hand. 'He'll come round, in time. When he knows the truth.'

Luke pulled her to him and wrapped her in an embrace, resting his head on the top of hers. Knowing the truth could make things worse.

# CHAPTER 67

Luke spent the week getting to know the girls. He'd never seen Belle in a maternal role before and it opened his eyes. The pampered, carefree girl he'd known long ago had grown into a wise, mature woman and a loving, devoted mother. What a pleasure it would have been to have taken that journey with her. To have seen her grow into motherhood, with Robbie and the girls. Mingled with his happiness was a profound understanding of all he'd lost.

The day after they arrived, Luke presented Anne and Clara with a present. It had taken a while to track down Bear's puppies, but in the end he'd found a litter of direct descendants, and purchased a fine male. Bruno was meant for Robbie. The pair of female puppies from a different lineage were for the girls.

However it was Belle who seemed the most delighted when he released the jet black trio of joyful pups onto the lawn. They each wore a different colour collar to tell them apart. 'How old are they?'

'Ten weeks. Bruno already weighs twenty-five pounds,' he said. 'You can name the girls.'

'They're beautiful.' Belle clapped her hands like a delighted child. 'If I half-close my eyes, I can imagine these are Sasha's babies and we're young again and back at Binburra.'

Anne sat down and the shaggy puppies piled on top of her. 'Help, help.'

Belle and Clara went laughing to the rescue. However, it seemed Anne didn't want rescuing. 'I'm calling this one Crusoe, after the dog in that book you read us, Mama.'

Clara frowned. 'You can't. That dog in the book is a boy.'

'It doesn't matter. Does it matter, Colonel?'

'Not at all,' said Luke.

Clara struggled to pick up the pink-collared pup. 'I'm naming this one Princess Irene like in *The Princess and the Goblin*. Do you think it's a good name, Mama?'

'The best.'

'Can we take them with us when we go to Papa's house on Sunday?'

Crusoe was burying Anne's shoe in a bed of petunias, showering soil behind her. Bruno was busy demolishing a cane garden chair and Princess Irene was using the verandah as a toilet. Together they were a three-puppy demolition crew.

'What an excellent idea,' said Luke.


On Saturday Luke waited anxiously for Edward to come, hoping to exchange a few words with Robbie. He was on tenterhooks to discover what the boy knew. But when Edward arrived, Robbie wasn't in the car.

'I told him,' said Edward. 'He knows you're his father. It was the toughest thing I've ever done.'

'How did he take it?'

'Pretty hard, but Robbie has a generous spirit. He forgave me.'

'Will he forgive me?' asked Luke.

'I don't know.'

Luke studied him, his expression, his manner. He looked healthier, stronger. 'You still chasing the dragon?'

Edward shook his head. 'I'm not even drinking. It's bloody impossible at times, but Robbie's not going back to Scotch College. He wants to live at home with me. It's the least I can do for him, considering . . . I want to set a better example.'

'You should know,' said Luke, struggling to get the words out. 'That I appreciate what you've done for my son.'

Edward nodded an acknowledgement.

The three puppies ran out on leads, dragging the girls behind them. 'We have to make room for Bruno and Crusoe and Princess Irene,' said Anne. 'Bruno's for Robbie.'

Edward looked on doubtfully as Clara dragged the pups aboard. 'I'll have to get a bigger car.'

Belle came outside with the girls' bags.

'Can't the servants do that?' asked Edward.

'We don't have servants at Coomalong,' said Anne. 'We do things for ourselves, even cook. It's fun. When we get home, I'm going to bake you and the puppies some bread.'

'Mrs Tibbs might have something to say about that,' said Edward, as he jumped out to help Belle with the bags.

'Are you all right?' Belle asked him.

'I will be.' Edward climbed up beside Clara, surrounded by a sea of puppies. 'Can I have the girls until Sunday? It's Aunt Hilda's birthday party.'

'Certainly,' said Belle. 'We're going on a short trip anyway. I'll telephone you when we get back.'

Edward started to ask where she was going, but didn't finish the question. Instead he saluted her. 'Goodbye, Belle.' He honked the horn as they drove away.

'He told Robbie that I'm his father,' said Luke.

Belle took his hand. 'That was good of Edward. Brave. You don't know how much he loves that boy.'

Luke kicked at the ground. 'I'm beginning to realise.'

'Cheer up.' Belle pulled him towards the house. 'Let's go to Binburra and walk to Tiger Pass. 'Do you know I've never been?'

## CHAPTER 68

The trek to the pass was bittersweet. Ghosts of lost friends travelled with them. Bear and Daniel. The bafflingly beautiful tiger cubs. Yet this time Luke had Belle by his side, and there was no longer any obstacle to their love. The greatest consolation of all.

She let down her hair, wore boots and men's trousers, threw off the trappings of civilisation. He revelled in her wild beauty. At night they shared a swag, her body melting into him beneath the burning Southern Cross.

'It feels like we're marching to the roof of the world,' she said, gazing over the distant peaks. 'We'll take the dogs next year. Show Bruno his great-grandfather's grave. We'll be pilgrims.'

Luke loved the idea. He loved it even more that Belle was making plans for a future together. It made their relationship seem less like a dream.

On the third day, with eyes wide open, he led her into Tiger Pass. Nothing had changed. Still the hushed expectancy as the birds fell quiet. Still the sense of hallowed reverence sending shivers up his spine. Belle sighed and they exchanged glances. The pass was working its magic on them both.

'You were being hunted last time,' said Belle. 'Does this place scare you now?'

He gestured wide, to the blue ceiling of sky. To the craggy cliff walls of the natural cathedral. To the ancient forest and timeless stream. Each seemed to whisper: *In our end lies our beginning.*

'Scare me?' he said. 'It would be like being scared of heaven.'

He led Belle to the rock platform above the waterfall. The stream broke into a rainbow as it cascaded down the overhang.

'It really is a hanging valley.' She turned to him with bright eyes. 'And I thought our little waterfall back at Binburra was lovely.'

The time had finally come. Luke took the rose-cut diamond ring from his pocket and slipped it on her finger.


It was dark and still in the cave by the old Huon pine tree. Belle collected some waratahs and Luke found an old pot for water. They placed the makeshift vase of flowers before the cairn Daniel had built to mark Bear's grave. They took off their hats, and stood a long while in silence, each thinking private thoughts.

Luke turned on his torch, showed her the rock art on the ceiling, the drawing of the tiger. Then he aimed it at the ground. The square stone-set brass plate gleamed on the rock floor.

Belle read the words out loud. *'In loving memory of Luke Tyler and his loyal dog Bear. My heart is forever yours. Bluebell.'* She knelt to touch the letters. 'I asked Papa to put it there. I was never sure if he did or not.'

'When I came here and read that plaque, it gave me courage to hope.'

He felt for her hand, and they moved through the shored-up tunnel, through the immense rockfall that could so easily have been his tomb. Down the ancient stone steps that led to the valley below.

Luke took Belle on a tour. 'This is where I found Old Clarry's treasure.' He pointed to the high stone ledge. 'The man lived like a penniless hermit, when he was surrounded by riches. See here?' He scrubbed away at the cave wall with the sleeve of his shirt, then trained his torch on it. A shining vein ran diagonally across the rocks. 'This is a valley of gold.'

Belle trailed her fingers along the bright seam. 'Edward can never find out about this place. Nobody can.'


They camped that night beside the singing falls. Luke lit a fire. He could almost see King and his sisters coming back from the hunt, flinging their panting bodies down in the circle of warmth cast by the flames.

They stayed up late, talking, reconnecting. The moon rode high in the sky when they finally crept into their swag.

'I'm taking you to Africa to see Themba,' said Luke, as Belle fitted her body to his. 'I want you to come face-to-face with an elephant. I want you to hold a lion cub and see giraffes drink by the river at sunset. I want to share the last sixteen years of my life.'

'Shh . . .' whispered Belle. 'Listen.'

All he could hear was the waterfall and the throaty music of frogs. Then, echoing through the night, came the eerie call of a tiger.

# ACKNOWLEDGEMENTS

Thanks go to the legendary Peter Bishop, Varuna's founding creative director and this book's first champion. A residential manuscript development week at Varuna, Australia's National Writers House, put the story on strong foundations.

I pay tribute to the late nineteenth century naturalist, Rev. Henry Dresser Atkinson, who inspired the character of Daniel Campbell. In The Woodpecker Papers, a collection of Dresser's published newspaper articles, he revealed himself to be one of Tasmania's first conservationists — worrying over the fate of Thylacines (Tasmanian tigers) when farmers still shot them as pests, and wishing to preserve native habitats.

A huge thank you to the following people:

The team at Pilyara Press, especially Kathryn Ledson, Sydney Smith and Kate Belle. I couldn't have done it without you.

My lovely agent, Clare Forster of Curtis Brown Australia.

My talented writing friends, the Varuna Darklings and the Little Lonsdale Group for their friendship and support.

Finally, I'd like to thank my family for their patience and willingness to brainstorm ideas. I love you all!

# ABOUT THE AUTHOR

Bestselling Aussie author Jennifer Scoullar writes page-turning fiction about the land, people and wildlife that she loves

Scoullar is a lapsed lawyer who harbours a deep appreciation and respect for the natural world. She lives on a farm in Australia's southern Victorian Ranges, and has ridden and bred horses all her life. Her passion for animals and the bush is the catalyst for her bestselling books, which are all inspired by different landscapes.

If you enjoyed *Fortune's Son* and have a moment or two, please leave a rating or review. Reviews are of great help to authors.

Head to my website, **jenniferscoullar.com** to join my VIP list and receive a free eBook!

CPSIA information can be obtained
at www.ICGtesting.com
Printed in the USA
FSHW012005290421
80989FS